Books by Elisa Braden

Midnight in Scotland Series

The Making of a Highlander (Book One)
The Taming of a Highlander (Book Two)
The Temptation of a Highlander (Book Three)–Coming soon!

Rescued from Ruin Series

Ever Yours, Annabelle (Prequel)
The Madness of Viscount Atherbourne (Book One)
The Truth About Cads and Dukes (Book Two)
Desperately Seeking a Scoundrel (Book Three)
The Devil Is a Marquess (Book Four)
When a Girl Loves an Earl (Book Five)
Twelve Nights as His Mistress (Novella – Book Six)
Confessions of a Dangerous Lord (Book Seven)
Anything but a Gentleman (Book Eight)
A Marriage Made in Scandal (Book Nine)
A Kiss from a Rogue (Book Ten)

Want to know what's next? Connect with Elisa on Facebook
and Twitter, and sign up for her free email newsletter at
www.elisabraden.com, so you don't miss
a single new release!

THE TAMING OF A HIGHLANDER

ELISA BRADEN

Cover design by Dar Albert at Wicked Smart Designs

For more information about the author,
visit www.elisabraden.com.

ISBN-13: 978-1-950805-07-5

CHAPTER ONE

October 7, 1826
Glendasheen Castle, Scotland

"He dispatches *forty* men? All with his dirk?" Hazel eyes glinted with amusement as John Huxley scraped a lean hand across his mouth and jaw. "Are you ... certain?"

Kate Huxley paused in the middle of demonstrating the imagined maneuver—left hand on hip, right hand extended forward to deliver the killing thrust. She blinked at her brother. "The dirk is the weapon of choice for Highlanders, is it not?"

"Scots do like their dirks; it is true." John rifled through the pages of her manuscript. "Perhaps the number slain by your hero's mighty hand could be smaller, hmm?"

Frowning, she crossed the drawing room to glare over his shoulder. "Forty is the number I specified in Act One, Scene Two. If I change it now, I shall be forced to include an additional scene in which Sir Wallace

McClure-MacLeod rescues Fiona Farquharson-McPhee
a *third* time." She folded her arms and eyed her
suspiciously firm-lipped brother. "Won't that strain
credulity?"

John was thirteen years older than Kate's one-and-
twenty, and before he'd settled in this remote-yet-
magical pocket of the Scottish Highlands, he'd traveled
to more places than Kate could name, places where lions
roamed and dolphins swam and French ladies bared
their bosoms willy-nilly. In short, John knew far more
about the world than Kate, which was why she'd asked
for his input. She'd hoped—foolishly, it seemed—that
he would take her work seriously. Instead, she
suspected he was laughing.

If only she were writing a comedy.

"Katie, you have him wearing a bearskin mantle."

"Yes. And?"

"There are no bears in Scotland."

"Perhaps I could change it to wolfskin."

"There are no wolves in Scotland, either."

She rounded in front of him and clicked her tongue.
"Well, there must be predators of one sort or another."

John leaned forward to set the pages on a tea table. He
remained silent, resisting a grin. At least he was *trying* not
to laugh at her. That was something, wasn't it?

"What of cats?" she pressed.

"What of them?"

"Africa has lions and leopards. They sound frightful.
Are there no wild felines prowling the wintry moors of
Scotland?"

"I've heard of one breed. Quite elusive."

She retrieved her notebook and pencil from the sofa.
"Yes? Is it very large?"

He rubbed his handsome chin, his eyes twinkling with mischief. "Hmm. How large was Erasmus?" He referred to their mother's ill-tempered housecat, which had been banished to the stables after an incident involving Papa's silk waistcoats.

Kate held her hands about twenty inches apart. "Yes. That's it."

She sighed. "Are they dangerous, at least?"

"I'm certain field mice regard them with great terror and loathing."

"John."

"Papa would also dislike them, I reckon." He tapped his nose. "The sneezing, you know."

"You are ruining everything," she retorted. "How am I to portray the legendaryness of Sir Wallace without implying he is capable of killing a dangerous predator and wearing its pelt?"

He arched a brow. "Legendaryness is not a word."

She snapped her notebook closed. "I am the author, and I say it is. I also say there are wolves in Scotland. Wolves are better than bears, anyway."

This time, he didn't bother disguising his laughter. The chuckles continued as he settled back in his chair. "I admire your pluck, little sister. But even you cannot *imagine* wolves into being where wolves no longer exist."

"I shall. It will be exciting. No one will question it."

"Apart from everyone who has ever been to Scotland."

"Nonsense. Sir Wallace is a master of the dirk. I shall say he hunted the last surviving wolf in Scotland with nothing but his wits and his blade." Tingles flashed as an idea sprang to life. "Or his *sgian-dubh*."

"Er, Kate?"

"It's perfect."

"The *sgian-dubh* is even smaller than a dirk."

"Yes! That's why it's perfect. 'He's mad that trusts in the tameness of a wolf, a horse's health, a boy's love, or a whore's oath.'"

John's hand slid from his chin to his eyes before dropping away. "Please. Not Shakespeare."

She jotted a few furious notes. "Should I include a whore, do you think? I could add one to Chapter Five. Audiences love whores."

"Chapter? I thought you were writing a play."

She waved off his nattering. "It might be a novel. I haven't decided."

Perhaps John had been the wrong person to ask. His new Scottish bride, Annie Tulloch MacPherson Huxley, would surely prove a better resource. Kate's new sister-in-law might be a bit brash, but she was a Highland lass through and through—red hair, fiery humor, and a brogue as thick as her venison stew.

Besides, Annie understood far better than John why Kate must complete her manuscript before spring. Kate hadn't had the heart to explain her goal of living independently to her brother. Was *he* a spirited woman who refused to be tamed and stuffed into an ill-fitting mold? No. He was a Huxley. Huxleys married. Huxleys bred. Huxleys did their duty.

Kate intended to be the exception, but to do so without becoming a burden to her family, she must establish an independent source of income. Finishing her manuscript was the answer, which was why she'd stayed on in Scotland.

Weeks ago, upon hearing news of John's long-awaited nuptials, Mama and Papa had immediately arranged for a Huxley family visitation. Eager to see the place she'd dreamt about for the past two years, Kate had traveled with them from Nottinghamshire to a land of green, wooded glens and glistening lochs. One glimpse, and she'd been enchanted.

While the rest of the family had returned home ten days ago, Kate had elected to stay with John and Annie through winter. She had a keen interest in learning more about Scotland's land, people, and history. One could not write a proper Scottish story without steeping oneself in Scottish culture.

Besides, Kate's four sisters, their husbands, and their children all had made the journey as well, and they'd planned to travel as a group with Mama and Papa on the return trip to England. Kate adored her family, but six days' travel in an enclosed carriage was dreadful enough without constant talk about the vagaries of infant teeth on one's nerves and nursing bosoms. She could only imagine what Annie had thought when they'd all arrived at Glendasheen Castle.

She needn't have worried. Annie had handled the Huxley Invasion splendidly. Annie was accustomed to managing a large family; hers included a stepfather and four stepbrothers.

Just then, Annie entered the room, abducting John's rapt gaze. To be fair, her hair did flash brilliant scarlet in the warm autumn light, so it caught Kate's attention, too. Several curls had escaped their pins, and Annie fussed with them as she crossed the room.

"Katie-lass. Ye always look so fresh and bonnie. Tell me how ye keep yer pins in place, and I'll let ye do another dramatic readin' after dinner."

"Of course—if you also agree to help me with Chapter Seven."

"Which scene is that, now?"

"The one in which Fiona Farquharson-McPhee rescues her father from a marauding gang of sheep farmers."

"Right. The sheep farmers." Annie cast a furtive look in John's direction and coughed. "Well, I do my best readin' when my hair isnae in my eyes."

Kate chuckled, set her notebook aside, and wiggled her fingers toward Annie's hair. "Here. Let me help." She went to work, tucking and repositioning the fiery coils. She and her sister-in-law were similarly petite, so Kate stood on her toes to get a better view of the top. "How did you manage to dislodge so many pins?"

Annie quirked a smile at John. "Care to explain, English?"

He cleared his throat. "No."

"I was havin' a wee nap." Annie's hand slid over her abdomen. "The bairn makes me … weary from time to time."

Kate glanced at John, whose cheeks were ruddy with the telltale Huxley Flush. "Right," she murmured. "Well, unlike my sisters, I've little advice to offer on that score." All her sisters had borne children. Many, many children.

Kate sometimes wondered what Annie would do when she grew too big to knead dough or carve venison any longer, or when she birthed the first of her inevitably large brood and spent all her time fretting over the babe's every sneeze. Motherhood had a way of taking over one's life.

So did falling in love.

As the youngest of five Huxley daughters, Kate had a unique perch from which to observe the phenomenon. One by one, her sisters had fallen madly in love and promptly descended into a state of foolish preoccupation. Longing glances, fluttery lashes, florid Huxley Flushes. It was all a bit bizarre, really. Worse, they'd lost interest in discussing much of anything apart from their men and, eventually, their children.

Even John—carefree, world-traveling, marriage-forswearing John—had fallen prey to the affliction.

To Kate, love was indistinguishable from a consuming parasite of the mind.

"Is it dreadful, then?" Annie asked, turning concerned eyes over her shoulder.

Kate tucked the final red curl into place. "There. Lovely."

Bright blue eyes warmed and sparkled. Annie gave her an affectionate pat. "My thanks, Katie-lass. Now then, ye must choose a happier scene for yer dramatic reading than the one from last night."

Kate frowned. "That was the Scottish play." Both Annie and John appeared unimpressed. "It is *Shakespeare.*"

"Aye. I ken ye've a fondness for auld Willy. But if I have to listen to one more lament about hand washin', I'll nae be responsible for the snorin'."

"Your father appeared to enjoy it." The towering old Scot had grinned throughout Lady Macbeth's scene, Kate had noticed. Which had been odd, given the dark subject matter. Still, Kate had thought it a positive reaction, even though his eyes had been fixed upon Annie's dressmaker, a widow from Inverness, who had joined Kate to read the other characters' lines.

"Angus was enjoyin' the whisky," Annie said wryly.

John came to slide an arm around his wife's waist. "I think he was enjoying the view."

"*Hmmph.* Mrs. Baird wants naught to do with him. What's he thinkin'?"

"Probably the same thing I'm thinking whenever I look at you."

"Dear God, English. Dinnae say such a thing. The very thought puts me off my breakfast."

His hand slid over hers where it lay upon her belly. "You cannot blame Angus for wanting—"

"I didnae say I blame him. Just that it makes me ill to contemplate."

As John and Annie discussed the unlikely affection developing between Annie's stepfather and her dressmaker, Kate sighed. This was yet more proof that love infected the mind of even the old and widowed.

Shaking her head, she moved to gather up her manuscript. "Well, I'll scurry off, then, shall I?"

They continued arguing with one another, ignoring Kate. Nothing new, there. John and Annie often forgot everyone else when they were in the same room, a common symptom of the mind infection.

"Must work on my manuscript if I ever wish to finish it." She didn't know why she bothered speaking. They were absorbed in a disagreement about whether a "crabbit auld man" of fifty-seven years and an "elegant lady" of forty-six years could make a sound marriage when they were so very *old* and settled in their ways.

Inches from embracing, John and Annie didn't notice as Kate backed toward the open doors.

"Perhaps the bit about the wolf will add an ineffable mystique to Sir Wallace's legendaryness," Kate observed.

No answer.

"That is the hope."

Now, John teased Annie about wanting to keep her dressmaker all to herself, to which Annie scoffed and repeated her assertion that "Angus and Nora suit one another about as well as an auld boot and a silk reticule." John retorted some might have said the same for an English earl's heir and a Highland lass.

Kate sighed and left them to their argument. It was a daft one, anyway. In her experience, there was no point ruminating upon whether a love match made sense.

Love itself made none at all.

On her way to the stairs, she passed Dougal MacDonnell, a brown-haired Scot with a plain face and friendly demeanor. One of many MacDonnells who now worked for John, Dougal functioned as head groundskeeper, footman, and general man-of-all-work.

He tugged off a dusty cap. "My lady."

She halted, her scalp tingling as another idea bloomed. "Mr. MacDonnell, may I see your *sgian-dubh?*"

Blinking, he replaced his cap then glanced side to side. "My ... er, aye. I suppose so." He bent and retrieved the small knife from his hose. "Have ye need of a blade?"

"Oh, no." She examined the small, rough knife with its wooden hilt. "I merely wish to ascertain how a man might employ such a weapon to kill a wolf."

A pause. "Beg your pardon, m'lady?"

"Hmm." She tilted her head, eyeing the blade. "It is rather small, isn't it?"

"'Tis not *wee.*" His tone suggested he'd taken offense. "'Tis the same size as every other man's, I assure ye. A fine size for its intended use." He paused. "Did ye say 'wolf,' m'lady?"

"One supposes if you struck the animal's throat with a sufficiently forceful blow, such a small blade could be effective—"

"Well, ye've no need to fash about blade size. There are no wolves in Scotland."

"Of course, Mr. MacDonnell." Her idea pressed at her, insisting she ask, "But, if there were, could a man who was very determined—one might even say *legendary*—dispatch a wolf with his *sgian-dubh*?"

Dougal lifted his cap and scratched his head. "Doubtful. A lamb, mayhap. Or a chicken."

"A chicken?"

"Aye. Make quick work of a chicken. Though, ye may have to finish the job with a hatchet. To be certain, mind."

She sighed, her idea reduced from the sparkling champagne of possibility to the flat, warm ale of disappointment.

"Has a beastie caused ye a fright, m'lady?" Dougal tucked his blade into its sheath. "Likely a doe rustlin' in the underbrush. 'Tis ruttin' season, ye ken. Dinnae fash. Lord Huxley is master of this glen, far as the eye can see. And where his land stops, MacPherson land begins. The MacPhersons dinnae tolerate threats to themselves, their cattle, or their kin. Fearsome lot, they are. Even if there *were* wolves in Scotland—which there arenae— ye'd have nothin' to fear. The MacPhersons would

protect ye." He patted his chest and gave her a kind
smile. "As would the MacDonnells."

She nodded, swallowing her deflation. "Very
reassuring. Thank you."

He tugged his cap as she made her way to the stairs.
She was halfway up the first flight when another idea
sent sparks down her spine. What if Sir Wallace had the
animal trapped in a sort of uphill-downhill scenario?
What if it first seemed that he would be defeated but
then gained the superior position on higher ground?

But that would require a very particular landscape.
She frowned, her fingers strumming the back of her
notebook. Dashing upstairs to her bedchamber, she
quickly retrieved her larger sketchbook and tucked a
few pages of notes inside. Then, she dressed in walking
boots and the tartan wrap Annie had given her as a
visitation gift. The blue-and-green wool paired
beautifully with her midnight-blue walking gown. She
draped it around her shoulders and pinned it with a
small brooch she'd purchased in Inverness. The jeweled
piece was a pair of knots, one silver and one copper,
intertwined and centered with a polished garnet. She
stroked the gem with her fingertip and admired the
folds of the woolen fabric in her dressing table mirror.

Several years ago, while miserably trudging her way
through her first London season, she'd read the
Waverley novels and become enchanted with
everything about this place. Bits of tartan ribbon and the
odd reading from Shakespeare's Scottish play had
satisfied her fascination for a time.

But nothing matched this—being here, wearing
actual tartan. Hearing the splash of a fish in the loch
below and the breeze rustling yellow-leaved birches

outside her open window. The same breeze played with her hair, tossing brown curls around her cheeks. She grinned at her reflection and donned a sensible straw bonnet before gathering up her pencil and sketchbook.

Today, she would find a landscape wherein a legendary man could gain an advantage over the last wolf in Scotland. Where he could dispatch a frightful predator with a "wee" blade and then make a mantle of the animal's pelt. Sir Wallace was a *Highlander*. A man to be admired and feared. A man whose legendaryness must bring audiences to their feet.

Or, at least, cause them to purchase her novel in some numbers. If she wished to live independently, she must sell well.

She hurried downstairs and outside, where sunshine turned the loch into liquid gold. Air as crisp as apples tickled her nose. Beneath lay the tang of pine, the burn of woodsmoke, and the loam of damp earth.

She grinned and filled her lungs, her step light as she hugged her sketchbook to her chest.

Ah, such majesty. The mountains, the water. Steep, green forests and deep-carved glens. She'd taken many rides and rambles here over the past weeks. She'd explored the waterfall and river north of the castle. The gentler fields and pastures to the southwest. The road that ran along the loch toward Angus MacPherson's land and, eventually, into the village.

She'd even climbed to the top of one of the smaller hills, where one could see the two neighboring glens, Glenscannadoo and Glendasheen, merge like reflections in a mirror. That hill lay to the east, and she now headed in that direction.

An hour passed before she reached the spot she'd been seeking, a hilltop bare of trees and covered in yellowing grasses, strewn with large rocks, and sloped just enough for comfortable sitting.

She plopped down and began sketching the two glens with their two lochs. Her pencil flew across the paper as she studied the landscape, hoping to spy the perfect site for Sir Wallace to meet his wolf. Should it be the crease before the curve above Loch Carrich? The slope on the way to the quarry? Or something closer?

She glanced west, raising a hand to block the sun. Without thinking, she began to hum. Then sing.

"Oh, there once was a man named Sir Wallace, who needed high ground as a solace, for his battle with the last wolf in Scotland, who would die by a wee knife in his hand, if only the author were slightly more clever. Or cleverer. Is it cleverer? Who can say? That's where cleverness serves one better. Will ever Sir Wallace have his triumphant day?"

Like most of her songs, it was extemporaneous, silly, and sung in an indecisive mezzo-soprano. But it kept her company while she sketched, so she continued on, *"Dear Sir Wallace. Will you be my legendary hero? Will you sell a thousand books or zero? Or must I marry some tedious fop, and become a drudge who's dull as a mop? Who says, 'Pass the peas, if you please, dear husband, for mashed is how little Thomas prefers them. He is teething, you know, and woe, woe, woooe to my aching bosoms.'"*

The tuneless nonsense continued until she noticed her paper turning gray. Then dark. A droplet splashed on its surface. She squinted up.

"Well, that moved in swiftly," she murmured.

Towering black clouds split the sky into dark and bright. A distant rumble heralded a storm. She scrambled to her feet and closed her sketchbook, but some of her loose notes caught and flew on a sharp, sudden gust.

"Drat," she muttered, chasing the pages as they drifted uphill then fluttered north toward the thick woods as though headed for a lovely jaunt through the countryside. One page landed in the grass.

Stretching out her arm, she raced to catch it. The notes were from her interview of Angus MacPherson, who'd gruffly explained the differences between raising cattle and sheep upon Highland lands. She *must* have them for Chapter Eleven, when Sir Wallace rescued Fiona from a fateful encounter with a herd of Farquharson-McPhee cattle. Her fingers brushed the corner of the page before the paper took wing again.

"Blast and dash it all. Dratted wind."

The second page flattened on the trunk of a tree. Changing direction, she raced to retrieve it first. "There! I have you." She shoved the paper inside her sketchbook and resumed her chase of the first page. Another blast shoved her hard, and she stumbled forward into the deeper shadows of the wood. Rain began to patter then beat upon her bonnet. She glanced around, noting the thick layer of pine needles and the diminishing light.

"Where did it go?" She spun in a circle. Twice more. Wandered in the direction of the wind. Finally, she spotted the paper near a thicket of ferns and brambles. By the time she retrieved it, she had two gouges on her wrist and a sore toe from an unseen rock.

"Damn and blast and curse every thorn in Scotland."

Tucking her sketchbook beneath her arm, she peeled back the edge of her glove to get a better look at her injuries. The air had gone rather purplish. She wandered toward a small clearing to her left where the light was better. Just past a coach-sized boulder and a gnarled tree that resembled an owl, she paused and looked again. Twin scratches welled red on her inner wrist. They'd already stained her sleeve. Huffing out a breath, she glanced up. The sky was nothing but low, ominous clouds. No sign of the sun, and night was falling swiftly.

Drat. How long had she been sketching? She frowned and looked behind her. Boulder and owl tree. She looked ahead. A slope angled down into a mix of trees, ferns, and rocks. A pair of pines on a small rise waved madly amidst the gusts now swirling and threatening to remove her bonnet. She walked toward them, trying to reorient herself.

Where the devil was she? It appeared to be a small valley in the upper foothills east of the glen. But she'd turned herself around so much, she couldn't tell one direction from the next. Frowning, she braced a hand on a rough pine trunk and struggled to see past the thick woodlands.

It was dark. Nothing looked familiar. And rain was beginning to pour from her bonnet's brim. She must try to find the way back to her hilltop. From there, she knew the way back to the castle. She started forward with a firmer chin and a great deal of self-reassurance. This would not be difficult. The hilltop must be past the clearing. Just beyond the wood.

It was not.

For the next hour, Kate searched for something—anything—to put her back on the path to the castle. She climbed to gain a better vantage point. But darkness kept her from making out anything but trees and more

hills. She slipped and carefully picked her way
downhill, thinking surely *down* would put her at the
bottom of the glen eventually. But down always seemed
to end with another *up*.

She had well and truly lost her way. When full dark
descended and rain soaked her to the skin, panic rose
up to grip her throat.

"K-Katherine Ann Huxley," she admonished. "Stop
being a ninny." A pine bough slicked past her nape, cold
and dripping. "John will surely have sent out a
MacDonnell or two in search of you. Highlanders are
superb at such things. *Obviously.* All you must do is
locate a path, which will take you to a house. Or a road,
which will take you to a village." She skirted around a
large rock and stumbled on a root. "*Ooph.* Or a brook.
That's brilliant. Water runs downhill; so shall you. A
brook runs into a river and a river into a loch. There are
two of them that cannot possibly be far. All you must do
is keep going *down* until you find one. Simple, really."
Her teeth began to chatter, and she hugged her damp
shawl tighter around her shoulders. "Provided you
don't freeze to death."

On her very next step, her foot slipped. Her legs flew
from beneath her. With bruising force, she landed on her
right hip and slid several yards down a muddy slope
before her clawing hand grasped a clump of grass and
yanked her to a stop.

The pressure in her chest built. The ache in her throat
tightened. Pain radiated from her hip and buttock, and
tears filled her eyes.

"Katherine Ann Huxley," she choked. "You will *not*
weep like some mewling milksop. Stop it this instant."

She gritted her chattering teeth. She firmed her aching muscles. She braced her sore hand on the ground and shoved to her feet, clutching her damp sketchbook harder.

Her surroundings were nothing but dark blobs of blue, gray, and green. Occasionally, a distant boom of thunder would precede a faint flash of light, but such flashes were coming less frequently. Squinting into the misty black, she tried to determine what lay ahead. More trees, she thought. They were downhill. *She* must go downhill. Like water, she would simply follow gravity. At least it was a direction.

She didn't know how long she'd been walking when she heard the odd, rumbling growl. It might have been minutes or an hour. All she knew was that her skin was cold enough to chill one of her favorite chocolate ices, and her muscles ached and shook and threatened to give up. When the sound reached her through softening rain, she froze.

Her heart battered its cage in a frantic revolt. So loudly did it pound—*wah-whump, wah-whump, wah-whump*—that she scarcely heard anything else.

Except this. The growl was deep as caverns, rough as gravel. It resonated past pinewoods and undergrowth and her *wah-whumping* heart. It sent a warning flash of ice across her skin.

"Th-there are no wolves in Scotland," she whispered. "No wolves in Scotland. No wolves in Scotland."

Her breathing shallowed to a pant as she listened closely.

There. A grunt. More of the rough, jagged rumble. An odd, wet crunch. A rolling thud.

She blinked. There it was again. The rumbling. Was that … a voice?

"… thought … escape, did ye?"

It was. It was a voice. A *man's* voice.

Oh, thank heaven. This wasn't a wolf. It was a man. And, unless he was a bit eccentric like Kate, he probably spoke to someone else. Another man, perhaps, or a dog or horse. Yes, that must be it.

Perfectly normal. A man was out here in the dark woods at night admonishing his dog for running off. Or fetching a horse who'd wandered away. Or arguing with his chum about who played a superior hand of whist.

Releasing a relieved breath, she chuckled at herself. Ninny, indeed. She wound her way toward the sounds, taking care to avoid acquiring any more bramble injuries. As it was, she'd look a fright when she asked the gentleman with the rumbling, distorted voice for directions back to the castle. He might even refuse to help her until she informed him of who her brother was.

"… bluidy swine."

Kate slowed. That had been a snarl. Were they arguing about livestock? She knew the sheep-cow debate was a sore one here in the Highlands.

A dull crack. "Get up. We're nae done."

Her eyes widened as she glimpsed a faint light. A lantern, perhaps, but a dim one. It flickered low through the wiry branches and steady rain. She searched the small clearing, a twelve-foot pocket of space between thick trees. When she saw a figure at the edge, beyond the lantern's light, she blinked.

Couldn't be real. Not possible.

Her breath whooshed out, ending in a wheeze. Lungs flattened. She couldn't blink. Couldn't breathe.

Not. Possible. He was … too big. Seven feet tall, at least. Enormous. Nothing but a hulking black shadow with faint light flickering along muscles that more rightly belonged on a Thoroughbred. No, he was human. Wasn't he? Something was … wrong with his face.

Her chest hurt. Oh, God. What the devil *was* he?

Lightning flashed white overhead, illuminated his jaw. It was a tangle of jagged lines. And where his eye should be was … nothing. Sunken skin and raised, puckered scars. Where his mouth should end, it didn't. Instead, a gruesome scowl had been carved downward, contorting his face into a permanent sneer.

But his monstrous appearance and unearthly size weren't what frightened her most. No, what terrified her was what he held aloft.

A man. At least, she thought the limp, light-haired, bloody-faced figure was a man. His throat was currently being crushed inside the bearish paw of the monster who dangled him two feet off the ground.

Good God, the strength that required. The menacing, furious, brutal strength of a seven-foot monster. Blood poured from the dangling man's broken nose. It shone red upon the man's exposed teeth. Exposed because he was … grinning?

The monster reeled back with his fist and drove it into the man's eye. Then, he dropped the man in a heap upon the ground and released a wordless roar. He kicked the man's ribs.

The man used the momentum to roll away, but the monster followed. Kicked him again.

"Get up, ye craven bastard!" He stomped the man's hand with a sickening crunch, and the man groaned. Another kick. "Get up!"

The rage inside the monster's graveled roars coiled around her heart and squeezed. Harder and harder and harder it squeezed until she gasped for relief. Mewling sounds escaped, and she tried to cover them.

The monster was leaning down, now, beating the man on the ground with furious blows. The light-haired man wheezed and stilled.

Oh, dear God. He wasn't moving.

The monster had killed him.

The monster had *murdered* someone while Kate had stood here and watched. Her stomach lurched. The cry that slipped past her fingers was as high as a child's. Fear battered her like fists, covered her like wet wool. Kate stumbled backward, away from the clearing.

Away from him.

But not soon enough. The monster's heaving shoulders stiffened. He straightened to his full height. Then turned.

White light flashed moon-bright, and for a moment, she was a rabbit pinned by a wolf. The monster's intact eye flashed and narrowed. He took several long, hitching strides closer.

Closer.

Closer to where Kate cowered in the brush, waiting for a dangerous predator to come and claim her.

CHAPTER TWO

Her throat felt as crushed as if he'd closed it inside his powerful fist. She must run. *Run!* She screamed the word inside her head then repeated it. *Run, run, run!*

She spun. Time slowed and the nightmare sank its claws into her.

She ran. Up the slope she'd just descended. Across a ridge she'd failed to notice. Around a stand of white-barked birches. Across a field of grass. Through the rain that was slowly turning to mist.

She ran until her lungs burned and her feet cramped and her knees were muddy from slipping so many times.

She didn't realize she was sobbing until she saw the owl tree. She braced her back against it and clawed her hand into the bark. Only then did she dare to look behind her.

The monster wasn't there.

And the darkness was lighter than before. She looked up. Clouds had moved off the moon.

Swiping her cheeks and gathering her breath, she searched for other familiar features. There! A knoll similar to one where she'd rested earlier. She shoved away from the tree and staggered toward it.

The rain stopped, leaving only cool damp. The moon continued to shine. It was so bright, she spotted her hilltop easily, and from there, she swiftly made her way down to the road.

Dougal MacDonnell and his brother were the first to find her. Dougal immediately wrapped her in his coat, placed her on his horse, and took her back to the castle. He questioned her gently, but she couldn't answer.

She felt muddled and choked. Cold and far away.

By the time John came to lift her down, she was shaking apart.

Her brother kissed her temple and rushed inside the castle, shouting for Mrs. MacDonnell to bring tea and prepare a bath. John was shaking, too, she noticed, though he carried her steadily enough.

"We'll get you warm and dry, sweetheart. Not to worry. Annie loves nothing better than taking care of her wee lambs."

Kate rested her cheek against his strong shoulder and sighed.

"Can you tell me what happened?" He nodded to one of the maids as he carried her into her bedchamber and lowered her onto a small sofa. "Where did you wander off to?"

Kate heard the control he was exerting. Their papa was the same way—in a moment of crisis, he remained calm and steady. Only later did he permit his emotions to show.

She found his solid strength reassuring. Yet, she couldn't force an answer to the surface. Instead, she sat very still and stared at her brother's chin.

Annie entered and immediately set to work removing Kate's soggy bonnet, which now dangled down her back. "Katie-lass, ye're soaked to the bone," she said matter-of-factly. "We must dispense with yer shawl and gown before ye catch yer death. English, I'll summon ye when she's done bathin'."

"Love, she hasn't said a word. I've never seen her like this. If anything, it's hard to persuade her to *stop* talking."

"Aye, I ken." Annie's eyes turned tender. She stood on her toes and cradled John's face in her hands. "Give us an hour, hmm? Let me help yer wee sister."

He nodded, kissed his wife, and stroked Kate's hair. Then, he left the room. Annie gently helped her remove her clothing.

Shivers wracked Kate until she wondered if her bones would break loose and float about inside her limp body. She blinked, realizing Annie and the maid had helped her to the tub. She blinked again, and she was soaking in hot water, surrounded by steam and the scent of her soap. Jasmine. Tuberose. Hints of clary sage and bergamot.

Another blink, and she was dry, her washed hair brushed and plaited down her back, her body dressed in a clean shift and swaddled in several woolen blankets. Presently, she sat on the sofa. She didn't remember sitting.

"Wh-where is my sketchbook?" she rasped.

Annie turned from speaking with the maid. She came and sat beside Kate, rubbing Kate's fingers between her hands. "Where ye always keep it." She nodded toward the dressing table beneath the window. "There, ye see?"

"Oh."

"Do ye care to say where ye were this evenin', Katie-lass?"

"I went for a ramble. I thought Sir Wallace should battle a wolf, but his knife was too small. He needs higher ground."

Annie's blue eyes caught Kate's gaze. Scarlet brows puckered with concern. "There arenae any wolves left in Scotland."

Kate tried to smile, but her mouth shook. "I know."

John entered and came to crouch in front of Kate. Warm, worried hazel eyes smiled at the corners as he stroked her cheek with his knuckle.

She clasped his hand desperately tight and held it against her. A tear wet their fingers. "I lost my way, John."

His jaw flickered. He closed his eyes briefly. "I thought as much. Why did you go off alone?"

"I—I've been taking these rambles by myself for weeks without incident. The storm moved in so quickly. I lost track of time, I suppose. Dark came on, and I ..."

"What happened?" His voice was a hard demand.

"Go easy, English," Annie said softly. "Kate's had a wee fright, havenae ye?"

Kate nodded.

Annie fetched her a cup of tea, but Kate could only drink half of it before her head began swimming. "This is mostly whisky," she murmured into the hot liquid.

"Aye. Best thing for ye."

Kate blinked as the little roses on the cup began to swirl.

"Did someone hurt you?" John demanded. He'd begun pacing, she noticed.

She shook her head. "No. Not me."

"What does that mean?"

"I climbed to the top of one of the easterly hills. The bald one with the large rocks. Lovely view of both glens. I was searching for a proper setting, but I didn't realize it had grown so late. Then the storm came, and the wind—"

"Katie." John's patience seemed to be slipping. "Just tell us what frightened you."

She'd been staring into her tea, seeing her own reflection. The white face surrounded by damp brown curls. Now, she raised her head. John crouched in front of her, his jaw hard.

"I heard his voice first. I was lost and thought to ask for directions back to the castle. Then I saw him. A monster. So very large." Her heart sped as memories flashed. "He was ... beating someone. Oh, God, John. I think he killed him."

John stilled. "Large, you say?"

"Seven feet, perhaps. Taller than Angus. But bigger. And so strong."

"And you were in the east hills."

She nodded. Her stomach churned.

"What did he look like?"

"Monstrous."

John released a half-chuckle. "For once, you are giving too little detail. But I need you to be specific, sweetheart."

She met his gaze, warm and reassuring. Like Papa's. "He was ... scarred. Very badly scarred. One of his eyes was missing. He wore black, I think. His hair was dark."

John stood and shifted his gaze behind Kate. "The man he was beating. Did he have light hair, by chance?"

Kate frowned. "Yes." She glanced behind her. Annie stood near the fireplace, swaying and whiter than Kate's tea saucer. "Annie? What's wrong?"

Annie shook her head and covered her mouth with a trembling hand. Blue eyes shimmered. Without speaking, Annie fled the room.

"John?" Kate tried to stand, but the whisky and layers of woolen blankets made it impossible. "What's wrong with Annie?"

Expression grim, John braced his hands on his hips and hung his head. "You must forget what you saw."

"I—I cannot."

"You must."

"Every time I close my eyes, I see it again."

"I promise you're safe. The man you saw will never hurt you. Do you believe me?"

She swallowed. John was her brother. He'd never lied to her before. "I suppose so."

"Good. Time to sleep, now."

"I don't think I can."

He nodded to her teacup. "Drink the rest."

She did, and before long, her eyelids fluttered as weariness and warmth invaded. Her muscles ached. She began to slump. The room spun.

He helped her to her feet and guided her to the bed. Then, he tucked her in as he'd done when she was a child. "Sleep, sweetheart. All will be well."

When he moved to douse the lantern on the bedside table, she stopped him. "Please. I need it." Her words sounded slurred. She'd never been one for strong drink.

He nodded and strode to the door.

"John?"

He turned.

"Why must I forget?"

For a moment, she thought he wouldn't answer. Then, he did. "Because the man you saw was Broderick MacPherson."

Annie's stepbrother? Kate knew the name, but she'd only met the youngest of the four MacPherson brothers. Rannoch was charming in a wicked, flirtatious way. The two oldest, Campbell and Alexander, were in Aberdeen on distillery business, according to Angus. Broderick was Annie's third-oldest stepbrother, a few years younger than John. She'd mentioned him to Kate in passing but hadn't gone into detail.

"I don't understand," Kate murmured. "If he murdered that man—"

"Forget him, Katie."

"But why?"

John's face turned to stone. Hazel eyes flashed angry gold in the firelight. "If what you saw was Broderick MacPherson killing a man, then that man deserved to die."

The following morning, Kate awakened bleary-eyed, head-pained, and more confused than she'd been when she'd fallen asleep, but at least morning had brought an end to the nightmares. Great, hulking monsters with bloody fists and a murderous gleam had hunted her for hours. One of them had even sprouted fangs.

She doubted Annie's brother had fangs, but how in blazes would she know? John and Annie hadn't explained anything about him or what she'd seen. Kate had hoped to question them about the matter this morning, but they'd already left the castle by the time she went down to breakfast.

Now, she exited the only shop that sold paper in the small village of Glenscannadoo—the haberdashery—and glanced around the tiny square. At the center was a statue of a pompous-looking MacDonnell laird. Surrounding it were several taverns, a motley assortment of shops, an inn, and a cottage or two. All were the same gray stone in the same state of dilapidation. They were also similarly wet.

Blast. Kate sighed and struggled to open her umbrella while keeping her package beneath her arm. She fumbled awkwardly. The package slipped. The umbrella flew. It collided with the knee of a passing pedestrian.

"Oh!" Her gaze flew up. "I do beg your pardon, sir. Dreadfully clumsy of me."

The middle-aged, black-clad gentleman straightened to a military posture with her umbrella in hand. His expression was steely, his mouth unsmiling between thick, gray whiskers. "Aye," he replied, his voice stern. Then, he snapped open her umbrella and handed it back to her before tugging the brim of his hat. "Here ye are, miss. Good day."

She blinked as he brushed past her. "Good day to …"

He entered the saddler's shop two doors down from the haberdashery.

"… you." Kate wondered if the Scot's brusque manner had been specific to her wayward umbrella or if he was simply displeased with life. Some men were. Her mathematics tutor, for example, had been of a similarly sour disposition. Of course, she'd always been dreadful with numbers, and the young man had found their sessions exceedingly trying. Why Papa had insisted she have both a music tutor and a mathematics tutor, nobody had quite understood. Papa would only say that some ladies discovered interests beyond music and theatre once they explored a bit further afield.

Which was certainly fine for those ladies. But Kate had discovered her interests—indeed, her *passions*—early in life, and she was quite content to pursue them to the exclusion of all else.

She wrinkled her nose as she glanced beyond the eave to the steady rain.

If only she could manage to keep a single sheet of paper dry long enough to finish writing Sir Wallace's grand adventure.

Raising her umbrella, she started forward past the statue. Only to halt, seized by a sudden flash of fear. Thirty yards away, a towering figure with black hair and broad shoulders loped toward the third most popular tavern in Glenscannadoo.

Her heart pounded. She clutched the umbrella tighter. Breathed faster.

Then, he glanced in her direction. And waved.

Her entire body went limp. Oh, thank heavens. It was Rannoch MacPherson. Wickedly handsome and often smiling. Yes, he was over six-and-a-half-feet tall. And yes, there was a family resemblance. But he was not his brother. Not the monster.

She smiled weakly and nodded in return. He disappeared inside the tavern, and Kate pressed the umbrella's wooden handle to her cheek. *Breathe,* she commanded herself. *Breathe and stop being a ninny.*

By the time she returned to where she'd tied her little mare, her heart had slowed from a racing gallop to a vigorous canter. She stashed her package inside her saddlebag and patted Ophelia's glossy black neck. The horse nudged her hip, and Kate winced. Cuts and bruises from the previous night's misadventures hadn't had time to heal. Further, her hands and legs—indeed, her every muscle—quaked like jostled jelly. A product of exhaustion, no doubt.

For a moment, she allowed herself to slump against Ophelia's damp warmth. Huddled beneath the umbrella, she squeezed her eyes closed.

Lightning flashed white inside the dark. A single eye filled with feral rage stared back at her. Blood dripped from—

Her eyes flew open. Her chest squeezed until she couldn't bear the pressure.

She grunted and shook her head.

A ride had seemed like such a good idea. Kate despised stewing in her own sauce. Much better to do something distracting. Ordinarily, she would play the pianoforte, but John hadn't yet acquired one. So, instead, she'd donned her brown wool riding habit and taken Ophelia out for a run.

Now, she stood in the pouring rain in the town square shaking like a perfect ninny.

What she needed was to understand. Perhaps John and Annie would return to the castle soon, and they could set her mind at ease. Or, at least stop the terrible visions she saw every time she closed her eyes.

She glanced at the tavern only steps from where she stood. John and Annie were not the only ones who might offer explanations.

Patting Ophelia's neck, she murmured, "I'll only be a moment, girl."

Glenscannadoo's third most popular tavern had only two patrons this time of day—one a plump woman in a shabby gown and white cap, slumped and snoring with her mouth open at a table near the hearth; the other was the man Kate had assaulted with her umbrella.

Blast. She peered deeper into the dingy, ale-stained room. The short man behind the bar, another cousin of Dougal's, immediately abandoned his conversation with the stern gentleman to greet her. "M'lady." He gave her a respectful nod. "What may I offer ye?"

She drifted to the bar and wrung her closed umbrella in her fists. "Thank you kindly, Mr. MacDonnell, but I'm looking for Mr. MacPherson." She squeezed the umbrella harder. "Rannoch MacPherson. I saw him enter. Is he here?"

He slanted a glance toward the stern man. "Popular fellow," he murmured. "Nae. I havenae seen him."

She frowned. "But, he was just—"

"Now, most days, ye'll find him at the distillery."

"Yes, I—"

"But I dinnae ken where he is today. Nor his brothers. Naught to tell ye, I'm afraid." Mr. MacDonnell's eyes darted strangely as his brows bobbed.

Kate wondered if the man had been tippling his own stock.

A shadow moved across the bar in front of her. "Beg yer pardon, miss. Or is it my lady? I hear England when ye speak. Perhaps ye're kin to Lord Huxley."

She blinked up at the stern gentleman. His gaze had sharpened from steely to piercing. Something about his intent posture worsened her trembling. "I am Lady Katherine Huxley, Lord Huxley's sister. And you are?"

"Sergeant Neil Munro, constable for Inverness. What interest have ye in Rannoch MacPherson?"

Alarm traced a shivery trail down her spine. She glanced toward MacDonnell and found him wiping a glass with undue fixation. Tilting her chin, she gave the constable the best answer she could summon on short notice. "I fancy him."

Steely eyes narrowed. "That so?"

"Yes." Her cheeks began burning. "Dreadfully handsome."

"Are ye acquainted with his brother Broderick, perhaps?" The man's whiskers moved as his jaw flexed. "Nae quite so handsome."

Her heart pounded. Pounded. *Pounded.* "N-no?"

"Ye're nae acquainted."

She shook her head. The skin on her throat felt afire. "I haven't had the pleasure." That, at least, was true. Nothing about her encounter with Broderick MacPherson had been a pleasure.

"He is kin to yer brother's wife, aye?"

"Y-yes, I suppose—"

"Yet, ye havenae met him."

"No." Blasted Huxley Flush. Her face prickled with heat.

"Hmm. Have ye any knowledge of a man named Lockhart?"

She frowned. "No. Is he—"

"Light hair. This tall." He placed a gloved hand near the top of his own head. "Lean. *Handsome* fellow. One a young lady might take notice of."

With every terse description, Kate's stomach gave a queasy lurch. She wrung her umbrella until it made a cracking sound.

"He's a Lord of Parliament," Munro continued, unsmiling and colder than drenched stone. "Last seen inside the Inverness jail."

"J-jail?"

"Aye. He escaped, ye see." Munro's head tilted. "Which is a wee bit peculiar, given he was likely to be released in four days." The grim constable lowered his head and his voice. "Now, I'm charged with findin' him, my lady. To my reckonin', the only man who'd trouble himself to free Lockhart from the jail is Broderick MacPherson, who would only do so to ensure his lordship met an untimely end. I'd prefer to ask MacPherson, but I cannae find him. Nor can I find any of his kin." For the first time, a small smile tugged inside the whiskers. "Except you."

"I—I am not his kin. His stepsister is my sister-in-law, which makes us nothing at all, really—"

"So, I'll ask again. Have ye heard or seen aught of Lord Lockhart in the last two days?"

She didn't have to close her eyes this time for the vision to come—the blood, the sickening sound of a fist being driven into a man's jaw and nose and teeth. The man she'd seen being beaten—no, killed—had been light-haired, lean, and roughly the same height as Sergeant Munro. His face had been too damaged to discern handsomeness, but it had clearly been him. Lockhart. What had he been jailed for? Why had he been scheduled for release?

Oh, God. She'd planted herself squarely in the worst possible circumstance. She must answer Munro's question. And she must lie. Convincingly.

Bracing herself and drawing upon every ounce of thespian talent she possessed, she tilted her chin. Straightened her shoulders. Cleared her throat. And gave the greatest performance of her life.

"You told him *what?!*" John groaned and ran a frustrated hand over his face. He paced the width of his study. Twice. "Kate. Please say you are jesting."

Kate twisted the end of her tartan shawl between her hands and nibbled her lower lip. "I'd already confessed I fancied Rannoch."

"But you don't fancy Rannoch. Do you?"

"Well, he is charming in a rakish sort of way."

John glared.

"No. Not particularly. I do find him amusing and handsome. But he is much too tall and his manner too coarse." She cast a sheepish glance at Annie, who'd sat listening for the past few minutes. "Apologies, Annie. I mean no insult."

"Katie. Good God," John continued. "Why would you not simply say you're acquainted with the MacPhersons through Annie and wished to speak with Rannoch on some family matter?"

She gave a small shrug. "I panicked."

"Right. Then, you lied about Broderick."

"Only a little."

"Bloody hell."

"Well, I didn't know what else to say!"

John's eyes flashed gold. "Anything. Anything would have served better than claiming you and Broderick had formed an 'impassioned connection'—"

"We did. In a manner of speaking. *He* was quite impassioned at our first encounter."

"Then, you claimed that, upon learning you 'fancied' his brother, he'd grown so jealous that he's now devoted himself entirely to winning your hand."

Absently, she wound a curl near her temple around her finger. "Yes. I may have gotten a jot carried away."

"And that he's spoken of nothing else since the day you met."

"Also true. He said nothing whatever when we met yesterday."

John folded his arms across his chest, leaned his backside against his desk, and stared at his boots. In this pose, he reminded Kate so much of Papa, her heart ached. Papa often wore a similar expression of exasperated disappointment. At the moment, she missed him terribly.

"John, I know you think I've made things worse—"

"You have."

"—but I was trying to help. Whilst my tale is rather fanciful, it may give Sergeant Munro pause. Perhaps he will accept that Broderick's attention has been monopolized by a pursuit *other* than murdering Lord Lockhart."

Her brother rubbed his eyes with his thumb and finger. "Katie. You've just trained Munro's sights squarely upon you, sweetheart."

She flinched. "No, I—I told him nothing about what I saw."

"But you lied," he replied softly.

She wrung the shawl then twirled a curl then bit her lip and wrung the wool again. Then, she nodded, her stomach twisting harder than the tartan in her hands.

Annie finally spoke, her small hand grasping Kate's. "English, I ken she told Munro a tall tale, but he cannae be certain it's false."

His mouth quirked. "Munro despises the MacPhersons, love. You know he resents them having eluded his men all those years with their whisky running. Now that the distillery is properly licensed, he'll see this as his opportunity to achieve some measure of justice."

"Aye."

"Lockhart disappeared days before his release and the likely dismissal of his charges. Broderick must surely have known suspicion would land upon him. But he's clever enough not to leave a bloody trail."

Annie nodded, her mouth pale and pinched. "I ken."

"Now, Kate's little performance has put Munro onto the scent. He'll know she was lying. He'll know all he must do is hound her heels until she breaks."

"How will he ken she's lyin'? 'Tis outlandish to claim Broderick would be the jealous sort, I grant ye, but—"

"Love, trust me. He knew the moment she spoke."

"Ye cannae ken such a thing for certain."

John gave Kate a wry nod. "A demonstration, perhaps?"

Kate shrank into her seat. "I don't think that's necessary."

"Demonstration of what?" Annie demanded.

"Go on, Katie," John nudged. "Lie to her."

She didn't want to. But as she stared down at the hand holding hers, offering strength and comfort when *Annie's* family was the one at risk, Kate thought she must. So, she gathered up a story in her mind. She raised her eyes to Annie's. Then, much as she'd done with Munro, she gave her performance her finest effort.

"I find haggis delightful," she began. "Never have I so ardently disagreed with the characterization of a dish as 'unspeakably vile.' I still recall the first time I had it. Delicious."

By the time Kate had finished her tall tale, her face was hot enough to cook a dish of vile haggis. And Annie's eyes were watering with laughter.

"Och, Katie-lass." She wiped a knuckle beneath her eye and released a series of hearty chuckles. "Why did ye never say ye hated the stuff?"

"I don't hate it … precisely."

Another round of laughter from her sister-in-law. "Oh, ye must stop. My belly's achin', and the bairn must be wonderin' what's so amusin'."

Feeling half-sick and half-embarrassed, Kate squeezed Annie's hand.

Annie squeezed back. "Now, I ken why yer brother is a wee bit puckered. We've had dealings with Munro before. He's no dull blade, that's for certain." She patted Kate's arm and cast a worried glance at her husband. "And I'm afraid John is right, Katie-lass. Ye're the worst liar I've ever seen."

Kate nodded. Regrettably, it was true. Every time a lie left her lips, her face flooded with red color and flashing heat. Her voice went abnormally high, and her eyes went abnormally wide.

"What do we do?" she asked John.

"You must return to England. I'll write Mama and Papa today."

Her heart sank. "But I haven't finished my novel. Play. It might be both, actually. I haven't decided. Regardless, I must finish Sir Wallace's story. John, please."

"I'm sorry, little sister. You'll have to use that vivid imagination of yours."

"There must be another way."

"There isn't. Munro hates the MacPhersons. He'll pursue this without quarter. If he suspects you have information that will help convict Broderick, he will compel you to testify. I cannot have you anywhere near this mire, let alone at the center of it."

"I'll simply refuse to answer. I'll stay hidden in the castle. I'll avoid him entirely." Kate swallowed. "Please don't send me away."

She'd written a third of her story in the past three weeks. The previous third had taken her a year. Scotland was her muse. Every green slope and drop of water. Every rolled R and throat-clearing *och*. Every warm tartan plaid and plaintive bagpipe wail.

In England, she was nothing but an earl's daughter. Future wife. Future mother. Future hostess of tedious dinners beginning with white soup and ending with pointless conversation. Future vessel to be filled with another family's aristocratic legacy then forgotten after the children were grown.

Here, she could be more. An author. A playwright. An artist of the page and stage renowned for more than her fertility and pleasant disposition. Well, perhaps *renowned* was a bit much. Independent. Yes, that was better. She needn't be renowned, merely self-sustaining.

Kate watched as Annie stood and moved to John's side. Then, she wrapped her arms around him and laid her cheek upon his chest. He enfolded his wife protectively, and Kate felt an odd pang. She dropped her gaze to her lap.

Faintly, she heard Annie whisper, "I cannae go through it again, English. I'd rather die than see him sent back to that godforsaken prison."

Kate's eyes flew up. "*B-back* to prison?"

"We won't let it happen, love."

Confusion spun inside Kate's mind, making her dizzy. Broderick had been imprisoned before? What had happened? Why had he been released? And what in blazes was going on?

After so many hours of shock and uncertainty, she'd had quite enough. Rising, Kate positioned herself in John's line of sight. "Explain, if you please. Broderick was imprisoned? For what crime?"

"Katie."

"No. Do not speak to me like I'm seven, John." She shrugged off her shawl and tossed it behind her. "I am not the one who took a man from the Inverness jail and beat him to death with my own hands. That was *him.* Indeed, I am the one who stumbled upon it, frightening me out of my wits. I'm the one who is forced to see the blood and hear the sounds—"

He reached out to stroke her arm. "Hush, little one."

"—of fists cracking bone." Her voice thinned. "Every time I close my eyes. Every time." She pulled away. "Why should I be punished for what he did?"

"You shouldn't."

In John's eyes, she saw the pain he carried for Annie, who hadn't moved from his embrace. "At least tell me what's going on," Kate whispered. "I deserve that much, wouldn't you say?"

Annie shuddered. When she turned, her eyes were mournful. "Aye, Katie-lass. Ye deserve to ken what ye saw."

After they returned to their seats, Annie began her explanations, describing how her "favorite" stepbrother had become the monster of Kate's nightmares.

"He was braw as a clear sky over snowy pines. Ah, ye should have seen him. Handsomer than Rannoch or Alexander, though dinnae tell them I said so. And better. He was better than all of us." Annie paused to smile. Blue eyes glossed. "Until last year. Until Edinburgh." Blue eyes squeezed closed, and her smile turned into a grimace of grief.

"What happened in Edinburgh?"

Blue eyes opened. Overflowed. "The devil came for him. And the devil won."

CHAPTER THREE

One year earlier
September 1825
Leith, Scotland

"Have a care with that crate—bluidy hell, man." Broderick MacPherson cursed the carelessness of younger brothers.

From the back of the wagon, Rannoch shot him a grin. "Gift for yer sweet dove, eh?" He shook the crate he'd just dropped from his full height of six feet, seven inches. The clink of broken china amidst a bed of straw was pure mockery. "Cost ye a wee bit, I reckon." Another grin, this one accompanied by laughter.

"Daft bugger," Broderick grumbled. "'Twas a gift for Annie. She's never had a proper china tea set before."

Rannoch's laughter faded. "Oh." He rubbed the back of his neck. "Sorry."

"Aye, ye are sorry. And ye'll be buyin' her another to replace it."

Sighing, Rannoch nodded and jumped down from the wagon before repositioning the crate with exaggerated care.

Their two older brothers, Campbell and Alexander, exited the warehouse where they'd been delivering a load of MacPherson whisky. Like all the MacPhersons, they were over six-and-a-half feet tall and built along their da's lines—heavy-boned and muscular with massive shoulders. All of them had dark hair and eyes, like their da. They all had square jaws and rough edges. And, to greater or lesser degrees, they'd all inherited a share of Angus's black temper.

Alexander had the worst of it in that regard, though he'd learned to channel his darker nature in more productive directions over the years.

Campbell was the slowest to anger, but also the quietest. At eight-and-a-half inches above six feet, he was technically the tallest, topping Broderick by a half-inch and Rannoch and Alexander by a wee bit more. They were all leaner than Campbell, whose powerful arms and millstone fists could put them on the ground with one swipe. *Everybody* was glad Campbell was the patient one.

By contrast, Rannoch was the charmer, particularly with the lasses. Every bit of trouble he'd ever landed in had been because of a lass or drink or, more often, both.

As for Broderick ... well. One of them had to negotiate business contracts and keep a cool head while the excisemen jockeyed for steeper bribes. If they ever wanted to be a properly licensed distillery with legitimate distribution to England, the Continent, and perhaps even America, one of them had to develop a bit of polish, smile for the solicitors, and court the government men. That had fallen to Broderick. His brothers called him the peacemaker. Annie called him her favorite. Broderick thought of himself as the sensible one.

Alexander glared at the crate Rannoch was sliding gingerly to one side of the wagon. "What the devil is that? A gift for yer wee dove?"

Being sensible was seldom easy with this lot. "I told ye, I dinnae have a dove, wee or otherwise," Broderick replied, checking off the last of the load from his list.

"Then, who's been sendin' all those letters that smell like Mrs. MacBean's headache tonic?"

Broderick shook his head. "'Tis lavender, ye eejit."

Alexander gave a sardonic smirk. "Noticed ye didnae answer my question."

Campbell's deep rumble intruded. "Leave off. He says he doesnae have a lass, so that's that."

Broderick nodded his thanks to his oldest brother and started for the warehouse, where he had some business to finish before the day was done.

"Wee bit of a curiosity, then," Alexander called after him.

Broderick kept walking.

"Want to hear why?"

"Nah," Broderick answered without slowing.

"But the question must be asked, brother," Alexander mocked. "If ye havenae any lass, nor any dove, who's that fair bit o' muslin waitin' inside, eh?"

He stopped. Closed his eyes. Removed his hat, ran a hand through his hair, and muttered a foul curse.

She'd returned. He'd told her to stay away.

"Meet me at the inn," he barked over his shoulder as he shoved through the old, rusted door. The warehouse was a cavernous building stacked with casks and crates. A few high windows let in dusty light. Near the back was a partitioned area with a small table and several chairs.

It was there she waited.

She was slim and graceful. Tall for a woman. She wore her flaxen hair in loose curls that always looked as though she'd been recently kissed. Her lips looked the same, full and ripe. Her beauty was rosebud innocence.

He'd been fooled at first.

They'd met last spring while he was shopping for a copper kettle along Princes Street. He liked bringing home gifts for his wee sister, who did so much for them—cooking and mending and managing her brothers with honest affection. Annie was a pure blessing, if a wee bit sharp-tongued from time to time. He'd wanted to buy her something to make her eyes light up, so he'd gone to an expensive shop in the most expensive part of the city.

A woman with flaxen hair and rosebud innocence had gazed up at him through a veil after pondering a pair of candlesticks for much too long. Then, she'd asked if he was making a purchase for his wife.

Within an hour, their conversation had progressed from politeness to attraction to flirtation. He hadn't recognized how deftly she'd steered him until much later. Outside the shop, she'd invited him to ride with her in a nearby green, and he'd learned she lived in one of the fashionable houses along Queen Street.

When he'd asked about her family, she'd demurred, saying only that they lived in the country while she preferred town. She hadn't explained how an unmarried woman could afford to live in such a fine house all alone.

Now, months later, he looked her up and down—her elegant velvet riding habit, her embroidered kid gloves, her slender waist, and satiny skin that required the costliest creams and powders to maintain. And he felt no bitterness, no betrayal. Only a pang of sympathy.

"Cecilia," he murmured.

Her back stiffened. Her head lowered. She didn't turn around. "Broderick." The single word ached with longing.

"We agreed ye shouldnae seek me out again, lass."

Full lips pressed together as she gripped the back of a chair. "I had to. Ye havenae answered me."

Slowly, he approached her. "Ye ken that's not true."

"I will leave him, Broderick."

"We've discussed this."

"If I kenned ye'd have me, I'd leave him this very day."

He came to stand beside her, noting how tightly she clutched her wee purse. It was silk. "If ye wish to leave him, then I will help ye. But—"

She turned and threw her arms around his waist, clutching him like the last rock before a precipice. "Please," she moaned. "Please."

Lightly, he stroked her thin shoulders. In that moment, he almost wished he loved her. She did need someone—someone who would not demand she wear a veil in public, who would let her eat what she wished and hire her own maids. Someone who would treat her as something other than an ornament to be used for his pleasure then stored inside a gilded vault.

Broderick couldn't do what she begged. But he could offer kindness. Every woman deserved that much. "I cannae be yer man, Cecilia. Ye ken why."

"Because I lied to ye," she whispered.

"Aye."

"And ye dinnae love me."

He hesitated. It was harsh, but the truth must be said. "No, lass. I dinnae."

She clutched him harder, her fingertips digging into his back. "Ye're the only man who's ever asked why I paint the sea," she choked. "The only man who's ever asked why I eat asparagus soup when 'tis plain it makes me queasy." She flattened herself along his front. With her height, her wee riding hat brushed his chin. "We needn't marry," she continued. "I cannae give ye bairns, anyway. But ye could keep me the same way he does. I wouldnae mind."

His heart twisted. *"I* would mind."

"Ye wanted me once. Do ye think I've forgotten? I'll give ye that pleasure again. More. Ye can take a wife, and I'll nae speak a word of objection. The house where ye keep me needn't be grand. I only want you. Just you."

"Cecilia. Stop."

"I ken I insulted ye when I implied I preferred his wealth. I've regretted it every day since."

"Hush, now. I took no offense. 'Twas plain why ye made the choices ye did." She'd never told him who her protector was, but the man had spared no expense on the woman whose favors he'd purchased. And Miss Cecilia Hamilton, an impoverished lass from a fishing village in Fifeshire, had gratefully traded her lot to become the pampered pet at the end of a rich man's leash.

When Broderick had realized she belonged to another, her reaction had been telling. She'd gone frantic. Then defensive. Then defiant. Finally, she'd tossed a bowl of cold asparagus soup at his naked chest and accused him of wanting to deprive her of everything she'd worked for.

He should have seen it sooner. He'd been cock-blind, of course. She was bonnie as the moon over water, and Broderick was hardly a saint. Still, Rannoch in his cups could not have been stupider.

Realizing the woman he'd imagined her to be had never existed, Broderick had walked away with few regrets. But Cecilia hadn't. She'd written him to apologize for her behavior. Then, throughout the summer, she'd begun a campaign to win his heart. He'd done his best to dissuade her, but she'd convinced herself she was in love. Now, once again, he must speak the truth plainly and hope it would be the last time.

"Leave him if ye wish to have a different life," he said gently. "I'll help ye make a new start. Help ye find employment. A place to live. But dinnae leave him for me. I'm not at the end of yer road, lass. Never will be."

She clung to him for a long while. Then, bit by bit, she withdrew. After dabbing her cheeks with the handkerchief he offered, she sniffed. "Ye're a good man, Broderick MacPherson." She gazed up at him with red, sorrowful eyes. "How I wish ye were a wee bit more of a scoundrel."

He walked Cecilia outside and helped her into her hired coach. Then, he watched the vehicle turn onto Constitution Street and disappear before he returned inside. The door squeaked and clanked shut. His footsteps echoed as he navigated twenty-foot piles of

crates and twelve-foot stacks of whisky casks to reach
the table behind the partition. For the next half-hour, he
made notes on his inventory list, ensuring all the
MacPherson casks had been accounted for. He didn't
want their buyer accusing them of shorting him again.
The last incident had been caused by thievery from a
rival smuggler, but their buyer hadn't been very
understanding.

Distantly, he heard the rusty squeak of the east door
opening. Moments later, a familiar, nasal voice
interrupted his final calculations.

"MacPherson!"

Broderick glanced up, surprised to see one of the
excisemen on the MacPhersons' payroll approaching
from the west end of the warehouse. Broderick frowned.
He'd thought he heard the opposite door open.

"Ferguson. What are ye doin' here?"

"You tell me." The wiry man tugged his waistcoat
tighter over his potbelly and cast an incurious glance at
the tower of casks. "Ye're the one who sent the note."

Broderick glowered at the man, wondering if he was
sotted again. "I didnae send anything. We already
settled on payment."

"Aye, that's what I thought." He patted his pockets.
"Where did I—"

A deafening crack echoed off stone walls and
wooden crates. Instantly, Broderick dropped into a
crouch and took a defensive position behind the
partition. He'd done enough hunting to know that
sound. Someone was firing at him. But who?

Broderick shifted to a better vantage point behind a
crate and chanced a glimpse over the top. Nothing.
Bloody hell. He couldn't see past the casks. His heart

pounded and his ears rang, but he slowed his breathing and listened for the shooter's movements. Had Broderick been the target or was Ferguson? The exciseman had been lured here under false pretenses, that much was obvious.

"Ferguson! Are ye wounded, man?" he called. "Can ye see who fired?"

The other man's answer was a gurgling groan.

"Bluidy hell," Broderick muttered. He reached for the dirk he kept strapped beneath his coat. If only the blade was his rifle or the pistol Alexander had given him, but devil take it, this was supposed to be a routine delivery. They'd made hundreds like it over the years with nary a shot being fired.

"Whoever ye are, ye bluidy bastard, best ye run now," he shouted. "If I get my hands on ye, ye'll need ten shots to save yerself. And ye'll be dead before the first one's left the barrel."

The east door whined open then clanked closed. Broderick took his chance, lunging from behind the crate and running toward the door. He raced past Ferguson on the way. The man lay on the floor gasping like a fish and clutching the wound in his potbelly. Wiry legs kicked, his heels sliding in the growing pool of blood.

Broderick didn't stop. He ran to the east entrance and threw open the door. Blinded by the sudden daylight, he scanned the wide lane where deliveries were loaded. "Where are ye, ye pile of shite?"

He leapt from the platform and stalked into the road, his head swiveling. The place was nothing but noisy gulls and empty carts this time of day. He watched for movement. Saw nothing for several seconds. Then, he saw a flash of black.

A horse. Thirty yards down, the animal raced away with a filthy rider holding a long gun. The rider glanced back just before exiting onto Constitution.

Broderick squinted. He looked ... familiar. Half his face was covered by a plaid, but the eyes. Broderick had seen those eyes somewhere before.

No time. No time to think and no time to catch the bugger. Ferguson had been hit. Broderick raced back inside to find the exciseman whiter than his neckcloth. He sheathed his dirk and moved the man's hands to view the wound.

Bloody hell. It was bad.

"D-dinnae let me ... die, MacPherson."

Broderick grunted. He was too busy trying to stanch the bleeding to bother with Ferguson's dramatics. "Stay still," he ordered, removing his own neckcloth to form a rough bandage. When he cinched it around the man's waist, Ferguson's wailing grew plaintive. *"Haud yer wheesht,* man. I must slow the bleedin' so I can leave to fetch a surgeon, else there'll be nothin' left of ye to save." He'd only just risen to his feet when he heard the rusty hinges of the east entrance again.

Had the gunman returned?

He unsheathed his dirk, holding it loosely by his thigh as he backed toward the crates.

Voices. Men. Two or three of them, by the sound of it. The voices grew more distinct as they approached his position

"Who reported it?" an unknown voice asked. "If that were gunfire we heard, 'twould be a prophetic coincidence to have the complaint beforehand, I reckon."

Frowning, Broderick glanced past the crates and saw three men, all of whom appeared to be High Constables. "Thank Christ," he muttered before striding into their line of sight. It appeared they'd just noticed Ferguson, for two of them crouched beside him while the third frantically swiveled his head searching for the shooter.

"The man who did this rode away not three minutes ago," Broderick advised.

The two constables beside Ferguson sprang to their feet and withdrew their batons. The third paled to a sickly shade of gray as he took in Broderick's size. Then, the tallest of the trio—a sharper, older fellow by the look of him—glanced at Broderick's right hand.

The one that still held his dirk.

A sinking sensation weighted Broderick's gut. He eyed the three constables and stretched his arms slowly out to his sides. "This wasnae me, lads." He waved his dirk in Ferguson's direction. "He'll tell ye."

Except Ferguson had gone quiet and still.

The oldest of the three constables advanced toward Broderick. The other two fell into flanking positions behind him. "Toss the dirk aside, sir."

Broderick considered his options. He could run. The west entrance was behind him. The constables didn't have guns. They'd be unlikely to catch him.

But while his size was an advantage in many ways, it was a disadvantage in one—he was recognizable. It wouldn't be long before the High Constabulary discovered whose whisky was in this warehouse. From there, it would be quick work to locate the MacPhersons.

No sense involving his brothers and risking the distillery over something so easily resolved.

He made his decision and dropped the dirk.

As the two younger constables seized his arms, he sighed at the hours of tedious bother that awaited him. He'd planned a night of drinking with his brothers and perhaps a wee flirtation with the barmaid at the inn. Now, he'd have to explain how he came to be standing near a gut-shot exciseman inside a warehouse filled with untaxed MacPherson whisky.

God, what a bluidy inconvenience, he thought. He hoped the barmaid saved him some supper.

But as they hauled him outside, something told him it wouldn't be that easy. Behind him, the rusted door clanged shut. He had the oddest feeling of dread. Certainty. And a sickening shiver he'd never felt before.

It felt cold. Writhing.

It felt like death's hand tracing a rune across his skin.

CHAPTER FOUR

One month later
October 1825
Calton Gaol, Edinburgh

Broderick studied the man in the cell across from his. Bony. Short. Grinning. His teeth were orange, for some reason. Such a man shouldn't be a threat. But he wasn't alone, and a single unwary moment on Broderick's part might result in a slash to the ribs from Orange-Teeth's friends.

Or, to be more precise, his gang.

A dozen of them had gotten themselves tossed in here deliberately. Broderick knew them by sight, in many cases, because they all worked for a piece of shite named David Skene.

Broderick rested his elbows on his knees and his head against the wall of his cell. God, he was tired. The iron bed groaned beneath his weight—far from luxurious, but he'd slept on worse. For the first few days inside the gaol, he'd run through the exciseman's shooting second-by-second in his mind. He'd struggled to recall where he'd seen the shooter's eyes before. Beady, black, and cold.

Then, it had occurred to him that they looked like a rat's. And he'd recalled how much Skene—a rival whisky smuggler who'd cost the MacPhersons a tidy sum over the years in lost supplies and aggravation— resembled that very rodent. Why the rat-faced bugger would summon Ferguson to a warehouse and set Broderick up as the killer, he could only guess.

Alexander had immediately suspected Skene had been hired for the task. "Sure, he's a nasty pile of shite," Alexander had said last time his brothers had bribed the gaolers for a visit. "But he's nae the sort to put this together."

"What sort is that?" Campbell had asked skeptically.

"Vicious for the sake of causin' misery. Clever enough to be patient about it."

Broderick had shaken his head. "Mayhap he is."

"Nah."

"How do ye ken?"

Alexander shot him a black look. "Like recognizes like."

Now, Broderick had only one certainty: The shooting had been the beginning of the plan, not its final aim. Broderick's brothers had hired surgeons to keep Ferguson alive, so thus far, the most serious charge against him was assault with intent to murder. His solicitors had appealed to the courts to assign bail, but the judge had denied him, citing the seriousness of firing upon an honorable member of His Majesty's government.

Broderick's solicitors had been surprised by the rigidity of the judge's stance, given the assurances offered by some of the MacPhersons' allies in the government. None were particularly high-ranking, but a few were well respected.

It was strange—one of many things that were.

Today, Angus was due for a visit. Broderick sighed and rubbed his eyes. He didn't know why Da and his brothers continued coming here. The Lord Advocate kept delaying his trial with one excuse after the next, and the judges kept agreeing to it over the objections of the MacPherson solicitors. Yet another oddity. Until the exciseman recovered enough to testify, it appeared Broderick's case was as mired in place as a wagon without wheels.

And he was stuck here in a whitewashed gaol with porridge twice a day and a target on his back.

The gaoler approached, a friendly Glaswegian named Wilson. "Visitor for ye, MacPherson. One hour."

Broderick nodded and unfolded his frame so he could stand.

Wilson's expression grew apologetic. "Stay put, else I'll have to put ye in irons whilst I open the door, eh?"

He sank back onto the creaking bed. "Aye." Wilson was a decent fellow. He knew Broderick hated being shackled. He also knew Broderick was a target for attacks from Skene's gang, so he did what he could to keep them separated.

The loud clank of the lock opening resonated in Broderick's head. He hadn't slept well in a month. Sound did strange things after that long. Sometimes overloud, sometimes muffled.

A man of towering height and glowering expression entered the cell. "Ye put my son in irons, and I'll break yer bluidy jaw, ye miserable—"

"Da," Broderick interrupted as Wilson's eyes rounded. Angus was a fearsome sight when he was angry. "What news have ye?"

Glaring daggers, Angus grunted and waved at the gaoler dismissively. "Well, go on with ye!"

Wilson closed the door.

"He's one of the better turnkeys, Da."

Another grunt. Angus patted Broderick's shoulder and sat beside him on the bed. Those broad shoulders stooped with weariness. "Met with the solicitors. There's a new lawyer they'd like to bring on. More accustomed to dealin' with the High Court."

"Another one?" Broderick noted his father's pallor and the way the old man's gnarled fingers absently rubbed his knees. "Ye're already payin' for the surgeon and bribin' every gaoler in the place. No. 'Tis too costly."

"Cost doesnae matter."

"Of course it does. Do ye think I want to beggar my family?"

"Yer brothers are preparin' the next shipment. We'll be fine."

"Bluidy hell," Broderick breathed.

Angus reached out to grasp Broderick's nape as he'd done when Broderick was a lad. He gave him a reassuring shake. "We'll be fine, son. But if we dinnae free ye from this place, *you* willnae."

Broderick met his father's dark gaze. "Who is doin' this?" he whispered. The question had plagued him for a month. Every night while he lay cold and sleepless.

Every day while he remained tense and watchful. He'd already fended off eight attacks from the men Skene had placed inside the gaol. How long could he last against dozens?

"Dinnae ken," his father answered, squeezing Broderick's neck. "Somebody with coin enough to buy a rival whisky gang. Somebody with influence enough over High Court judges to make them rule against their own laws, their own interests, for God's sake. The lawyers are baffled." He shook his head. "Nah. 'Tis a peer at the root of this vile contrivance. Nothin' else makes sense."

"I dinnae ken any peers. I've never even met one."

"Who did ye rankle? A customer? Tell me, son. I willnae be cross."

"Nobody. For God's sake, Da. It was a shipment like any other. A day like any other. None of this makes any bluidy sense!"

Angus drew him close, as though he might shield his son with his own broad frame. "Aye, well. We'll discover who did this. Then, yer brothers and I will make him wish he'd never heard the name MacPherson. That's a promise I mean to keep."

One month later

Wilson vanished two days after Angus's visit, replaced by a turnkey who "fell asleep" at times convenient to Skene's men. The day after that, they moved him into a new cell with two other men. One was a thief, the other a drunkard. He'd been forced to break the thief's jaw after the bugger went for his throat with a sharpened broom handle. The drunkard had gone for Broderick's face with a rock twice. The second time, Broderick had made certain he'd never try again. For this, he'd been tossed into the gaol's Dark Cell, a windowless chamber intended to isolate and punish troublemakers. His best sleep had been on that cold straw, surrounded by darkness.

Shortly thereafter, the prison governor had sent him to the adjacent Bridewell to work. It was yet another anomaly. He hadn't been tried yet, let alone sentenced to hard labor. The exciseman was still alive, so far as he knew. Alexander was hunting down Skene, who had gone to ground. Rannoch brought letters from Annie every so often. But as winter came on and the attacks on Broderick from Skene's men grew more frequent, hope dwindled.

He'd been moved to yet another new cell with three other men. He rarely slept more than a few minutes at a time. The food was bland and scarce. Porridge in the morning. Barley broth at night. He'd lost a third of his muscle over the past two months.

Broderick wanted to believe he could fight this, that he could win. But he was too bloody weakened. Thus far, his strategy had been to wait it out, hoping the man behind his torment would run out of funds. But the bastard had deep pockets and endless patience. Waiting would not win this battle. If Broderick wanted to survive, he'd have to take command.

Even now, the hair on his neck lifted as he watched the orange-toothed sod across the workroom slip something beneath his shirt.

"MacPherson!" a gaoler barked from outside the door. The large-nosed man was one of several turnkeys in Skene's pocket. "Ye're to pick oakum next."

Glancing at the hammer in his hand and the pile of rubble he'd been tasked with breaking into finer gravel, he answered, "By whose command?"

He shouldn't have said it. The last time he'd questioned the arbitrary orders of his gaolers, they'd put him on the treadwheel, a pointless, endless toil with punishment its sole purpose. The time before that, they'd given him twenty lashes.

But he'd almost prefer a whipping to the grueling tedium of picking apart tarred rope so that it could be rewoven into new rope.

The gaoler paused as he was turning the key. "Did I tell ye to speak?"

"Nah. But ye didnae tell me to tup yer wife, either. And I did that twice."

Laughter erupted from a few of the prisoners. The gaoler's eyes narrowed while sizable nostrils flared.

"In fairness, the second time was only because she begged me." Perhaps they'd toss him into the Dark Cell. He could use the sleep.

"Put down the hammer and step back," the gaoler snapped. His keys clanged as he twisted them in the lock.

Broderick tossed his hammer aside and moved behind the worktable. Then, he waited for the gaoler to open the door.

Waited.

Waited. Frowned.

The man was smirking. Turning his back. Disappearing. What the devil?

Too late, he felt the warning prickle along his neck. He half-turned as Orange-Teeth swung his hammer into Broderick's shoulder. He'd been aiming for his head.

Pain exploded through muscle and bone, rippling down his arm. Rage burned upward from his guts. He used the momentum of the blow to spin. Leap. Evade a second hammer swing with a crouching maneuver.

Another prisoner came at him from his left. He felt the slash along his ribs. A sharpened stone, likely. A third man tried to kick his knee. Hissing in a breath, he hurdled the table to take a defensive position behind the rubble pile.

Pain receded. His vision focused until gray haze crystalized. Seven men surrounded him. He dealt with Orange-Teeth first. The man's grin disappeared as he realized his error. Nervous eyes flickered over Broderick's length. A nervous hand flexed on the handle of his hammer.

"Warned ye," Broderick uttered. "If ye take a swing, dinnae miss." In the next moment, he grasped the other man's hammer by the head, ripped it loose, then swung his fist into a slack jaw. Multiple orange teeth flew. The man who once owned them collapsed into an unconscious heap.

Broderick turned. Two more attackers charged. He tossed the hammer end-over-end and caught it by the handle. Quickly, he dispatched first one man then the other with efficient blows to a chin and a gut. Both men fell, groaning and writhing.

Another scrapper leapt upon his back. Broderick looped an arm behind the man's neck, bent and slammed the bugger like a bag of tatties onto a cart. When he straightened, three more attackers stared up at him with comical awe. The one who'd managed to gouge his ribs staggered back. The one who'd kicked him darted to the pile of stones and hefted a ten-pounder.

Lungs heaving more from rage than exertion, Broderick went for the stabbing fellow first. The man took a few frantic swipes with his blood-edged blade before Broderick's hammer struck his ribs. He collapsed with a pathetic whimper. Broken ribs would send him to the infirmary for a good while, no doubt.

A grunt sounded behind Broderick moments before a ten-pound stone thudded harmlessly beside his foot.

Broderick turned. The man had wet himself. He babbled something about his mother and a dead brother and how he'd never wanted to attack Broderick, but he'd needed the coin Skene offered.

Broderick rubbed his forehead with fingers still zinging from the radiant pain down his arm. He breathed and thought of Da, how he'd always taught his sons to manage their rage with thoughts of their home.

Frost that turned heathered hillsides shimmery. The scent of Annie's bread baking. The lowing of long-haired cattle and the musical sigh of wind over the loch.

Slowly, he forced the rage back down. Then, he grasped the man's shirt and pulled him close. "Ye'll be my ears, now."

Wide eyes and a frantic nod.

"Aye. Ye'll listen for what Skene has planned. Ye'll find out who's funding him. Ye'll tell me everythin' and hold back nothin'."

Wide eyes rounded.

Broderick shook him the way Campbell's hound shook a rabbit. "Do ye ken?"

A nodding whimper came from the wretch. Distantly, Broderick heard keys clanging as the gaoler fumbled to unlock the door.

"Thought I told ye to drop the hammer, MacPherson." The gaoler's words were stern, but his voice shook.

"I think I'll keep it," he replied softly.

The gaoler staggered inside. He gulped and panted as he eyed the six fallen prisoners and the man dangling from Broderick's fist. "Y-ye're to pick oakum. Order of the governor."

Broderick released his new informant, shoving the wretch aside and approaching the guard. Sometimes his size was a nuisance. Other times, it was extremely useful. "Nah. I'm to be put in the Dark Cell, instead. Disobedient lad that I am, ye had to do it. Immediately."

The turnkey fingered the cudgel he carried then locked eyes with the prisoner who had wet himself. The prisoner shook his head as if to say, "Best not provoke the man who just dispatched six attackers in less than a minute."

The gaoler opened the door and gave Broderick a nod. "Dark Cell it is."

Finally, Broderick thought. Some real sleep.

The gaoler led him down a series of long, dank corridors, through an iron gate, then down steep stone stairs. Without a word, he unlocked the thick wooden door at the end of a narrow passage. Inside, the cell was small—eight feet by six feet, perhaps. But it was far from the other prisoners. Quiet. Best of all, Broderick could sleep without fearing he'd be set upon, for his senses would alert him the moment the door opened.

He ducked through the doorway only to halt when he heard shuffling. He peered into the dark. A quiet gasp came from the corner of the cell.

"Eh? Who's in here?" demanded the gaoler.

A feminine murmur preceded scrambling amidst the straw.

The gaoler shoved past Broderick then hauled a gaunt, gray-gowned woman into the light.

Broderick frowned. She was stark white tinged faintly blue. Plain to the point of ugliness, she appeared young—perhaps Annie's age. Her face was narrow, her chin pointed, her nose long and prominent. She was, however, remarkably tidy. Mouse-brown hair was neatly tucked inside her cap. Near-translucent skin was clean. A bit of straw dotted her skirt, but otherwise, few signs of her confinement in the Dark Cell were visible.

"What's yer name?" barked the gaoler, dragging her from her corner.

Sunken eyes darted and squinted. A thin hand came up to shield them as she blinked and blinked and blinked up at Broderick. The gaoler's grip dug into her arm. She shook her head as though dazed. "Magdalene Cuthbert."

"How long ye been in here?"

"I—I don't know. Several days, I think."

"Who put ye here?"

"Mr. Burnside."

One of the turnkeys assigned to the airing yard, Broderick recalled.

"Well, yer time's up. Get yerself back to the women's ward." The gaoler shoved her forward into Broderick. He gently braced her elbows.

She flinched away, eyed his hammer then gazed up at him with wide, confused eyes. "Are ye here to take me home, then?"

Her speech was a soft blend of the Lowlands and England, scarcely Scottish at all. Her voice was muted, gentle, and clear. But she made little sense.

"I'm here to take yer place, lass."

Frowning, she lowered her gaze to his shirt. Blood wicked into the blue fabric where he'd been slashed. "The cell is filthy," she murmured. "Ye must bandage this."

He was dizzy with fatigue. His fists ached. His shoulder felt on fire—likely dislocated. And the bleeding slice along his ribs stung. But somehow, he thought this plain, skeletal woman might be worse off than he.

The gaoler gripped her arm with bruising force. "Go on with ye!" he growled, shaking her bone-thin frame.

Once again, Broderick steadied her as she gasped and staggered. He grasped the gaoler's wrist, squeezing until the man's hand loosened. Then, he tilted his head and flashed his hammer. "Dinnae touch her again."

The big-nosed man swallowed. Backed up a step.

"Miss Cuthbert," Broderick murmured. "Can ye find yer way back to yer sleepin' cell?"

Several breaths passed before she nodded. She swept her hands over her skirts, shaking the hem free of straw. Then, she calmly stepped past him into the passage before turning back. "Wh-what is your name, sir? If I may ask."

"MacPherson. Broderick MacPherson."

She nodded, her face haloed in gray light. She looked like a nun, he thought. A nun who had seen too much suffering.

"I shan't forget your kindness, Mr. MacPherson."

He raised a brow. "Ye should, Miss Cuthbert. Ye should forget all about me."

She didn't smile. But her eyes warmed briefly before she turned and walked away.

One month later

The airing yard teemed with men, despite deep snow and bitter wind. Frozen, the usual foul smells of unwashed bodies and human waste were near tolerable.

Broderick folded his arms across his chest and leaned back against the prison's stone wall. "What have ye heard?"

His informant, James Tweedie, blew into his hands and kicked a pile of snow. "Skene's been run off. Naught's been seen of him for weeks. But the payments keep comin'."

"I ken that much from my sister's letters, ye worthless cur. What have ye discovered about Skene's backer?"

"Naught, sir. Nobody kens who it is. Not even Gordon, and he's runnin' things now."

Broderick shook his head and stared across the yard to where several women hauled loads of bedding to be laundered. One of the many child prisoners tripped and fell in the snow. A familiar, plain-faced woman stopped to help the wee lassie to her feet.

"Keep yer ears sharp, Tweedie."

"Aye, sir."

"And bluidy well stop callin' me sir."

"Aye, sir."

Broderick shoved away from the wall, scanning his surroundings for signs of a threat. The prisoners gave him a wide berth, and the gaolers cast him wary glances. He headed for the arched entrance to the sleeping cells but stopped when he heard his name. Cursing silently, he turned.

"Miss Cuthbert," he said, watching her dust the child off and send the lassie on her way. "Ye're due for release soon, aye?"

She straightened. Hesitated. As usual, she looked neater than a solicitor's spectacles, but her hands were vivid red from her laundry duties.

In the past month, he'd learned she'd been imprisoned for stealing a pair of costly jeweled combs from her former employer. It had taken some coaxing, but he'd finally discovered why such a quiet, pious, dignified woman would resort to thievery. Her employer had been a hateful old crone fond of striking her paid companion with her cane. For years, Magdalene Cuthbert had endured the abuse until she'd reached her limit and made her escape. Unfortunately, she'd only sold one of the combs, tucking the other away for the future. When the constables had found it in her possession, her former employer had been spitefully eager to see her punished. Miss Cuthbert had been arrested, convicted, and tossed into the Bridewell for six months' imprisonment with hard labor. She'd been slated for release in early January.

"I was, aye." She focused on her hands.

He sighed. "What happened?"

"Mr. Burnside caught me delivering soup to you in the Dark Cell on Christmas Eve. My sentence has been … lengthened."

He gritted his teeth. He'd warned her not to help him. He'd begged her to stop appearing friendly and avoid speaking to him around others. "How long?"

"Three months."

"Christ on the cross."

She winced. "Please don't say such things, Mr. MacPherson. Ye're an honorable man who deserves yer place in heaven."

"I havenae said half of what I'm thinkin', so dinnae preach to me like that damned chaplain."

Her eyes warmed. "He's been so very kind to me. He visits every day he's here, often requesting I assist him with his tasks."

Broderick snorted. "Well, at least somebody bothers to do what I tell them."

She adjusted the scarf over her head and glanced behind her before stepping closer. "I could not let them starve ye, Mr. MacPherson. Not after everything ye've done for me. Ye're already too thin."

He hated the gratitude shining in her eyes. The poor woman didn't understand what she risked. Three more months in this place? He'd asked the chaplain to look after her, true, but the man couldn't be with her every second. "Bein' my friend will make ye a target, ye ken?"

She swallowed, the thin bones of her neck rippling. "Aye. I haven't forgotten what ye told me."

"Stay away," he urged as gently as he could manage. "Ye must protect yerself."

Her spine straightened, her features turning placid. She met his gaze with that inherent dignity that made him think she must have queens in her lineage. "I shall keep you in my prayers, Mr. MacPherson."

His gut turned colder than the snow beneath his feet. "Prayers havenae helped me so far, Miss Cuthbert." He started for the iron gate leading to the men's ward. "Dinnae waste yer breath."

One month later

The surgeon's hand shook as he knotted his last stitch on Broderick's biceps. "Watch for putrefaction." The doctor reached for his scissors and snipped the thread. "If ye've signs of fever, come see me."

Broderick glared at the man's handiwork. "Next time, have a drink before ye take a needle to me. I've had steadier rides on the back of a donkey."

A new batch of men from Skene's gang had launched a fresh attack early that morning. They'd managed to gash his arm with a sharpened spoon before he'd put them down. Now, he sat in the infirmary with a red-eyed surgeon, numerous bruises on his face and jaw, and a poorly stitched arm.

Oh, and a team of three unctuous lawyers—two short solicitors and a tall, bespectacled barrister. They'd all gathered around his bed, fidgeting as though they needed to visit the privy. In fairness, they were there to deliver wretched news, and he probably looked ready to kill.

The barrister adjusted his spectacles. "We did submit Mr. Ferguson's original statement exonerating you of all blame for the attempt on his life. But, as the Lord Advocate obtained a contradictory statement shortly before Mr. Ferguson's death, we do not expect the High Court to rule in our favor." He cleared his throat. "You are to be charged with murder, Mr. MacPherson. I am sorry."

Broderick glared out the window on the far side of the room, unable to speak. The exciseman had been on the mend, damn it. The physicians Campbell and Alexander hired had saved Ferguson's pathetic life. He'd recovered enough to give the solicitors a signed statement declaring Broderick had been an innocent bystander and that he could not have shot him, as he'd been positioned in the opposite direction from where the gunman had fired. Days later, according to the physician, the Lord Advocate had visited Ferguson. The prosecutor had left an hour later with a statement accusing Broderick of firing upon him after Ferguson discovered his cache of untaxed MacPherson whisky. Yesterday, Ferguson, who had previously been well enough to eat breakfast with his wife, had been found dead in his bed.

The physicians were baffled. Currently, Alexander was questioning everyone involved to find out what had caused his death.

It didn't much matter, of course. Whoever had orchestrated Broderick's torment intended for him to die, either in prison or by hanging.

Vaguely, he noted the bird swooping past the infirmary window. It was white and gray. "Get out," he murmured to his lawyers. Useless, all of them.

"We shall prepare a robust defense. Your father is most keen to—"

"Leave."

He felt them glance at each other. Felt them go.

The surgeon offered Broderick his flask. Broderick drank it all down.

"I'll inform the governor ye must sleep here tonight," the surgeon said, tucking his flask away.

Broderick watched the snow swirl, the white and gray bird fighting the gusts. It appeared to be dancing in place.

As the surgeon departed, Alexander arrived to tell Broderick what they'd found beneath Ferguson's widow's bed. "Five hundred pounds," he growled, eyes flashing like the devil's blackest fire. "She poisoned her man and condemned you to hang for it for five hundred pounds. Christ's bones."

Broderick closed his eyes, but he still saw the white and gray bird. Only now, it was black.

"We're makin' a plan, brother," Alexander continued. "Dinnae despair. If the bluidy solicitors cannae free ye from this place, then we will. Campbell and I met with an old mate from our regiment. He makes regular runs to the Continent. Fine ship. Good crew. Once ye're far away from here, we'll find Skene. We've already dismantled his operation. A rat can only stay hidden so long. We'll discover who—"

"No," Broderick rasped.

Suddenly, Alexander's face hovered inches from his. A long finger pointed at Broderick's nose. "Aye," he gritted furiously. "Ye'll let us do this because we'll nae fuckin' survive watchin' ye hang for somethin' ye didnae do."

Broderick grasped his brother's hand in both of his. Alexander tore away. Paced to the window. Slammed a fist into the whitewashed wall.

"Think of Da. Annie. Rannoch," Broderick said. "You and Campbell are soldiers. Ye're accustomed to the sacrifices of war. They're not. They'll suffer."

"They needn't be part of it."

"Alex—"

"Stay breathin'," he ordered as he stalked to the door and pounded it to signal the guard. It opened in seconds. "We cannae save a dead man."

"Bluidy hell. Alexander!" His shout echoed off whitewashed walls. But his brother was already gone.

One month later

He awakened in darkness. Deep, endless black. His heart pounded. He remained still. Breathed slowly. Silently reached for his hammer. The worn handle inside his fist was a comfort.

Outside the door, he heard whispers. A scrape. A click. Jangling keys.

Light cracked the dark, faint and gray.

Wider. Wider.

He rolled. Crouched. Readied.

"Mr. MacPherson?"

Gray skirts swayed into view.

His fist gripped the hammer harder, unable to let go. His heart beat him to death inside bruised ribs, unable to slow.

She moved inside, stupid and stubborn, clutching a Bible to her chest with a white, bony hand. Her eyes darted, widened as they settled upon him. "Oh, Mr. MacPherson. What have they done?"

"Get out," he growled. A hank of his own hair obscured his eyes, foul and filthy. No one should see him like this.

"I will not." She set the Bible on the floor outside the cell, murmuring something to the gaoler before returning to stand before him. "We'll take ye to the infirmary."

He shook his head. "Shouldnae be here."

She didn't touch him, but she moved close. "No, ye shouldn't."

"I meant you."

"Me? I was only delivering a Bible when I discovered ye here, insensible with fever. It's my Christian duty to see you're looked after properly. The chaplain would do the same, were he here."

He ordered his heart to calm. Needed to loosen his grip on the hammer before he went mad. She was not someone he wished to hurt.

"Come."

"Go away, Miss Cuthbert. Ye shouldnae see this."

"See what?"

He breathed. Breathed. Thought of home. Lost the vision. "Me."

She went quiet, standing straight and still as she often did. "Come along, Mr. MacPherson." She led the way into the passage then turned back expectantly. "Please. Let me do this much."

It took him long minutes to leave the Dark Cell. His muscles felt frozen. Rigid. His skin itched. Every breath hurt. Worse, he couldn't decide if he was awake or if this was another dream. He'd had so many.

Gradually, he unlocked his muscles. Stood by pushing himself against the back wall. Took one step. Then another. His eyes watered as they met light after so long without it. A week, at least.

She didn't reach for his arm. Neither did the gaoler, who shrank away from the stench. Miss Magdalene Cuthbert didn't so much as twitch her long nose. Instead, she quietly nodded and started forward, modulating her pace to match his slow, hitching one.

The last attack had nearly killed him. Twelve had come at him with hammers, rocks, and planks from the workrooms. Broken ribs. Shattered left hand. His knee might never be the same.

"I'm to be released soon," she murmured. "I thought ye should know."

He gritted his teeth at the repeated agony of every step. "When?"

"Next month."

"Good. Dinnae do anythin' foolish."

Magdalene Cuthbert never smiled. He suspected she thought her teeth too big, her lips too full. But from time to time, she'd slant him an amused glance, as she did now. "Such as?"

"Helpin' murderers."

"You are not a murderer."

"Fine. Helpin' *me.*"

She fell quiet, glancing ahead to where the gaoler kept a stench-free distance. "I do not have many friends, Mr. MacPherson."

He grunted, wincing as his knee protested the next step.

"None at all, really. Before you, I knew very little kindness." She slowed. Stopped. Gazed up at him with the faintest shimmer. "Permit me a wee bit of foolishness before we bid farewell, hmm?"

One month later

They had him cornered—in the infirmary, of all places. "Tweedie," he snarled. "When I get my hands on ye, ye'll be sorrier than all of 'em put together."

His "informant" took three nervous steps toward the door. "I had nae choice, sir. They said they'd kill me if I didnae get ye here."

The prisoners surrounded him. Three were familiar. Two were new. The last five appeared to have been brought in specially for the occasion of his death. Bruisers, all of them. Big and rough and dim.

The sharpest of the lot hefted his hammer. He had black hair and a chipped tooth. Broderick had seen him before—he was one of Skene's old partners, he thought. Gordon. Aye. This was Gordon.

"Doin' yer own jobs these days, eh, Gordon? Funds run dry?"

The man sniffed and cocked his head to a taunting angle. "This is one job I'd do for the pure pleasure of it.

Damned MacPhersons have been a thorn in my ballocks for too long."

Broderick raised a brow and palmed the surgeon's scissors. "Good thing yer ballocks are so wee." He eyed the other men, who seemed to be herding him toward the window. "What's the matter? Have my brothers made trouble for ye?"

Gordon squinted. His expression hardened. "Look out the window, MacPherson."

"Nah. I'd rather see the damage I intend to do."

"Dinnae ye wish to see yer ugly lass on her way out the gate?"

An icy chill chased down his spine.

"'Tis her last day, aye?"

The infirmary was on the top floor of the prison. From here—from the window behind him, specifically—the main gate was visible. Because of the angle toward the north, one could watch visitors and newly released prisoners come and go, if one was of a mind to.

His heart stuttered to a stop. It kicked again when Gordon smiled. "What have ye done?"

The black-haired bastard sauntered closer, raising his hands when Broderick shoved him backward. Gordon chuckled. Nodded toward the window. "Have a look. We willnae set upon ye. My word as a Scot."

Heart twisting and lurching erratically, Broderick edged closer. He kept his back to the wall but sidled so he could turn his head and glimpse the gate. There. She was there. The main gate, which resembled the turreted gatehouse of a castle, opened. She paused. Nodded regally to the turnkey. Then slowly started through.

"Trouble is," Gordon said casually, "a prisoner might go free from the Bridewell. But it isnae much safer out there on the road. This time of the evenin', just ere dark. A lass alone. Frightful things might happen."

A cold, sickening fist gripped his stomach. Men had been known to be set upon when leaving the prison. Women had been assaulted. Abducted. Raped.

"Ye putrid pile of shite," he snarled. "Call them off."

"Now, now. We've a bargain to set. I've been paid— quite well, mind ye—to make yer misery a masterpiece. And I do intend to finish the job. But I'll need yer cooperation." Gordon sniffed. "How much do ye fancy her?"

He didn't fancy her. He respected her. He considered her a friend, and she considered him the same. Friends protected one another.

"Call them off," he growled, watching a half-dozen men emerge from the shrubbery along the upper road as the gate closed behind her. She didn't see them, too focused on the ground in front of her. "Do it." He gripped Gordon by the shirt. Shook him hard. "Do it!"

Gordon laughed. "Drop the scissors. Turn yer back. Then, I'll signal them with that sheet, there." He nodded to a blue sheet wadded in another man's fist. "A wave out the window, and she'll nae be harmed." He held up a hand. "My word as a Scot."

Broderick read his own downfall in the man's eyes. This would be how it ended. At least his family would be free. At least he'd be done fighting. For months, he'd been wearied to the point of madness. Perhaps now he'd find rest. True rest. But first, he wanted a name. "Tell me who it is, Gordon. Who paid ye?"

"He never said." The man shrugged. Chuckled. "All I ken is he hates you all the way to the bone. And his coins are good."

"What does he look like?"

"Havenae set eyes upon him. All was arranged by delivery. And before that, through Skene." Gordon glanced toward the window. "Now, then, ye may wish to decide upon our agreement before long. Things turn dangerous after dark, ye ken."

Broderick swallowed the sudden thickness in his throat. The lurching nausea in his stomach. Slowly, he released Gordon's shirt. And gave a nod.

"Splendid." The chipped tooth appeared inside the man's grin. He took the blue sheet, opened the window, and waved the thing several times. It came back stained with rainwater. "Now, bear in mind, if I wave this again, I cannae vouch for her safety."

Broderick nodded again. Deposited the surgeon's scissors on the windowsill.

And turned his back.

When the first blow fell, he was staring out the window at a gull fighting the wind—and losing.

CHAPTER FIVE

One month later

All was pain. It was the air. It was the water. He wanted to be gone. But a rope clung. Cinched. Bound him with iron knots. Wouldn't bloody well let him go.

"… and I said, 'English.' That's what I call him. He's English, ye ken." A cool, efficient hand stroked his forehead. Water splashed nearby. Annie's voice chattered on. "Anyhow, I said, 'After ye scurried off into the dark at the first wee bit of trouble, I didnae suppose ye'd dare provoke Angus again. I reckon it takes Englishmen a few months to locate their ballocks, eh?'" She chuckled and ran a wet cloth over Broderick's arm. "Come to think of it, ye've met John Huxley once or twice. Aye, when he came to MacPherson House, and ye were there for supper, I think. Do ye remember, Broderick? Ah, he's a bonnie man. Strong, too. I'm teachin' him to toss the caber. Can ye imagine? A dainty

Englishman. Well, nae so dainty. Dinnae tell him I said so."

Pain sang along his skin. Through his bones. The melody vibrated his blood. He wanted to leave.

God, he wanted to leave.

But the knots wouldn't loosen.

And she kept talking. Chattering on and on about her Englishman and Da and the new license for the distillery. Explaining how the High Court had accepted the exciseman's original statement. How he'd been freed after the charges were suddenly dismissed.

Freed.

He was not free.

He was in hell.

One month later

"… would ye listen to me. I sound like a pure dafty, natterin' on about him like he's some magical answer to my fondest wish." Annie sat on the bed beside Broderick, smoothing and tugging his blankets. "He's still here in Edinburgh. I dinnae ken why. But I think— I think he stayed for … me."

She leaned down and kissed his forehead, her thumb tracing the spot.

His heart squeezed. He wished he could ignore it. But he loved her, his wee sister. Always had.

"He brings me such comfort." Her voice thickened. "How I've needed it. Seein' what was done to ye, I … I want to kill the man responsible. I want to kill him with my own hands." She sniffed then whispered, "Do ye want to hear a secret, Broderick? I intend to. I will discover who he is. And I will kill him."

As she gathered up the remains of his soup and lowered the flame on the lantern, a single thought resounded in the dark cell of his mind.

Not if I find him first.

One month later

He was home. Not his house on his land, but the house where he'd grown from a lad into a man. He lay in his old wood bed. A leather patch covered the hole where his eye had been. The eye that remained saw well enough. A brace kept his left hand from re-breaking. He was afraid to test the damage to his throat.

Outside, a bird sang to the rising sun.

Inside, the scents of wool and peat reminded him he was alive.

He took a breath. Deeper. Expanded his chest.

He hadn't seen Annie since yesterday. Where was she?

Beyond the bedchamber door, his father's deep, booming voice grumbled about Englishmen taking liberties with his precious daughter. Then, he mentioned something about cleaning his hunting rifle.

Broderick couldn't fight the small ache in his chest. The need to see Da's face. To speak to him. To thank Annie.

His stomach growled.

How long since he'd eaten a proper breakfast?

Slowly, he rolled onto his side. Tossed aside his woolen blanket.

His legs were long bones with white skin and dark hair. So much of him had wasted away.

He shook as he sat upright. His head swam. Every muscle was weak, every breath painful. But pain was the air, the water. When something was everything, it might as well be nothing at all.

So, he ignored the pain. Shifted his feet to the floor.

The maid entered—Betty. Freckled and shy. Although they looked nothing alike, she reminded him of Magdalene.

"Mr. MacPherson!" she squeaked. Ordinarily, her eyes were downcast, but now she rushed toward him. "Are—are ye well, sir? Dinnae stand. Let me fetch ye a shirt."

He didn't want to speak. What if his voice was gone? They'd stomped his throat until he'd choked on his own blood. Could a man heal from that?

He started to nod in answer, but she was busy digging through a trunk and wouldn't see. So, he gathered himself. Opened his mouth. At first, nothing emerged but air. He tried again. This time, sound came, distorted and rusty as a saw cutting metal. Nothing like his voice. But he could speak. "Fetch Da."

Betty blinked. "Sir! Ye're talkin'!"

Again, he started to nod but decided using his voice might be best. "Aye."

She pulled a shirt from the trunk and returned to his side. While she helped him dress, she gently questioned him about how he was feeling.

"Hungry," he answered. His throat felt raw, but the more he spoke, the stronger the sound emerged.

"Shall I fetch ye broth?"

"No." He'd had enough broth to last a lifetime. "Eggs."

Betty's shy gaze met his then softened with womanly sympathy. "Gladly, sir. I shall fetch yer father and prepare eggs for ye. Dinnae move."

Angus entered moments later. "Son?"

A breath shuddered in Broderick's chest. Tight. Tighter. "Da," he managed. He felt like a wee laddie, watching his father rush forward and wrap him up tight.

"Ah, God, son," Angus cupped his nape and squeezed. "Ye're home. By God, ye're home, now."

One month later

His axe whizzed past the outermost bark of the log he'd placed on the wide stump. The log teetered but didn't fall. With a thud, the blade buried six inches deep in the ground. He tore it loose with a curse.

"Och, that was a close one, laddie," said the old woman standing on his blind side. "If ye dinnae take better care, ye'll split that log in two."

A river of sweat cascaded down his back and face, making the skin beneath his leather patch itch. He swiped his forehead with his free hand before turning to Mrs. MacBean. "For the last bluidy time, that's the point," he snapped. "I mean to chop the wood." He gestured toward the half-finished pile of firewood stacked between two trees.

The old woman frowned as though she hadn't already heard him repeat himself several times. Her milky left eye wandered away from her right. She scratched her head. "If that's true, ye're doin' a poor job of it, I regret to say."

With a gust, he tossed the axe a few feet away. "Ye're supposed to be helpin' me improve my aim."

Mary MacBean was the local herbalist and midwife. Some in the village called her a witch, and Annie seemed to think she had a wee bit of "sight." But all Broderick saw was a befuddled, wild-haired old crone. True, Mrs. MacBean's liniment was helpful. Her salves and odd-smelling concoctions had eased his pain while he recovered. And she'd offered to teach him how to navigate the world with only one functional eye, which had been the purpose of her visit today.

He should have known better. She was half-blind and mostly mad.

He glanced through the stand of pines toward his house, which the old crone had surrounded with rowan saplings. Several weeks ago, after Annie's wedding to John Huxley, he'd moved back into his own house here in the wooded foothills, intent upon regaining the strength he'd lost.

His home was fully staffed, so he'd expected to find it unchanged. "Who the devil planted so many trees?" he'd growled to Campbell as his oldest brother had helped him to the door.

"Mrs. MacBean," Campbell had answered. "She claims the rowans offer protection."

"There are at least a dozen." They flanked either side of the main entrance, extending the full width of the house. His house was large—three stories of polished stone—but when that hedge reached maturity, he'd get no light on the ground floor. "'Tis ridiculous."

Campbell had grunted his agreement. "'Tis Mrs. MacBean. One follows the other."

In the past, she'd been fond of giving him and his brothers wooden "bride charms," claiming her magic could summon "a wife to please yer very soul." None of them had the heart to tell her to stop. Harmless enough, he supposed, given she also claimed she could speak to the dead, complained His Majesty George IV had targeted her for assassination, and offered disconcertingly frank advice on avoiding venereal disease. Madwomen were rarely effective magicians.

Now, Broderick retrieved his shirt and asked, "Do ye have anythin' *useful* to offer?"

"Oh, aye."

He waited.

She blinked.

"Which would be ...?" he prompted, grinding his back teeth.

Frowning as though she'd just remembered something, she dug through the leather pouch she often wore around her waist and offered him a small wooden carving. The lopsided, two-inch spiral resembled a corkscrew carved by a drunkard.

"Is this meant to help me see better?" He was trying to be patient, but the heat and the midges, his weak, straining muscles, and his frustratingly bad aim had worn his temper through.

"Och, no," she answered, slapping a midge that was biting his shoulder. "'Tis for yer bride, laddie. She'll be here soon."

"I have no bride, and I dinnae want one." He wanted only one thing—to kill the man who had done this to him. It was all he lived for, the reason he worked and sweated and pushed his body past the tearing burn of bone and muscle.

There was nothing after this. No wife. No life. No purpose apart from delivering punishment where it was most deserved.

And now, according to Annie and John, his tormentor might be within striking distance. Recently, Annie had gathered the family together and announced she had a suspect—a Lord of Parliament named Kenneth Lockhart, who had visited Glenscannadoo with his sister last September.

Broderick had never heard of the man, let alone met him.

But he trusted Annie. He also trusted John, who had used his connections within the English peerage to free Broderick from the Bridewell, have his charges dismissed, and discover who the enemy might be.

They might be wrong, of course. The family had a plan to lure Lockhart into returning to Glenscannadoo for the Highland Gathering next month. Lockhart was friendly with the local laird, a wee, pompous dafty who liked to host a grand ball at Glenscannadoo Manor after the annual Highland games.

They would make their stand there. Broderick only hoped they had the right man—and that he'd be recovered enough to do what must be done.

Mrs. MacBean patted his biceps. "Yer strength's returnin'. That's good. Strong is what's needed." She wandered to where he'd flung his axe then gave him an assessing squint. "One eye makes it harder to judge distances, ye ken? Cannae see what's comin' and goin'. Remember what was once a part of ye. Notice how its absence changes how ye perceive things."

He frowned, wondering if this was one of her rare lucid moments.

"Be aware of yer blind side, laddie. Accommodate it." She bent and lifted the axe handle from the dirt, dragging the tool back to him and placing it in his hand. "When ye swing for yer mark, ye may not strike what ye're aimin' for. But ye might discover what ye couldnae have seen ere ye were blind."

He blew out a breath and muttered a curse. Not so lucid, then. He shrugged on his shirt and embedded the axe in the chopping stump. "Right. I thank ye for the liniment, Mrs. MacBean."

"Oh, that reminds me." She dug in her pouch again and handed him a small brown bottle. "This is for yer bride, laddie."

"There is no bride, Mrs. MacBean. Not now. Not ever."

"Aye, aye. Dinnae tell her what it's for. She likes surprises."

"Ye havenae said what it's for." He cut her off before she could answer. "Doesnae matter. For the hundredth time, I dinnae intend to marry." He retrieved his water flask and took a long drink.

She frowned. Glanced at his thighs. Frowned deeper. "Stoat's a wee bit shy about comin' out of his burrow, eh?"

He choked on his next swallow.

"Dinnae fash. I'll make ye a tonic." She dug through her pouch. "Hmm. I've enough stag's antler, but I must collect butcher's broom from the north side of a west facin' slope. Also, four pounds of roseroot."

Recovering from his coughing fit, he capped his flask and rasped, "There's nothin' wrong with my stoat."

With a triumphant cry, she withdrew a shriveled mushroom from her pouch. "Now, *this* will wake yer wee beastie from his slumber."

Shaking his head at her daft nonsense, he started for the house.

The old woman mumbled as she trailed after him, "Come to think of it, yer bride may need a salve when the tonic takes effect. 'Tis a powerful formulation. Not for the weak-kneed or those prone to chafing."

"For God's sake." He stopped. Turned. Glared. "There willnae be a bride! Any lass worth havin' would take one look at me and flee in the other direction."

She froze, her eyes going wide. "Och, laddie. Have ye become a seer, too?"

One month later

Broderick hated Annie's plan. Too dangerous, he'd complained to her less than a half-hour ago. She'd argued the only way it could work is if Lockhart were lulled into false confidence, and for that, he must be confronted by someone he thought inferior. In other words, Annie herself.

God, he hated this. So much so that, if Campbell and Alexander hadn't been assigned to guard him, he'd be inside Glenscannadoo Manor's ballroom right now. Instead, he stood in the small manor house's back garden, cloaked in shadows and listening to three MacDonnell cousins playing a reel.

"Let me go in," he gritted. "I'll get answers."

"Huxley is with her," Campbell murmured, watching Rannoch thread his way through the dancing villagers with a grim stare. "He'll slash Lockhart's spine if the bastard so much as breathes on her."

Alexander, leaning against a young oak tree, chuckled darkly. "Aye. He dispatched Skene readily enough. Must admit, the Englishman is good with a dirk."

True. David Skene, the rat who had been Lockhart's weapon of choice, had shown his rat face after months of being hunted by Broderick and his brothers. Unfortunately, he'd only emerged from his hole to abduct Annie and use her as leverage. If John Huxley hadn't awakened from a drug-induced slumber and charged like an enraged bull to Annie's rescue, she might have died instead of Skene.

Broderick's debt to the Englishman was growing vaster by the day.

And he was grateful. He was. But, God, he wished he'd been the one to put the rat down. He'd have made Skene's death slower. Excruciating. He'd at least have taken an eye.

Through the ballroom doors, Angus emerged and stalked toward them.

"Da's wearin' his good kilt," Alexander observed. "Do ye suppose he's decided to chase after the bonnie dressmaker?"

Campbell's answer was a grunt.

Broderick didn't bother replying, for there was no need. Alexander was trying to distract him. Because Alexander understood what Broderick was fighting.

His skin thrummed like a maddened hive.

Angus approached with Rannoch in tow. "Lockhart arrived. The sister, too. Another few minutes, and we'll go inside." Da's dark gaze focused on Broderick. "Are ye ready, son?"

Was he? Every muscle burned. His chest felt agonizingly tight. The leather patch burned like a brand. He must contain the pressure.

"Aye," he muttered, knowing it was a lie.

Da eyed him warily and braced his shoulder. "Ye're strong. A MacPherson. Dinnae forget."

Broderick nodded. MacPhersons were too big to let their tempers drive the wagon. How many times had he and his brothers heard that admonishment when they were wee? A thousand, at least.

"Time for Da and me to clear the ballroom." Campbell nodded toward the terrace doors, where John and Lockhart's sister emerged. "We'll signal ye when it's time." Campbell and Angus kept to the shadows, avoiding notice by the woman on Huxley's arm.

Sabella Lockhart was a slender, elegant blonde with emeralds glittering around her long neck and an air of untouchable delicacy. Annie insisted the lass knew nothing of her brother's vile deeds and, indeed, might well be one of his lesser victims.

"Bonnie lass," Rannoch observed as John handed Miss Lockhart off to Dougal MacDonnell and returned to the ballroom. "Do ye suppose she kens what her brother did?"

Alexander, as usual, took a cynical view. "I dinnae give two shites if she kenned his scheme or not. She kens his nature. But it hasnae stopped her wearin' the silk and jewels he buys her, has it?"

Their conversation buzzed dimly in Broderick's ears. Pressure roiled inside him. Built and built and built. For a moment, he swore he heard rain howling past barred windows. It drowned everything. Flooded his blood and turned him cold as filthy stone beneath filthier straw.

Minutes later, he found himself standing beneath glittering chandeliers, watching his sister taunt a lean, blond Lowland lord. The man's back was turned to the room, but by the set of his shoulders beneath a light-blue linen coat, Annie's sharp tongue had already done its work well.

"Your vulgarity should be shocking, I suppose, except for one thing. I'd expect nothing less from a MacPherson."

Annie, lounging on a settee in front of Lockhart, raised a scarlet brow. "Are ye speakin' of my brothers?"

Broderick's heart squeezed when his sister's beautiful blue eyes flickered ever-so-briefly to meet his own. He must control himself. For her sake.

"I'd rather not," the arrogant lord retorted.

"Aye. Only natural. Them bein' so much *larger*." She smirked. "A pure shame. Some men carry cabers. Some struggle to lift their teacups."

"I think this conversation has run its course."

"Did a MacPherson steal yer woman, then?"

The way Lockhart stiffened in that moment was its own reply.

When Annie had quizzed Broderick about Lockhart, he'd had few answers for her. He didn't know the man, had never met him. The name wasn't familiar, so they'd never done business together. When she'd suggested Lockhart's enmity seemed deeply personal, he'd searched his memories for anything he'd done that fit such a description. Nothing had made sense.

And it still didn't. All this over a woman? What woman, for God's sake?

"Any woman I considered mine would remain so until *I* deemed otherwise," Lockhart gritted.

Annie grinned. "Unless she didnae. What happened? Bit of a problem hoistin' yer teacup?" Briefly, she dropped her gaze to his breeches. "Or perhaps she simply prefers Highland whisky to weak Lowland tea."

Broderick wanted to stop her then. She was playing with fire. That was the point, of course, but if Lockhart moved a single inch in her direction, Broderick would snap the bastard's neck.

"You're treading on dangerous ground, Lady Huxley."

"Like Broderick did? I'd wager ye discovered yer lass fancied him."

Fancied him. Bloody, everlasting hell. The answer arrived in a rush of memories. A veiled woman on Princes Street. Practiced lovemaking and lavender-scented breasts. Asparagus soup running down his naked chest. Her tears as they said their final goodbye.

Cecilia. This had all been about Cecilia. The woman he'd sent back to her protector—who was Lockhart.

Annie continued, "I'd wager ye werenae too pleased by her preference."

Lockhart's next words were as cold and slithering as an adder in frozen grass. "I'd wager your brother is no longer the sort of man a lass fancies."

Roaring disturbed Broderick's ears, but no one else around him seemed to hear it. Annie kept talking. He didn't hear what she said. The roaring sharpened until it sounded like rain beating bars and stone. Cold deepened. He could almost smell the straw.

Annie's voice flickered past the roar. "How did ye ken ye'd lost her, eh? Did she stop botherin' to please ye? Stop doin' that wee trick with her smile that made ye believe she worshipped ye?" She was pressing Lockhart, now, provoking him. "Here's the truth, Lockhart. I'll say it plain so ye cannae miss it. A woman can only pretend to love an empty bag of worthlessness so long."

How did she know these things? Even Broderick hadn't suspected Cecilia was the cause of his torture.

"When she finds a real man with real substance, she kens what she's missin'," his wee sister said. "And no title or fortune can hold her."

Lockhart bent closer to Annie, bracing his arm on the back of the settee.

Broderick tensed, picturing ten ways he could snap the man's neck before any harm came to Annie.

"She didn't leave," the bastard seethed.

"Aye, she did," Annie retorted calmly. "Mayhap ye kept her with ye. Mayhap she still lets ye wet yer teacup from time to time. But ye ken very well who she'd choose, had she the choice to make. And it wouldnae be you."

"It *was* me."

"Nah. 'Twas Broderick."

"No."

Yes, he thought starkly. Cecilia had chosen Broderick. Had she known what her protector would do when he found out?

"That's why ye had Skene set him up to take the fall for an exciseman's murder," Annie continued. "That's why ye made certain he would die in the Bridewell."

The shoulders inside light-blue linen heaved with agitated breaths. "He deserved his punishment."

"Ye couldnae bear the comparison. Couldnae bear thinkin' how she'd always want him more."

"Shut your mouth."

"A wee, empty man cannae hide his shortcomings when he's standin' next to a giant." Annie flashed Broderick a tender glance.

God, he wished she would stop this. Just stop.

"Bloody harridan," Lockhart growled.

Broderick's fists curled. Readied.

"His only hope is to bring the giant down."

When Lockhart pounded the back of the settee right beside Annie's shoulder, Broderick lost control. He lunged forward, only to have two of his brothers lock him in place with unbreakable force. Huxley, too, was being restrained by Campbell, he noticed. But Lockhart didn't seem aware of who stood behind him.

He was too busy crowing in a vicious snarl, "And down he fell, like a great, bloody tower smashed into bloody ruins."

Annie, seemingly satisfied by Lockhart's confession, sat back. "'Twas a clever plan," she said. "Very effective."

"Aye. It was."

"Do ye wish to see those ruins, Lord Lockhart? Surely ye do."

"Aye."

"Turn round."

Lockhart faced him. The man's eyes were a blaze of green as they scoured Broderick's face. Fine tension vibrated through his frame. The tension spoke of pleasure. Vicious, triumphant pleasure.

Annie's plan had been to goad Lockhart into a confession within earshot of enough prominent witnesses that he could be charged with arranging the exciseman's murder. She'd accomplished her goal.

Standing amongst the MacPhersons were two High Court judges, a Lowland duke, and a local magistrate. Annie and John believed it would be enough to convict Lockhart, enough to see him punished.

Broderick knew better. He'd experienced Lockhart's obsession and extraordinary influence first-hand. Before he'd known the bastard's name, he'd known the extent of his power. As a lord, Lockhart was middling, a minor social presence with a fading title and no official duties.

No, his power emanated from a different source—blackmail, perhaps, or secret favors. There were rumors of his investment in a particular club.

Regardless, the man before him now shook with near-orgasmic satisfaction upon viewing the results of his destruction. That sort of hatred did not die an easy death. And men of Lockhart's influence would never be punished by any court.

That would be left to Broderick.

"I'm goin' to kill ye, Lockhart," he vowed. "One way or another, I'll see it done."

The bastard's teeth gleamed as he grinned his victory. "Perhaps. But I've already killed you, haven't I? She'll never want you like this. Never again."

Two constables came to haul the man away, but inside, Broderick knew this was not the end. They would see each other again, and when they did, he meant to keep his vow.

One month later

Rain poured down Broderick's naked back as he brought the axe down with a harsh grunt. The log split cleanly down the center. The axe buried deep in the chopping stump. He jerked it loose, breaths heaving. "Nae more lies, Rannoch." His voice was a harsh rasp. He couldn't look at his brothers. "You and Alexander have been searchin' for weeks. What did ye find?"

"I told ye, I—"

"Is she alive?"

Silence.

Broderick battled the sick surge in his gut and looked at his younger brother. Rannoch's hair plastered like dripping ink to his forehead. His eyes spoke of sorrow. Broderick looked to Alexander. "Tell me."

"It's as he said," Alexander answered. "We couldnae find a trace of anybody named Magdalene Cuthbert. Nor anybody of her description."

Rannoch swiped a hand through his hair, slicking it off his forehead then paced away to stand with his back turned.

Alexander stood still, letting the rain soak him to the skin. "But we did find Gordon's lead man. He claims there was a lass that night. Not outside the Bridewell, but later, just down the way. Like thwarted hounds, their blood was up. They took her."

Something was stabbing Broderick's guts. Tearing and ripping and making him bleed. "Are ye certain it was—"

"Nothin' is certain. There was nobody left to ask." Months ago, shortly after Broderick's release, his brothers had turned every man involved in Broderick's torture into a cautionary tale on the dangers of targeting a MacPherson. According to Campbell, Alexander had taken his time with Gordon.

Now, Broderick's most lethal brother stood before him, black hair dripping into his eyes, dark gaze bleak as a windowless cell.

"What do ye ken?"

"We made inquiries," Alexander replied. "The minister who found her outside Trinity College Kirk said she died the following day. Her wounds were … severe. Too severe for a proper description."

Stillness took him. Inside, he froze until he burned. His breathing slowed to nothing. His eye closed. He saw gray. White. Kindness.

Red.

Someone released a deafening bellow, the cry of a great beast grievously wounded. When he opened his eye, the axe was fifty feet away.

It had cracked a tree in two.

One month later

Broderick cursed the freakish storm that made his poor vision worse than normal. Shortly after he'd sent Campbell and Alexander off, clouds had crowded the sky, bringing an early nightfall. Rain had followed. Now, in the downpour, darkness was thick enough to make the clearing impenetrable. He set the lantern on the ground near where the cart was mired.

His cargo shifted. Grunted.

"Soon enough," Broderick muttered, though he wasn't certain if he spoke to himself or to the evil bag of shite in the cart. Originally, he'd planned to take him further south, beyond the quarry. But the rain had turned the ground soft, and he'd decided rubbish could be buried here as easily as anywhere.

He pulled the shovel from the cart and leaned it against a tree. Then, he grasped an ankle and yanked the cargo onto the ground. The bag of shite landed with a groaning thud.

"Ye'll hang, MacPherson," it hissed, rolling onto its knees in the mud. "They'll dump you in that hole where you should have rotted. Then, they'll kill you."

After removing the bag from the shite's head, Broderick withdrew his dirk and severed Lockhart's bindings. He relished the man's flash of fear as he bent over him to complete the task—perhaps more than he should. But he'd already condemned himself to hell. What was another sin added to the pyre?

"Your sister's indulgent husband won't save you," the soon-to-be-dead man snarled as he staggered to his feet. "No duke's favor or judge's bribe. *Nothing* will spare you this time."

Returning his dirk to its scabbard, Broderick met his enemy's gaze, lit unearthly green by the lantern. "Mayhap. But ye'll be here, rotting 'neath the soil. That's what matters." He shrugged out of his coat and tossed it onto the cart. "For a long time, I didnae ken who ye were, Lockhart." He rolled up the sleeves of his blue linen shirt, rendered black by the downpour. "I wondered what sort of weakling must hire his retribution done. Now I ken."

He looked the man up and down. The Inverness jail had left no mark upon Kenneth Lockhart. When Campbell and Alexander had carried the blackguard out of the place, he'd been clean, well-fed, and garbed in the finest wool coat, white linen cravat, and pressed trousers.

With fury, Alexander had described the "cell" where they'd found him—a fine oak table and upholstered chair, blazing hearth, feather-stuffed mattress, silk bedding with plump pillows, and a china tea set.

After dropping his unconscious cargo unceremoniously into the cart, Campbell had said nothing apart from, "Ye were right. He must die."

Lockhart must die. Not because Broderick wanted it with every breath in his body. Not even because the bastard deserved the punishment a thousandfold. But because if they did not put this mad predator down, everyone they loved would suffer—Annie, in particular.

Blond hair that had remained neatly trimmed over the past two months plastered to a broad forehead. Thick lips sheened as Lockhart's head tilted. "God, ye're bloody hideous." A feverish glint entered the man's gaze, a queer sort of joy. "She's written me, you know. Begged me to take her back."

"Cecilia has her reasons."

"Don't you understand, you grotesque *teuchter*? You were a novelty." He spat in the mud near Broderick's boots. "She never loved you. How could she? You are nothing!"

Calmly, Broderick slid his fingers beneath his leather patch and stripped it away. He tossed it on the bed of the cart with his coat. "If I'm nothin', why did Cecilia take me to her bed?"

"Do not speak her name."

"Ye've gone to a fair bit of trouble to destroy *nothin'*, eh?"

Unexpectedly, the bastard's thick lips curled upward. "Oh, but I haven't finished."

Until now, Broderick had been methodical about his rage. He'd channeled it into rebuilding his strength, devising a plan to take Lockhart from the jail, arranging alibis for his brothers, who had insisted on helping him, and taking precautions to protect his family. He'd managed the pressure inside him carefully, surrounding the volatile mass with a dam constructed brick by brick. He'd chopped a ten-year reserve of firewood. He'd worked his own cattle and plowed his own fields. He'd hauled whisky casks and swum the loch. He'd hunted the last of Skene's men and ensured they'd never harm another woman.

All the while, he'd envisioned every minuscule detail of Lockhart's death. Again and again as he lay in the dark, he'd pictured his hands snapping bones and gouging an eye. Maybe two. He'd felt the blade of his dirk sinking into the black bastard's heart. He'd thought of Magdalene, Annie, his brothers, his father—everyone who had suffered for their association with him. Even

Ferguson. The pot-bellied exciseman hadn't deserved to die. None of them had deserved this.

While he'd worked and hunted, chopped and hauled, he hadn't controlled the scalding pressure of his hatred with thoughts of frosted heather or the scent of baking bread. Instead, he'd imagined blood.

Lockhart's blood.

But as he listened to his enemy's promise, he knew death would not be the end. The savage triumph now wreathing Lockhart's arrogant features told him as much.

The dam he'd built inside himself didn't merely crack. It vanished.

White-hot acid flooded inside. Filled his veins and organs, his muscles and mind. It drove him forward. It took its vengeance as an ordained right.

There it was. Blood. Aye, there it was. From his enemy's nose. From his enemy's teeth. From his enemy's taunting grin.

"Kill me," his enemy hissed from the ground. "Makes no difference. It will never stop. Your sister? That bairn in her womb? Dead."

Broderick's next kick elicited a groan.

The sound soon became a wheezing chuckle. "Yer brothers, dead. Yer father, dead."

Through a haze, Broderick heard roaring. It was him, but not him. The dark was red. Blood red.

"Ye're *nothing* because I've made sure of it. Every trace of your existence will be wiped away, MacPherson. And ye'll watch it be taken piece by piece." Lockhart's swelling eyes gleamed up at him through blood, mud, and malice. "I may be dead, but ye'll be watching … through the one eye I've left ye."

He bent and pummeled the sneering face of his enemy. Bones cracked. Blood flowed. Shapes altered. Flattened. Swelled into grotesque lumps.

He didn't feel it.

His enemy slackened. Stilled.

He didn't feel it.

He didn't feel anything except white-hot pressure.

He didn't see anything except red.

But just as his fist was about to swing again, he did hear a sound.

A cry. Soft and high and distressed.

He halted. There. Gasping. Whimpering like a wounded pup. Or a woman.

Blinking rain from his eye, he straightened and turned toward the sound, which came from a thicket at the base of the hill. Past the trees, he glimpsed white. Oddly, the sight forced the red to recede. Breaths heaved inside his pounding chest. Inky black surrounded him once again as the sounds of rain and wind replaced the strange buzzing in his ears.

The white moved. Scrambled backward.

More distressed mewling.

The white appeared to be a gown. Skin. A face, small and frightened.

He stalked toward what he now recognized as a lass. His vision was shite outside the lantern's reach, but he drew close enough to make out a slender figure, delicate jaw, wet curls beneath a limp bonnet, and a flash of terrified eyes before she spun and scrambled up the hill, quick as a doe fleeing a hunter. Instinctively, he started after her—whoever she was. The last thing he needed was a witness. He'd planned this too carefully.

But he had no time for distractions. He must deal with Lockhart first.

He cursed. Pivoted back toward where he'd left his enemy.

And saw only mud.

He rushed back at a dead run. Searched the perimeter for signs of the man's footprints. Anything. Any bloody thing.

But there was nothing. Rain had washed away every trace. He couldn't fucking see in the dark.

And an unknown, wayward lass had stolen the only chance he had of discovering Lockhart's plan before his family paid with their lives.

CHAPTER SIX

October 10, 1826
Glendasheen Castle, Scotland

Kate awakened gasping. Her shift plastered her skin. Cold. Damp. Her blankets lay mangled at the foot of the bed as though she'd fought them to the death. She rolled onto her side and waited. Breathing. Giving her heart time to slow.

He'd chased her for hours this time, but he'd only caught her once. That had been enough to make her never want to close her eyes again. Because the monster hadn't hurt her. He'd simply reached for her throat, gripped with a near-sensual caress, and growled like the animal he was. Then, the strangest thing happened. He'd drawn her against him.

And he'd been … warm.

She'd dreamt the same dream for three nights. Details changed—he'd worn black in some dreams, a kilt in others; a few dreams had taken place in that wooded clearing, others beside a moonlit loch, and last night's inside the darkened corridors of the castle—but never had he caught her before. Never had she imagined his hand circling her throat with more gentleness than threat. Never had she thought of him as warm.

Swiping a hand over her face, she shoved up from the bed and stripped off her damp shift. At the washstand, she rinsed away sweat with soap and water until her scent was once again tuberose and jasmine, clary sage and bergamot. Then, she dressed while distracting herself by singing her plans for the day.

"I shall begin with breakfast," she sang as she donned a fresh shift and summoned a maid. *"For, sweet Annie's bread is divine. I'll add butter and jam and a good bit of ham, so long as my stomach doesn't mind."*

She sat at her dressing table and brushed tangles from her hair. *"Next, I'll go for a ride, for it's been far too many days, and Ophelia must be going mad. Is it wise to mount a horse that's crazed?"* She sorted through her box of pins and combs, searching for her tartan hair ribbon. It wasn't there. *"Then, I shall visit the haberdashery, for I must have a ribbon to ride. And nothing rhymes with haberdashery, but my restlessness cannot be denied. Later, I'll return to the castle, and then ..."*

Her voice thinned to a trickle.

She paused. Glanced at her reflection.

And then what, Katherine Ann Huxley? She couldn't go outside the castle, for pity's sake. What if Sergeant Munro was waiting for her? As John had predicted, he'd come to the castle two days in a row asking to speak to her. She'd avoided him, but that would be hard to do if he caught her on the road. What if he questioned her and accused her of lying? Could he arrest her? Could *she* be jailed?

No, she must remain here. Again. Wistfully, she gazed out the window. Perhaps she *should* return to England. She would be safer. Annie's brother would be safer. Her muse would suffer, to be sure, but was that the worst thing? Her desire to pen a grand Scottish adventure could not be more important than a man's freedom, especially if everything Annie had told her about Broderick MacPherson was true.

Besides, she thought as she strummed the loose papers protruding from her sketchbook, she suspected her talent for storytelling approximated her talent for lying.

Her heart ached and twisted. She swallowed a lump.

Perhaps she wasn't meant to be an author, just as she wasn't meant to sing operatic arias or play Lady Macbeth at Drury Lane. Loving something did not make one good at it. Perhaps being a prolific breeder of future aristocrats *was* her singular talent, and she was a feather-headed ninny for thinking otherwise.

The maid, a buoyant young lass with sandy hair, entered and curtsied before crossing to the wardrobe near the fireplace. "Good mornin', m'lady."

"Good morning, Janet." Kate attempted a smile. "How did your conversation with young Stuart go?"

The maid grinned over her shoulder and bounced on her toes as she threw open the wardrobe doors. "Just as ye said it might. He wants to dance with me at the *cèilidh* on Halloween. I dinnae ken how ye sensed he fancied me, m'lady, for he's never so much as spoken my name. But I'm grateful ye pressed me to speak to him. He's a shy one, that Stuart."

Nodding, Kate watched a bird land on a branch outside her window. The bird was small and green. Another landed beside it, red and brilliant. They were different, yet clearly belonged together. "I'm pleased it went well."

"Oh, it did. He promised to teach me a new reel." Janet giggled and sighed. "I pretended I havenae been dancin' the reel since I was a bairn. Wouldnae wish to disappoint him." She winked and began sorting through the wardrobe. "Now, then, will it be yer blue riding habit this mornin'?"

Kate glanced down at the sketchbook and tattered stack of notes strewn across her dressing table. "No," she said, pushing them aside. "The green muslin with the long sleeves, I think. I shall remain at the castle today."

Hours later, Kate had just finished penning morose letters to her dearest friends, Francis and Clarissa, lamenting the woeful tides of fate when Janet informed her that John and Annie required her presence in the drawing room.

"At once?" Kate frowned, her pen poised above the paper. "That is what they said?"

"Aye, m'lady." The maid glanced behind her then whispered, "A family meetin', I reckon. I was told to serve cider. And whisky."

How odd. Had Angus or Rannoch come for a visit?

The answer came as she approached the drawing room doors—and heard the distorted growl from her nightmares.

Her skin flashed hot then cold. Shivers struck. Her breath quickened until her head felt light.

"… dinnae give a damn what some bluidy constable does," the monster was saying. "Tell him he can kiss my hairy ballocks—"

"I'll tell him nothin' of the sort, ye great crabbit beastie!" That was Annie. She sounded enraged.

For some reason, her sister-in-law's bold ire made Kate's palms stop sweating and her heart calm a little.

"And ye'll be doin' likewise if ye dinnae want to return to the hell we pulled ye from!"

John spoke next, though his volume was lower. "We must deal with this. There is no choice." Calm and steady. That was her brother.

The tension in her stomach eased a bit more.

"'Tis mine to deal with, Huxley," grated the monster. "Not yers."

"The moment my sister witnessed what you'd done, it bloody well became mine. She is innocent, Broderick. Whatever I must do, she will *not* take damage for this. I trust I'm clear."

Silence fell.

Even through the door, she felt the tension inside the room. For a moment, she considered fleeing. She didn't want to meet the monster. She didn't want to look upon him or hear his voice or remember what he'd done.

But John could not flee. Annie could not flee. Their child could not flee. They were her family, and long after she returned to England, they must contend with everything Broderick had done and everything that had been done to him.

The least she could do was walk in there and speak to them. To him.

So, she inhaled as though preparing to sing a high note then entered the drawing room. The first person she saw was a bald, bespectacled man with a long nose and waxy pallor. He sat on a green damask settee to the right of the fireplace.

John stood in the center of the room, hazel eyes sharp and flashing with hard resolve. His hands rested on Annie's shoulders. Her cheeks were flushed, her eyes brilliant with outrage. Both of them shifted to look at Kate.

Kate clasped her hands at her waist and kept her eyes trained on her brother. John crossed to greet her, and she took his arm. *Steady,* she told herself. *Screw your courage to the sticking-place.* But Shakespearean wisdom wasn't helping. She repeated the phrase over and over as John drew her toward the corner of the room where she sensed a dark, volatile presence waiting.

Inside, she shook hard enough to rattle her bones.

John covered her hand where it rested on her arm. "Lady Katherine Huxley, may I present Mr. Broderick MacPherson."

She should lift her eyes. *Stop staring at his boots, you ninny.* But God, they were so dreadfully large.

"Broderick, this my youngest sister, Lady Katherine."

Silence.

Her lungs wouldn't work. Her eyes refused to budge. "Screw your courage," she whispered to herself. "Screw your courage."

His ankles were crossed, she noticed. As though he leaned against something and couldn't be bothered to stand upright. She blinked and noticed his knees. Did monsters have knees? They seemed such an ordinary part. Not frightening at all, really. He wore breeches. Slightly dusty. Buckskin, she thought. His thighs were the thickest, most muscular thighs she'd ever seen, so she forced her gaze to race past them. Then came his waist, surprisingly trim given the overall size of him.

"Screw your courage," she whispered. "To the sticking-place."

His shirt was white. Clean. His waistcoat and riding coat were brown wool. Not particularly fine. Not particularly humble.

His arms were massive. Crossed across a massive chest and attached to even more massive shoulders.

"Screw your courage to the sticking-place. Screw your—"

"Calm yerself, lass."

Her heart hammered so loudly, she thought for a moment she'd imagined that deep, damaged rumble. Before she could stop herself, she looked at his face. Ah, God. It was … her nightmare.

"Screw your courage."

Her nightmare. Dear God. Her nightmare had come to life. Only it was worse because in daylight, she saw everything: The slashing wounds that had healed jagged. The flattened, crooked nose. The empty eye socket mercifully covered by a leather patch. He was a monster, massive and mean, leaning casually against a bookcase and looking for all the world like a predator examining an unwary rabbit.

Her fingers dug into John's arm. "S-screw your courage—"

"Aye. Screw that courage all the way to the sticking-place." His tone was wry. That single, dark eye flashed, and the scars along his jaw and the corner of his mouth tightened. "I only devour wee, frightened lasses on Sundays."

"Broderick," Annie snapped. "Ye owe her better."

He held Kate's eyes. "Do I?" His jaw flexed as he examined her from head to toe. "What do ye think, Lady Katherine? Or are ye only capable of quotin' Shakespeare?"

She blinked. He knew Shakespeare?

"That's quite enough," John said quietly. "We are here to settle the legal troubles you've caused. Now, I suggest we all take our seats and hear what Mr. Thomson has to say on the matter."

The bespectacled man cleared his throat behind them. John led Kate to the blue sofa before he and Annie took their seats. Broderick, she noticed, wore a ferocious scowl that deepened the scars slashing his brow and disappearing beneath his patch. He straightened from his position against the bookcase. His full height stole her breath.

He was coming toward her. Slowly. With a slight hitch in his gait. Then, he lowered his enormous frame into the largest of the three chairs, the one directly across from her.

She frowned. One of his knees didn't bend quite right. A faint shudder worked through his shoulders, a faint wince narrowing his eye. For some reason, sympathy squeezed her heart.

"My lord," Mr. Thomson began, "I have made the inquiries you requested."

"And?" John prompted.

"I regret to say our options are few."

From that point on, the conversation grew more distressing. Mr. Thomson explained that, even if Kate returned to England, she could still be summoned to testify against Broderick.

"It would be a simple matter for the court to request the notice be served at her home in Nottinghamshire."

"And for her to defy the court would be considered—"

"Contempt, my lord. She could be fined or jailed. Commonly the latter."

John cursed. "Humiliated, too, no doubt. An English aristocrat defying a Scottish court."

"Indeed."

They discussed alternatives ranging from having her declared mad to sending her on a lengthy tour of the Continent. In the end, Mr. Thomson shook his head and adjusted his spectacles. "She is one-and-twenty, certainly of age to be considered competent."

"What of my father's influence? He is an earl with a peer's privileges. Might that benefit us here?"

"Only if he were the witness in question."

Annie poured herself a cup of tea from the side table and took a sip before asking, "How can they charge Broderick with murder when they havenae found the evil bugger's body?"

"They cannae," Broderick answered, speaking for the first time.

Kate shifted to face him, unnerved to find him staring at her. Her heart lurched. Her belly quaked. What was he looking at? Without thinking, she twirled the curls near her ear. His gaze tracked the movement.

"And they willnae," he finished. "He's nae dead."

It took a moment for his flat statement to digest, as she was busy trying to decide whether his eye color was black or merely dark gray. Then, his words registered. "He—he's *alive?*"

"Aye."

"How?" Kate shook her head. "How is it possible for anybody to survive …" She examined the hands resting on his thighs, huge and battered and powerful. "… those?"

Broderick folded his arms across his chest, tucking his hands out of sight. "Ye distracted me. I lost him in the dark."

"No. I saw him collapse."

"Aye. Then, ye started bleatin' like a lamb missin' its mother—"

"I do not *bleat*."

"—and I turned to see what sort of puny animal was makin' such sounds. Yer wee fit of fright cost me—"

"The sight of you pummeling a man to death would frighten any sensible creature, Mr. MacPherson."

"Right. And ye're a perfectly *sensible* creature, eh? Wanderin' alone on *my* land in the middle of the bluidy night, lost in the wood. A daft, wee lamb strayin' too far from the pasture."

"Do you honestly intend to sit there, adding insult to the injury you've already done me?" She sat forward. "You really are beastly."

"Nah. I might be missin' an eye, but I can see ye just fine." His gaze dropped to her gown then returned to her hair. "Go home to England, Lady Kate. 'Tis where ye belong."

She straightened and arched a brow. "Perhaps you're correct, Mr. MacPherson. But, as Mr. Thomson has stated, returning to Nottinghamshire will not stop the court from compelling my testimony. Nor, I suspect, will it prevent Sergeant Munro from accosting me every time I leave my home."

"Simple answer: Tell Munro ye dinnae ken anythin'."

"I did."

"And?"

"He didn't believe me."

"Tell him another story, then. Make him think ye're lyin' about somethin' else—"

"I have already done precisely that."

He frowned. "And?"

"He has continued his pursuit."

"What sort of wild tale did ye tell?"

She felt her cheeks burning. "It is not important."

His gaze intensified, wandering curiously over her neck and face. "Tell me."

"I don't wish to."

"Ye must."

"No."

"If I'm to be convicted of murder on the basis of yer testimony, I should ken—"

"I told him you fancy me."

Disbelieving silence fell.

Her skin could light a thousand candles. She brushed her skirts and wound a curl around her finger before forcing her hands back to her lap.

"Lass, the first time I ever clapped eyes upon ye was that night in the wood."

"Yes, well, I'd already told him I fancied Rannoch, so—"

"Rannoch?"

"—the subject was on my mind." She shrugged. "It was extemporaneous."

He was glowering. With all his scars and the distorted nature of his features, his expression was initially difficult for her to read, but the longer they conversed, the easier it grew. Presently, he was either displeased or confused.

"Extemporaneous means unplanned," she offered helpfully.

"What the devil possessed ye to make such a daft claim?"

"I told you already. My tale was extemporaneous. Another word would be improvisational. It is a common technique for actors to use whilst—"

"So, ye tell a constable ye fancy *Rannoch*," he snapped.

She blinked. That was his complaint? "I had to have some reason for pursuing Rannoch into the tavern."

"Pursuin'? What were ye—no. Never mind. Go to the Continent. Buy yerself some new frocks in Paris. Munro's a bluidy-minded auld sod, but he'll nae follow ye there."

"I don't wish to leave." She sniffed and brushed her skirts. "And I have no need of new frocks."

He shook his head, his frown deepening. "Christ on the cross, lass."

She'd heard Angus and Rannoch both use similar blasphemies when they were overwrought. She attempted to explain her reasoning. "Scotland is my muse."

His eye flared.

"I am a playwright. An author. I must complete my manuscript."

Silence thickened. Broderick appeared at a loss for words.

"I need only a month. Perhaps two. If Lord Lockhart is alive, as you claim, then it should be a simple matter of locating him."

Broderick tilted his head. "Brilliant. Why didnae I think of such a solution?"

She frowned. "Sarcasm is the lowest form of humor."

"Nothin' about this is amusin'."

"We agree."

"Except, perhaps, for ye claimin' to fancy Rannoch."

"He is quite charming, you know."

He snorted. "My brother has tupped every lass in the county. He's plowin' his way through Perthshire as we speak."

"As I said," she retorted pertly. "Charming."

He appeared to bite down on further commentary regarding his brother. "If ye willnae leave Scotland, then ye'll simply have to refuse to speak to the constable."

"Every time I leave the castle, he waylays me. He is very … forceful."

Broderick tensed again, his gaze roaming over her. "Has he hurt ye?"

"No. He grasped my arm a time or two, but I would not say—"

"He put hands upon ye?" Spoken in that roughened rumble, low and menacing, his words sent a strange charge spiraling up her spine.

"Let us say, I should like to ride to the village without fear of being accosted. Certainly, there must be some measure we can take to prevent Sergeant Munro from hounding me." She glanced to her left, thinking she'd put the question to the solicitor.

She found three sets of eyes staring at her and Broderick in silence. Annie, John, and Mr. Thomson wore varying expressions of fascination and perplexity.

Annie spoke first. "Are ye certain ye havenae conversed with Broderick before now, Katie-lass? The two of ye seem a mite … familiar."

Kate frowned her confusion. Familiar? How ridiculous. He was slightly infuriating, and she'd responded appropriately. That was all.

Before she could reply, Broderick took control of the conversation. "Thomson, answer the question. Can ye keep Munro away from her?"

The solicitor hesitated, nudging his spectacles higher.

"Out with it, man," John insisted, still casting odd glances between Kate and Broderick.

"I'm afraid not. By importuning Lady Katherine, Sergeant Munro is executing his official duties. There is no legal recourse."

"Blast," John muttered.

"That is, short of Mr. MacPherson *marrying* Lady Katherine." The solicitor chuckled nervously.

Wait. There *was* a solution? Kate sat up straighter, feeling hopeful for the first time in days. If there was a way to protect him while remaining in Scotland …

But marriage? To the monster? She glanced to Broderick, who was scowling at the lawyer. Then she looked to Annie, who was scowling at Broderick.

With a disgusted sigh, John stood. "Thank you, Thomson. You've been exceedingly unhelpful."

"Apologies, my lord."

"Wait," Kate sputtered, following John as he led Mr. Thomson toward the door. "How would marriage change anything?"

The solicitor turned. "A wife cannot be compelled to testify against her husband, my lady."

Hope soared, warm and tingly along her middle. "Even for crimes committed before the marriage?"

"Indeed."

"Kate," John chided. "You are not marrying Broderick. I'll send you back to England. We'll keep Munro occupied so he'll be disinclined to follow."

"But I—"

John ushered the solicitor out of the room as though the conversation were finished. But Kate was not finished. Thomson had given her hope. He'd given her a choice—run home to Mama and Papa to prepare for yet another disappointing season on the marriage mart; or stay in Scotland, complete her manuscript, and perhaps be relieved of the duty she'd been assigned at birth.

She turned. Broderick and Annie argued in low tones near the fireplace.

All Kate must do was marry ... him.

Annie poked a finger into Broderick's chest. He enfolded her hand in his enormous paw and, with incredible gentleness, cradled it, nodding at whatever she said. The anger melted from her eyes, and she cupped his jaw, saying something that looked like, "Ah ken, brother. Ah ken."

He embraced her, kissing her temple.

Kate watched as the monster of her nightmares held his sister as tenderly as she might hold one of her newborn nephews.

Annie had explained a bit about what Broderick had endured, how Lockhart had targeted him out of jealousy, and how richly the lord had deserved his punishment. But Kate hadn't understood. Not really.

Not until this moment.

Broderick was not a monster. He was a man. One who had been tortured, wrongfully imprisoned, and nearly killed. One dearly loved by his sister, his family. He must be protected, whatever the cost.

She could do this, she thought. She could marry him. And it might not even be terrible. She could remain in Scotland as long as she pleased. She could write whatever stories took her fancy. She would not fall in love. She would not have to bear hordes of children. She would not have to endure white-soup suppers filled with vapid conversation. She could attend the theatre, spend her days riding and exploring, and perhaps travel wherever the wind took her.

Her breath quickened. Their marriage would guarantee she could never be used as a weapon against him. And she'd never have to endure another season of tiresome suitors buying her Gunter's ices and prattling about their winnings at Ascot. Because she would no longer be the last eligible Huxley girl. She'd be a bride.

His bride.

True, he was still the rageful beast she'd seen beating a man to the edge of death. His disposition might best be described as surly. He was even bigger than Rannoch, towering over her like a great, scarred oak. He was rude. Dismissive. And parts of her quaked in the most peculiar fashion whenever he spoke in that deep, damaged brogue.

But she didn't have to kiss him or lie with him or even live with him, necessarily.

Indeed, if he was agreeable to a modest arrangement, Broderick MacPherson would make an entirely acceptable husband. According to Annie, his lands were expansive, his house quite fine, and his income reasonably secure now that the MacPherson Distillery was properly licensed. Despite his injuries, he appeared strong and fit—frightfully so. He was in his prime at two-and-thirty. Untitled, but that was no great matter. Titles were rarely worth the nuisance.

Mama might be disappointed at his lack of wealth and manners. Papa might object to the distance from Nottinghamshire; he preferred to keep his girls closer to home. But her parents would come around. They'd accepted Annie readily enough.

Now that she thought about it, this might solve more than the trouble with Sergeant Munro. This could be the answer she'd been looking for all along.

Annie patted Broderick's shoulders before crossing to the doorway where Kate stood. She squeezed Kate's hand with a sad smile then departed for the kitchen to "make certain Marjorie MacDonnell hasnae ruined dinner."

Kate nodded and kissed her cheek before gathering a breath. Across the room, Broderick braced an elbow on the mantel and gazed down into the fire. Kate approached, feeling both excited and queasy.

"Mr. MacPherson."

He turned. "Shouldnae ye be packin'?"

"I—no, I … I have a topic to discuss with you."

Silence.

"A proposal, really."

More silence. The way he glared down at her from his great height reminded her that it was a good thing she didn't have to kiss him. She'd need a ladder and an entire bottle of wine.

Best to come to her point. "I think we should marry."

Again, the silence.

Had he heard her? She squinted up at him, trying to discern whether his ears had been damaged. She didn't think so, but he wasn't responding as she'd hoped.

"Our sacred union offers multiple benefits," she elaborated. "It would shield me from being forced to send you back to prison. Which I do not wish to do. Perhaps I haven't been clear on that score. But it is true. I shouldn't like to see you imprisoned. Again."

His expression remained unreadable. "Charitable of ye."

"Yes, well. I am fond of Annie. I don't like for her to be distressed."

Silence.

"Also, I do wish to remain here. In Scotland, that is. Our sacred union would ensure I am able to do so."

"How sacred do ye expect this union to be, lass?"

"Oh. We needn't live together or anything of that sort."

More silence.

She clarified, "Our sacred union would be purely an arrangement. Mutually beneficial, of course. We may obtain an annulment at some future date, if you wish."

"If *I* wish."

"I'll have no need of one. I shall be most content to be your wife for the duration."

His head tilted. "An hour ago, ye refused to look at anythin' above my boots."

"I was frightened of you. If you'll recall how you turned Lord Lockhart into a piteous, broken heap, you may begin to understand why."

"Hmm. But ye're nae frightened of me any longer."

"No."

"Screwed yer courage to the stickin' place, eh?"

"Are you going to address my proposal?"

"No."

"Whyever not?"

"Because it's pure, daft madness, that's why."

"Though this be madness, yet there is method in't."

"Ye belong in England."

She inched closer, even though it forced her to crane her neck to continue holding his gaze. "No, Mr. MacPherson. Scotland is where my spirit sings. Where my muse comes alive and *breathes*." On impulse, she reached for his hand, shocked to find it so warm. Enormous, callused fingers clasped hers. His knuckles were the size of coins. Some of them remained split and scabbed. But his hand held hers loosely. Gently. The warmth reminded her of last night's dreams.

She raised her eyes to his. Though he had only one, it was thickly lashed, deep-set beneath a heavy brow, and brown. So dark a brown, it was black. Beautiful, really.

"I want to stay." Her whisper felt torn from her soul. "I need to stay."

For a moment, his jaw flickered. "Mad creature." He dropped her hand.

She frowned. Why was he so resistant? Their marriage would solve everything. Besides, it wasn't as if he'd have dozens more opportunities to marry. The scars distorted his features dreadfully. Most women would refuse to look past them. Was he concerned he wouldn't benefit equally from their sacred union?

Perhaps her offer had been insufficient. Perhaps he expected a wife to bear him children.

Blast. Could she? She examined the enormity of him, pausing at his thick, muscular thighs and giving them duc consideration.

Ignoring the sudden strange twist in her belly, she tendered an offer. "We—we could have one or two, I suppose." Surely, he could not expect more.

"One or two what?"

She couldn't seem to look away from his legs. There was a long, thick bulge between them, tucked along one of the thighs. "Children."

Silence. The bulge appeared to shift and ... lengthen?

"You may have heard that we Huxleys are peculiarly fertile. I don't expect much effort would be required on your part."

It grew further. She frowned. Just how long could it be? And it was thickening, too, she suspected. Yes, indeed. Thicker and longer than before. Already, she regretted her tendered offer. They did not appear compatible.

"Huxley should have put ye on the first stagecoach headed south. Ye're pure trouble." He pivoted on his heel and strode for the door.

Startled, she watched her only chance to remain in Scotland and his only chance to secure his freedom slipping away. "Mr. MacPherson." She rushed to follow, determined not to let him doom them both. "Broderick."

He reached the doorway.

"I—I will tell Munro everything!"

That stopped him. Impossibly wide shoulders stiffened. Enormous hands curled into fists before relaxing. Slowly, he turned to face her.

Oh, heavens, the fury in that dark, beautiful eye. "Are ye threatenin' me, lass?"

For a moment, she couldn't catch her breath. For another, she couldn't form words. Finally, she managed, "No-ot exactly."

He prowled toward her. "Then, what *exactly?*"

"Sergeant Munro is dreadfully persistent. I cannot evade his interrogations forever. I fear the truth may inadvertently ... slip out." Not a lie. The longer it went on, the greater the likelihood she would make a mistake. Everyone else thought Munro would give up if she returned to England. They were wrong.

"Then, leave."

"No."

He moved closer, looming above her. "No?"

"No. I shall stay."

"Yer brother might have somethin' to say about that."

"Yes, let's discuss my brother. The man who arranged for your release the first time round. The man who ensured your family's distillery was granted a license. The man who saved your life. You owe him a great deal, do you not?"

"*Him,* not ye."

Couldn't he see this was necessary? Couldn't he see she was trying to save him—and herself? Kate's belly shook and shook. Her skin flashed cold and hot, writhing with shivery sensations as she took the most daring step she'd ever attempted.

She would not return to England. She would not go back to the marriage mart. She would stay here. And she would marry this monstrously large, scarred, beastly Highlander, whether he liked it or not.

"All I must do is walk a hundred feet outside this castle," she said. "Munro will find me. He will insist I answer his questions." She shrugged. "I fear I am simply too weak to continue resisting."

"That's pure shite," he rasped. Black fury radiated from him, pulsing the vein near his temple. "Ye wouldnae do that to Annie."

"Do you wish to take that chance?"

For a dreadfully long minute, he looked ready to kill. Then, he straightened, released a sneering huff, and replied, "Have it yer way, lass. Dinnae say I never warned ye."

CHAPTER SEVEN

One week after Kenneth disappeared from the Inverness jail, Sabella Lockhart watched a wagon draw to a halt behind the garden of her rented house. Half of her had prayed her brother would never return. The other half remembered the boy who had huddled over her in the freezing rain, whispering a bitter promise that she would never again be cold, never again be without shelter. Kenneth had vowed he would rebuild the fortune their father had lost and save them both from the poorhouse.

That boy had succeeded. But he'd become something dark and terrible in the process.

For Sabella, the changes had been easy to ignore. She'd been comfortable. Safe. Even now, as she stood at the rain-battered kitchen window of the rented house in Inverness, she wanted to believe he was the brother who'd cared so dearly for her comfort that he'd gone without a coat and nearly lost his fingers to frostbite.

She wanted to remember the day he'd shown her the house he'd purchased in Charlotte Square, one of the most fashionable areas of Edinburgh. "It is ours, Sabella," he'd announced, holding the umbrella carefully above her head and ensuring not a drop of rain landed upon her skirts. He'd beamed down at her with pride in every handsome line. "Ours. Let them try to take it from me, now."

Aye, she wanted to remember *that* Kenneth. Not the monster who'd orchestrated the torture and imprisonment of an innocent man. Nor even the tyrant who forbade her from wearing red or taking sugar in her tea or waltzing with a suitor.

That Kenneth made her want to flee Inverness. Flee far away from him. And sometimes, in her worst moments, flee this world altogether.

She watched the old merchant climb down from the covered wagon and help a huddled figure to the scullery door. A knock sounded. She closed her eyes. Inside, she felt cold. Sick. Another knock.

She went to the scullery and opened the door.

"Evenin', miss." The merchant nodded, bracing the huddled figure with a wary expression. "I was told ye'd have a shillin' or two for my trouble."

Sabella nodded, retrieving two shillings from the reticule around her wrist and handing them to the merchant. She offered a third but held it back. "If anybody comes asking, tell them naught of this delivery."

She knew it might not be enough, but she was unaccustomed to such transactions. Kenneth had always handled these matters.

The merchant nodded, accepted the extra shilling, and departed. Sabella took the arm of the huddled figure wearing a horse blanket as a cowled plaid and guided him to a chair near the kitchen hearth.

"Rest, now," she murmured. She retrieved the kettle from over the fire and poured a bit of tea into a chipped cup. "Drink."

He grunted harshly. Slammed a palm upon the table.

She flinched at the show of temper.

With pained motions, he drew back the cowl. She felt her gorge rise. His face was … hideous. His jaw was thrice the size it had been, his eyes mere slits amidst the swelling. Dried blood sealed gashes along his cheeks and brows and lips.

He made a writing motion with his hand.

She gave a jerky nod and retrieved a quill pen and paper from her sitting room. With unsteady hands, she placed them on the table and quickly retreated. He seized her wrist, twisting and painfully grinding her skin against her bones.

She gritted her teeth, her eyes watering. He pulled her to the chair beside him and forced her to sit. When she did, he loosened his pressure but didn't release her. If experience was any guide, she'd have to wear long sleeves and gloves to cover the bruises for a while. He didn't like to see the marks he left upon her.

Breathing harshly, he began writing: *Laudanum.*

She nodded and tried to rise. His hand tightened again, making her gasp. "Ye must release me, Kenneth. The laudanum is in the larder."

Gradually, he let her go. *Hurry,* he wrote.

After retrieving the laudanum and adding it to his tea, she poured herself a cup and added a few drops to her own. Her wrist throbbed badly enough to make her eyes water.

His hand slammed the table again, jolting her heart into her throat. She turned. He slid his paper closer to her. *Pack everything. Must return to Edinburgh.*

"D-don't you wish to contact yer solicitors first? The charges against ye haven't yet been dismissed."

This time, he grasped her arm, yanking her close enough to smell the rancid, putrid stench of him. The green of his eyes was barely discernible, but inside, she saw what her brother had become.

There was nothing left of the boy who had nearly frozen to death so that she could be warm, or the young man who had often walked around with a wet shoulder so that her skirts could stay dry.

No, this was the Kenneth she'd refused to see for too long. Malignant. Poisonous. Possessive.

He shook her. Shoved her. Sent her stumbling backward until her lower back struck the corner of the table. Then, he wrote furiously for a long minute. Tapped the paper with a demand.

Insides quaking with sickening dread, she inched closer and read what he'd written.

The magistrate's sympathies were lost with my "escape." Huxley's doing. Anne Huxley and her bairn will be the first to die. You are the reason. I have no use for a sister who would betray me to a supposed "friend."

Sabella's stomach cramped. She feared she might vomit. How did he know? And, dear God, how did she protect Annie? "I—I didn't betray you, Kenneth," she lied. "I wouldn't."

More writing.

MacPherson knew of my plans. The only way he could have known was that you told her, and she warned him. Now, she'll suffer. That is your punishment.

She shook her head, panic rising like boiling water. "No. Please, Kenneth. I never said anything to her. Perhaps yer man Gordon or one of the solicitors—"

His fist slammed the table. He pointed at her then pointed to the word *betray*.

Her breath shook inside her chest. "Please. Please do not hurt her."

He pointed to *Edinburgh*.

"Aye, we'll return to Edinburgh. I'll help ye recover. Ye must be in dreadful pain, brother. Let me take care of ye the way I did when ye were ill. Remember when ye were a young lad? Remember the fever?" She tried to swallow but nearly choked. "If ye leave her be, I'll do anything ye ask."

He stared at her for a long while, the green slits of his eyes burning with hatred. Then, he took a slow, wincing drink of the tea she'd prepared for him, set down the cup, and resumed writing.

Aye, you will. Gordon is dead. But there is another. Before our return to Edinburgh, you will take him a message. And if you ever betray me again, Sabella, be assured your friend's life will not be the one you're begging to save.

The day Katherine Ann Huxley married Broderick MacPherson, the Scottish sun beamed from a sky as blue as Annie's eyes. Unfortunately, that was the only joyful thing about it.

The wedding took place inside the ruins of an old church near the castle on All Hallow's Eve. The banns had been read thrice. The wispy-haired minister spoke words of sacredness and unions. Kate and Broderick dutifully repeated what they must. But everyone looked miserable.

Especially Broderick. Until the very moment she stepped up into the church's roofless interior, she'd wondered if he would refuse to attend. But there he stood beside the old, crumbled altar, his nearly-black hair thick and shining in the sun, his massive shoulders encased in dark wool, and his lower half dressed in MacPherson tartan. The patch over his eye formed a dark slash across his face. His other eye glinted searing fury.

Feeling scorched from head to toe as he looked her over, she had to steady herself on John's arm before continuing forward.

Kate's own misery might be blamed on the oily, sickening sensation in her stomach, which might have started when she'd blackmailed a man into marriage, and might be guilt.

John had been apoplectic at first. He'd refused to grant permission for them to marry. Kate had pointed out that she was of age and did not require anyone's permission. He'd threatened to write Mama and Papa. She'd pointed out that in Scotland, marriages could be performed on a moment's notice by a blacksmith, if need be, and that Mama and Papa could not possibly journey here from Nottinghamshire in time to prevent her nuptials. John had brought Annie into the argument, insisting she "talk some sense into my baby sister." Annie had refused to intervene, other than giving Kate a penetrating stare and asking, "Are ye certain about this, Katie-lass?"

Kate had nodded, and that had been that. The solicitor had recommended their wedding be performed by a clergyman with the full reading of banns in place, as the marriage was less likely to be challenged.

Today, Kate wore her finest gown of creamy-gold silk embroidered with metallic-thread leaves in silver, bronze, and peach. She'd draped a luxuriously soft, woolen sash of MacPherson tartan—coppery red with accents of blue and green—across her body, pinning it with the brooch she'd purchased in Inverness. She breathed deeply of crisp Highland air. Screwed her courage to the sticking-place. Then, she traveled the grassy path to where a monstrously large Highlander waited in his MacPherson kilt.

Sunlight passed through the ruined, broken arches of the old church, casting artful shadows across the weedy ground. Across his scarred, thunderous face.

How he must hate her. The entire ceremony, he glared down from his great height, making her neck tingle. She was surprised her nosegay of white heather didn't burst into flames.

Afterward, his brothers and father surrounded her like a phalanx of giants, each offering his well wishes. First, iron-haired Angus bent down to kiss her cheek and declared, "Welcome to the clan, lass. I hope ye like whisky."

Next came Campbell, who was even bigger than Broderick—which should not be possible. He was less handsome than Rannoch and much quieter. But when he took her hand in his, he was gentle as could be. "*Meal do naidheachd.* Congratulations, lass."

Alexander's features had a more sardonic edge, and his half-smile as he commented what a "bonnie bride" she made might have been sarcastic. Still, she thought his dark attractiveness was enough to make some women swoon.

With a wide grin, Rannoch opened his arms and embraced her as he often did with Annie, lifting her onto her toes. "A new sister! This is grand, Lady Kate. Och, but can ye be *both* a Lady and a MacPherson?"

She chuckled. "For you, Rannoch, 'Kate' will do."

"That's a relief, I must tell ye. No more fashin' about which fork to use around ye." He laughed his deep, charming laugh, which made her laugh, in turn. Then, he followed Angus's example and bent to kiss her cheek.

Before his lips made contact, however, Broderick stepped between them, forcing his brother back several steps. "This isnae one of yer lasses, Rannoch. Do ye ken?"

Grin vanishing, Rannoch raised a wary brow. "Aye, brother. She's yer bride. I ken."

"Nah. Not my bride. She'll have my name. But that's all."

Angus came forward to lay his hand on Broderick's shoulder, but it was swiftly shrugged away. "Son—"

Broderick rounded on Kate, leaning in with menacing fire. "Ye'll live at the castle, not with me. There'll be no bairns. No visits. No allowance for yer frocks or demands for favors. In fact, ye'll nae trouble me again. Ever. Do ye hear me?"

Her insides shriveled. A cold wind rippled her silk skirts. She looked at his shirt, snowy white and paired with a fine, dark coat.

With a long finger, he nudged beneath her chin. "Say ye understand, lass."

"Yes," she whispered. "I understand."

He let her go and stalked away, his hitching strides long and swift. The last she saw of her new husband was his MacPherson kilt disappearing through a ruined church entrance.

Behind her, the priest awkwardly cleared his throat. Angus murmured a gruff condolence. John advised they should all return to the castle before the weather turned. Annie slid an arm through Kate's and said, "It will all come right, Katie-lass. Ye'll see."

But Kate didn't think so. She couldn't lift her gaze from her hands, from the ring he'd placed on her finger. The design included a knot much like her brooch, but plainer. Older. The gold was dark and scarred. She wondered where he'd acquired it. Probably from a pawn shop for as little coin as possible.

Chest painfully tight, she managed to survive the rest of her wedding day without incident, chiefly because all the guests departed immediately upon reaching the castle, giving her leave to retreat to her bedchamber. She did not see Broderick again that day or any of the next ten.

She spent her first week as a wife hounding Annie to tell her more about Broderick—his favorite meals (eggs and smoked haddock, venison and onion gravy), his worst habit (working too much), her happiest memory of him (the day he'd presented Annie with a copper tea kettle and made her weep). She'd asked for more details about his ordeal in prison; Annie had struggled through her answers so dreadfully that Kate had swiftly changed the subject to inquire about his history with women.

She'd changed the subject again when Annie's answers made Kate's throat burn.

When her sister-in-law tired of her questions, Kate wrote letters until her hand was sore. To Francis and Clarissa, she poured out all the worry, hope, and self-recrimination that plagued her soul. To her sisters, she begged advice on mending a husband's offended sensibilities. To Mama and Papa, she begged forgiveness for neglecting to inform them sooner.

In the end, she gained no relief. This morning, ten days after promising herself to a man who hated her, she smoothed a hand over her unfinished manuscript as Janet arranged her hair into a coil with four small plaits.

"How go the adventures of Sir Wallace, m'lady? Have ye decided how he'll win the heart of the fair Fiona?"

Kate glanced up and collided with her own reflection in the mirror. Dark smudges beneath her eyes were stark amidst her pallor. She hadn't slept well for a fortnight. First, she'd been plagued by visions of Broderick killing a man, then visions of Broderick being tortured by Sergeant Munro. She'd awakened with her cheeks wet and her chest aching more than once.

Now, she shook her head, unable to muster a smile for her maid. "No, I'm afraid not," she murmured.

"Shall I tell ye how Stuart captured my heart?" Janet's dance lesson with the taciturn footman had gone well, evidently.

"How is that?"

Janet winked and chuckled. "After the *cèilidh*, we went down to see the fires in the village. I got a wee bit blootered, and ... well, Stuart has a braw face, m'lady. Chin is a mite weak, aye, but he grows handsomer the more ye look upon him." She shook her head with a secretive smile then waved the comb in the air. "Anyhow, I made an offer no other lad would decline, I'll tell ye that one for certain. But he did. Purely flattened me." The hand holding the comb settled on her bosom. Janet's ordinarily sharp gaze softened into syrup. "Said he wanted no question of his intentions toward me. Can ye imagine, m'lady? I've had my share of kisses, some better than others. But his refusal told me right then and there he'd be my forever man."

Kate managed a faint smile. The mind infection had struck again. She supposed she was happy for Janet. Except that, from now on, the subject of Stuart MacDonnell would dominate every conversation. In the interest of variety, Kate said, "Let's walk to the village today, hmm? I feel the need for ribbons."

An hour later, as they entered the square, Kate felt a strange prickle along her neck. She frowned, glancing around as Janet prattled on about Stuart's rare talent with the pipes. Her gaze snagged on a dark figure dismounting a horse outside the second most popular tavern in Glenscannadoo. By the time she realized who it was, he'd started toward her.

Pretending she hadn't seen him, she tugged Janet toward the opposite end of the square.

"Lady Katherine," Sergeant Munro called from much too close behind them.

Kate ignored him, dragging Janet, who twisted to see who was following.

"Lady Katherine!" The constable's shadow merged with theirs. He grasped her arm, halting her with a firm grip.

She tried to free herself, but his grip held. Finally, she turned. "Release me," she gritted, her anger at the constable's incessant pursuit wiping away all fear. "You are within a hair's breadth of losing your position, Mr. Munro."

His whiskers twitched. Hard eyes narrowed. "I hear ye're a MacPherson now."

She didn't answer.

"I also hear ye still reside in yer brother's castle," he continued. Somehow, Sergeant Munro made everything sound like an accusation.

Her chin tilted up. She arched a brow. "Broderick MacPherson and I were married ten days past, Mr. Munro."

"Sergeant."

"As his wife, even if I knew whatever it is you think I know, my account cannot be coerced by you or any court in the land." She yanked her arm free with a fierce jerk that made both her and Janet stumble. "Now, I shall bid you good day, *Mr.* Munro. I trust we shan't meet again."

"We will, m'lady. I regret to say I believe yer marriage to be fraudulent."

She froze.

Janet whispered a curse.

A frigid blast of wind rocked them both.

Kate glared up at the man whose relentless hunt had made her life a misery. He was perhaps fifty, barrel-chested, and very certain of his own righteousness. To serve his own ambition, he sought to persecute a man who had already suffered unimaginable torment. She'd never hated anyone as much.

"Why should I care what you think of my marriage? It is none of your concern, nor will it ever be."

Janet tugged insistently. "Let's be off, m'lady."

The whiskers twitched again, this time with a faint smile. "Sham marriages have been challenged routinely in court. Questions of legitimacy are often settled there. A husband and wife livin' separately? That's evidence no judge could deny. If yer marriage is a lie, m'lady, I shall see it set aside. Then, ye'll have no choice but to tell me what ye ken about the night Lockhart went missin'."

Thank goodness for Janet, or Kate might have folded into a heap at Munro's boots. Wobbly knees and little sleep made her head swim. Could he be telling the truth? Would he go to such lengths?

Yes, she decided. Yes, he would.

Janet tugged again. "We must go, m'lady."

This time, she let the maid pull her away. They started for the haberdashery, but her heart pounded a rhythm that sounded very much like, "Not again, not again, not again."

Munro called after her, "I'll be watchin', Lady Katherine. Broderick MacPherson may believe he's free, but he cannae escape justice. Not so long as I breathe."

Kate slipped inside the small shop with a gasp, wadding her reticule and rushing to the darkest corner, near the tartans. Janet followed, attempting to comfort her with small pats on her back. "He means to rattle ye, m'lady. Dinnae let him win."

She swallowed the fear tightening her throat. "He is winning, Janet."

"Dinnae say that." The maid fell quiet for a moment. "A proper marriage cannae be set aside."

Kate frowned. "What are you—"

"Make it proper, m'lady. He'll have no choice but to leave ye be."

"I don't think you understand what you're suggesting," Kate whispered.

"Oh, I ken it well, and it willnae be easy." The maid straightened, her gaze direct and firm. "Ye must go to live with Broderick MacPherson. And ye must convince Sergeant Whiskers the two of ye are *properly* wed, if ye take my meanin'."

Kate's cheeks burned at the mere thought. She nodded.

Janet tidied a curl near Kate's temple and gave her a reassuring smile. "I recommend havin' a dram or two before ye visit Mr. MacPherson, m'lady. Whisky makes the hard tasks a wee bit easier."

"How long has it been, do ye suppose?" Alexander rested his elbow on the side of the wagon and nudged Rannoch.

Rannoch winced and adjusted his hat. "Since he's tupped somethin' other than his own hand? A year. Mayhap longer."

Broderick hefted a cask of cider onto his shoulder and started past the rowans flanking his front door. There was little point in answering. They'd drawn their own conclusions from his short temper.

Carrying the second cask, Campbell weighed in. "Longer, I'd wager."

Broderick shot his oldest brother a glare as they carried the cider through the house into the kitchen. He nodded to his grizzled old naval captain of a cook and the cowering kitchen maid before depositing his load next to the sideboard. The maid squeaked as Broderick straightened, scurrying to the hearth and pretending to stir an empty pot. With a grunt of disgust, he returned outside where his brothers debated which of them would suffer the most damage when Broderick's lack of sufficient tupping caused his temper to explode.

As if he were a bloody uncontrolled wildfire. Ridiculous. He was focused on what mattered—finding Lockhart. For the past week, he'd scoured Inverness-shire. What he'd found were *traces* of Lockhart: bloody linens in the stable at Glenscannadoo Manor, which meant the lord had found shelter with the pompous arse who lived there. The two men had once been friends, and when they'd questioned the arse, he'd admitted to allowing his surgeon to tend Lockhart's injuries but claimed he'd tossed Lockhart out once it became clear the blackguard would live.

Thereafter, Campbell had found a traveling merchant who transported an "auld, ailin' woman" from Laird Glenscannadoo's land to a modest house in Inverness. Alexander had discovered the house had been rented for the past month by none other than Sabella Lockhart—the bastard's sister. Both Campbell and Alexander had accompanied Broderick inside, only to find it empty. From there, the trail went cold. They'd inquired at the port for passenger lists. They'd questioned the owner of the house, a widow, who answered, "Bonnie lass, Miss Lockhart. Paid through the end of this week. No, I didnae inquire as to her destination. She helped me trim my roses, ye ken. The thorns are a wee bit much for these auld fingers. Lovely, kind lady. Fond of silk gowns, as I recall. I dinnae ken how she keeps them so clean in this rain."

In other words, he'd hunted Lockhart for the better part of a month and found only frustration. His brothers thought his ill temper was sexual. That wasn't the cause. True, nightly dreams about a certain brown-eyed lass with a habit of winding her curls around her finger weren't helping. But he had it under control.

"Shall I take a message to yer bride, Broderick?" Rannoch called from the front of the wagon. "I'll be dinin' at the castle this evenin'. 'Twould be nae trouble."

Every muscle tightened against the visceral need to shut his brother's grinning mouth with a fist. Rannoch could be exasperating at times, which usually sparked a bit of brotherly irritation. But lately, it was more. Whenever Rannoch mentioned a visit to the castle or spoke about Broderick's "bride," violent resentment welled, quick and hot. It couldn't be jealousy— Broderick wasn't the jealous sort. If a woman preferred another man over him, she lost her allure as surely as meat gone off. Cecilia had been no exception, in that respect.

Besides, it wasn't as though he'd taken Kate to his bed. Granted, she was a bonnie lass. Large, expressive brown eyes that went tender one moment and lively the next. Ivory skin that flushed berry-bright at the slightest provocation. The first time he'd heard her laugh, he hadn't been able to look away. And when she'd mentioned having his bairns—"one or two," mind— he'd gone hard enough to sharpen his dirk. But that didn't mean he wanted her. He didn't. She'd cost him a precious opportunity with Lockhart. She'd blackmailed him into doing the one thing he'd sworn not to do.

He should hate her. He *did* hate her.

These strange flashes of anger toward Rannoch were likely misdirected vexation toward his wife.

Damn it all, she wasn't his *wife*. Not really.

"Appears yer wife prefers to hear her messages directly," Alexander commented, nodding to the end of the drive that curved through thick woods before angling down the hill.

Broderick frowned, shifting his glare in that direction. His skin heated inside his clothing. Everything hardened. He gritted his teeth, trying to control his breathing. Too fast. Too hard. Hadn't he told her to stay away?

Campbell's hand settled on his shoulder. "Easy, brother."

"Bluidy hell," he bit out.

She wore a blue riding habit beneath a MacPherson plaid. She rode a black horse. Tiny brown curls wisped along her temples and cheeks. But it wasn't her beauty that grabbed hold of his guts and twisted. It was her foolishness.

"She didnae even bother to bring a maid with her."

Campbell gripped him harder. "Aye. Ye can chastise her recklessness. But ye must manage yer temper."

"I'm fine."

"Ye're nae fine."

"Leave us. Take Rannoch with ye."

After a long, considering pause, Campbell grunted, removed his hand, and gestured to Alexander and Rannoch. By the time Kate's horse approached the house, they were tipping their hats in farewell.

The smile she sent Rannoch trembled at the corners, he noticed. She was nervous. She should be.

When she pulled her glossy mount to a halt a few feet away, her breathing quickened. He waited.

She opened her bonnie lips to speak. Closed them. Swallowed. Whispered to herself—likely something about courage and sticking places. Finally came the answer he hadn't asked for: "I've come with news."

"Unless yer news is that ye'd like an annulment, ye've wasted a trip."

Frowning, she glanced down at her mount then at his shoulders. "W-would you mind very much—"

"Aye, I do mind. Very much."

Those rich brown eyes narrowed. A straight, dainty nose flared. Had he pricked her temper? Good. She'd lit his on fire.

With a mutinous glare, she shifted in her sidesaddle before sliding to the ground. Her dismount was awkward, but she managed to land on her feet. "There's no call to be churlish. I know you don't want me here."

"And yet, here ye are."

"Yesterday, I encountered Sergeant Munro in the village square." Her dainty chin rose as she patted her horse's neck with a gloved hand. "He intends to challenge the legitimacy of our marriage. He believes our sacred union to be fraudulent."

Why she kept calling their union "sacred" when it was the opposite, he didn't know. He folded his arms across his chest. "He's right."

"Well, yes. But that is why we must make it proper."

"Proper how?"

She glanced behind him at the house. "How would you feel about my living here?"

"I'd feel the same way I did when I married ye."

She focused on him again. "It's a lovely house, Broderick."

Why the devil did she have to say his name like that, all soft and warm? She was a frivolous young woman caught up in fantasies about muses and penning nonsense plays and quoting Shakespeare with reckless abandon. Kate Huxley belonged in England, married to a London fop who wore lace-trimmed drawers and purchased a box at the theatre to host his wealthy friends. Not here. Not with him.

"Surely there is ample room for me," she continued, attempting a smile. "I shan't require much. A small chamber for writing. A bedchamber with a hearth." Her smile steadied enough to brighten. "You'll scarcely notice I'm here."

"But ye shouldnae be here." He crowded closer, watching her smile fade. "And if ye were going to be so foolish as to ride here, ye should have brought yer brother, or a footman at least."

Blinking rapidly, she thrust her chin forward. "You don't frighten me."

"First of all, that's daft. I'm ten times yer size—"

She snorted. "Three, at most."

"Secondly, I have enemies. Take a good look at my face, lass. The man who paid for this to be done would think nothin' of harmin' ye in unspeakable ways. In fact, he'd revel in it."

Examining his face for long moments, she shocked him when she stepped closer, their bodies almost touching, and reached for his cheek. He jerked away, but she followed, her hand landing upon his chest.

"Broderick, what I did … the way I coaxed you into … I—I'm so very sorry."

His heart kicked in the strangest fashion as if it were being violently squeezed. "Now? *Now* ye're sorry?"

Her eyes pleaded as her hand stroked and petted him in a distracted fashion. "My intentions were … I wished to ensure I could not be used against you. But I should not have forced your hand. I haven't slept soundly in weeks."

Neither had he, though the cause was vastly different. That cause gazed up at him now with a vulnerability that made him want to pick her up and haul her inside. She was so small—slender and shapely and petite. He wanted to build a wall around her that even Lockhart couldn't break.

"Tell me what Munro said," he murmured.

She blinked, her thick lashes fluttering down as she examined the place where her hand lay upon him. "He is relentless," she whispered. "He wants to have our marriage nullified by the court. He came round to the castle this morning and left a note for me."

"And?"

"He's threatening to bring charges against both of us. Fraud. Obstruction." Her lower lip trembled. "I cannot put your family or mine through this, Broderick." Velvety eyes lifted. "Please help me."

Bloody hell. How did she do this? When she'd arrived, he'd felt like a barrel of gunpowder next to a kiln. Now, all he felt was a driving need to put his arms around her. Which was daft. "What would ye have me do, lass?"

"Let me live here with you," she said softly. "Help me persuade Munro our marriage is proper."

He was afraid to ask. "What do ye mean by 'proper'?"

His answer came in another flood of berry-bright color flagging her cheeks and throat. More lash fluttering. Feminine breaths quickening. "He must believe we are … that we are … a love match. Or, at least, that the marriage has been … consummated."

Focused on controlling his body's predictable reaction, he didn't answer straight away.

Which sent her stumbling into further explanations. "That is, I assume you are capable of … You seem quite …" She stroked his chest again. "I cannot think of the best word for it. Vigorous? Robust? *Thoroughly* recovered, that much is certain."

"Kate."

"Hmm?"

"He has no way to ken whether we've consummated anythin'."

She gave a tiny, wide-eyed shake of her head. "He will. You don't know what he's like."

"He's questioned me seven times."

"He has?"

"Aye."

"Well, perhaps I don't have your vast experience with resisting a constable's interrogation, but I assure you, if he approaches me, I cannot—"

"If he approaches ye again, ye'll come to me, and I'll take care of it."

"Oh, no. You mustn't."

He glowered. "Why?"

"Broderick," she whispered, placing a second hand flat over his heart. "How am I to protect you if you won't let me?"

150 ELISA BRADEN

God, she stole his breath from his body. Rain had started. It was pelting him now, but he didn't feel it. All he felt was her hands. All he saw was her eyes.

She meant it. She honestly intended to protect *him*. This woman needed a keeper. He'd sworn he wouldn't put himself in this position again. The risk was too great. But what could he do? Technically, he was her husband. And even if he should, he could not leave his wife to suffer the consequences of her own foolishness.

"When ye return to the castle, pack yer belongings. I'll speak to my brothers. They can help move ye in tomorrow."

"Oh, that won't be necessary." Her smile blinded him. "Dougal and his cousins are right behind me. They'll arrive with everything shortly."

"Bluidy hell."

She patted him with both hands and laughed. God, her laugh. It was a crack at the beginning, a wee hitch in the middle, and a cascade of fluttery giggles at the end. It was as wide, warming, and free as sunlight on water.

He was still staring down at her like a daft sod when she withdrew to take her horse's lead and cast Broderick a teasing glance. "You mustn't be vexed with me, now. Annie assured me you would see sense, so I saved you the bother."

He should be angry, but he was too damned busy being dazzled. "The stable is round back."

She clicked her tongue at her horse, still grinning at Broderick in a way that made all his appendages tingle. "Come, Ophelia. Let's have a look at your new home, shall we?"

CHAPTER EIGHT

After ensuring the young groom in the stable understood Ophelia preferred apples to oats and oats to forage, Kate returned to the drive and found it empty. With no sign of Broderick, she ignored the queer pang in her belly and set out to explore her new home on her own.

She'd imagined so many things—a great stag's head above a massive fireplace, an ancient tapestry depicting Robert the Bruce's mighty battles, a settee upholstered in tartan.

What she found instead was a home newly built and mostly empty. The house itself was a stout stone rectangle, two stories stacked beneath a gabled third. An attic, perhaps? As she climbed the few steps into the entrance hall, she could scarcely credit the familiarity. The place smelled of beeswax, new wood, and warm bread. Wood paneling stained nearly black skirted white plaster walls and matched beamed ceilings. High, square archways led into the drawing room, library, and a stair hall.

The drawing room had only two chairs and a carved table. The library had beautiful shelves with the same dark stain of the paneling but held fewer than twenty books. She wandered deeper, admiring polished plank floors and a sturdy staircase rising in a square alcove to her right. A small parlor at the rear of the house promised to be her favorite spot, with its tartan-upholstered sofa and cozy hearth. Further on, she explored the dining room, which had a table long enough for twelve chairs but no carpet or draperies.

Next, she found the kitchen, where she met the cook, Mr. McInnes, who must be nearing eighty. "Nae Ginnis, lass," the short, salty man grumbled. "Mack-Innes, ye ken?"

"Ah, yes. My sincere apologies, Mr. McInnes."

"*Hmmph.* Better." He slit the belly of a plump trout and began removing the insides with a quick sweep of his fingers. "Now, what sorts of meals take yer fancy, eh?"

"Oh, anything, really. I've loved everything I've eaten here in the Highlands with the possible exception of—"

"We dinnae make fine food." He chopped the fish's head off with a whack of his enormous knife. "Here in my kitchen, we make *proper* Scottish fare."

"Yes, I—"

"'Tis what keeps ye warm in the long bluidy winters." He slapped a second trout onto the worktable. "The long nights turn a man's ballocks into frozen baubles fit for naught but clangin' together like two wee pebbles in a saggin' sporran."

She firmed her lips against a smile. "So, it gets cold here, you say?"

He snorted. "Ye'll see." A third fish landed. *Splat, slice, sweep, chop.* "Ye'll be thankin' me." He waved his knife in the direction of her waist. "Add a wee bit there. Aye, ye'll be grateful."

Next, she met the housekeeper, a charming orange-haired Scotswoman with four daughters, two sons, and eighteen grandchildren. Mrs. Grant's bulky height and broad shoulders might be intimidating if not for her kindly smile. As she led Kate upstairs, she explained, "The MacPhersons started buildin' this house several years past when the distillery became the largest in the county. They employ most of the lads here in the glen. Angus and his sons finished the top floor whilst Broderick was … away last winter."

"Oh, are there more bedchambers upstairs?"

"Aye, a few, along with sleepin' quarters for the staff. And a nursery." The housekeeper's tone quieted. "I think 'twas Angus's idea."

As she opened the door into a large chamber at the rear of the house, Kate wandered in, distracted by Mrs. Grant's trove of information about the MacPherson men—one in particular. "So, Mr. MacPherson—Broderick, I mean—didn't intend to have a large family?"

"Och, no. When he hired me last year, he said his house must be fit for entertainin' government men with hunts and such. His aim was to secure a distillery license, nae a wife." Mrs. Grant folded her hands at her waist. Her smile softened into fondness. "Never kenned a lad so single-minded."

"Yes, I noticed a similar …" Just then, Kate caught a glimpse of the view from two large windows on the back wall. She drifted toward them, blinking. "Is that

another loch?" Water glimmered silvery gray beyond
the thick canopy of pine and birch.

"More a wee tarn, but aye. 'Tis where McInnes finds
his trout, most days."

It was splendid—a hidden gem nestled in a cradle of
wooded hills. When she'd ridden up the long, winding
lane earlier, she'd imagined her new home would be a
small hunting lodge, rustic and rough. Not this magical
place.

She turned to ask Mrs. Grant another question but
lost her breath when she spied the bed. Oh, dear. It must
be eight feet square with a deep mattress as high as her
waist. The smooth posts were pinewood, whorled and
stained golden. The blankets were coppery MacPherson
wool. Quickly, she scanned the rest of the room. A chest
of drawers in the same pinewood. A washstand with a
yellow glazed pitcher and basin. A fireplace of the same
stone she'd seen inside the castle.

This was not just any bedchamber. This was *his*. She
imagined lying beside him in that enormous bed. When
she'd stood outside with her hands upon his chest
earlier, the thought hadn't seemed quite so intimidating.
Something about his warmth or scent, perhaps. He'd
smelled heavenly.

Mrs. Grant cleared her throat. "Shall I ask the lads to
move yer trunks in here, m'lady?"

Kate's stomach swooped. Her skin flashed hot. "N-
no, I think another chamber would be best."

"Very well." Had the housekeeper's tone gone
colder? "There are two more on this floor. Four
upstairs."

Gaze still riveted to the bed, Kate nodded. The scent
in here was wonderful: wool and woodfire and hints of

the cool, herbaceous aroma she now recognized as his. She spied one of his coats draped over the back of a large chair near the fireplace. Suddenly, it felt too intimate. Would he want her in here? Of course not. He didn't want her in his life, let alone in his bedchamber. She sighed. How did she entangle herself in such messes?

Mrs. Grant sniffed and gestured to the corridor. "This way, m'lady."

Kate followed, but something made her turn back, a squeeze of longing she couldn't explain. With a last peek at the beauty beyond the windows, she reluctantly trailed after the housekeeper, who was already opening a door at the opposite end of the long corridor. Kate's chest went tight.

No. Too far away.

Where had that thought come from? She didn't know, but it was strong. Insistent. She should sleep *here*, the impulse demanded. Her skirts brushed the door of the chamber next to his. Her hand settled on the latch. She opened it, uncaring of what she'd find. It was smaller than the master bedchamber, of course, and less furnished. The bed was plainer and sized for a human rather than a giant. A writing desk sat beneath the long window. "Mrs. Grant!" she called.

A moment later, the housekeeper hovered in the doorway.

"This one, I think."

White-laced red brows arched. "As ye wish, m'lady."

"And I should prefer to be called Mrs. MacPherson."

The frost in Mrs. Grant's expression eased. She nodded. "I'll inform the household."

After exploring the third story, which remained empty but had the loveliest view of the small lake

behind the house, Kate wandered back outside to see if
Dougal had arrived yet. Instead, she found an old
woman with wiry gray hair and one milky eye
muttering to the row of saplings someone had planted
in front of the house.

Wondering if the woman was a MacPherson relation
or perhaps part of the household staff, she approached
with a cautious, "Good morning."

The old woman turned. "Och, lass. I've seen snails
cross a pasture faster than ye arrive after ye've been
summoned."

"I beg your pardon?"

"Aye, well ye should."

Kate glanced behind her. "Have we met?"

"Nae time for that rubbish." The old woman dug into
a pouch fastened around her waist. She tossed a dried
weed and a strip of leather on the ground. "Where did I
put it?"

"Er, have you seen Mr. MacPherson about, by
chance? Broderick, I mean." Kate debated whether
retrieving Mrs. Grant was in order. This woman
appeared a bit senile. "I seem to have lost him."

"Not yet, lass. And if I have aught to say about it, ye
willnae. Now, where the devil did I—ah!" A gnarled
hand held out a corked brown vial triumphantly.
"Here."

Kate examined the vial. It had a small label marked
with an M. The other letters were too smeared to read.
"What is this?"

"A tonic for the laddie's stoat."

"I'm afraid I don't understand."

The woman clicked her tongue and waggled the vial.
"Put it in his tea. Then brace yerself, lass. That beastie

willnae remain shy for long. I recommend a wee bit of salve. For the chafin', ye ken." She dug inside her pouch again and offered a small tin.

Kate's dear friend Francis was fond of elaborate jests, and if Francis were here, she'd suspect this was meant to make her laugh. But nobody was here, apart from this peculiar woman and her peculiar talk about weasels and chafing. Perhaps if they started again, the woman would realize she was speaking to a perfect stranger.

"I think there's been a small misunderstanding. I am Katherine MacPherson, Broderick MacPherson's wife. And you are?"

"Mary MacBean, maker of potions and cures for ailments of every sort. I ken who ye are, lass. 'Tis *you* that needs the introduction. What took ye so long?"

"Long?"

"Two years, I've been callin' ye."

"Calling?"

She grasped Kate's hand and slapped the vial and tin into her palm. "Think ye every English lass has a yearnin' for tartan and bagpipes?" She snorted. "Aye, who *doesnae* love music that sounds like two cats tuppin' inside a rain barrel?"

Kate blinked. She didn't know what to say, so she pocketed the items the old woman had given her and said the first thing that came to mind. "Sarcasm is the lowest form of humor."

"*Hmmph.* Ye havenae heard McInnes's joke about the Irish priest, then."

Kate started to ask what the devil was going on when a cart driven by Dougal and his two cousins turned out of the woods and rounded toward the house. A curricle carrying Annie and Janet appeared behind them, followed by John on horseback.

"Thank heaven," Kate breathed. Sanity, at last.

A few minutes later, as Kate greeted everyone, Broderick emerged onto the drive from the western wood with two young men. Immediately, they set to work helping Dougal unload the cart.

All the men demonstrated impressive strength, but Kate's attention focused upon Broderick. Heavens, for a man so badly injured, he was … she hadn't the words. Astounding? No, *breathtaking*. Yes, that was it. Light rain had dampened his hair, turning it even darker. Beneath his breeches, muscles swelled and rippled as he heaved her heaviest trunk onto his shoulder and carried it by himself into the house.

He didn't glance at her as he passed, but she inhaled deeply, hoping for more of that faint, cooling scent.

"… think Janet should remain here."

Perhaps it was his soap or something he ate. Perhaps the scent was simply part of his skin.

"She doesnae mind, and I suspect Broderick will give ye nae trouble over the expense."

Kate wondered if she should follow him inside to ensure all the trunks were placed properly. Yes, she probably should. Then, she could ask him if he thought their marriage would be more believable if they shared a bedchamber. What if he said yes? Or, rather, "aye" in that deep, graveled brogue that made her nape tingle.

"… best solution, in the end. Dinnae ye agree, English?"

"No," said John. "But, then, my opinion hasn't mattered very much thus far, has it?"

"Dinnae be cross. She's his wife. She belongs here."

"Right. I'll let you explain that to Mama. I'm certain she'll be mollified by assurances that her youngest daughter, who wed an oversized Scot with a potential murder charge hanging over his head, will now be living as far from her maternal embrace as it is possible to go whilst remaining in Britain."

"Nah, she could go farther. Orkney. Now, there's a place ye dinnae visit intentionally. Ye're either born there, searchin' for herring, or ye're lost. Mayhap all three."

Kate wrapped a curl around her finger and considered the question of how much wifeliness Broderick might tolerate. Would he be willing to let her manage the household? Should she want to? She did have a few ideas about draperies and a carpet for the dining room. Would he like that? Or would he resent her even more?

"Katie-lass, I thought I saw Mrs. MacBean when we arrived. She's been away this past month visitin' her sister in Nairn, and Angus is out of liniment. I cannae bear his crabbit complaints any longer. Do ye ken where she's gone?"

Broderick emerged through the door, instructing one of his men and pointing to the cart. His gaze flickered to Kate briefly before he continued past her.

Would Munro believe Kate had lain with a man like Broderick if she hadn't? She considered the question while taking the full measure of his shoulders, tapered hips, and thick arms. Extremely doubtful, she concluded. A woman could not lie with a man like Broderick MacPherson and remain unchanged.

"Kate!"

Her head snapped up at John's glowering snap. "Yes?"

"What is wrong with you?"

Her cheeks tingled. "Nothing whatever."

He glared between her and Broderick. Without a word, he started toward Broderick with purposeful strides.

"Oh, no. John—"

Annie looped her arm through Kate's and nudged her toward the house. "Let's see about settlin' ye into yer new home."

Kate twisted to watch as her brother entered a tense conversation with Kate's somewhat-husband. "I should really—"

"Nah, ye should come inside and let yer brother have his say." Annie gave her another tug. "'Tis a miracle he's restrained himself this long."

Frowning at her sister-in-law, Kate released an irritated breath. "None of this has anything to do with John."

Annie raised a brow. "No? He's responsible for ye, lass. Yer parents entrusted ye to his care. Now, look what's happened."

"I'm fine." She pulled away, her temper flashing.

"Are ye?"

"Yes." Before she could think better of it, she spoke the truth she hadn't told anyone: "I am *glad* for what happened."

Annie glanced over her shoulder toward the cart then back to Kate. Her brow crinkled. Slowly, her eyes took on a hint of pity. "Ah, lass. Dinnae say it. Already?"

"I don't know what you mean."

"Hmm."

"Stop looking at me like that."

"Ye're not the first, ye ken. He's had to discourage so many, I'm surprised he doesnae have a herd of heartsick lasses trailin' him about the countryside with buckets of rose petals."

"If you're implying I'm in love with him, you could not be more wrong." Kate lowered her head to confess, "That is why he suits me so well."

"Hmm."

That skeptical frown called for Shakespeare. "'*Love goes by haps. Some Cupid kills with arrows, some with traps.*' But I choose neither. Cupid must find his target elsewhere."

Silence and an arched brow.

"Stop saying that."

"I didnae say anythin'."

Kate blew out a breath. "Let's go inside."

"Aye. Mayhap we'll find Mrs. MacBean. And mayhap she'll make a wee bit more sense than you do at the moment."

As a general rule, Broderick liked John Huxley. The Englishman's nature was good-humored, steady, and honorable. He'd made Annie happier than she'd ever been. He'd saved Broderick's life and aided the MacPhersons in numerous ways.

Presently, however, Broderick fought the urge to shove his brother-in-law hard enough to put his arse in the mud.

"If she hadnae blackmailed me, she'd be back in England where she belongs." He stacked two small trunks together and handed them to one of his men, who grunted at the weight. "Mayhap ye should be havin' this discussion with her instead."

"Kate's led a sheltered life. Her innocence is part of her charm, but it makes her vulnerable." Huxley propped his elbows on the side of the cart and gave Broderick a hard stare. "You must protect her, not least from herself."

Exasperated, Broderick scoffed. "What would ye have me do? Lock her in her bedchamber?"

"Don't bother. Before you've pocketed the key, she'll have convinced you to give it to her for safekeeping."

Broderick almost laughed. An accurate assessment. And wasn't that the problem?

Huxley's eyes turned thoughtful. Concerned. "I don't know where this infernal determination to remain in Scotland is coming from." He seemed to struggle for words before continuing, "You must understand, Kate is … a pure delight. Fanciful, yes. A bit obsessive. She overestimates her talents, particularly singing. But she's clever and loyal and, above all, kind. Blackmailing you? Refusing to listen to reason? Marrying without so much as a word to our parents? No. This is quite unlike her."

Broderick frowned. He'd assumed she was a bored, frivolous young woman with poor impulse control. He hadn't considered that she was acting out of character. "Is there somethin' she's avoiding in England? Somethin' she doesnae wish to return to?"

"Not that I'm aware of." Huxley sighed. "Her letters over the past year have been a bit desperate, but my mother said her most recent season was a great success.

Numerous suitors. She could have married ten different times, by all accounts. Kate wraps men round her finger as easily as a lock of her hair. Remarkable, given that it's unintentional."

Gut burning, Broderick shoved away from the cart. "That's the last of it," he barked at his men, who were chatting nearby. "Back to the fences."

Huxley followed him as he started toward the house. God, he wished John would stop blethering about Kate and how many damned suitors she'd wrapped around her finger. For some reason, it raked his temper over hot coals. "What do ye want from me, Huxley?"

"Your word," he said quietly. "That you will protect her."

"I've other priorities. Ye ken that very well."

"She must take precedence."

"I cannae promise such a thing." Lockhart came first. Finding Lockhart. Killing Lockhart. "She'll nae be safe until he's dead. None of us will."

"I do understand. And I will help in whatever way you require." Huxley stopped him with a hand on his shoulder. "But she belongs to you now."

The statement hit him like a boot to the belly. "Nah," he breathed.

"Yes." Huxley's eyes were hard. Direct. "It's not fair. You deserved to choose your own wife. Bloody hell, that's the least of what you deserved. But that is not what's happened." His hand tightened over Broderick's shoulder blade until the force was bruising. "My baby sister might be vexing. She might make your head spin with her nonsense. But she is *yours*, and you will take care of her. Do we understand one another?"

Broderick's jaw hardened, along with his gut. He grasped Huxley's wrist and forced it away. "Fine," he growled. "Ye want me to say it? She's mine." An odd sensation rippled over his skin. Hot. Pleasurable. He ignored it. "Now, kindly take yer men and yer wife and leave me alone with my bride."

CHAPTER NINE

Kate dusted her nine-volume collection of Shakespeare's dramatic works and listened to Janet's soliloquy about Stuart's fine head of hair. Annie and John had departed hours ago, and Kate had spent the afternoon unpacking with Janet and Mrs. Grant. Presently, they were in the library adding her books to the bare shelves.

Outside, drizzle had turned into pounding rain. Fighting the chill, she'd changed from her damp riding habit into a long-sleeved gown of leaf-green wool. She gathered her tartan wrap tighter around her shoulders, listening to Mrs. Grant's amusing anecdote about her grandson's first taste of whisky.

She couldn't decide which room was her favorite— the hushed library with its dark shelves, the little parlor with the view of the wood, or her cozy bedchamber with its cheery yellow coverlet and elegant desk.

"Mr. MacPherson doesnae care for idleness," the housekeeper advised Janet. "Ye'll be expected to keep busy when ye're nae attendin' yer lady's maid duties. He favors a clean house. More so than before he ..."

Janet turned solemn. "Ere the Bridewell."

"Aye."

Kate sometimes forgot that everyone had known Broderick before he'd been imprisoned—everyone but her.

"Do ye remember summer before last?" Janet asked, digging into another trunk full of Walter Scott novels. "The Highland Games."

Mrs. Grant hummed low. "The hammer throw. Aye. Who could forget? I may be a grandmother, but I'm nae dead."

Janet groaned. "And the loch swim. I needed a wee dip, myself, after that." Their laughter was rich and appreciative.

Apparently, they'd forgotten Kate was in the room. She delicately cleared her throat, but they were too busy debating whether a man's forearms looked better with rolled-up sleeves or completely bare to pay her any mind.

She slid her three-volume collection of Shakespeare's poetry onto the shelf and settled the argument. "If it is forearms only, they benefit from sleeves. The mystery is *why* this is so when a fit man's torso is best viewed naked." At their twin shocked expressions, she smiled calmly. "Formal clothing is also quite beneficial. It's the anticipation of imminent removal, I suspect."

The two women's mouths fell agape, their eyes rounding. Kate's smile widened. Her sisters would be proud—especially Eugenia.

"Mrs. Grant, I should like to be alone with my wife."

Kate's heart seized at the deep, rough brogue behind her. Her stomach dropped into her feet. He'd been away from the house since John and Annie's departure, repairing fences and moving cattle, reportedly. Why must he return now, here, to witness her rehearsing brazenness? She must be cursed.

The housekeeper and maid scurried from the room with apologetic glances before she managed to take a full breath. Finally, she gathered her courage and turned to face him.

Oh, God. He'd rolled up his sleeves.

"We need to talk," he said, closing the library door.

She raised her chin and brazened it out. "About?"

He glanced around the room then slowly came toward her. He was damp from the rain. "Our marriage, lass."

Another flitter seized her heart. "Yes, I ... did wonder."

"Wonder?"

Heavens, he made her nervous. Couldn't he look somewhere other than directly at her? She distracted herself by dusting her hands and then her skirts. "How much wifeliness you would prefer."

Frowning, he braced his hands on his hips. Dressed as he was in a plain shirt and woolen waistcoat, buckskin breeches and muddy boots, he should not appear quite so attractive. But there was the small matter of his forearms, dusted with black hair, heavily veined and thick with muscle.

She swallowed and considered how hard it must have been for him to rebuild his strength, how much work it must have required to regain those muscles in half a year.

"I should be gainin' somethin' from this arrangement, wouldnae ye say?"

She blinked. "Your freedom isn't sufficient?"

"Some men dinnae consider leg shackles freedom."

"Hmm. *'Men are April when they woo, December when they wed.'*" She quirked a smile. "It seems my winter will be as cold as Mr. McInnes warned."

"I havenae wooed ye, Kate. Else, ye wouldnae be speakin' of winter."

For a moment, both of them fell silent. Kate was busy battling a heated flush in her lower half. Was her blushing now afflicting her *everywhere?* This was bad. Further, she suspected wifeliness meant something different to him than to her. Heavens. Had she unwittingly offered more than carpets and draperies?

"Regardless of how it came to be, ye are my wife," he said gruffly. "I see no reason ye shouldnae behave as such."

Oh. Oh, dear. She *had* offered … And he *did* expect … that. Could she? Her eyes tumbled down the length of him. The great, towering length.

"I've matters to tend that will take me away from home most days," he continued in measured, businesslike tones.

"Lockhart," she whispered, eyeing his scars.

The one near his mouth pulled tight. "Aye. He must be brought down, lass."

She nodded. "How?"

"That's nae for ye to fash about."

"You have to find him, yes? Perhaps I could help."

The scar scowl deepened. "As my wife, ye'll stay where I put ye. Which is here. Content yerself with fillin' bookcases and plannin' supper."

"This is a lovely house, Broderick, but I shouldn't care to remain imprisoned here whilst you go traipsing about hither and yon—"

"I've work to do," he snapped. "The distillery. Dealin' with crofters. Findin' bluidy wanderin' coos." He stretched an enormous arm above her shoulder to pat the empty bookshelf behind her with a solid thump. "Why do ye think this place hasnae been properly furnished, eh?"

She struggled for breath, overwhelmed by his cooling scent and heated nearness. He was gripping the shelf, now, staring down at her with a glittering eye.

"Nah," he rumbled, his gaze falling to her mouth. "Stay here. Be my wife. Perhaps I'm owed a bit of comfort, hmm?"

She swallowed against a dry throat. Examined the slashes through his brows and strong, square jaw. He still shaved his whiskers, she noted. Even with the ridges and valleys carved by evil men, he kept up with that one, simple daily task. "C-comfort. Yes. Perhaps you are."

"Aye, then. Ye'll follow my instructions."

She would? There were *instructions?* She'd always imagined it would simply begin with kissing and end with … well, more than kissing. "Are you saying there is a specific procedure you'd like me to follow?"

An impatient sigh. "Just do as I ask, and all will be fine."

"I've only just unpacked everything."

He frowned. "Aye."

"Are you … content to have me remain in the bedchamber I selected?"

He raked a hand through his hair, causing a lock to fall across his patch. "Take whichever room pleases ye, lass. 'Tis nae matter to me."

Ah, so he wished to conduct their marriage as many in the ton did—with separate chambers and, ultimately, separate lives.

"I see." She folded her hands at her waist, swallowing a lump of … joy. Yes, it must be joy choking her and not disappointment at all. This was what she'd wanted. She'd be free to pursue her writing, and he'd be free to pursue his revenge, and she'd simply follow his instructions when he needed wifely comfort. Very sensible. They were hardly a love match, after all.

"I want ye safe." His low, quiet rumble jerked her head up. "Mayhap we didnae have the best beginnin', lass. And I cannae promise ye easy because that's as daft as promisin' the moon. But I will stand betwixt ye and all others. Munro. Lockhart. So long as I'm alive, any man who seeks to harm ye will deal with me first. Ye ken?"

Yes. She understood. She couldn't breathe, really, because he'd stolen all her air. But she understood the promise he'd just made to her. Better than anyone, she knew the punishment he could deliver to his enemies.

"I do," she whispered. "And I—I will bring you comfort, Broderick. Perhaps we may comfort … each other."

His nostrils flared. He nodded, his eye burning as it traveled her throat and flickered briefly to her bosom. It didn't linger, however. "We'll discuss this more at dinner." His arm retreated. He rubbed his nape and backed up with a grimace. "I smell like the coos."

She couldn't help it. She laughed.

He didn't. Rather, he stared down at her with dark intensity.

"Apologies." She covered her mouth with her fingertips and peeked up at him. "I wasn't laughing at you. I just adore the way you say cow."

"Coo?"

She giggled. Nodded.

The slightest quirk of his mouth lifted the scar. "Highland coos shouldnae be mocked, m'lady."

"I wouldn't dare. And you don't smell like them," she insisted. "You smell … splendid."

He raised a brow.

"I don't know what it is. Something cooling like mint or pine or snow. I find it soothing." She leaned closer and breathed deep. "Your soap, perhaps?"

"Liniment." Was his voice thicker than before? Raspier, certainly.

She hoped he wasn't falling ill. "Well, you should have a hot bath and more liniment at once. Is it really necessary to work in this weather?"

"If I dinnae wish to lose my cattle, aye. A broken fence is a useless fence."

"Couldn't your men handle the repairs? They appeared capable."

His brows crashed into a glower. "I prefer to do it myself."

"Why?"

"Keeps my hands busy. My mind from strayin'."

"Straying to what?"

A muscle in his jaw flickered. He looked at her mouth, her bodice, her skirts. Then, he backed up a step. Another. And another. "Things I shouldnae be thinkin' about, lass." When he finally pivoted and strode to the door, it almost seemed he had to force himself to open it.

"We'll speak at dinner, yes?" She didn't know why she asked, only that she wished he would stay longer. Wished they didn't have to wait to continue their conversation.

He didn't reply. Just halted. His hand squeezed the doorframe until his knuckles whitened. Then, he gave a single nod and left her alone with only the hush of rainfall for company.

If Broderick hadn't thought it would shock Kate's sensibilities, he'd have washed in the wee loch beyond the garden. But then, if it weren't for Kate, submerging his body in frigid water wouldn't have been necessary.

Bloody hell, he hated when his brothers were right.

Even now, after a hot bath and a round of self-delivered relief, he had trouble tucking his cock into his trews. It wanted … her. The thing was hard as a hammer. Throbbing. Maddening.

She was maddening. Gazing up at him with those rich, dancing brown eyes. Laughing with that crack-hitch-and-tumble rhythm. When she'd gone breathless at his mention of wooing her, he'd nearly forgotten how hideous he was. The way she looked at him, she didn't seem to see the scars at all.

Disgusted, he shrugged on a waistcoat and then his brown wool coat. They'd be dining together this evening. He'd explain more clearly that she had leave to manage the household as she pleased, so long as certain instructions were followed. In the library earlier, he'd conveyed that she could rely upon his protection, but before he could elaborate on the specifics of how the household should be run to ensure her security, she'd distracted him with her laugh. Witchcraft, it was. Brilliant. Glowing. Unrestrained.

Coo. She loved the way he said coo. She'd laughed—twice—and his body had lit on fire. Everything inside him had wanted to take. Take and take and take. Her mouth, her breasts, her tongue. He'd wanted to fill her and drive gasps from those lips. He'd wanted to watch her come.

He sat on his bed and ran a hand through his hair. God Almighty, he needed a woman.

But what he had was a wife. A beautiful, virginal wife who should not be offering to make their marriage "proper." She deserved better than a broken, vengeful man.

His body didn't care what she deserved. His body wanted to flood hers with seed. Feel her rippling around him. It wanted to steal pleasure for itself and damn the bloody consequences. But he couldn't do that to her. After all this was over, after Lockhart was dead and the danger to his kin had passed, she mustn't suffer for having married him.

He shoved up, ignoring the pain in his knee and shoulders. Pain was nothing. The goal was everything.

He found her in the dining room, smiling and chatting with Mrs. Grant. She now wore blue silk rather than green wool.

"My niece, Merry, insists on being carried everywhere. She is three. So, you see, your granddaughter is not so unusual."

"Are ye sayin' I should indulge the wee bairn?"

"Well, if she turns eighteen and continues her eccentricity, some intervention might be in order."

Mrs. Grant chuckled, placing a platter of trout on the table and casting Kate a considering glance. "Ye ken a fair bit about bairns for a lady who has none, Mrs. MacPherson."

Broderick's chest tightened when Kate's smile softened. She leaned forward to light the tapers at the center of the table. From his vantage in the shadows of the doorway, he could see the swells of her bosom and the dark, tempting cleft between.

"We Huxleys are rather … prolific. Legendarily so, I'm afraid."

"How many nieces and nephews have ye?"

Gracefully, Kate pivoted to move a pitcher of cider from the sideboard to the table. "Fifteen? No. Seventeen. Drat, I've lost count. I did, however, devise a solution. It's a small trick I employed when I was a girl to help me remember my sums."

"What is the trick?"

A faint blush touched her cheeks. "I sing their names. Would you care to hear?"

"Oh, aye. I do enjoy music."

Kate folded her hands at her waist and cleared her throat. *"The first to arrive was sweet Beatrice, who was a blessing despite being toothless. Next came a boy named Gabriel, whose pointed head made his mother squeal. Followed by an angel named Emma, whose father had quite the dilemma, because twins were quite unexpected, and that would make any man apoplectic."*

Mrs. Grant's polite smile gradually gave way to a grimace. "Er, I seem to have forgotten the neeps. I do beg yer pardon." She fled to the kitchen, leaving Kate alone.

Broderick watched Kate's lower lip tremble then firm. After a moment in which she appeared to gather her pride, she resumed lighting tapers while humming her previous tune, wavering between a warbling falsetto and a threadbare alto.

By God, his wife was a dreadful singer. He winced as her voice skated past the proper key and cracked. She paused to clear her throat.

"Ye changed yer gown."

She jolted and spun. "Broderick. Good heavens, you startled me."

He strode the length of the room, halting across the table from her. Best to have a piece of furniture between them, else he might do something rash. Kissing her, for example. "I didnae wish to interrupt yer performance."

Her blush deepened, washing the swells of her bosom. "Hardly that." Her gaze roved across his shoulders and down to his waist. "You appear refreshed." She gestured to the platters. "Mr. McInnes has prepared a veritable feast. I do hope you've brought your appetite."

His greatest appetite wasn't for food. "Aye."

Her fingers fluttered nervously before rising to spiral a curl along her cheek. "My mother often says there is nothing that cannot be improved by a good meal."

Mrs. Grant returned with two more platters, followed by the kitchen maid with a basket of bread. The fearful maid shot him nervous glances then fled as though her drawers were on fire.

Kate, he noticed, glared in the maid's direction. She didn't explain her irritation, merely gesturing to the two place settings at the head of the table. "Shall we?"

Minutes later, Broderick wondered if dining with his wife had been a mistake. Partly, the problem lay in watching her lips close around dainty bites. The other trial came while listening to her amusing stories about Annie's battle to keep Marjorie MacDonnell out of her kitchen. Kate would pause occasionally to laugh.

Every time she laughed, Broderick grew harder.

"The rub of the matter is that Mrs. MacDonnell makes very fine shortbread—even better than Annie's." Kate grinned and giggled. "So, it is not a simple matter of banishing her entirely. John has suggested they hire a cook, but Annie won't hear of it." She slid a forkful of roasted turnips between her lips and chewed thoughtfully.

Broderick drained his cup of cider and poured himself another.

"I suspect she'll reconsider after the babe is born," Kate continued, her fingertips strumming the rim of her plate as though she were playing the pianoforte. "That is what always happens." A sigh. "And thus, the process is complete."

He frowned, scarcely able to focus on what she was saying. Those fingers. Those lips. The heady scent of her hair and skin. "What process?"

"The mind infection."

He waited for her to elaborate, but she simply took another bite and released another sigh.

"What is the mind infection?" he asked.

Her color deepened, and she gave a small shrug. "A small theory of mine. I've watched it happen to my sisters. First, they fall in love. Then they marry. Then they produce children. Then they transform."

"Into?"

"I don't know. Something other than what they were, that much is certain."

He frowned. She seemed content with her conclusion, though it made no sense.

Rather than explain, she patted his wrist. "Not to worry. I won't suffer such a change. That is why our sacred union suits me so well."

"Ah. Is that why?"

"Oh, yes." She shot him a brilliant smile and took a drink of her cider. "You and I will never fall in love with one another." She fluttered her fingers in a graceful, dismissive wave. "The very idea is absurd. We suit precisely *because* there is so little chance for attachment."

The food in his stomach started to churn. He took another swig of cider and wished it was whisky.

"We'll be free, you see. Even though we're married, you and I may go about our lives, pursuing our pursuits and enjoying our interests separately."

Her blithe, ridiculous assertions grated his temper raw. They shouldn't. He'd never wanted to marry her in the first place. "And what are yer *interests*, lass?"

Rich brown eyes glowed and sparkled in the firelight. "So many things. Theatre. Music. All manner of artistic performance, really. At the moment, I'm writing a play. Or a novel. It might be both." She leaned closer, clutching his wrist as if to hold his attention.

She needn't have bothered. He couldn't look away.

"Perhaps you could advise me, Broderick. There is a pivotal scene with Highland cattle, and I'm certain you—"

His temper snapped. "I havenae time for nonsense. Or have ye forgotten the wee matter of Lockhart?"

Her sparkle dimmed. Her hand withdrew. "Of course, I ... I wouldn't wish to distract you."

"Focus on yer wifely duties."

"Yes. About that. You mentioned instructions."

"Aye." Damn it, he wanted her smile again. He wanted it lighting up her eyes and warming his insides. The need clawed at him. He hated his craving. Hated it. "Ye must do as I tell ye. So ye'll be safe."

Her eyes flared wide, darting frantically along his shoulders and to his hands. Berry-bright color swept from her forehead to her throat and pinkened the swells of her bosoms. "D-do you anticipate I shall be ... damaged?"

What an odd way to phrase it. "If we dinnae take precautions, aye."

Her throat rippled. Her breathing quickened. She kept staring at his hands.

He set his fork beside his plate, losing his patience. "If ye'd prefer to return to yer brother's care, lass, we can move ye back—"

"No!" Her shoulders straightened. "I must remain here. With you."

"Because of Munro."

"M-Munro? Yes! Yes, entirely because of Munro."

"Ye shouldnae fear him." He noticed her cup was empty and filled it. Reaching for the pitcher put him closer to her scent. What was it? Sweet, floral, luscious. It made him think all sorts of thoughts he shouldn't. "If he so much as looks in yer direction again, he'll regret it."

She blew out a sigh. "Have you made any progress in your search for Lockhart?"

"Not enough," he murmured. Then, he grew distracted by her skin, which was smooth and lightly blushing, warmed by candlelight. For some reason, the glow of her loosened his tongue. He shared what he and his brothers had discovered about Lockhart's presence in Inverness, how they'd lost track of him and his sister.

"I'm sorry he's proven so elusive." Her fingers played with the curls at her temple. "When I saw you that night … with Lockhart … it frightened me rather badly."

His breath froze. His ribs tightened. She meant to discuss this *now?*

"I'd never seen anything so …" Her eyes lifted to meet his. They were not frightened. They were remorseful. "I didn't know, Broderick. No one told me. All I knew was that I'd lost my way and stumbled upon you in the dark, k-killing another man."

He'd reassure her if he could speak. But he couldn't.

"What he did—I cannot … Heavens, how you must hate him." Her hand reached for his, and he didn't have the strength to pull away. "I will not be the weapon wielded against you. I refuse to add a single drop of suffering to what you've already endured." Her smile trembled at the corners. "I know I sometimes seem a fribble. Perhaps I am. But I shall protect you, as well. With all my strength."

His heart felt as though it had been kicked with a hard boot. Lust warred with something deeper, painfully sharp. He forced himself to remain still. Mustn't take hold of her. Mustn't lay her upon the table and raise her skirts. Mustn't kiss her until his hunger was satisfied.

Mrs. Grant entered and began tidying the table. Kate's hand squeezed his then withdrew into her lap.

For the remainder of the meal, Broderick couldn't take another bite. But his ears drank the sound of her voice describing her favorite scenes from her fanciful story about a Scot named Sir Wallace. His lungs breathed the aroma of sweet, rich skin. His gaze devoured every flicker of her lashes, every dash of her tongue across her lips.

By meal's end, he wondered if she'd been sent by the devil as punishment for his sins. Because even Skene's men could not devise a greater torment than craving the wife he couldn't have with a fire he hadn't known was possible.

CHAPTER TEN

Kate had assumed he'd want to bed her straight away, but before Mrs. Grant served the dessert course, Broderick muttered something about reviewing the distillery's accounts and fled the dining room as though his trousers were ablaze.

She hadn't known what to think. He'd specified he wanted her to fulfill her wifely duty, hadn't he? He'd even specified why she must follow his instructions—a warning that produced a flare of panic low in her belly.

Well, perhaps it wasn't panic. She'd begun to wonder.

Throughout dinner, he'd listened so intently, she'd occasionally lost her train of thought. How many times had she repeated her insight about Lady Macbeth's love for her husband being both her redemption and her downfall? Twice, at least.

Heavens, how he flustered her with that dark, flashing gaze and deep, graveled voice. How he fascinated her with the deft motions of those massive hands. In the candlelight, his scars and patch had been stark reminders of his pain, a contrast to the strength exuded in every inch of his powerful frame.

Now, she paced from her bedchamber window to the opposite wall, pausing now and then to listen for his approach. She'd waited an hour so far. Where was he?

Glancing down at her finest, sheerest shift and the lace-trimmed dressing gown she'd layered over it, she ran her fingers through her loosened hair and wrapped a curl around her finger. Again. And again.

Would he prefer her naked? She nibbled her lower lip. Should she disrobe and wait for him in his bedchamber? No, she'd already gone over this dozens of times. In the past several years as she'd searched for a husband, her sisters had shared vital information about marital congress. From all she'd gathered, it was best to follow a man's lead at the start. Later, she could adjust their sails, as it were.

She nodded to herself. She'd done all she could do—letting her hair fall long and loose, even if the curls wanted to spring outward from her head like sheep's wool. She'd removed her stays and all but two sheer layers of clothing. She wore no slippers, though her toes were frightfully cold. She'd cleaned her teeth and washed her face. She'd even dabbed a drop of French perfume on each earlobe. It had been a gift from Francis for her last birthday, the same scent as her favorite soap.

Blast. She was ready. So, where was Broderick?

Just then, out in the corridor, she heard it—a grunt, followed by a whispered curse. Then, she heard a muffled creak as the door to Broderick's bedchamber opened and closed.

Her heart stuttered. Pounded.

Steady, now, she admonished herself. *You are a wife. Just follow his instructions, and that will be that.* She swallowed. Rushed to the bedside table, where she'd placed her tea. Gulped—cold. The cup rattled as she set it back in its saucer, which clinked against something glass. It was the brown vial Mrs. MacBean had given her that morning.

Surely it wouldn't be necessary. She nibbled her lip and rubbed her damp palms against her thighs. Surely he wouldn't need such a remedy to perform his husbandly duty.

She tucked the vial into the small lace pocket of her dressing gown. "Just in case," she whispered.

Before she could lose her nerve, she ducked into the corridor, found his door, and slipped inside. It was darker than she'd anticipated. A low fire in the hearth was the only light. "Broderick?" she queried softly, searching the room.

A quiet thud sounded from the darkest corner. "Un-bluidy-believable," he whispered before releasing what sounded like a despairing chuckle.

She squinted. "It is you, yes? I can't see anything without ..." She lost her breath, her train of thought, and possibly her senses when, out of the dark, her husband stood and moved into the faint light of the window.

Dear heaven and a choir of angels. He wasn't wearing a shirt.

Her back met the door. She'd never seen anything like him. The muscles were like great slabs of stone, smooth and swollen and hard. So very hard. His torso was a V, tapering to a narrow waist and centered with a dark mat of hair. She noted the scars—some long and slashing across his ribs, some short and wide in his upper arm. Two were long gouges on his shoulder. He had so many scars, they quickly faded from notice until all she could see was his magnificence. It was near blinding.

"... are ye doin' in here?"

She forced herself to blink. "Hmm?"

He was reaching for a shirt. His face was in deep shadow, but she saw a splash of white on the foot of the bed seconds before he plucked it up.

"Oh, please," she begged. "Don't."

He stilled. For a moment, she thought he might obey her plea. But then, he drew the white linen over his head in swift, efficient motions.

Her very soul mourned the loss.

"Answer me, lass."

She couldn't. She was in mourning. "Why would you do that? So unnecessary."

"Kate."

"You're wearing too many garments."

"Bluidy hell."

"And there is too little light. Deuced frustrating."

"Why are ye here?"

"To perform my wifely duty, as we discussed."

Silence. He shifted to retrieve something from the shadows.

When she saw it was a bottle of whisky, she frowned. When he tipped it up and drank it like water, she glowered. "Are you in your cups?"

He wiped his mouth with a thick wrist. "Not nearly enough." Sighing, he moved through the firelight to set the uncorked bottle on the bedside table. "Look, lass. I think ye mistook my meanin' when I spoke of wifely duties."

"No. I comprehended you perfectly."

"Obviously not. I was suggestin' ye take over runnin' the household."

She drew closer, leaning a hip against the foot of the bed and crossing her arms over her bosom. "Rubbish."

He retreated back into the shadows of the corner near the window. She noted he wore only one boot. It thudded a moment later.

"Furnish the library," he continued. "Change the cleanin' schedules to suit yer liking. Hire a new kitchen maid who willnae panic at the sight of me. Put wee flowers in the entrance hall and wee pillows on the parlor sofa. That's all I intended for ye to—"

"Do not spin tales, Broderick. If you are having trouble with your stoat, then simply say so, and we shall solve the problem together."

She could barely see his face, but his deep silence and the air of incredulous thunder emanating from his dark corner suggested he didn't care for her challenge.

"I mean no insult, but plain speaking will serve us best." She sniffed and softened her tone. "A bodily malfunction of this sort must be trying."

"There is nae malfunction."

"Come, now," she chided, rounding the bed as he backed toward the window. "All this talk of how I am likely to be harmed by your great, towering manliness is rather silly, don't you think?"

"Lass, stop."

"And how I must follow your 'instructions' so as to avoid injury—"

"That wasnae why—bluidy hell, dinnae come any closer."

She paid him no mind, certain now of her conclusions. "Clearly, an overcompensation. But you did not marry some ordinary milksop miss. I am a Huxley. Adversity is our fuel. Challenge us, and we only burn brighter."

He'd obviously suffered injuries to more than his face and chest. Had his ability to father children also been affected? A peculiar pang struck her heart. No matter. Whatever his capabilities, consummating their marriage remained crucial. She felt the necessity of it beating like a drum in her bones and skin. Pounding, throbbing, and aching.

She inched toward him, reaching into the dark. "Broderick, you mustn't let your manly pride prevent us from making this a *proper* marriage."

His groan was deep and agonized.

"Darling man," she cooed, scarcely able to make out his eye patch in the faint light. Her fingertips brushed something before he pulled away. His arm? "Let us try, hmm? I shall do whatever is necessary to … er, *excite* your stoat. Would you prefer me naked?"

"Christ on the cross."

"The air is a bit chilly, but I shouldn't mind too much. Perhaps I could caress you. Oh, and kissing! I understand it can be most stimulating when tongues are involved."

He reeled back, knocking into something and creating a loud clatter.

"Hmm. A lantern would not go amiss. I should very much like to see you."

"Ye must leave," he snarled.

"I will not."

"Aye, ye will."

A split second before he reached for her, she realized his intention—he meant to force her from the room. She evaded his hand by ducking, sliding, and spinning past him toward his bedside table. It was a dance maneuver she'd practiced with her dear friend Clarissa many times.

"Kate," he growled. "I'm orderin' ye to return to yer bedchamber."

"Oh?" she inquired, withdrawing the brown vial from her pocket and surreptitiously pouring its contents into his whisky bottle. "Are you making this demand as my *husband?*"

"Aye. Yer husband."

She spun to face him. He'd remained near the window, she noticed, almost as if he feared being close to her. "To qualify as my husband, you must do your husbandly duty, I daresay."

"'Tis a shite idea."

"No. It is necessary."

"I mean to take hold of ye, Kate. Then I'll be carryin' ye out of here and puttin' ye where ye belong."

"You'll have to touch me first."

He groaned. Cursed. "Aye. I ken." Then, he moved.

Alarm surged. Blast! He was faster than he looked. With a squeak, she scrambled up onto the high bed. Her gown snagged on her toes, and the delicate hem tore. But she clambered across the width of the mattress like she was traversing deep snow. Even Broderick's arms weren't long enough to reach her. She stood on the far side of the bed, dizzy at the height.

"Woman!" His growl was furiously deep. He slammed a palm onto the mattress. It shook the frame. "By God, ye're beggin' for trouble."

"Calm yourself, Broderick." She panted, brushing her curls away from her face. "This needn't be a battle."

"Ye've made it one."

"Sit down." She used a tone she'd heard her mother and every one of her sisters use with their husbands—Annie had used it on John, too. "Let us discuss this rationally. Have a drink. It will make you feel better."

"I dinnae want a drink."

"Have one anyway."

His chest heaved for several seconds. His hand braced on the bedpost, squeezing until the thing creaked.

She feared for the wood.

Slowly, his grip eased, and he lifted the bottle, drinking long and deep.

"There, now," she soothed. "Better?"

"No."

"Have you a lantern?"

"Aye."

"Light it for me, won't you?"

The empty bottle scraped as he slid it onto the table. Silence lengthened while he decided whether to grant her wish. Finally, he moved to the hearth, bent and lit a lantern then set it on the mantel. "There," he rasped. "Now, will ye leave?"

Something in his face—for, she could see him more clearly now—made her heart twist. A kind of ... feverish desperation. Slowly, she stepped across the bed, hiking her skirts up to her knees and struggling to keep her balance. "Broderick," she murmured as she reached the edge. "Might we try kissing?"

His hands were braced on his hips, his head lowered to stare at his feet. He grunted. Shook his head. Released a deep chuckle. "The devil's own torment. That's what ye are."

"I could be more." She swallowed, examining the massive lines of his shoulders and chest. "I could bring you comfort. Wouldn't you like that, after all the pain you've endured?"

Silence.

"It will be easy," she coaxed. "I shall stand here. All you must do is kiss me. You won't even have to bend down."

He shuddered and refused to look at her.

For the first time, she wondered if it was possible he didn't want her, might not *ever* want her. It had happened before.

God help her. What if she *couldn't* tempt him to do his husbandly duty? Her stomach went queasy. Her palms went damp.

"One kiss, lass." His voice—gravel and caverns. Rough and deep.

Her breath whooshed. Her skin tingled.

His head came up, and that dark, beautiful eye flashed wildfire. He started toward her.

Oh, dear. Mrs. MacBean's formulation worked quickly, it seemed.

With her standing on the mattress, their mouths could align easily. He stopped a whisper away. His breath smelled of golden whisky. His skin smelled of mint or pine. This close, she saw every scar: the slashes through his brows, the fainter creases along his cheekbones, the deep gouge that marred the corner of his mouth.

Her hands floated upward as though carried by an updraft. They cupped his jaw. The rough texture of his whiskers fascinated her fingertips. She stroked him over and over. His scars and his skin. Bones that had broken and mended. Lips that were fuller than she'd realized. Firm and soft.

Powerful hands seized her waist. For a moment, she thought he might lift her and toss her away from him. Strength and tension shook him. Shook her.

She captured his gaze and held. Held. Stroked his jaw and held him fast.

His hands tightened upon her waist, his fingers lacing along her back. Digging in. Kneading. His breath caught. Heaved. A massive palm slid up her back to cup her nape. Another angled down to her lower spine and drew her tight against him.

This time, she was the one who groaned. He was hot. Hard. So very hard. His chest flattened her breasts, making her nipples beg for more. More pressure. More friction.

Suddenly the room felt scorching. Her skin tightened and zinged. Her breasts swelled and ached.

He angled her head, breathing against her lips. "Dinnae say I never warned ye, lass."

Between one moment and the next, Kate's world both exploded and shrank to a pinpoint. There was only this. His lips sliding against hers. His tongue sleeking inside. His taste—whisky-sharp—teasing her senses.

She answered by clasping him closer, looping his neck. He pleasured her mouth with his, stroking and teasing, making the invasion a sensual dance. But he was too careful. Too slow. Too gentle.

Needing him deeper, harder, she ground her mouth against his. Chased his tongue with hers. Dug her fingers into his scalp and clutched his thick, cool hair.

His hand slid into her hair, too. It grasped and forced her away.

Whimpering, she realized how breathless she'd gone. How cold she felt without his mouth. How little she'd known about desire until now.

He gazed at her with that single, ravenous eye. "I was imprisoned for six months," he rasped, holding her hair and her body and her sanity in his hands. "Recuperating another six. If we do this, I cannae be gentle. Do ye ken?"

She stroked her knuckles across his lips. Rested her forehead against his. "Can you make it pleasurable?"

His breaths quickened. He uttered a low growl. The hand on her back squeezed until she could feel his fingertips. "Aye."

Brazenly, she traced her tongue along his lower lip then whispered, "Right answer, Broderick MacPherson."

Everything sane inside Broderick burned away. He'd had the thought—fleetingly—that he should be the one to leave. To save her.

But then she'd kissed him. Stroked him. Offered herself so sweetly and so persistently that he'd lost track of why she needed saving.

His hands tightened on her tiny waist. His fingers dug into her hips. She was small. Probably untried. He should take care.

She gave him one of her glowing smiles, and he cracked. Split like wood down the middle. The wood burned to ash, revealing what lay inside.

Need. Dark, shocking need.

With quick, jerking motions, he tore loose her dressing gown. Beneath lay a shift that might as well not exist. Positioned as she was, her breasts were level with his mouth. He saw her nipples. Hard, pouting.

He took. Suckled her through the linen.

Not enough.

He grasped her hems and stripped her shift and gown up and off. Ah, God. His wife was exquisite. Curving hips, dark hair, lean thighs. Milky-white skin and soft, pink-tipped breasts. The one he'd suckled was darker, flushed hard with pleasure. He took the other in his mouth and tasted flowers and velvet.

He clutched her naked body tighter. Closer. Lifted her off her feet and dropped her flat on the mattress.

Faintly, he heard her gasping. Then, she laughed.

Sweet Christ. That laugh.

He growled, deep and low. Yanked his shirt off. Tore open his fall. He was so hot, he wondered if he might set the bloody room on fire. "Need ye," he rasped, all senses focused upon her beauty and her scent. "Spread yer legs."

"Broderick," she crooned. "Look at me."

"Kate. Do as I tell ye."

"Here, darling. Kiss me."

He wanted to. Her mouth and her nipples and her sex. But the monster of lust, primal and uncaged, had taken control. This was precisely what he'd feared. He should have paid some whore to ease him. He should not be mauling his wife.

But she wasn't his wife, was she? Not yet. Suddenly, that fact was an untenable agony. She must be his. Nobody must question it.

He gripped her legs and drew them apart, tugging her closer until her knees bent wide. That was when he noticed. Like an animal, he fixated upon it. She was pink, as berry-bright as her blush. The folds glistened like flower petals after a hard rain. And she smelled like flowers, only deeper. Richer. He wanted a taste. How long since he'd tasted a woman?

Too damned long.

He grasped her waist, lifted and slid her higher on the bed. Then he dropped to his elbows, held her hips with desperate hands, and began to feast. A groan rumbled from the deepest part of him.

Sleek. Swollen. Wet.

She tasted of exotic blooms and salty lust. She tasted like honey from the depths of paradise. With his tongue, he stroked and delved, watching her ripe crimson nub swell and beg. He suckled it hard, controlling her as she arched high. Ignoring her as she yanked at his hair and demanded to know what he was doing.

He was devouring her, that's what. Feasting like the desperate, starved beast she'd married. How tight was she? he wondered. As soon as the thought occurred, he sank his longest finger into her sheath, feeling for the small signs of her virginity. Found it. Added another finger. Stretched her as he suckled her sweet nub and felt her rippling. Rippling. Rippling. Seizing. Ah, God. So bloody tight.

Her screams of ecstasy echoed in his ears, and it was not enough. He wanted her juices on his cock. He wanted her to feel him there inside her long after he'd left. The desires should have signaled how far from reason he'd strayed. Instead, they satisfied the wild, primitive creature he'd become.

Aye. He wanted her beneath him. Taking him. He wanted this tight, slick sheath wringing him dry.

"... rick, pl-please. Kiss me. I want you here."

His guts twisted hard. He looked at her—the flushed, white skin. The soft curves and downy curls. Then, he let his gaze travel higher. Her breasts heaved, the nipples red and beaded. Finally, he dared to meet her eyes.

He couldn't stop the growl. It came from so deep inside him, he wasn't even sure it was human. She was painfully beautiful. And the way she glowed—like the damned sun, she was.

"Kate." Her name was agony. How he hurt. How he needed the glow in her eyes and her soft, sensuous smile.

She reached for him.

He came over her.

She kissed his mouth.

He dove in deep.

Her fingers dug into his back as his clawed the MacPherson wool on either side of her head. "Need ye, lass."

"Mmm. Yes."

He reached between them, took out his cock, and stroked her folds with the tip.

"B-Broderick?" Her eyes flared. "Is this going to ... just let me ... perhaps give me a moment—"

He didn't have a moment. The world was on fire. He wedged his hips deeper into the cradle of her thighs, forcing her legs wider. Then, he tucked his cock at her entrance and, as slowly as he could manage, he pushed inside. She squirmed, grunted, huffed. He controlled her movements with a hand on her nape and one on her thigh.

He forged deeper, the heat and vise-like grip of her body making his head float free, his senses spin. The base of his spine tingled and sparked. His ballocks felt heavy as cannonballs, primed to fire.

She squirmed again, and he growled. Repositioned her firmly. Gave another thrust.

"Too … big. Broderick. Good God."

Her eyes caught his, pleading for mercy.

He had none. It had been beaten out of him before he'd ever met her.

With another ferocious growl, he pulled free of her, earning him a surprised yelp. Before she could either thank him or protest, he flipped her onto her belly, yanked her up onto her knees, and bent over her.

"Say no, lass." He gathered her hair in his fist, pulling it to the side so he could nip her earlobe. "Tell me to go to the devil. For, that's where I belong. Say it."

Her shoulders heaved on stormy breaths. "I—I can't."

"Say it. Or I'll take ye like this."

Her body trembled beneath his, her shoulders and her smooth, creamy back shuddering as her head hung between her braced arms. "Then, take me," she panted, her voice in threads. "I want you to."

It was all he needed. His first thrust was hard, but she was tight as a fist, and he only forged inside five inches or so.

She stiffened. Whimpered. Gasped and clawed the blankets.

He withdrew and thrust inside again, deeper this time. She was slick from her earlier climax, and it helped ease his path. But it took several more thrusts before he'd filled her completely. When he was seated as deep as he could go, a strange thing happened. The urgency receded the slightest bit. His head cleared of its steamy heat long enough for him to notice her shaking.

He bent closer. Slid his lips along her nape and down the side of her neck. Holding himself deep inside her, he used his free hand to caress her breasts. He worked her nipples, squeezing them hard. He cupped and plumped the breasts he'd failed to pleasure sufficiently. Then, he slid his hand down to her sex, the downy ringlets wet and warm, now. Her swollen nub begged for his stroke. He answered with a firm nudge that made her jerk and gasp. Her sheath wept its approval, seizing upon him with an uncertainty he couldn't tolerate.

He began moving. Thrusting. Out and in. A few inches and a few more. The thrusts pounded, first solid then rougher. Harder. He drew back to watch as he pulled almost free and sank back inside her tight, slick sheath. So pink. So swollen and ripe. His own body's thick, dark stalk was a marauder, invading her small, delicate passage. The sight obsessed him. She was his, and nothing had ever felt so damned perfect. He took his wife hard. Taking and taking and taking. But her body welcomed him. Her pleasure glistened upon him.

"… take anymore. Please." She moaned. Pleaded in rhythm with his thrusts. Her hips writhed and pushed back into him as he went deeper. "Need you. To finish."

Not until she did. By God, not until he'd felt her coming on his cock.

Gritting his teeth, he circled and swirled amidst the center of her folds, using his fingers to force her body higher, closer to her peak. He thrust faster. Rammed deeper. Growled in her ear, "Is this what ye wanted, Kate? To be tupped by a monster?"

"Oooh, heavens. Broderick! Not a monster. Not … a monster. A man. My husband." She keened. Seized. A warning ripple. "Aaah! The pleasure. It's too much. I can't …" She sobbed and stiffened. Her body undulated. Wrung his cock with wondrous, repeated paroxysms. Her arms collapsed. Her head lowered onto the blankets.

His hips didn't stop. His fingers didn't stop. He wanted everything from her. He wanted to fill her and fuck her and make her understand no other man would ever give her this.

But his body's deprivation caught up to him, and nothing could have stopped its eruption. He felt its rise as her rippling pleasure began to ease. His arm banded her waist. His mouth settled in the cradle of her neck and shoulder. He gritted his teeth, and with several mighty thrusts, the pleasure he'd been denied for longer than a year—longer than a lifetime—burst through his entire body. The violent explosion was every wondrous sensation he'd ever had, distilled down to one long, exquisite minute. It pulsed and raged. It eased and relieved. It made every second he'd spent apart from Kate Huxley MacPherson an eternal torment.

Because this was not the result of deprivation. This was extraordinary. *She* was extraordinary.

He collapsed onto his side, his arms drawing her back into the cradle of his body. And, when he felt her soft chuckle, he squeezed her hard. Breathed her in. Kissed her temple. Nuzzled her hair, helpless to do anything else.

God, how could she be like this after the way he'd treated her?

"Well, I suppose you did warn me, didn't you?" she said wryly, her voice in tatters and edging toward drowsy. She stroked his wrist where it banded between her breasts. Her fingers tapped out a ticklish tune on his arm. "Nobody can say we aren't married now." Satisfaction threaded her voice. She turned her face and kissed his jaw then sighed. "Including you."

CHAPTER ELEVEN

Kate had always been an early riser, but the morning after being ravished by her husband—three times, no less—she slept through breakfast. And then through luncheon. In fact, by the time she managed to roll from his bed, wrap her nakedness in a blanket, and summon Janet, the day was half-gone. She searched for her shift amidst the bedclothes and didn't find it. So, she dropped to her knees and peeked beneath the bed. There! She reached for the wad of white material, and her knuckles brushed something hard.

She frowned. Felt wood and metal. It was a hammer. The tool was heavy and worn, the metal head nicked and the handle smoothed by long use.

Why did Broderick have a hammer beneath his bed?

She had little time to contemplate it, as Janet knocked at the door. Kate shoved the hammer back into place and greeted her maid with a sheepish glance. "No commentary, if you please," she warned.

The maid grinned back. "Wouldnae dream of it, mistress."

In truth, Janet was most helpful, arranging a soothing bath and helping her choose a chocolate-brown wool walking gown appropriate to the damp, cloudy weather. Of course, the maid fought a knowing smirk while tending Kate, and that was vexing. But Kate couldn't blame her.

The signs of her debauchery covered her body, rendering it sore, pleasantly achy, and sensitive. His whiskers had reddened her breasts, her neck, and most especially, her inner thighs. Her nipples could scarcely tolerate the brush of her shift. Though his hands had never caused her pain, his fingers had left faint marks on her hips. To her, every one of them was a prize.

Oh, how he'd wanted her. And it had been glorious.

She wanted to see him again. He'd departed long before she'd awakened, and she wanted to know whether he'd been as pleased as she was.

After Janet untangled, washed, and dressed her hair, Kate donned her walking gown along with a fur-lined, brown velvet cloak, a blue silk bonnet, and a sturdy pair of half-boots. Her stomach grumbled, reminding her she hadn't yet eaten.

"If ye mean to take Ophelia for a jaunt, wouldnae yer riding hat be better, Mrs. MacPherson?" Janet's smirk pursed her lips.

"No!" Kate swallowed her chagrin and lowered her voice. "No riding today. I shall walk. You said he'll be at the distillery, yes?"

"Aye," came the amused response. "Pleasant day for a walk. Mind ye dinnae exhaust yerself, now."

Kate snorted and rolled her eyes.

The cheeky maid chuckled and tidied the dressing table.

"I must fetch a bite to eat before I go. When Mrs. Grant returns from shopping, please inform her I shall be moving my belongings to the master bedchamber, but I shall keep this room for writing."

Janet's eyebrows arched until they disappeared beneath her fringe of sandy hair. "That good, was it?"

Kate's lips longed to smile, but sharing such confidences with one's maid was inappropriate. Instead, she shot Janet a chiding glance and opened the door. On her way out, however, she couldn't resist. "Not that good." Her grin broke free. "Better."

She hummed a new, inspired tune as she floated along the corridor, down the stairs, and to the kitchen. There, she noticed a plate of sliced lamb and a basket of rolls on the sideboard. She quickly wrapped both in a napkin and slid the bundle inside her reticule.

A loud clatter sounded from the passage leading to the scullery and larder. A series of grumbled curses and grunts followed. Then, silence.

Kate frowned. Perhaps she should help poor Mr. McInnes. He was getting on in years, and if he'd taken a tumble—

An old woman staggered from the passage, bracing herself against the corner of the table. She looked more frazzled than usual, her hair dusted with flour and her cheeks red as apples. Her leather pouch now hung halfway down her skirt.

"Mrs. MacBean?"

The herbalist gave her a half-milky blink. "Och, lassie. Didnae expect to find ye here this mornin'."

"It is afternoon."

Mrs. MacBean frowned. Glanced out the windows. "Well, look there. It is. Where did the time go?"

"Are you here about Broderick's liniment?"

"Eh?"

"Liniment," Kate repeated, louder this time. "Or perhaps his tonic?"

Half-blind eyes flared wide. Mrs. MacBean rushed toward her and grasped her hand. "Ye didnae use it, did ye?"

Kate frowned. "Well, yes, actually. It appears most effective."

"It does?"

A twinge of misgiving struck her middle. "This surprises you?"

The woman blew out a breath and ran a hand across her forehead. Flour dusted down from her hair. "Aye. Ye might say that."

Mr. McInnes entered from the same passage Mrs. MacBean had staggered through moments earlier. He had flour on his cap, a misbuttoned fall, and a brown vial in his hand. "What sort of devil's formula did ye give me, woman? Ye might've killed us both!"

Mrs. MacBean's gaze shifted sheepishly between McInnes and Kate.

The conclusion was both baffling and obvious. They'd been in the scullery doing … that. Kate groaned, her fingers moving to her lips. "Dear God. What did I give Broderick?" she murmured.

"Och, nothin' poisonous, lass."

McInnes grumbled as he dusted his cap off against his leg then stomped to where he'd hung his apron and tied it in place. "Ye owe me another batch, woman. My piles willnae be shrunken after this, I'll tell ye that much."

Mrs. MacBean leaned closer and whispered, "A wee bit of horse chestnut."

"And it'll be days ere I have a proper shite!" he bellowed, yanking a crate of apples from a low shelf and slamming it on the table.

"The lad might be eager for the privy today," she whispered with a pat. "He'll be feelin' fine by supper. Dinnae fash."

"Might as well be *years!*"

Kate managed to swallow her horrified amusement long enough to make her escape from the kitchen. For the next half-hour, as she traveled the winding lane down through the wooded foothills to the main road, she marveled that Broderick's passion had *not* been a product of Mrs. MacBean's herbal intervention. It had been real. Just him and her and whatever lay between them.

Suffused with warm tingles, she imagined what he would say when she saw him again. Something gruff and growly, perhaps. A compliment on her hair. A request for ongoing wifeliness. Would he say anything at all? Perhaps he would simply lift her and kiss her senseless.

She sighed, dug out her roll and lamb, assembled her meal, and chewed thoughtfully. She would like that best, she decided. No words. Only kissing.

She'd finished her meal and dusted her crumbs by the time she passed through the outskirts of the village to take the long, rising distillery road. Kate's first glimpse of the MacPherson Distillery came after she passed an old farmer driving a flock of sheep down the hill. The buildings were the same gray stone as those in the village. But these structures were longer, stretching dozens of feet. One of them, a massive rectangle with white stucco over stone, had sizable windows lining the top story. Offices, perhaps? There were more than twenty buildings clustered in the embrace of the surrounding hills. At the center, a towering spire rose high above the other rooftops. It breathed smoke.

"If it isnae my bonnie new sister, Kate."

She grinned at the tall, handsome charmer emerging from a nearby cottage. "Rannoch. How lovely to see you."

His eyes warmed and crinkled as he approached. "What brings ye here?"

"I was hoping to speak with my husband. Is he about?"

Rannoch hesitated. "Aye." He glanced toward the white stuccoed building. "He's meetin' with somebody. Shouldnae be long." Another smile filled with persuasive charm. "Will I do for a wee while?"

She chuckled and looped her arm through his. "Of course. Perhaps you could show me round. I've never explored a distillery before."

For the next hour, he showed her the barley being steeped and spread out in a cavernous malt barn, the grain turned by ten red-faced men with wooden shovels. He took her to the adjacent kiln—the smoking spire at the center of the distillery complex—where green malt was dried with peat fire. Next, he showed her where the milled barley combined with heated water in a process called mashing.

"The water is piped into the boilers and used to fill the mash tuns, as ye see."

She gazed in wonder at the fire-heated copper boilers and enormous vats supplied by a series of pipes and valves. "Piped from where?"

"Three burns run down through these hills. Purest water to be found for two hundred miles. We divert a wee bit of it for our own purposes. That's why the distillery sits here, lass. The water is plentiful. Do ye ken this place started as a brewery? Middlin' beer, fine ale, and superior cider. That's all we made." He grinned and winked. "At least, that's the tale we told the excisemen."

She examined the man beside her. His features were strong and even, his hair thick, his eyes dark and flashing with MacPherson pride. Annie had mentioned once that Broderick's face had been similar to Rannoch's before his imprisonment. She'd also said Broderick had been even handsomer. Kate marveled that such a thing was possible, but immediately decided it didn't matter. To her, Broderick's attractiveness had little to do with his face. It was his strength and competence she found compelling. The uncomplaining resilience. The protectiveness in every gesture, every word.

In her belly, impatience to see her husband began heating like malted barley.

But Rannoch insisted on showing her the rest of the distilling process—the pinewood washbacks where fermentation occurred and the copper stills where the resulting wash magically became whisky. By the time he offered to show her the cottages for the distillery's workers, Kate felt quite certain he was stalling.

She halted outside near a row of wagons. "Rannoch MacPherson, you are purposely delaying."

He flashed her a guilty wince. "Mayhap a wee bit."

"Why?"

He crossed his arms and lowered his brows. In that moment, he looked so much like Broderick when Broderick was being obstinate, she blinked.

Suspicion tickled the back of her mind. "Who is he meeting?"

"Naebody ye need fash about."

She narrowed her eyes. By heaven, she had seen that look before—stubborn protectiveness and manly resolve. "Rannoch, take me to my husband. Now."

"Have patience, lass."

"Never mind. I shall find him myself." She turned on her heel and headed toward the white building. She'd wager all those windows were for offices. And she'd wager Broderick was inside one of them, meeting with God knew which woman. A former paramour? A heartsick lass lamenting his marriage and offering "comfort"?

Her stomach burned like peat fire. He wouldn't accept, would he? Not after last night.

Rannoch caught up to her just before she reached the entrance. "Kate, 'tis nae for ye to—"

She glared. "My husband. Take me to him now." She ground her teeth and recalled her manners. "If you please. I should like to see him, Rannoch."

He sighed, opened the door, and waved her through. "Aye, well. If he asks, grant me a boon and tell him I tried, eh?"

Moments later, outside a door on the mezzanine above an enormous warehouse filled with casks, Kate took a deep breath. Rannoch knocked twice and opened the door at Broderick's impatient, "Aye!"

Inside, Kate's husband stood with his legs braced and arms folded across his chest—a dominating, challenging posture rendered deadlier by his black glare. The person across from him wasn't a paramour. Nor a tart. Nor even a woman.

Her eyes widened. "Sergeant Munro?"

The constable turned and frowned in her direction. "Didnae expect to see ye here, m'lady."

She raised her chin. "It is Mrs. MacPherson, if you please. And I see nothing unexpected in visiting my husband at his legitimate, properly licensed distillery."

Broderick's glower had gone thunderous the moment she entered, but initially, it focused on Rannoch. "Brother, ye'll be explainin' yerself later."

"Aye, I ken." Rannoch sighed, nodded his farewell to Kate, and left.

Broderick's eye flashed to her bodice and throat. His greeting was a low rumble. "Kate."

Ignoring the heated thrill that ran up her spine, she crossed to stand at his side, facing Munro. The constable appeared frustrated. A good sign. "I fear you must be neglecting your duties, Sergeant, what with your many hours traveling between here and Inverness. Would not your time be better spent at your post?"

"'Tis my first duty to locate an escaped prisoner, Mrs. MacPherson. I suspect yer husband kens pertinent facts he refuses to share." Munro's sharp gaze focused upon her. "As do ye."

"Yer business is with me." Broderick's warning came low and hard. "Approach my wife again, and ye'll discover how I survived six months in the Bridewell."

The other man's whiskers twitched. "Is that a threat?"

Alarmed at the escalation, Kate intervened. "No!" She clasped Broderick's elbow and stroked his upper arm. "No, no, no. Merely a suggestion."

Broderick frowned as though she'd lost her mind.

"I believe what my husband would prefer is that you focus your efforts where they will produce the greatest benefit." She cleared her throat as soon as her voice started rising—though she could do nothing about her flush. "Have you even considered the possibility that Lord Lockhart escaped on his own accord and that he is, even now, fleeing the punishment he so richly deserves whilst you remain here, accosting innocent, legitimate whisky producers and their devoted wives for crimes they have certainly not committed, nor have any intention of committing—"

"Kate."

"—including such scurrilous charges as murder and fraud and illicit distribution of untaxed liquor—"

"Kate." A growl, this time.

"—before you have bothered to verify whether the scapegrace in question remains corporeal on this earth, or indeed, has been assisted in his flight from justice by his sister, who may have rented rooms in a house mere minutes from the jail which you claim—"

Suddenly, her nape was in Broderick's hand and her lips were captured by Broderick's mouth and nothing mattered except Broderick's kiss.

Oh, heavens. His hard, thorough, plunging kiss.

She might have whimpered. She certainly clung. Her knees turned to water and her belly went hot. By the time he finished with her, they could have poured her into a still and turned her into whisky.

"Kate," he hissed against her mouth.

"Hmm?" She opened her eyes and melted more. God, he smelled delicious.

"Haud yer wheesht."

Dizzy and dazed, she couldn't quite recall what the phrase meant. Still, she could see he wanted a response, so she nodded. When he straightened, she blinked, realizing Munro was still there. Still staring at them.

Her smile trembled. "We are ... very affectionate."

The constable raised a skeptical brow. "Is that so?"

Broderick banded an arm around her waist and hugged her quite forcefully against his side. She assumed he meant to reinforce her point and demonstrate the properness of their marriage for Munro, so she played along, patting his ribs and stroking his chest in little circles. "Oh, yes. My husband is exceedingly demonstrative. Why, only last night—"

"Kate." This time, her name was accompanied by a light squeeze of her backside. It distracted her momentarily as she tried to determine how she was meant to respond.

She decided to return the gesture. Broderick's reaction was to tighten every muscle, including the ones she was patting.

"Munro," he said, his voice a bit more graveled than before. "Ye've asked yer bluidy questions for the hundredth bluidy time. I didnae kill Lockhart. I dinnae ken where he is. Now, either leave off or ye'll be findin' yerself a new post—and not the one ye're hopin' my arrest will earn ye."

Munro's eyes turned icy. His nose flared. His whiskers twitched.

What was this? John and Annie had hinted that Munro was ambitious. Apparently, he believed apprehending Broderick for Lockhart's disappearance would be the feather in his cap he needed to attain a loftier position. Was that why he'd been so persistent and vexing? Or was it worse?

Was he working for Lockhart?

Kate's head lifted off her shoulders. Dear God. Was Munro a much bigger threat than she'd supposed?

The sergeant glared between the two of them. Then, he clenched his jaw, turned on his heel, and strode away.

She waited until she heard the footsteps echoing down the mezzanine stairs before she rounded on Broderick. "You didn't tell me he might be working for Lockhart."

He stared at her oddly—with a great deal of heat and consternation and a faint whiff of … she didn't know. Amusement, perhaps. "Kate," he murmured. "What are ye doin' here, lass?"

"Answer me."

"Anybody could be workin' for Lockhart. That's why ye must do as I tell ye."

"But, do you know for certain—"

"Nah."

"We must find out."

"Woman, ye're tryin' my patience. First, ye show up in my office bein' squired about by *Rannoch*. Then, ye start bletherin' away to Munro like an uncorked bottle."

She nibbled her lip and patted his chest. "I did warn you. It's a bit of a problem."

His gaze suddenly went dark. Cold. Then so hot, she thought he might actually combust. "Ye do fancy Rannoch, then."

"What? No!" She shook her head. "I was referring to my tendency to ramble when I'm nervous. And Munro makes me dreadfully nervous."

The tension in his neck and forehead eased. "Is that why ye wouldnae be quiet when I told ye to? Or why ye kept touchin' and provokin' me past the point of reason?"

"I thought that was what you wanted."

"What part of *haud yer wheesht* is confusin', lass?"

"The whole thing, really." She lifted her chin. "You kissed me. How was I to think sensibly, let alone translate your nonsense Scottish commands into English?" She sniffed. "When you consider everything that transpired, it was entirely your fault."

More consternated amusement. "Pure rubbish."

"Kiss me again, if you don't believe me."

He shook his head. A smile tugged at the unscarred corner of his mouth. "I dinnae think that's wise."

"Go on. I shall prove my point."

"Did ye ride or walk here?"

"Why should that signify?"

"Answer the question."

"I walked."

He loomed closer, his heat and scent dizzying. "There ye have it." His gaze roved from her bonnet to her boots then back to her bosom and, finally, her lips. His nose flared as he drew a shuddering breath. "Kissin' is unwise."

"I don't underst—"

"If I kiss ye right now, lass—if I even touch ye—ye'll nae be leavin' this room without bein' tupped. And I'd wager yer wee body cannae handle me this soon. So, no.

We willnae be doin' any more kissin' for another day or two."

"A day or *two?*"

"'Tis all the time I can give ye."

She frowned and moved into him. When she slid her hands up his chest, he groaned. "That is much too long, Broderick. No, no, we must continue to build a proper marriage."

"After the way I treated ye last night, I already feel like the arse end of a donkey."

"Oh, that's only because of Mrs. MacBean's formula. It was the wrong vial. She assures me you'll be much improved by supper."

Silence.

She petted his chest and played with the buttons of his waistcoat.

"What vial?"

"Hmm?"

His voice was harder this time. "What vial, Kate?"

Realizing he might be displeased, she rushed to explain. "Mrs. MacBean gave me a tonic to invigorate your stoat. She may have mistaken your tonic for that of Mr. McInnes, who suffers from two rather humbling complaints. His age, I assume. In any case, I may have added Mr. McInnes's tonic to your whisky last night, unaware that the vials had been switched or that your stoat needed no such invigorating. Really, the dear creature is far more robust and determined than Mrs. MacBean led me to believe."

A long silence settled between them. Briefly, she considered apologizing. Then, she decided it might make matters worse.

"Broderick? That vein in your forehead cannot be a good sign. Do you suppose horse chestnut causes apoplexy? Perhaps you should lie down."

"By God, woman. I dinnae need. Any help. With my STOAT!"

"There is no cause for shouting." She raised a brow. "If anyone understands how vigorous you are, it is I."

A few heaving breaths passed before the thunder quieted. He nodded. Then, he bracketed her waist and gently squeezed. "Kate," he rasped. "I regret how I handled ye last night." He drew her closer until proof of her earlier statement pressed against her belly. His jaw flickered as he lowered his face near hers. "I was … ye were … Bugger all, I've never treated a woman so roughly. How can ye nae be furious with me?"

Her heart broke open, and she cupped his jaw, drawing him down for a soft kiss. "Furious? I'm elated, darling man. As we speak, I'm devising clever schemes to lure you into debauchery."

He released a sharp crack of laughter, rusty and surprised.

The sound delighted her so much, she joined in, giggling helplessly.

"God, I love yer laugh." His gaze roved her face. His fingers looped through her curls. "I love yer scent."

Aching with a tide of melting heat, she murmured, "Tuberose and jasmine, bergamot and clary sage."

A puzzled frown tugged.

"My soap."

"Ah." A small, devastatingly sensual quirk of his lips nearly had her begging him to take her. "'Tis a fine soap, indeed."

"Broderick?"

"Aye."

"Must we wait?"

He sighed. "Aye, lass."

"We are alone, now. Would it not behoove us to solidify the properness of our marriage at every opportunity?"

"When ye've recovered, and not until."

"But I came all this way."

His brows crashed into a glower. "Aye, ye did. And where's yer escort?"

She blinked. "I came alone."

"Precisely. Kate, ye mustn't leave the house without an able man by yer side, preferably armed. Ye could be attacked, abducted. Killed." His gaze roiled with darkness, his voice thrumming. "Lockhart might still be lickin' his wounds, but none of the damage he did was by his own hands. He'll hire men. He'll target ye because ye're mine. Do ye ken what I'm sayin' to ye? Bluidy tell me ye understand. *Never* leave the house alone. Not ever again."

By the time he'd finished, she worried about the vein in his temple and the strain in the hand that braced her lower back. His eye was filled with such ferocious intensity, she wanted only to hold him. Ease him.

"Of course," she soothed. "I shall never leave the house alone again. I promise."

"A male. Armed."

"Yes. An armed male. I understand."

He seemed to relax the slightest bit. "Ye do?"

"I'm very reasonable." She patted his chest. "Now, which male would you prefer? Patrick, perhaps?"

Frowning, he shook his head. "Too young."

"What of Connor?"

"Bluidy hell, he couldnae defend a pint of ale from a determined barmaid."

"Hmm. Mr. McInnes?"

He snorted.

Her fingers began plucking open his waistcoat buttons. "Well, you cannot possibly expect me to remain ensconced inside the house—lovely though it is—for the duration."

He swallowed visibly. "Kate."

"Such a conundrum." She began tugging at his shirt, drawing the fabric loose from his breeches. "You know, there is only one man who makes me feel safe whenever I am with him. So, perhaps I should simply follow you about."

"I dinnae think that's a good idea."

She tugged off her gloves, tossed them on the desk behind him, dug beneath the hem of his shirt, and ran her fingers over his hard, ridged, naked belly. "No?"

A jolt and a groan.

"I suppose one of your brothers would do."

"Nae Rannoch," he barked.

She raised a brow. "I fail to see why. He seems quite capable. And we do get along rather—"

"Nae Rannoch," he repeated in a deep rumble. His hands, meanwhile, fell to her backside and drew her hips hard against him, lifting her onto her toes.

"Campbell, then," she panted. "Is he about? Alexander is also an option, though I must tell you, I find him most intimid—"

"Ye'll accompany me," he gritted. "When I cannae be there, ye'll wait for me. If I'm away longer than a day, ye'll rely upon yer brother's protection."

She opened her mouth to agree, but he swooped in to kiss her so hard and thoroughly, she lost track of the conversation. And just when she'd made frantic progress on unbuttoning his fall, she found herself abruptly thrust away from him and held at arm's length.

"Not until ye've recovered," he said. "Wicked temptress."

"Me?" She tingled everywhere he'd touched her— lips, hips, bosom, backside. And *she* was the wicked one?

He remained resolute, however, and after buttons were fastened and gloves donned, he took her outside to one of the distillery wagons. Broderick called orders to several men to load it with loose straw and ready it for transport. As two of his men hitched the horses, a third retrieved blankets from the stable. Broderick spread one over the straw. Then, he lifted her high in his arms with no more effort than he might lift her smallest trunk. Gently, he lowered her onto the soft nest.

"I'm takin' ye home, lass."

Breathless and more than a little enchanted, she found herself unable to do more than nod.

"Are ye warm enough?" He took an additional blanket one of his men handed him and spread it over her lap with deft flicks. Then, he stroked a knuckle down her cheek. "Are ye comfortable?"

Her throat tightened as she gazed up at him. His dark hair ruffled lightly in the chilly breeze. His dark eye roved over her with a hint of concern. She nodded again.

He gave her a final, lingering caress then climbed onto the wagon's bench and took the reins. "My thanks, lads," he called to his men. "Tell Rannoch to be here early tomorrow. We'll speak then."

The wagon jerked into motion.

But Kate scarcely felt it. She scarcely smelled the peat-smoke air, the damp earth. She scarcely heard the nicker of the horses.

Because inside she'd halted like an unwound clock.

While she hadn't been looking, while she'd been merrily contemplating carpets for the dining room and pillows for the parlor, the worst possible thing had happened.

An illness.

A disaster.

A calamity few recognized and fewer conquered.

The mind infection had struck. But this time, Kate was the poor ninny in its grasp.

CHAPTER TWELVE

FF our days after Kate came to see him at the distillery, Broderick's urgency overcame his better judgment.

This could not go on. He could not leave for Edinburgh while his wife hated him.

He sucked in frost and breathed out clouds as he pulled his horse to a halt in front of his father's house. The old stone farmhouse had been his home, but right now, it harbored the woman who had defied his express orders to visit Angus for "tea."

She'd barely spoken to him—barely looked at him— since he'd lifted her out of the wagon. She'd taken supper that night in her bedchamber. He'd listened to her pacing until well past midnight. When he'd returned from the distillery the following day, Mrs. Grant had informed him Kate had spent the day writing. He'd assumed she'd been inspired and wanted solitude. But the following morning, she hadn't appeared at breakfast.

Then, she'd avoided him, her eyes skating away when he found her reading in the library. He'd asked if she wanted to visit the castle or ride into the village. With a faint crinkle of her nose, she'd glanced out the window. "Not today, I think," she'd murmured, gathering her shawl tighter. "Too much rain."

This morning, she'd ridden to MacPherson House without telling him; instead, he'd had to hear from Mrs. Grant that Kate had wanted to take tea with his da.

That was why he'd come. Because her withdrawal could not be borne. Yes, he'd behaved like a woman-starved, half-sotted brute. Yes, she'd claimed she wasn't vexed with him—obviously a lie. Nothing else explained her behavior.

Perhaps it would be better for her if she hated him before he left. If he never returned, she wouldn't mourn. She'd be free.

But the howling ache in his chest wouldn't go away. He couldn't stand her silence, her distance, the shadowy smudges beneath her velvety eyes. So, she must forgive him for handling her roughly. She must return to being the sweet, glowing Kate she'd been before.

It would hurt to leave her. More than he'd anticipated. More than it should. But he couldn't leave without seeing her smile one more time.

He handed his horse to one of the stable lads and entered his father's house. Warmth and the scents of wool, bread, and wood surrounded him. The smell was his childhood. He breathed deep, remembering.

"Well, now, isnae this a grand surprise." Annie emerged from the shadows beyond the staircase—the direction of the kitchen. She was grinning and wiping her hands on her apron. "Angus said ye'd come. I wasnae so certain."

Broderick frowned, shrugging out of his coat and placing his hat on the hook by the door. "Why would he say that?"

"'Tis Sunday."

He blinked. It was?

Annie arched a brow and planted her hands on her hips. "Venison and gravy? All the MacPhersons come round to eat my food and drink yer whisky?"

"Aye. Sunday. Truthfully, that wasnae why I came, though it does smell delicious, sister."

"Come. Dinnae stand there puddlin' Mrs. Urquhart's clean floors. The woman is a saint to put up with the auld man's crabbit ways, but even saints have their limits." Mrs. Urquhart was Angus's newly hired housekeeper and cook.

"I must speak with Kate," he said, wiping his boots on the rug. "Where is she?"

Annie crossed her arms. "Last I saw, she was interviewin' Da again. 'Tis the most confoundin' thing. He hasnae bellowed once. I think he likes yer lass."

"Wife." He muttered the correction before he could think better of it.

Red brows arched as bright blue eyes rounded and blinked. She drifted closer until he could smell the scent of the dough she'd been kneading. Her expression eased into tenderness as she searched his face. "Aye. She's yer wife."

Something twisted around his guts and squeezed. "Where is Rannoch?"

"He's runnin' late. Hasnae arrived yet."

"So, he hasnae been with Kate?"

"Nah. She rode here with me and John, and she's been talkin' to Da ever since." Her head tilted. "Broderick MacPherson," she breathed. "Tell me I'm nae seein' what I'm seein'."

"Can ye bluidy well answer the question, Annie? I didnae come here for—"

"Ye're jealous."

He snorted. "Rubbish."

"Aye. Possessive, too." She chuckled and shook her head. "It's like watchin' a unicorn dance a reel with an elephant durin' an eclipse, and I would have wagered every copper pot in my kitchen that it was impossible, but … there it is, plain as boiled tatties."

He ground his teeth. "Just tell me where Kate is."

"She's in the parlor with Da."

He strode to the doors on his left and thrust them open. Angus and Kate sat beside each other on one of the sofas. She was holding her teacup to her lips with a wry smile. He was holding up her sketchbook to the gray light from the window and pointing to a scribble that vaguely resembled Campbell's hound.

"There are nae wolves in Scotland, lass." The old man tapped the scribble with a gnarled forefinger. "Doesnae matter where ye position him. Nae wolves. Nae fight. Nae legend." He glanced at Broderick. "Right, laddie?"

Broderick barely heard him. His heart pounded as she finally noticed her husband standing in the doorway. Her slim shoulders tensed. Gracefully, she lowered her cup to her lap. Her lashes fanned along her pale cheeks.

"Da, I'd like to speak to my wife."

Angus closed the cover on the sketchbook and got to his feet. He crossed his arms. "Then, speak."

"Alone, if ye please."

"I think I'll stay."

Broderick approached to stare his father straight in the eye. "Alone," he repeated quietly. "If ye please."

Angus's scowl deepened. "Watch yer step, son. A maddened bull full of piss thinks to challenge when he should be mindin' his manners. Never ends well."

"I'm fine."

"Ye're nae fine."

"Angus?" Kate said softly. She touched the old man's wrist then squeezed his gnarled fingers. "It's all right. I don't mind."

Angus grunted, shot Broderick a hard stare, and gave him an even harder clap on the shoulder. "Mind yer manners," he growled. "This bull is auld and wily, son. I ken things ye havenae bothered contemplating. All of 'em vicious." A warning pat, and then he left.

Broderick closed the parlor doors before sitting on the sofa directly across from Kate, who pretended to smooth her skirts. She wore green velvet, he noticed. Bottle green with brown piping.

Absently, he rubbed his aching knee and wondered what to say. How did a man persuade the wife he hadn't wanted—the one who currently occupied every thought in his maddened mind and obsessed every inch of his broken body—to forgive him for being a broken, maddened, obsessive brute? Especially when he might leave her a widow.

"I quite like your father," she said in a tremulous voice that reminded him of the first time they'd spoken, when it had taken her a full minute to raise her gaze above his knees. "He's been remarkably patient. I may even have a solution for the scene with the wolf, though

I fear I must permit Sir Wallace the use of a dirk. It seems the *sgian-dubh*, while a venerable implement for coring fruit, is insufficient for this purpose."

"Look at me, Kate."

Her throat rippled. "Broderick," she whispered to her skirts.

"Please, lass. Look at me."

She lifted her gaze—and her misery flayed him open.

"I shouldnae have handled ye as I did," he confessed in a rush. "It frightened ye, and for that, I beg yer forgiveness." He angled closer, resting his elbows on his knees. "But forgiven or no, ye'll cease fearin' me now, ye ken?"

"Broderick." His name was a plaintive sigh.

"Should I promise not to touch ye? Is that what ye want?"

Suddenly, she shot to her feet and clapped both hands over his mouth.

"Kmmph?"

"This is not *helping*, Broderick," she gritted. "You are not helping."

Lightly, he braced his hands on her waist, which was, after all, right there within easy reach. Automatically, his thumbs began stroking her ribs, brushing the undersides of her breasts.

Her eyes slid closed, and she moaned as though he'd hurt her.

Or pleasured her.

What the devil?

Her hands slowly eased away from his mouth then began stroking his face—everywhere. His brows, his patch, his chin. Even his broken, reshaped nose. Her forehead came down to rest against his as her thumbs traced his lips. "Do you have any idea how much I ..." She panted and rocked her head against his. "I do not fear you. And nothing you did was wrong."

"Then why havenae ye spoken to me in four bluidy days?"

She leaned into him until he had no choice but to gather her into his lap. Then, she wrapped her arms around his neck and buried her face against his throat, clinging like a wee kitten to a skein of yarn. "Hold me," she murmured.

He wrapped her up tight, stroking her soft curves and wondering what in blazes was going on.

"I am afflicted, Broderick. Only a matter of time, now."

Alarm sent cold chills down his spine. She was ill? "Afflicted how?"

She sniffed, snuggled closer, and combed her fingers through his hair. "The mind infection."

The what? He searched his memory. Aye, she'd mentioned it once. Wait. Hadn't she been referring to—

"Ye're infatuated?"

"Thoroughly. One might even say ..." She shuddered against him. "In love. It's dreadful. I cannot bear to speak it aloud."

For a moment, he froze. Breathed. Rage started low in his belly and bloomed until it filled him, hotter than a kiln. "Who is it? Rannoch?"

She straightened away from him with a perplexed scowl. She glanced down to where her bosom brushed his chest. To where she currently perched in his lap, arousing him unmercifully. "Do you see Rannoch here?"

"Nah," he breathed. "So, not Rannoch."

She rolled her eyes. "No, silly man. Not your brother."

The rage dissipated as quickly as it had risen. She often had that effect on him.

"I've battled with every weapon I have," she said, snuggling back into her previous position, except now she laid her cheek against his shoulder and began stroking his ribs. "I fear the war is lost."

Air left him in a wordless whoosh. She was in love with … *him?* Bloody hell.

"Perhaps you could behave boorishly," she suggested, fussing with his waistcoat buttons. "Or cover yourself in haggis."

His arms tightened around her, his head spinning. There'd only been one eventuality worse than her refusing to forgive him. This was it.

"Lass."

"Hmm?"

"Ye shouldnae love me."

She sighed. "I know. The height of foolishness. I thought I'd been so clever. You aren't the sort to demand white soup."

White soup?

"We've nothing in common. Further, you are much too tall. Too big. Too brooding. Not my sort at all, really."

His frown deepened into a scowl.

"Yet, I can scarcely concentrate. I've decorated your drawing room eleven times in my mind, and in every iteration, I include a stag's head upon the wall." She clicked her tongue. "Do you know why? Because I dream of boasting about the prize my darling husband hunted with his mighty prowess."

"I'm missin' an eye, Kate. My prowess isnae what it once was."

She sighed. "Yes, yes. The conquered weakness will add drama, so I shall include a mention of it to my sisters. But don't you see? I should be inventing pointless nonsense songs about breakfast! I should be playing the pianoforte and dreaming about seeing *Othello* performed as an opera. I should not be simpering about my forever man!"

He knew why *he* didn't want her becoming overly attached, but he was having trouble understanding her objection. "Remind me why bletherin' about yer forever man is a bad thing."

When she pulled back again, he could see her fear, sorrowful and real. "I shall lose myself." She gave a tiny shake of her head. "I shall become someone else before I've discovered who I am. Just me. Kate. Could I have been a playwright or a novelist or some brilliant combination thereof? Nobody will ever know. From now on, I shall spend all my waking hours obsessing over your stores of liniment and wondering if you prefer turnips or potatoes."

"Mrs. MacBean keeps me well supplied with liniment. And I'll eat either neeps or tatties, but if ye give me a choice, I prefer tatties. There. No need to fash."

Her raised brow indicated how unsatisfactory his answer had been.

He tried again. "Besides, havenae ye spent the past four days workin' on yer manuscript?"

"As of this moment, Sir Wallace not only has an eye patch and a bevy of scars, he has acquired an additional foot of height and a penchant for growling."

"I dinnae growl."

She deepened her voice and mimicked his brogue flawlessly. "Aye, husband, ye do."

Amusement tugged his lips. He played with a curl near her cheek. "Ye still have him killin' a wolf. I've never so much as seen one. Mayhap ye're nae so infected as ye suppose."

"Love is a smoke raised with the fume of sighs."

"I think that's the onions ye're smellin'. Annie puts them in her gravy."

She swatted him playfully, making him laugh. The sound was odd to his own ears, the expanding warmth in his chest a foreign pleasure.

"Romeo's next line implies the smoke may clear only after the fire is allowed to burn." Like a sunrise, her gaze slowly brightened, becoming soft and rapt as it fixed upon him. "Perhaps that is my answer. I must quench my appetite so thoroughly that I exhaust myself and, thus, return to sanity."

Until that moment, he'd managed to keep his body's reactions reasonably tame. But the image of his wee wife "quenching her appetite" for him turned him hard as stone.

She licked her lips, brown eyes sparking. "Broderick, what would you say if … that is, I should like to … would you be so kind as to tolerate my constant affections? Temporarily. I think." She shook her head then nodded. "I will be quite avid until my appetite is satisfied, I'm afraid, which may be trying for you, but I don't expect it to take longer than a year or two. Perhaps three. By then, we'll likely have at least one babe, provided we don't have twins, of course, which will divert my attention somewhat and may prove helpful to our mutual cause—"

He kissed her. He couldn't help it. She was the most enchanting, bewildering, unintentionally seductive woman he'd ever known.

This woman clawed at his neck and opened her mouth to his tongue. This woman cupped his jaw and panted for more. This woman claimed to be in love with him.

Him. With all his scars. All his darkness. All she'd seen him do.

And he had to leave her. The thought twisted his guts, stoked his hunger. He crushed her to him. Reveled in her sweet moans and soft mouth. Lowered her onto the sofa so he could kiss her properly.

"Shall I take that as a yes?" she panted, hooking one of her ankles over the back of his thigh and shifting her hips until his cock settled into a heated, heavenly cradle.

"Bluidy hell, woman." He buried his face in her sweet-smelling neck. "Ye drive me mad."

Nothing had ever been like this. So intensely pleasurable, he couldn't control himself. So urgent, he couldn't allow a single inch of space between his skin and hers. So powerful, he'd felt like a suffocating man when she'd withdrawn from him for four days.

He couldn't need her this much. She couldn't love him.

The thought cooled his ardor enough to say, "We cannae do this."

"If you lock the door, no one will know."

He groaned and forced her hips to stop writhing against him. "I cannae tup ye in Da's parlor."

"Let's find a bedchamber, then, if you're going to be prudish about it."

He gathered every ounce of discipline the Bridewell had hammered into him and levered himself away from her. Then, he stood, turning his back to her. If he looked at her—the kiss-swollen lips and bone-melting beauty— he'd be tupping her in Da's parlor and damn the consequences.

Instead, he paced to the window, forcing himself to ignore the ache in his groin, the clawing sensation in his chest. Every step of distance, the pain worsened.

"What ye feel for me is lust, Kate," he lied, hardening his voice. Making it cold. "That's all. Ye're new to this, so 'tis understandable ye'd mistake it for more."

Her quiet gasp knifed him through the middle.

Nevertheless, he must make her hate him. It was for the best. "The attraction between us is strong, I grant ye. But dinnae go thinkin' it's rare. The tuppin' is like whisky. Makes yer head spin. Hardly uncommon, in my experience. 'Twill pass." He ran a hand over his jaw, feeling the ridges of the scars. "A month or two, and ye'll be sickened by the smell of liniment, vexed by the thought of seein' my face again, and wonderin' what all the fuss was about."

Behind him, he heard rustling. He squeezed his eye closed. Clenched his fist where it braced on the window casing.

He waited for her to say something. Instead, he heard the door opening. Felt the brush of air shifting. Heard it close behind her.

And felt a chill as bitterly sharp as an enemy's knife. It shocked him. Cut him. Reminded him of precisely why he must let her go.

CHAPTER THIRTEEN

K ate didn't believe in weeping. It was pointless and foolish and only ninnies cried like little children when their feelings were injured.

Which was why, after a brief bout of childish tears behind the stable, she swallowed the ache in her throat and chest, reminded herself that Huxleys thrived on a challenge, and returned to Angus's house to help Annie chop onions.

If she must shed tears, she would have a sensible reason, by God. Certainly not a cause as foolish as a humiliating, heart-bruising, soul-crushing conversation with her somewhat-husband. No, no, no.

She refused to play the lovesick fool any longer. Enough was enough.

"Katie-lass, I ken the onions are strong, but dinnae murder them. Half-inch pieces, nae mince."

Kate blinked, swiping at her cheeks with the back of her hand. "Apologies, Annie," she mumbled, taking more deliberate slices.

So, a man didn't want her. This was hardly the first time. She'd survived the previous mortifying debacle and even salvaged a lovely friendship from the ruins. She could do it all again.

Her chest tightened. Her eyes stung. A sob gathered like steam inside a sealed pot. She pressed her lips together and laid her knife on the board beside her pile of half-inch pieces.

Annie was busy ordering Mrs. Urquhart to fetch her a pint of cream, so Kate quickly untied her apron, retrieved her cloak, and slipped out the door. Behind the stable, between a pine and a willow, she let it out. The first sob was a gasp, the pain ceaseless. She leaned against rough pine bark, bent at the waist, and stopped fighting.

She'd spent four days wrestling with the notion of loving him. She'd feared losing herself, becoming daft and tedious like so many others before her. She'd paced, sleepless and hollow, missing him with every breath. She'd tried to write, wasting half a stack of paper before realizing the mind infection had infected her story, too.

That was when she'd recognized the severity of her wretched condition, the likelihood that it was permanent. Worse, she'd considered the appalling possibility he would reject her and that it might be worse than anything she'd experienced before. She'd even contemplated returning to England to spare them both. But sitting across from him in the parlor, she'd looked upon his beautiful, scarred face and known she must be bold.

This was what boldness bought her. And it wasn't just worse than before. It was worse than anything she'd imagined.

"Kate?" The deep, masculine voice from the other side of the willow was filled with concern. Rannoch's tall shadow emerged around the corner of the stable. "What's wrong?"

She covered her mouth and shook her head. She couldn't speak. Pain was crushing her lungs.

He gathered her into his arms, holding her the way she'd seen him hold Annie, with one hand on her back and the other cupping her head. "Nod if ye're injured, lass."

His coat was damp wool, cool against her hot cheek. He reminded her of Broderick sometimes, but he was leaner. Lighter. Easier. Why couldn't she have fallen in love with him?

"Aye, then. Nae injured. That leaves other sorts of wounds, the ones ye cannae see." His hand lightly rubbed her back. "Dinnae fash. Tell me who hurt ye, and I'll see them tossed in a mash tun."

Her next sob was a half-laugh.

"There, now. Ye'll be all right, lass. Once yer enemy is bellowin' about the blisters, the sweet sounds of his agony will soothe all those sore places."

She swatted his arm and wiped her nose on her sleeve. "Rannoch," she croaked. "Please d-don't tell anyone you saw me ... like this."

He handed her a linen handkerchief with an R embroidered in one corner. It was strangely clean and fine. "'Twill be our secret." He patted her back and released her. "Now, then, are ye well enough to eat? Annie's gravy is known to cure all manner of ills. A coo crushed my wee toe once. Hurt so bad, I thought the bugger might fall off. Annie fed me her gravy, and the next mornin', the toe was still there, not a bruise to be found. A miracle, it was."

By the end of his preposterous story, she released a wet chuckle. Then, she realized she'd ruined his handkerchief with her stupid tears and nose blowing. "Oh, I'm dreadfully sorry."

"Nah. Keep it. I've a dozen more."

She ran her finger over the embroidery. "Lovely. Where did you get them?"

"'Tis cold out here for a blether, lass. Let's go inside, eh?"

He seemed uncomfortable, glancing around as though expecting an attack, so she let him lead her back into the house.

Fortunately, other guests had arrived while she'd been weeping behind the stable, which kept Annie from noticing her absence. Kate blamed the onions for her red eyes and pretended she didn't have several large blades puncturing her chest. She avoided Broderick as much as possible, making a point of speaking with the pretty, blonde Mrs. Baird, Annie's dressmaker and the object of Angus's interest.

After Angus growled at Mrs. Baird for taking "too bluidy long" to arrive, the kindly woman drew Kate aside and asked how she was settling into her new home. Kate assumed her responses were adequate— Mama had trained her well.

At dinner, she sat between Angus and John, who described the amusing letter he'd received from Papa and the even more amusing one he'd received from Mama refuting everything Papa had said. She thought she chuckled in all the right places.

After dinner, she gamely drank a dram of whisky—at Angus's insistence—and laughed along with her gruff father-in-law when he teased her for taking such delicate sips.

A short while later, they all gathered in the parlor, where John, Campbell, Alexander, and Rannoch traded tales about their past dominance in the events of the Glenscannadoo Highland Games.

The cider and whisky had made Kate a bit warm, so she retreated to a spot further from the fireplace. The move was not because Broderick leaned against the mantel, she assured herself. Not at all. She simply needed a bit of air.

"Do ye plan to play the pipes next year, Broderick?" Alexander asked. "Stuart MacDonnell won last summer. We cannae claim total victory for the MacPherson clan if a ginger-haired lad with naught for a chin wins the bagpipin' contest."

"Nah," came the deep, tingle-inducing timbre Kate both craved and dreaded. "Mayhap Rannoch should have a go."

Rannoch laughed. "He said he wants to win, brother. Ye're the one with music in ye. My talents lie in impressin' the lasses with my sword … dancin'."

Music? Broderick played music? Why hadn't he mentioned it? She was his wife. She should know such things. Or perhaps not, she thought with a pang. Perhaps she didn't belong with him, and he'd known it from the start.

"Aye," Campbell replied to Rannoch. "Keep to lasses and swords. 'Tis what ye're best at."

Meanwhile, Alexander pressed Broderick. "Do ye still have the bagpipes Da gave ye?"

Silence lengthened. "Somewhere, mayhap."

"Same place as yer fiddle, eh?"

Kate half-turned, daring a glance across the room. Campbell glared at Alexander while Rannoch rubbed his nape. The brothers seemed wreathed in tension.

"'Tis full dark," Broderick said. "Best we head home."

Kate stiffened, realizing "we" meant her. She'd have to ride with Broderick. Alone. In the dark.

She forced herself to smile as she kissed Angus's cheek, hugged Annie and John, and said her farewells to Mrs. Baird and Broderick's brothers. As she donned her cloak, she gave another nod to Rannoch, a thank-you for his earlier kindness. He nodded in return, offering an encouraging grin.

It lent her courage as she avoided glancing in Broderick's direction. To her, he was a blank space, a darkened corner of the stage she could ignore in favor of more interesting players. She ducked beneath the blank space's arm as he opened the front door. A blast of icy wind burned her cheeks and made her nose prickle.

One of the stable lads held Ophelia ready for her. Another held a much larger mount. She marched toward her lovely mare and waited for the boy to help her into her saddle. He was swept aside with a grumble before two massive hands cinched on her waist.

She gasped and lurched sideways away from Broderick's touch. Breath heaving and heart seizing, she glared at the ground in front of his boots. "Do not," she begged. "Please do not."

The boots stayed planted in place for a long while. Finally, they moved toward the larger horse.

The ride home was cold, dark, and silent.

Just before the last turn up the hill, his voice cut through. "I'm sorry, lass."

So was she. Never had she been so sorry for anything.

Wind began truly howling, bending the pine trees to and fro. When a low-hanging bough whipped around suddenly, Ophelia shied and danced out of its path. Kate controlled her with steady pressure and calm reassurance. Then she heard a sharp crack. A tumbling collision. Saw heavy wood rushing down from high above.

Time distorted. Sound became a deafening roar.

The tree limb struck with such force, she scarcely felt any pain. Only the thrust. The weight. The fall.

She landed with a crushing whump. Rolled. Air collapsed outward. Wheezed inward. Gulped and gasped. Still, she didn't feel any pain. The heavy limb had struck her shoulder, she thought. Or was it her side? She didn't know. Everything was black and somehow, she was lying on the ground. Her skirts twisted around her legs, weighing them down. Wool covered her face.

Why did wool cover her face?

And what was lying on top of her? Something heavy and loud.

"Ye will answer me now!" boomed the roar. Strong, callused hands cupped her cheeks. Stroked along her neck. Slid behind her back and lifted. "Kate. Bluidy hell. Answer me!"

"Wha—what was your question?"

"Ah, God." His forehead lowered until it brushed her temple. Hot, fast breaths washed over her skin. Heated lips slid over her cheek. Hard arms lifted her high against his chest and then high above the ground. He squeezed her so hard, she wondered why she didn't feel any pain.

Shouldn't she be bruised? Hadn't the tree limb struck her? She blinked and automatically clasped his neck as he carried her with fast, hitching strides. "Broderick?"

He kept walking.

"Where is Ophelia? I don't ..." She clung harder as she began to shake. "I don't understand what happened."

"Inside. Must get ye inside, *mo chridhe.*"

She frowned. Why was he calling her "mockery"? Was she so piteous to him that he considered her a jest?

Perhaps she was. Useless, frivolous Kate. Nothing but a ninny with a head full of fancies. She drew a shuddering breath. Her shaking worsened. She buried her face against his shoulder.

Moments later, he carried her sideways through the front door. Warmth replaced the cold, and she distantly heard Mrs. Grant's reassurances that tea and whisky would be delivered straight away.

He carried her up the stairs. Down the corridor. He passed by her door and instead entered his. Even when he stood between the bed and the fireplace, he didn't set her down. Rather, he sat with her on his lap, crushing her against him until her breathing shallowed.

"Broderick?" she wheezed.

His grip loosened marginally. "Aye."

"What happened?"

"A limb broke loose. Almost struck ye."

"Is Ophelia injured?"

"Dinnae ken. She ran off."

"How did I ..." She swallowed. "You saved me, didn't you?"

"I'll be fellin' every tree along the lane tomorrow. Every bluidy one."

She tried to pull back and look at his face, but he held her too tightly, his chin resting upon her hair.

"This willnae happen again." He ran his hands over her back, her legs. His touch was smooth yet methodical. He was checking her for injuries. "Ye must be safe, *mo chridhe*. I cannae keep my sanity unless I ken ye're safe."

Again, with the "mockery." She didn't understand him.

He began to undress her, and she squirmed to escape. He grunted as she shoved against his chest and struggled to stand. Then she caught a glimpse of his expression. It reminded her of the first night she'd seen him—a beast in the grip of madness.

He made her heart pound.

Her hesitation allowed him time to remove her half-boots and strip away her cloak. A white scrap of linen flew onto the carpet as he tossed the cloak toward a bench near the window.

He frowned. Focused upon the white cloth. His head tilted in a predatory fashion.

She used the distraction to scramble off his lap and stumble away, bumping against the washstand.

A knock sounded at the door. Mrs. Grant entered with a tray, and Janet followed with blankets and a gown. Both wore worried frowns.

As the two women fussed over Kate, insisting she drink whisky-laced tea and wrap herself in wool, Kate only wanted to know one thing: "Is my horse all right?"

"Dinnae fash yerself," Mrs. Grant soothed. "Connor has her right and sound in the stable. Poor beastie has a scrape on her flank, but otherwise, she only suffered a wee fright. Appears the saddle took the brunt of it."

Relieved, Kate went limp, collapsing onto the chair near the fireplace. Janet unpinned her hair and brushed the curls with gentle strokes. "There, now," she murmured. "I've brought yer dressing gown. Shall I help ye prepare for bed?"

"Leave us," Broderick said. He'd removed his coat, Kate noticed. He stood with his back turned in a dark corner near the window.

The two women obeyed his command, closing the bedchamber door behind them.

In the silence, the fire crackled and popped. She placed her teacup on the washstand and gathered her blanket tighter around her shoulders. "It's late. I should retire to my bedchamber."

"Stay," he said roughly. His fists were clenched, his neck tense.

She swallowed, her throat burning. "Thank you for saving me. From the sound of it, if you hadn't knocked me to the ground, I might have been very badly injured."

"Killed." The word was a harsh grind. "Ye would have died, lass."

"Yes. Likely true." She licked her lips. "I'm very grateful, Broderick."

If anything, his tension increased. She watched the muscles in his arms, shoulders, and back tighten until they vibrated.

"Not bluidy good enough."

She blinked.

"I meant to do the right thing," he continued. "I meant to leave ye here, happy to be rid of me."

Granted, it had been a difficult night, but he wasn't making sense. She glanced at her cup. She hadn't had *that* much whisky, had she?

"Pain is nothin', I thought. But that pain and this pain arenae the same. Christ, they arenae on the same continent." His voice was raw, his arm flexing as though he were clenching his fist over and over. "So, I'll keep ye, *mo chridhe*. I'll keep ye, and ye'll be mine."

A strange, pulsing wave moved through her.

"'Tis selfish, I ken. To take my pleasure with ye, to demand yer love and expect ye to take me as yer own. I might leave ye with bairns. I might break yer wee heart. Selfish, aye. I'm a blackhearted bastard. I've nae excuses."

Her own heart clenched so hard, she covered it with her palm.

"By God, I've sacrificed everythin' for nothin'. And I want one bluidy thing for myself. One precious thing."

"Broderick?"

"Mayhap ye prefer Rannoch. Too bad."

"I—I don't."

"Ye're *my* wife," he snarled as though he didn't hear her. "Ye'll sleep in my bed. Ye'll take my cock into yer body and grow my bairns in yer womb." His voice was pure gravel, his breathing harsh. He still hadn't turned to look at her. "Ye'll resign yerself to lovin' only me, and nae for two or three years, lass. Forever. Do ye ken?"

It took her several deep breaths to speak. "This is … quite the reversal."

"Aye, well. If God expects a man to be honorable, He shouldnae send the devil to break him."

Her chest ached. "Broderick, I'm so confused."

Finally, he turned. His eye was pure fire. "Nah. Ye ken just fine." He opened one of his fists, revealing the handkerchief Rannoch had given her.

"Th-that was … Rannoch only offered it because I was distraught." She scowled, remembering why. "After you assured me my affections were unwanted and foolish. And *commonplace*. Let us not forget that."

He tossed the scrap of linen away and came toward her. "I must leave for Edinburgh."

Reeling at the sudden change of topic, she shook her head. "Edinburgh? Whatever for?"

"Lockhart is there. I have reports from two contacts that his sister has returned to their townhouse, and his business partner has amassed a large sum of money. I must find him before he launches his next attack."

Her stomach sank. Her arms went limp. "When do you leave?"

"We. Ye're comin' with me."

As she struggled to absorb the abrupt shift in her husband, he moved close and lowered his towering frame into a crouch, bracing his hands on the arms of her chair. It put his face roughly level with hers. Her knees brushed his abdomen.

"I'm not certain that's a good idea," she said softly.

"Nah, it's not. But I must keep ye with me, else go mad."

"No, I meant you shouldn't go. What do you plan to do once you find him?"

He shrugged.

"Broderick," she breathed. "If you kill him, they will put you back into that prison. They might hang you."

"Aye, they might. But it must be done."

She clutched her blanket harder, her fingers strangling the wool.

"Bringin' ye with me changes my plans a wee bit," he continued calmly. "I'll have to recruit Campbell and Alexander to come, too. A half-dozen stout men besides. Mayhap more. Ye'll be safe, so long as ye mind what I tell ye."

"I cannot let you do this." Already, the thought of him returning to the place where he'd received his scars sent clawing urgency through her. She grasped one of his hands, squeezing his fingers hard enough to bruise. "I will not lose you that way."

"Who says I'll be caught, lass?"

The pressure inside her eased marginally. A frown tugged.

The beginnings of a smile curved his mouth. "The first time they tossed me into the Bridewell, I didnae see Lockhart comin'. He stayed well hidden. I couldnae anticipate his attack, nor predict what he might do next. Matters are altogether different now." His thumb stroked the back of her hand. "This time, he'd do well to fear me."

"Please." She squeezed her eyes closed and clenched her teeth against a welling cry. "Broderick. I can't lose you."

"Have some faith in yer husband."

"Husband." She shook her head. "Suddenly, you want me as your wife."

"Oh, I do. Enough to make the devil blush."

She opened her eyes. "Yet, you claimed only hours ago that what we have is far from rare—"

"Aye. All pure rubbish."

"Rubbish? Broderick, you've tried more than once to rid yourself of me."

"To protect ye."

"From Lockhart?"

His gaze, still burning oddly in the low firelight, heated her cheeks as it traced over her face, lowered to her throat and then her bosom. "Aye. Him. But truthfully, lass? More from me." His voice thickened to a rasp. "I'm nae the man I once was. Everybody mistakes that. They think I still have light in the dark places, ye ken? Mayhap if I did, I'd be worthy of ye. I'd be able to love ye easy. Soft. God knows ye deserve it, *mo chridhe*."

She grasped his hand in both of hers and brought it to her lips. Kissed his knuckles over and over. "I didn't fall in love with a soft man. I fell in love with you." Tears wetted her fingers and his. "Now, I concede I made a cake of myself over you, but please stop calling me a mockery."

A rusty laugh burst from him. He shook his head. "The term is *mo chridhe*. 'Tis Gaelic."

"Oh." She sniffed. "What does it mean?"

"My heart."

A shower of tingles dappled her skin. "Oh." She drew his hand to her chest and held it over her own heart. "Broderick?"

"Hmm?"

"You really want me?"

"If ye're feelin' fine, I could show ye."

"No, I mean ..." Looking down at where she clutched his fingers, she gathered her courage. "You mentioned forever." She raised her eyes and let him heat her with the fire in his. "That's a long time."

His nose flared. His arm curved around her back and slid her close. "Not long enough."

He said it with such ferocity, she almost believed him. Her heart wanted to. It leapt and twirled. It danced like the daftest ninny.

"Now, for the past wee bit, ye've been sleepin' elsewhere. There'll be nae more of that." He unfastened the hooks at the back of her gown then scooped her up from the chair and transferred her to the bed as easily as he might move a pillow. "Yer place is with me."

Breathless and more than a little warm, Kate threw aside her blankets and propped herself up on her elbows. "Broderick, perhaps—"

"Earlier, I said things that wounded ye. 'Tis natural ye'll be vexed for a time." He straightened to remove his waistcoat. "But if ye ever seek comfort with Rannoch again, I'll make him swallow those teeth he's so proud of."

"No, that's not—"

"Then, I'll break his ribs. And his fingers. All of 'em." He drew his shirt off over his head with a quick motion.

Thought ceased. Aching heat surged. She'd nearly forgotten how magnificent he was.

"I'll win yer heart again, *mo chridhe*." He dispensed with his boots, trousers, and drawers. "I'll make ye glad ye're mine."

He already had. His nakedness lit her on fire. Good heavens, how was it possible she had taken him into her body? He was massive, his manhood thick as her wrist, long, hard, presently swollen with heavy, pulsing veins, and rising proudly from his groin.

While she studied his scarred body with utter fascination, he gently undressed her—first her gown, then her petticoats and corset. He left her shift in place but removed her stockings to carefully examine her legs, arms, and hips for bruising. By the time he drew back the coverlet and sheet to tuck her in and lie down beside her, she was aching everywhere. Immediately, she reached for him.

"Are ye comfortable, lass?" He gathered her close, sharing his heat.

"Hmm." She nuzzled his neck, absorbing the cooling scent of him like a balm for her battered spirit. "A bit warm, I think. Perhaps you should remove my shift."

His breath caught as she wriggled her hips and widened her legs to allow his hardness to settle between her thighs. He grunted. "Ye've had a rough night. Mayhap ye'd rather sleep."

She used his thick, muscular neck to drag herself higher and closer, plastering her bosoms against the hard ridges of his chest. Her nipples ached, tight and needy. Her thighs wanted his hands. Her melting center wanted his tongue. Every part of her wanted every part of him.

Had he bruised her feelings? Yes. But he'd also saved her. And most importantly, he wanted her. She hadn't realized quite how perfectly that missing piece would fit the yawning crags of her emptiness.

"I shall sleep better naked," she purred.

He huffed—nearly a laugh—then groaned as she ran her thumbs across his nipples. "Christ on the cross. Will ye leave me no control, my bonnie Kate?"

She nibbled his chin, licked a bead of sweat from his throat. "None whatever. Are you certain you wish to keep such a brazen wife?"

He stripped off her shift with a frantic sweep. "Bluidy hell," he gritted, rolling her onto her back and running callused palms over her naked breasts. "Ye're so damned beautiful." His thumbs circled her nipples, the pressure firm and dragging. "Look how ye are. Pink as a summer berry. Ripe and sweet for me."

She arched into the waves of sparking pleasure he drew with repeated passes of his fingers and palms. Firelight painted him black and gold as he lowered his head to capture one tip in his mouth.

Distantly, she heard wind howling at the window, fire snapping in the hearth. She saw the coppery red of MacPherson wool and the wadded white of her shift on the foot of the bed.

But all she felt was his mouth. His teeth. His strength and hardness and heat. She wrapped her legs around his waist and dug her fingers into the lush black of his hair. Pleasure rushed in upon her from all directions. His tongue swirling, his fingers squeezing, his weight pressing. And his hard stalk riding between their bodies, the tip seeking her center.

"Broderick," she panted as he moved his mouth to her other breast. "I want to touch you."

He ignored her, continuing his suckling and nibbling and stroking as if it were the only task he'd ever felt obligated to complete.

"Dear God," she moaned, grinding her hips to try to force the tip of his shaft to lodge where it belonged. "This is madness. I want to be on top."

More suckling, deeper and harder this time. Another nibble, rougher and sharper. The ping of sensation sizzled down to her core.

She gasped. "Broderick! I demand to be on top."

He squeezed one of her nipples with near-painful pressure.

She arched. Her sheath rippled and seized. Pleasure exploded so suddenly, all she could do was writhe and scream and grit her teeth like she'd been struck by lightning. The waves battered her, and still, he wouldn't let up.

Her body gripped and wept, empty of what it most wanted.

In the storm, she grew frantic. She clawed at his shoulders. Her heels dug into his back. "Need you," she begged. "Let me … on top. Need you."

Firmly, he gripped her thigh. Pushed her leg up. Then, he pushed himself up, sitting back on his heels and gripping her hips, sliding her up onto his thighs while her arms spread wide to grip the blanket.

"What are you doing?" she murmured, marveling at the stark tension in his chest, arms, and face. His eye burned with obsessive lust. Sweat coated him. Between her widespread thighs, his manhood arched upward along his belly. Flushed and dark, it glistened on the rounded tip. He gripped the massive stalk hard—harder than she'd imagined might be pleasurable—stroked several times and forced the tip down to touch her where she most needed him. Damp and blunt, it kissed the jewel at her center. First gently. Then firmly.

Waves of intense sensation rippled outward, stoking her need once again. She shook her head. Begged him to come inside her. He didn't reply. Didn't stop. Just played with her body like a great, beastly lion playing with its helpless prey.

"Broderick," she growled. "Enough. I cannot … please … I need you."

The first time they'd lain together, he'd been similarly unrelenting. He'd pleasured her until she'd begged. He'd taken her to heights she hadn't imagined then forced her higher. Like a man possessed, he did the same now.

He stared down at where his body caressed hers, swirling and pleasuring and making her shamefully wet. And he didn't seem to hear her pleas.

She tried to rise on her elbows, to reach for him, but he grasped her thighs and spread them wider, pulled her higher. Then, he slid his thumb down through her folds, gathering moisture. He placed his thumb in his mouth, closing his eye and groaning.

She nearly peaked at the sight of his pleasure. "Good God," she sobbed. "I don't know how you do this to me."

He did it again. And again. Then he painted her nipples with her own juices. And she did peak again. Her belly rippled and writhed as her core convulsed for want of being filled.

Just as she began to relax, he tucked the head of his cock against her greedy opening and pushed. Oh, she remembered this. The impossible stretch. The aching fullness. The incredulity that her body could take his inside. But just as before, she wanted him so badly, nothing mattered but the urgency. The mad desire to merge with him. To bring him ease. Pleasure. Contentment. To drain his body of its seed, which belonged to her.

Only her.

She watched his face as he watched himself entering her. Rapt. Savage. He couldn't disguise what he felt in this moment, for nothing remained of his usual control. She felt it in the grip of his hands and the urgency of his thrusts. After the first few, they went from slow and steady to hard. Fast. The rhythm stuttered as his body jerked, seemingly in the grip of ferocious forces.

The friction of his body pumping deep inside hers built a fiery pressure. She looked down at her flagrantly hard, red nipples, her white belly undulating and shivering with tension, her slick thighs spread wide around him.

She watched with sheer erotic pleasure his big, scarred body invading hers. Taking hers. Loving hers.

"Come for me," he rasped, his eye now focused upon her face. He looked maddened. Desperate. "Let me feel ye, *mo chridhe.*"

Like a flame to kindling, his words sparked an explosion. The pressure flared out and convulsed inward. Repeated. Repeated. Her cries echoed amidst the wind and fire. Ecstasy burst open, cascading all around her in shades of copper, gold, and black.

"Good lass," he whispered. He stroked her belly. Caressed her breast, which heaved with her exertions. Then, he scooped her up until she sat astride him, filled so deeply, she could scarcely breathe.

With arms as limp as spent blooms, she clung to him and mewled in vague distress. Pleasure like this shouldn't be possible. She still rippled around him, unable to stop her body from continuing to milk his.

"Hold on to me, ye ken?"

She nodded, helplessly kissing his throat and shoulder and jaw. Bristles scraped her lips, making them tingle.

His arms tightened. He lifted her, withdrawing a few inches and returning with a forceful thrust.

She gasped.

He did it twice more before the rhythm quickened. Faster. Faster. His hips worked her at a galloping pace. Because of his angle, each pass dragged across her pleasure-swollen nub, and another impossible peak loomed.

"Broderick," she sobbed. "I can't … again. Oh, God."

But she did. He stiffened, rammed deep, and roared his pleasure, flooding her with his seed. His groans rumbled through her as he spasmodically thrust and released. Thrust and released. Thrust and released. The scalding joy of his peak tipped her body into another of her own. This one was long and less sharp but no less satisfying.

By God, her husband was brilliant.

Someday, she would ask where he'd learned to perform such bewitching sorcery, but for now, she could only cling. Breathe. Savor his arms around her and his harsh breaths in her ear.

He stroked her back and smoothed her curls for a long while before his ragged voice rumbled, "M'lady demanded to be on top. I do hope m'lady is pleased."

Startled, she burst out laughing. The giggles took her by storm.

"Ah, now ye've done it, my bonnie Kate." He grinned down at her, stroking her cheek with the tenderest expression. Inside, she felt him begin to harden again. "We'll never get any sleep now."

Hours later, Kate awakened from a deep slumber. The room was still dark, the only light a faint glow from the coals remaining in the fireplace. Wind howled. Rain pelted the windows in long bursts. Her bed was soft and too warm, but she felt oddly chilled, as though she'd had a nightmare. Blankets covered her. She was naked, but they were piled ridiculously thick.

Slowly, she blinked. A chuffing sound came from her right. A grunt. A soft, queer grate like grinding teeth. Groggily, she brushed her mass of hair from her eyes and shoved at the copious blankets so she could turn over.

There, at the edge of the bed, lay her husband. She could just make out the line of his shoulder, the white of his massive body amidst deep shadow. His back was to her. Broad and rippling with tension, it bore the marks of lashes he'd taken in prison. Like her, he was naked. Unlike her, he had no blankets. And he was shivering, his body quaking in bursts like the ones driving rain against the windows.

The grinding came again. His teeth, she realized. He grunted. Huddled tighter.

Instantly, she began tugging several of her blankets free. Why had he piled them upon her? Good heavens, he must be freezing. Frantic, she crawled to him and threw the blankets across his body.

The grinding stopped.

It wasn't enough. She must get him warm *now*. She slid a hand down his arm. God. His skin was ice. "Broderick," she murmured in his ear. "Turn on your back, my darling."

He didn't awaken, but somehow, he did seem to hear her. His face angled toward her.

Heart seizing with concern, she crawled atop him, flattening her body across his and tugging several more blankets over them both. Feeling his face with her hands, she traced his scars. Nuzzled his throat and kissed his jaw. "You mustn't do this again," she whispered, scarcely aware of what she was saying. "When you are cold, I shall warm you. Your place is with me. Not there. Here."

What was she babbling on about? Still half-asleep, she didn't really know. The words welled up from nowhere. "You must stay with me forever. That was your promise. That I could love you forever." Her throat tightened as she heard him sigh. Felt his shivering begin to ease. "You're not there any longer. You are *here.*" She held him, kissed him mindlessly. Instinctively. "And when you sleep, I shall be your blanket."

He drew in a shuddering breath and sighed it out. His arms circled her. His lips nuzzled her hair. "Cold," he slurred.

He was still asleep. She could tell by the way he breathed.

She stroked his hair and kissed his lips. "Not for long, my darling. I am here."

Another sigh, this one relieved. "Here, *mo chridhe.* With me."

Holding him as tightly as she dared, she laid her cheek in the crook of his shoulder. Their shared warmth gradually lulled his muscles to relax and his breathing to deepen. As she, too, drifted toward sleep, she dreamt the strangest sounds: the slow drip of water on stone, the clattering clank of a key turning in a lock, the call of gulls, the din of men, and wind whistling through iron bars.

CHAPTER FOURTEEN

A pair of birds landed at Sabella's feet. Ravens. One let out a screech. She skirted past them to continue toward the post office.

To punish Sabella, Kenneth meant to kill Annie. Sabella must stop him. She must warn Annie.

Her heart thrashed in her chest as she quickened her pace. The ravens followed, flapping their wings and cawing at one another.

She glanced behind her. The hour was early, and only a few pedestrians lined this end of George Street. Still, Kenneth was having her watched. She knew his sense of betrayal had not diminished while she'd cared for him. He didn't trust her. In fact, the moment he'd recovered sufficiently, he'd left their house in Charlotte Square to sleep elsewhere. But he often visited without warning, and all the servants in the household reported to him, which effectively made her home a prison.

She thought perhaps her lady's maid might be loyal to her, but the lass was so fearful, she didn't know whether to trust her. Which was why Sabella must post her own letters and fight her own battles.

Another glance behind her, a scan of the street. She turned a corner and hurried toward the small building next to a tea shop. The nuisance birds followed. One of them boldly plucked at her skirt. She gasped, veering away before the creature damaged the silk. The second bird screeched and launched into the air, forcing her back into a doorway. She was about to swipe away the bird who'd plucked at her gown when the door behind her opened and a barrel-chested man with a whiskered face and stern demeanor exited. He turned with his back to the street and braced her elbow.

"Pardon, miss." He tipped his hat. "I didnae see ye there."

She gave a nod. "My fault entirely." Automatically, she patted her silk reticule, taking comfort from the crackle of paper inside. "I'm in a wee bit of a rush."

The man's gaze lingered upon her face, a frown creasing his deep brow.

Sabella was accustomed to men staring at her, but this one's gaze was probing. Almost as if he recognized her.

Panic fluttered in her chest. What if Kenneth had hired him? She glanced at the tobacconist's shop behind her then at the pouch of snuff in his hand. Her suspicions eased slightly, but he continued staring.

"Well, I shall bid you good day, sir."

He seemed to gather himself then tipped his hat with a polite nod. She rushed past him, driven by merciless urgency to post her letter and return home before Kenneth learned of her outing.

She posted the letter with trembling hands, shaking so badly that the clerk asked if she was well. Nodding with a jerk, she said nothing else before exiting the post office with a pounding heart and fast breaths.

Relief warred with fear. What if Kenneth discovered her treachery? Would he kill her?

Oh, God. The old Sabella would have laughed at such a thought. Kenneth adored her. Spoiled her. Yes, occasionally, he'd bruised her wrists or arms in a fit of pique, even seeming to enjoy her pain. And she'd long known she must take care not to spark his temper. But he'd always expressed regret for his lapses in control, sometimes apologizing with a lovely necklace or a rare breed of rose.

The new Sabella hated knowing the truth. Kenneth *would* kill her. And she was playing with fire to warn Annie of his plans. But what else could she do? Annie had been her friend when she'd been utterly alone.

Nerves quaked beneath her skin as she examined the street. A carriage approached from the west. She mustn't be seen. Spinning in place, she scrambled toward the tea shop, praying it was open at this early hour.

Just as she reached for the door, a man's gloved hand got there first.

She looked up. Her stomach sank.

The whiskered man pulled open the door and tilted his head. "Miss Lockhart. I am Sergeant Neil Munro of the Inverness constabulary. I believe ye and I should have a chat."

Broderick had intended to begin his campaign of Kate persuasion immediately. But his wee, bonnie wife turned his scheme back upon him with ruthless enchantment. The morning after he'd staked his claim upon her, she awakened him by kissing all the scars on his face. And his arms. And his shoulders. And his belly.

Two hours later, after a long session of lovemaking and a rare doze, he awakened a second time to the sounds of his wee, bonnie wife singing as she carried a breakfast tray to the bedside table.

"When the sun rose this morning, I first said, 'Tea's the sole reason I'll leave this bed.' Yet not even for a cup could I rouse myself up, foooooorrr 'tis too lovely to lie here and wallow, though my stomach be noisy and hollow." She turned in a theatrical spin, to drape a napkin across the pile of blankets on his thighs. *"Until I recalled what was once said, that stoats on the hunt must be well fed."* She waggled her eyebrows. *"Lest he wither and flag, I bring smoked haddock and eggs. Aaaaaannnnd, I've been told the dear creature likes petting, if only he weren't hiding 'midst the bedding —"*

He chuckled and rolled to the edge of their bed, snagging her around the waist and pulling her into his lap. She squealed and wriggled and laughed.

"Two problems, lass. 'Flag' and 'eggs' dinnae rhyme." He made sure she felt his readiness. "Secondly, this dear creature is always primed for the hunt."

She cupped his jaw, kissed him with a glowing smile, and traced her fingertips lovingly over the puckered flesh where his eye had once been.

Only then did he realize she'd removed his eye patch sometime during the night. Vaguely, he recalled her worrying that wearing it for too long must irritate his skin. It did, but he hadn't wanted to subject her to the sight of his worst scars. He still didn't understand how she could look upon him without a trace of revulsion. But she appeared only enchanted. Attracted. Appreciative.

He'd never been so hungry for a woman's desire as he was for hers.

They spent the entire day pleasuring one another. He left their bedchamber once to send a message to his brothers, but otherwise, she held him spellbound.

He'd intended it to be the other way around.

The second day, he spent a full quarter-hour away from her while delivering orders to his men for clearing the trees along the lane and securing the house while he was away. Then, Kate lured him into the drawing room to describe her intended changes.

"The stag must have a minimum of twelve points," she explained, gesturing to the stone above the fireplace. Her arms swept in wide arcs as she gracefully twirled like a stage performer. She cast him a teasing grin over her shoulder. "Can you manage that, husband?"

He locked the doors. "Let me show ye what I can manage, lass."

The third day, he controlled his lust enough to prepare for the journey to Edinburgh. While Kate and her maid packed, he discussed logistics with Campbell and Alexander, recruited five of his most capable men to accompany them, and met with Thomson to revise his will and set aside funds for his wife.

The fourth day, he loaded Kate and her three trunks into a wagon and headed to Glendasheen Castle to borrow John and Annie's travel coach. Part of his plan to woo his wee, bonnie wife involved making good use of their trip. He would learn everything that pleased her. He would keep her comfortable, happy, and safe. Then, she would want to stay with him. She would trust him with her heart.

Because right now, she didn't.

He saw it in her uncertain glances. The way she nibbled her lip and wound a curl around her finger as she rode beside him. Her nervous chatter about how splendid the loch was even on overcast days. "We haven't anything to compare in Nottinghamshire," she said. "And London?" She shook her head. "The entertainments are dazzling, true, but the smells are far from majestic."

"What was it like for ye there?" he asked.

"Oh, lovely enough, I suppose."

When she didn't elaborate, he frowned. "Ye fancy the theatre, aye? London has many."

"Yes."

"Kate."

"Hmm?"

"What's wrong?"

She turned so he could see her face past the brim of her bonnet. Her eyes were shadowed. Wistful. She hugged his arm and snuggled closer against his side. "Nothing whatever. A bit chilled is all."

When they reached the castle and he lifted her down, her smile was bright. But something lay beneath. Uncertainty.

He hated her uncertainty. He wanted to erase every bit.

Campbell and Alexander emerged from the stable, followed by Rannoch. Broderick stiffened as Kate greeted all three with a cheerful wave.

"What are ye doin' here?" he asked his youngest brother.

Rannoch cocked his chin to a challenging angle. "I'm comin' with ye."

"Nah. Ye're not."

As Rannoch approached, Broderick tucked Kate closer. Campbell and Alexander looked on with wry amusement.

Kate patted the hand squeezing her waist. "If you attack him, I shall be very cross, Broderick."

He gritted his teeth. "Rannoch, ye should stay here. Guard Annie and Da."

"Da can take care of himself. And Annie's bein' well-guarded by the ten new men Huxley hired." Rannoch crossed his arms. "'Tis you who needs my help."

"I need ye like I need a thistle in my boot."

"Well, now, thistles can be useful from time to time, brother. Keeps the lordly sorts from venturin' where they arenae wanted."

Kate tugged on his sleeve until he bent down. "Let him come along."

He shook his head, his gut burning.

"Broderick." His name was a gentle chide. "You have *no reason whatever* to refuse his help, I promise you."

He understood her reassurance, but it didn't lessen the grinding resentment.

"Och, if it isnae all my blackhearted brothers in one place!" From across the stable yard, Annie's voice carried on a wave of sisterly amusement. "And my favorite sister-in-law."

Kate laughed. "I am your only sister-in-law."

"Aye, but ye count twice, Katie-lass." Annie grinned and embraced them all. "Come inside and warm yerselves before the frost freezes yer nether bits."

A short while later, Broderick stood in Annie's kitchen watching her pack two loaves of bread and a wedge of cheese into a basket for their trip. Campbell, Alexander, and Rannoch were busy loading weapons and supplies into the wagon. Kate was speaking with her brother in his study. Broderick rested an elbow on the back of his chair and studied his sister. Her cheeks were fuller, and when she turned to begin slicing venison, he saw the swell of her bairn beneath her gown.

What would Kate look like when she carried his child in her womb? Would he live to see it? His teeth gritted as hollow pain warred with fledgling hope.

"She's good for ye, brother," Annie said, wiping her hands on a towel and wrapping the sliced meat in paper. "Mrs. MacBean thinks she's the reason ye stayed."

He frowned. "Stayed?"

Blue eyes met his. "Aye. She says yer soul kenned ye had a bride waitin'. I said, 'Nah. He's just that stubborn.'"

He huffed out a chuckle.

"But our wee Katie-lass does light ye up; that much is certain." Annie rubbed her lower back and sat in the chair across from him. She stretched out a hand, and he took it in his own. "I've had another letter, Broderick."

Alarm rang through him. His fingers tightened on hers. "When?"

"Two days past."

"What did it say?"

Annie's eyes went glossy. She squeezed his fingers and swallowed, visibly gathering her composure. "He kens ye've married. He kens ye love her."

Broderick shoved away from the table. Flew to his feet. Ran both hands through his hair. Paced to the hearth. "She must stay here at the castle. I'll leave the men and go alone to Edinburgh. I'll kill him. That will end it."

"No. Ye must do as ye planned. Ye must protect her *and* yerself."

"I dinnae bluidy matter!" he shouted.

"Aye, ye bluidy do!" she shouted back. "Use yer head. If she's here, she's where he expects her to be. 'Twill be as easy as sendin' a huntin' party to track a coo in a fenced pasture."

Urgency thrummed through his body. He closed his eye. Tried not to picture Kate being hunted. Being violated. Being slaughtered the way Magdalene had been slaughtered. God, he wanted to vomit.

He felt Annie behind him, her hand upon his back. "This is no surprise," she murmured. "We kenned the evil livin' inside him. Follow yer plan. Take her to Edinburgh. Nobody will protect her more fiercely than you." She patted his arm. "Take Rannoch, too."

"I dinnae want to."

"I dinnae care. Ye need him." This time, her pat was more of a swat. "Stop bein' a jealous dafty and do what's sensible."

His fists flexed. "I'm nae the jealous sort."

She snorted and pulled away. "With other lasses, I'd agree. The instant Florence Cockburn or Lucie Robertson fluttered their lashes in another lad's direction, ye were naught but a cloud of dust. For years,

I thought ye were a wee bit coldhearted, truth be told. But with Kate? Ye're so bluidy jealous, ye've gone blind."

He ground his teeth, willing it to go away.

"There's nothin' for ye to fash about," Annie assured him. "Katie doesnae fancy Rannoch."

He wouldn't ask. He wouldn't. "How do ye ken?" Damn and blast.

"She told me. Before she met ye, she apologized for thinkin' Rannoch was too tall and coarse for her likin'."

Frowning, he glanced at his sister, who had her hands planted on her hips. "I'm taller than Rannoch."

"Aye."

"And my manners are nae better. Mayhap worse since the Bridewell."

A red brow arched. "Aye. And yet, whenever ye're near, she's sighin' and watchin' ye and sniffin' the air round ye like a daft, moony lamb."

"So, she doesnae fancy him."

"Bluidy hell." She swatted his arm with typical Annie force. "No! She doesnae fancy him! Take him with ye and, for God's sake, quit natterin' about it!"

He couldn't help grinning at her show of temper. Annie's hair wasn't the only fiery thing about her.

She loaded several more items into the basket she was preparing and said in a softer tone, "One last thing, Broderick."

"Aye?"

Fastening the basket's lid, she took a deep breath and met his gaze. "Sabella. If it isnae too much trouble, see she isnae harmed."

Twice, the brittle beauty had helped them at great risk to her own safety. Annie didn't have to ask, but he nodded anyway.

An hour later, he gave instructions to Jack Murray, the coachman John had lent him to drive the oversized black travel coach, and the footman, Stuart MacDonnell. Broderick's men and his three brothers mounted their horses and positioned themselves around the carriage. Broderick looked around for his wife and found her near the castle doors, arguing with a wildly gesticulating Mrs. MacBean.

Broderick frowned as he crossed the yard. The old woman thrust a leather pouch into Kate's hands.

"… ye'll be thinkin' push when ye should be thinkin' pull. Ye ken?"

His sweet wife nodded as though the madwoman made perfect sense. "Pull instead of push. Of course."

"Aye, there's a good lass. That spoon is straight from Holland with no stops in between. The salve is for when ye find yer miracle. The knot willnae be loosened unless ye cut it free."

"Er, Mrs. MacBean, I really must be off—"

The old woman seized Kate's wrist. "Wait for the gulls. They'll tell ye when morning's come. Wait for his song. That's when 'tis time to wake."

Kate clasped Mrs. MacBean's hand and nodded, which appeared to calm the madwoman. Mrs. MacBean threw her arms around her, whispered something in her ear, and then released her to disappear into the castle.

When Kate reached his side, he asked, "What was that about?"

She shook her head. "Either a great deal of nonsense or …" She frowned at the leather drawstring pouch in her hand. "Well. Probably a great deal of nonsense." After bidding John and Annie farewell, she smiled up at Broderick and patted his chest. "Shall we?"

He opened the carriage door. "M'lady."

She climbed onto the step and paused. Turned. Grasped his coat in her fist and pulled him close. Then she kissed him with shocking intensity. "I prefer Mrs. MacPherson," she whispered against his lips.

As she ducked inside, he struggled to slow his heart. "As do I, lass," he murmured. "More than I should."

Kate expected Broderick to ride outside the coach with his brothers. Instead, he spent most of their first traveling day seated beside her, offering his warmth when she was cold, his arms when she was weary, and his company when she desired it.

To be clear, she desired it—desired *him*—constantly. The mind infection was all-consuming in that regard.

Their conversations meandered from one topic to the next much like a river flowing through flat terrain— easily, lazily, naturally. At first, mindful of Janet's presence on the opposite seat, she kept to polite subjects. His opinion regarding haggis. His recommendations for the wolf scene in her story. The efficacy of the *sgian-dubh* as a weapon of last resort.

He answered with patient consideration, as though she were someone of great importance, and he must be thorough in his responses: "I've had good haggis and bad. The good is a fair treat. The bad is best avoided. But if ye have no likin' for it, lass, we'll nae be servin' it at our table."

And, "I dinnae see why ye cannae include a wolf in yer story. 'Tis fiction, aye? A wolf adds a wee bit of danger. Makes yer hero seem more of a legend. Now, if he's to dispatch a predator, ye might consider addin' a hound as his companion. Campbell's would be a good model. I'll introduce ye when we return home. Also, give him a second dirk. A well-armed Scot lives longer."

And, "Well, now, a *sgian-dubh* is more than a wee blade. *Dubh* means 'black,' or, in this case, 'hidden.' That's its purpose. To be tucked away and used when better weapons have failed ye. 'Tis in the name Glenscannadoo, as well. Roughly speaking, 'tis from the Gaelic, *gleann an sgàthan dubh*, valley of the black mirror. Some say the glen is where our world and the next overlap, a window for ghosties and faeries and such. Dinnae ken about that. More likely, the name refers to Glenscannadoo and Glendasheen being reflections of one another."

He spoke so freely, she scarcely recognized him as the man she'd married, or even the one who'd awakened her that very morning with erotic commands and thrusting pleasure. The Broderick she knew was far from forthcoming.

But, how well did she know him? Not well enough. With that in mind, she took her next opportunity to remedy the situation.

Four hours into their journey, while changing horses at their second coaching inn, Janet moved outside to sit with Stuart on the coach's rear bench. And Kate began a campaign to acquaint herself with the man she loved.

"Is it true you play music?" she inquired as he tucked another blanket around her.

He stilled. Sat back. "I did."

"The bagpipes, yes?"

"Aye."

"And the fiddle."

Silence.

"I should love to hear you play," she offered, noting his tension. "I should also love to know why you haven't mentioned it before now."

For a while, he stared out the coach window at the brown hills covered in bare trees. Finally, he looked at her. "Music doesnae live inside me any longer, *mo chridhe*."

Her heart cracked in two. "Broderick," she whispered. "How can that be?"

"The Bridewell changed many things. That's one."

"Will you tell me about the Bridewell?"

His gaze darkened. "Ye dinnae want to ken about that."

"No. I don't. But I think I must." Music should be a solace. If even that had been stripped away from him, she must work to restore its place in his heart.

"Very well, I'll tell ye a wee bit. But ye must agree to tell me about London."

She blinked. "London?" Her cheeks prickled. "What a silly thing to ask—"

"Kate. Ye're the worst liar I've ever seen."

"A fine thing to say to your wife."

"Somethin' happened in London that ye're reluctant to tell me."

She sniffed. "It was nothing. Certainly nothing compared to your experiences in prison."

"Do we have a bargain?"

She considered his offer. Swallowed her misgivings. "Very well." Adjusting her blankets and snuggling closer to his heat, she began at the beginning. "First, you must understand my sister Eugenia. She is rather bold. Two years prior to my debut, she landed herself in a delicate position with a footman in full view of gossiping busybodies."

"A wee bit scandalous for an earl's daughter, aye?"

She snorted. "Yes. In the same sense that a bonfire is a wee bit warmer than a candle."

"What was that to do with ye?"

"The scandal was deeply damaging. Eugenia was forced to retreat to the country. We delayed my first season by a year, but it scarcely helped. Most gentlemen avoided me. Others were crueler, calling my sister vile names and implying my nature would be similarly wanton. I spent a good deal of that spring sitting with the wallflowers and trying desperately not to let my misery show."

She smoothed the blanket, expecting him to comment. But he simply waited. Listened.

"Generally, I loathed every minute, but something good did emerge from the rubbish heap." She smiled, remembering. "I found friends. Clarissa Meadows spent years keeping her grandmother company whilst other ladies danced away with their bridegrooms. She showed me how to survive the wallflower experience with aplomb. Then, Francis came along with witty observations on the ton's resemblance to a Drury Lane farce. Francis is very amusing." She chuckled and shook her head. "We became inseparable. They are my dearest friends, particularly since Eugenia married and went to live with her husband in Dorsetshire." She sighed. "The mind infection, you know."

"Ye miss her."

"Yes." Heart aching, she continued smoothing the folds of the blankets over her knees and shifted the subject back to something less painful. "In my second season, suitors began to find their courage, and one by one, they sought to win my admiration. Yet, no matter how I tried, I could not muster the slightest interest in bearing their children." She chuckled. "Heavens, I couldn't even be bothered to kiss any of them more than once or twice."

Broderick's arm flexed against her side, and he sat very still, but his expression remained neutral. He was listening. For Kate, being listened to with such careful attention was a refreshing pleasure.

Relaxing into him, she continued, "You must understand, being a Huxley is … well, it comes with certain expectations. I'd watched my sisters make excellent marriages. Annabelle wed a future marquess. Jane married the Duke of Blackmore. Maureen and Eugenia both wed earls. Marrying well and bearing hordes of children is simply what we do. Yet, the longer I searched for a husband, the more dissatisfied I became. Before long, I realized that perhaps marriage itself was the problem—at least, the sort of marriage that required me to mold myself into a duplicate of every other society wife. I found being forced into such a role objectionable, a bit like being cast as the hunchbacked King Richard rather than the lovely Lady Anne." She paused. "Although, Lady Anne was forced to wed King Richard, who was admittedly the more brilliant and fascinating of the two characters. All in all, I should prefer to play

King Richard, I think. So, perhaps my analogy is not as applicable as I—"

"Kate."

"Yes?"

"Explain what happened in London."

"Oh, right. Yes. Last spring, I embarked on my third season with a new aim: I would seek a different sort of marriage, one which would permit me to remain myself, rather than becoming another of the white soup wives."

He quirked a smile. "Ye dinnae care for white soup, I take it."

She rolled her eyes. "If only the dish were interesting enough to dislike. Alas, it is ubiquitous because it is unobjectionable."

"I see," he murmured. "Like a wife who nobody notices any longer."

"Yes." She blinked, shocked at how well he'd understood. She gazed up at him, wondering how she'd managed to marry the finest man in Britain while running as far from the marriage mart as possible. By heaven, he was a rare prize. She wondered if anyone would notice if she seduced him before their next stop. She also wondered why they were wasting time talking instead of kissing.

"Lass."

"Hmm?"

"Ye were seekin' a different sort of marriage," he prompted.

"Indeed." She licked her lips and squelched her sudden hunger for Scottish fare. "I surmised that if I found an amiable husband who would not demand very much wifeliness, *and* I avoided succumbing to the mind infection, I might carry on pursuing my own interests whilst satisfying my family's expectations. Really, it was a perfect plan. I even had a gentleman in mind."

"Who?" His dark tone made her cautious.

"Oh, someone I'd known for years. A dear man who shared my love of the theatre and music. At society gatherings, I would play the pianoforte, and he would sing. It was ... just lovely."

"Mmm. What was his name?"

She patted his arm and slid her hand over his, which fisted on his thigh. "You mustn't bother yourself about that. The important thing is I selected him precisely because we were compatible but *not* a love match."

His jaw flexed as the ominous air lifted slightly. "Go on."

She gathered her courage. This was the humiliating part. How to explain one of the worst rejections of her life without him viewing her as a piteous, embarrassing fool? She played with the curls tickling her cheek. A distraction seemed just the thing.

"Firstly, I should like you to kiss me. Perhaps more. Yes, definitely more. If I lift my skirts and climb atop you, nobody will see anything. We'll make good use of the blankets. They'll assume you're keeping me warm. Which is a true yet insufficient description."

He shifted, his posture stiff, his expression suddenly pained. "Bluidy hell. No. I'll nae be distracted. Tell me the rest."

"But, if you kiss me, you'll recall that you want me. And if I mount you, that will go a very long way—"

"Finish yer story, woman."

She held him tighter. Squeezed her eyes closed. And pressed forward in a rush. "Very well. Whilst watching an insipid play at the Adelphi Theatre, I suggested to him that we would be an ideal match, and he replied that he couldn't possibly be a suitable husband for a lady of such grace and loveliness, and so on, etcetera. I assured him I was none of those things, and he was splendid, and I'd thought a good deal about an arrangement between us, and furthermore, he must marry and produce an heir because he is in line for a title and must have a wife. And, in any event, we suited one another well enough, and I shouldn't be a bother to him, nor him to me, and then I kissed him, and he behaved as if I'd fed him a spoonful of haggis. And so, I tried again, much more diligently this time, and then he very gently explained that he hadn't those sorts of feelings toward me and that I deserved much more from my husband, and so on, etcetera."

She took a breath and sallied onward before she lost her nerve. "And then, on the coach ride home, he apologized profusely and reiterated that he'd never wish me to think he didn't admire me more than any other female of his acquaintance, and I asked if perhaps his feelings might change if he tried a bit harder or ate a hearty meal or improved his sleep. He laughed a bit at that, but I simply didn't understand, because other men seemed so keen to kiss me. Indeed, I occasionally had trouble persuading them to stop, which is only to say that his response was quite different and unexpected, and so, when I found him kissing his footman behind a hedge several days later, I was quite, quite, *quite* perplexed."

Silence.

"I know what you're thinking."

"I doubt that very much, lass."

"Certainly, I considered that he might have stumbled and *accidentally* collided with his footman. Or that his footman was offering assistance, resulting in an unintentional embrace. George is remarkably attentive, as footmen go."

Broderick sighed. "Kate."

"But the embrace went on too long. I concluded it must be intentional." She winced, remembering how both men had turned seven shades of crimson when they'd noticed her gaping at them. "I felt simply dreadful, Broderick." She braved a glance at her husband's face. "He assured me that I hadn't driven him to such a pass, that he'd long had such tendencies. But part of me still wonders: Is my kiss really so revolting?"

He looked out the window for a moment, and her stomach twisted as she saw him calculating his answer. Leaning across, he drew the curtains on each window then removed her bonnet with a few practiced flicks of his fingers.

"Broderick?"

He tossed aside her blankets.

"What—what are you doing?"

He lifted her onto his lap, slid her skirts up to her thighs, and guided her to straddle him. Then, he tucked the blankets around her and cupped her face to hold her gaze with his. "Listen closely. Are ye listenin'?"

She nodded, her breath coming faster as she felt how ready he was for her.

"Some men have a different nature. The reason he declined yer offer is because he wouldnae want any female." Her husband's dark eye burned with a molten fever. "And thank God for that. Because *I* want ye." His thumb stroked her cheek, brushed her lower lip with a sensual tug. "Do ye hear me? I want ye more than I've ever wanted any bluidy thing in my existence. Ye're a fire in my blood, *mo chridhe*. These wee curls along yer cheeks. The way ye shine when ye smile. The sweet scent of ye and the sweeter way ye touch me when ye think I'm asleep."

Her eyes were welling and her throat aching, but she managed to whisper, "You know about that?"

"Aye. I ken."

She traced her gloved fingertips over his brow. His ear. The scar along the corner of his mouth. "I want you, too."

"Then kiss me, my bonnie Kate. Let me show ye why ye were always meant to be mine."

CHAPTER FIFTEEN

Not until the third morning of their journey did Kate realize Broderick hadn't told her anything about his time in the Bridewell. Instead, he'd kept her thoroughly distracted by satisfying her every need and fantasy.

He'd read her manuscript without laughing.

He'd listened to story after story about her family, including the time she'd brought home a litter of kittens to make her mother happy—only to instead make her father sneeze.

He'd told her about his boyhood with his brothers spent hunting, farming, raising livestock, and later, building the distillery.

He'd described the day his father had married Annie's mother and how enchanted they'd all been with the idea of a "wee, red-haired lassie" becoming their new sister.

He'd asked about her favorite plays and why she believed Shakespeare was the finest playwright to ever live. Her answer had taken an entire afternoon.

He'd kissed her and fed her and kept her warm, dry, and contented as a kitten in a pool of sunlight.

After only two days, she was so enthralled, she feared her heart couldn't survive without his constant presence. Every time he exited the coach to speak with his men or fetch her a flask of ale, she gazed out the window like an absolute ninny, her chest aching. Every time he looked at her with that beautiful, lustful fire in his eye, she craved more of him.

The man was deliberately obsessing her; she was certain of it. He even claimed not to mind her singing. Could there be a clearer sign of sinister intentions? She thought not.

The mind infection had overtaken her soul, rooting deep and binding her to him inexorably. It was everything she'd feared, only worse.

This morning, he awakened her in a now-familiar fashion, and she suffered a moment of panic. His hard, naked body wrapped around her from behind as they lay on their sides in the Lowland inn's finest bed. One of his hands cupped her breast. The other caressed lightly between her thighs.

She moaned, still emerging from the sensual dream she'd been having. Arousal heated her skin, turning it sensitive to every sensation. The prickle of his chest hair against her back. The tickle of his lips against her neck. The heat of his breath and the hardness of his staff and the coolness of early-morning air.

"Are ye awake yet, lass?"

Her breath hitched on another moan as his fingertips played and swirled. "Broderick."

"Aye, there ye are."

Her heart kicked frantically as he drove her pleasure higher. Tighter. He did it effortlessly. By now, he knew her body better than she did. He played her like a stringed instrument, with subtle motions and exquisite pressure. His tongue traced her earlobe and his teeth scraped her neck. The roughness of his unshaven jaw chafed her shoulder.

She arched and reached back for him, wanting his mouth. He granted her a kiss, sliding his tongue inside to duel with hers. Too soon, he pulled away, nuzzling her hair and whispering, "Come for me. I need ye wet and eager."

Her body needed no further urging. Driven by his fingers and his voice, the power of his arms and the fierce hold he had upon her, her pleasure launched. Soared. Spun out and unwound. Her sheath demanded to be filled even as it wept and seized.

He waited for her to calm. Kissed her neck and slowed his hand. "Good." His other hand slid from her breast to her hip then down to her thigh, just above her knee. He gripped. Lifted. Hooked her leg over his arm and slid his hot, massive shaft inside her with a long, slow thrust.

She should have been used to him by now. But the way he filled her so completely, stretching her and working his length in deep enough to cause a near-unbearable pressure, made her gasp every time.

"Try to relax," he murmured, infuriatingly calm. "Let me in."

She couldn't. She shook her head, gasping for air.

"Aye." He raised her knee higher and gave her a harder thrust. The hand that had never left her folds began stroking again. "That's the way. Easy, now."

Drawing little circles around the center of her pleasure, he drove her to the brink of madness. The spiraling sensations wound tighter. Tighter. She begged him for mercy, but as usual, he didn't heed her pleas. Rather, he kept on without a word, pushing her to the edge and sending her flying into the abyss as if that alone were his mission.

It was too much. Heart frantic, she grasped at his arms. Clawed at his hands. Reached for his hair and only managed to dig her fingers into his hard nape.

"Luik at ye, lass. Luik."

She forced her eyes open. Looked down at her own body, utterly possessed by his. Dark-red nipples stood hard and eager on the white swells of her breasts, which trembled as he steadily, rhythmically claimed her sheath. He held her splayed wide open, fully accessible to his dark, thrusting cock and commanding hands. His arms were darker than her skin, his muscles bulging, his strength enormous. The sounds of their joining—the wet sighs and faint collision of his hips with hers—blended into the soft rain outside and the fire crackling nearby.

Feeling him inside her had grown essential. The way water was essential. Or air. Or light. Without him, she would die.

She'd wanted to believe she could keep a part of herself whole. She'd wanted to believe she could gorge herself on him until her love grew more manageable. More sane. But he wouldn't leave her a blessed inch. On the contrary, he seemed intent upon making it worse.

Now, the tempo of his thrusts increased, stoking a blaze of friction. Deeper and deeper he went. Harder and harder he drove. Faster and faster his harsh breaths sounded in her ear. "Tight," he growled. "Sweet Christ. I feel yer need. Give me everythin'."

Soon, she was right back where she'd started—begging, sobbing, out of her mind with the craving only he could invoke.

And that was when the panic set in.

She couldn't see his face, but it didn't matter. He controlled her completely. He managed her pleasure the way a conductor managed a symphony.

Her body wasn't hers. Her mind wasn't hers. Every part of her belonged to him alone.

She stiffened against him, resisting the urgent pleasure he commanded from her. His arm flexed where it wrapped around her body. His hand tightened on her thigh, draping her leg over his. He banded her shoulders and lightly gripped her neck. Increasing the pace of his thrusts, he cupped her jaw gently and stroked her below with his other hand. His fingers and thumb worked her harder.

"Pleeeeaaase," she groaned, her body wracked with shivers. "Broderick. Oh, God."

She was pinned. Trapped by her own hunger. Her muscles tensed, but she couldn't make them do the one thing they should—break free.

"Give me yer pleasure," he growled. "Dinnae fight it. Ye always fight it, lass. Let it come."

She clawed his forearm. Drove her hips back into him, forcing his cock impossibly deep. She turned her head into his shoulder and bit. Tasted his skin and wanted more.

All the while, he held her tight and drove her higher.

The cataclysm broke over both of them with concussive force. She screamed and fought it. But the pleasure consumed her like a wall of fire devouring dry grass. It left her nothing.

No pride. No room. No Kate.

Nothing but him.

He remained inside her, his arms squeezing, his breath hot against her neck and shoulder, long after he'd roared his pleasure and flooded her with his own release.

Gradually, she caught her breath. Gathered her strength. And untangled herself.

He grunted as she rolled away and sat at the edge of the bed. She hunted for her dressing gown but only found her shift draped across a bench. She tugged it on and moved to the washstand behind a screen to clean herself.

"We dinnae have to leave for another hour or so, ye ken."

She was shivering, half from the chill of the water and half from panic. "I'd like to get an early start. Do you think we'll reach Edinburgh today?"

"Aye." The bed creaked as he rolled to rise. As usual, he moved slower first thing in the morning before he'd applied his liniment.

She continued washing—her face, her teeth, her body—with automatic motions. But inside, she quaked. Her hands trembled. Her belly shook.

"Are ye all right, lass?"

Drawing a shuddering breath, she gripped the edge of the washstand and closed her eyes. "Yes, of course."

She smelled the aroma of his liniment, cool and delicious. It made her want him again, which intensified the panic. Swiftly, she dug through the valise on the floor, searching for a bottle. There! She dabbed drops of perfume on her neck, her belly, her thighs. The scent was strong, but not strong enough. She could still smell him everywhere.

"Ye dinnae need all that."

Startled to find him directly behind her, she fumbled and nearly dropped the bottle. She would have, in fact, if he hadn't shot an arm around her and cupped her hand and the bottle from beneath.

"Steady, now."

She tugged away. "I shouldn't need steadying if you hadn't given me such a start," she snapped, depositing the bottle back in her valise and spinning to confront him. "This perfume was a gift from Francis. I almost dropped it because you cannot seem to grant me the slightest bit of room."

He frowned.

She noted he'd donned his patch, a shirt, and trousers, but he hadn't yet shaven. Shamefully, the roguish look of him further sparked her lust.

"What's wrong?" he demanded.

"Nothing. I'm fine."

"Ye're nae fine."

She shoved past him, scanning the chamber for her gown and corset. She found the gown draped over a chair, but the corset and her dressing gown remained missing. She rushed to the bed and yanked at the bedclothes.

"Tell me what's ailin' ye, Kate."

"Nothing!" she shouted, her breathing fast and her pulse faster. She tore at the sheets, wadding them into tight balls and tossing them into the corner. First one, then the other.

"Calm yerself."

"I must find my corset. Where is it?"

"We'll fetch Janet. Mayhap she—"

She threw a pillow at his head.

He caught it against his chest, but his eye flared with alarm. "Kate."

"Stop being reasonable!"

"One of us has to be."

She threw another pillow. It bounced off his knee and plopped at his feet. "You are infuriating!"

A corner of his mouth twitched. The devil was fighting a smile.

"Oh, do I *amuse* you, husband?"

"I could say no, but ..." He shrugged. "I dinnae like to lie to ye."

She blew a curl out of her eyes and started toward him. Pain erupted from her toes as they collided with something metallic. The momentum sent the thing sliding from beneath the bed out into the middle of the floor. Releasing a whimpering yelp, she stumbled and caught herself against the bed.

Before she could blink, Broderick scooped her up and set her on the mattress, tucking the pillow she'd thrown at him behind her back. He grasped her leg and raised her foot for closer examination.

"Broderick," she gasped. "There's no need for ... *ow-ow-ow-ow.*"

"Easy," he murmured. "I reckon they're a wee bit sore, but naught's broken."

"How could you possibly know that?"

"Lass." He arched a brow. "Ye're askin' *me* that question?"

Her throat tightened as she reviewed his scars. "I suppose not."

He cradled her foot in his hands then reached for his liniment. After applying the soothing mixture to her toes with whisper-light strokes, he slid a hand up her calf and squeezed. "Now, do ye wish to tell me what sparked this wee fit of temper?"

No. She couldn't tell him. She'd sound like a mad, desperate, besotted fool.

Which she was, but she had no desire for him to realize it.

Avoiding his gaze, she locked on the source of her injury: a hammer, the same one she'd previously seen beneath their bed at home. "Why do you keep a hammer beneath your bed?"

"Dinnae change the subject."

"That is the subject. I should like an answer, please."

His jaw flickered. He withdrew and left the bed to retrieve the hammer, hefting it with a considering gaze. "Makes a fine weapon."

Something in his voice sent a chill down her spine. Bleak. Flat. Dark. She studied his face, his grip upon the handle. He caressed the thing with his thumb as though he'd worn it smooth. That was when she knew. This was about his time in the Bridewell.

"Why do you keep it where you sleep?"

For a long while, she didn't think he would answer. He kept his gaze averted, rubbing and rubbing and rubbing the tool he held. Finally, he said, "They'd come at me, ye ken. Sometimes one by one. Sometimes two or three. More when they planned better."

She drew her knees up to her chest, holding tightly as though that could keep her intact. She'd wanted to hear this, hadn't she? She'd wanted to know.

"Nights were worst. The noise. The attacks. There was nae sleep to be had. Nae weapon apart from one ye'd made." A small smile tugged. "Or one ye took. Kept within reach. Used to make certain if they didnae bring twenty bruisers to the fight, they'd pay a dear price."

Outside, she heard rain. Inside, she heard crackling fire. But in his voice, she heard pain. She breathed away the ache in her chest and asked, "Was there nobody to defend you, nobody to help?"

"Nah," he said. "Lockhart has deep pockets. The turnkeys who wouldnae accept his bribes were replaced with ones who did. Skene's men were cheap fodder, easily purchased, easily discarded. Da and my brothers did what they could, but they were overmatched in a game of that scale."

A game. What a strange way to describe such evil.

Before Kate had known Broderick, Annie had described what had happened to him. Kate knew Lockhart had formed an irrational jealousy of Broderick, that he'd arranged for the murder of an exciseman to be laid at Broderick's feet and had methodically targeted him for destruction over months of unjust imprisonment. Kate knew his injuries might as well have been inflicted directly by Lockhart's hand and that Lockhart had confessed before witnesses that he'd done everything possible to "fell the tower into ruins."

When she'd asked Annie about the source of Lockhart's jealousy, Annie had hesitated before explaining that Broderick had unwittingly involved himself with Lockhart's mistress. She hadn't gone into much detail at the time, only saying that the mistress had fallen in love with him "as many poor lasses have done before. 'Tis a sad thing to see, Katie-lass. They cannae help themselves. To be fair, he doesnae make promises he cannae keep, and he's gentle about sendin' them on their way, but the pinin' fair breaks yer heart."

Kate hadn't thought much about Annie's explanations until recently. Until she'd become one of the "poor lasses" who'd fallen so deeply in love, she couldn't imagine her next breath without him. Pining didn't begin to describe it.

Even now, she had to physically grip herself to keep from going to him. Touching him. Offering whatever comfort she could.

"I wish I had been there," she whispered. "I wish I had been with you."

His gaze flew up to her, burning with a mad fire. "Dinnae say that," he growled, stalking toward her. He tossed the hammer onto the foot of the bed and sat next to her, gripping her shoulders. "Never think it, *mo chridhe.*" He stroked her cheek, her hair. His eye traced her features and squeezed closed for a moment as pain crumpled his brow.

She couldn't bear it. She rocked forward onto her knees. Wrapped herself around him, cradling his head against her and burying her hands in his hair. She wanted to take every ounce of pain from him, even if she must feel it in his stead.

His grip upon her tightened until she could scarcely breathe.

"I had someone, there in the prison," he whispered against her neck. "A friend. Her name was … Magdalene."

Kate froze. Hearing him say another woman's name with such anguish pierced her through the middle. A sickening wave of jealousy followed, hot and unwanted. She bit down upon it. Waited for him to explain.

"I told her nae to help me, that she'd be harmed. I warned her over and over, but she wouldnae listen." He cinched her waist harder, held her tighter. "She brought me soup at Christmas. She took me to the infirmary when I was nothin' but a foul-smellin' madman. She was kind. And they killed her for it. They told me they wouldnae. They said if I let them do all the damage they wanted, they'd leave her be. She was walkin' free that day. I watched her from the window. I watched, and she passed through the gates. She was free. But they killed her. They raped her over and over, and—Christ, they took my eye. They took everythin'. And they killed her anyway."

Kate rocked him back and forth, his pain becoming her pain. Jealousy was a pebble washed away in the tide. She wept silently, intent on offering only comfort. He grieved. He didn't weep or wail, merely shuddered. But grief roared like the sea inside a lightless cavern.

"Ye wonder why I keep a hammer beneath my bed? That's why. Because those animals willnae take another goddamned thing from me. Not one more thing." He gripped her nape, pulled back, and brushed away the wetness on her cheeks. "Especially you."

She couldn't stop her tears. They kept flowing, even while he kissed her.

Even while he whispered, "I'll keep ye safe. I'll nae let them touch ye."

Whatever slim hope she'd had for keeping a piece of her heart for herself vanished. She was his. And he was her forever man.

"I love you so much," she choked. "My God, Broderick. How I wish I could take this pain from you."

"Ye do, *mo chridhe*." His eye roamed her face, heated and raw. "In the Bridewell, the only safe place was the Dark Cell. No window. No light. I came to crave it, would have the gaolers toss me in there as often as possible." He stroked her hair, knuckling the curls near her damp cheek. "That's where I live. In the black. But every now and then, my wee, bonnie wife smiles, and a bit of light comes for a visit. Then, she laughs, and that light dances." He quirked a smile of his own. "Ye're a flame in my darkness. I wouldnae have predicted it, given how we met. But nothin's ever been truer."

Her throat burned. Tightened. "I'm so dreadfully sorry about Magdalene."

He touched his forehead to hers. "That was the worst of it." His voice was pure gravel. "The rest was scars and bone damage. Losin' her stole all hope that any of it meant anythin'. That's why I didnae want ye to set yer heart on me. I had nothin' much to offer. But I'll nae be such a fool again. I'm keepin' ye, and ye'll be glad for it. I promise ye that."

Because he seemed to need it, she gave him a smile. But inside, she ached with the knowledge that his worst wound—the one nobody could see—might be the loss of a woman who would never return.

A woman Kate could never hope to replace.

CHAPTER SIXTEEN

"Do you suppose a legendary Highlander who slays the last wolf in Scotland might also be a skilled dancer?" Kate rested her chin on her hand and stared out the morning room window, her fingers tapping her cheek.

No answer came from the mountainous male seated near the fireplace.

"Campbell," she nudged.

Broderick's oldest brother glanced up from the piece of wood in his hand. He rested his carving knife on his knee. "What sort of dancin'?"

"Waltzing?"

"Nah."

She smiled and hooked an elbow over the back of her desk chair. "You sound very certain."

"Highlanders who waltz are the soft sorts." He resumed carving what appeared to be a wing. "Same ones drink brandy instead of whisky. Takes ten of 'em to hunt a wee fox."

She sized up his shoulders, which made his chair look ridiculously small. "Could you lift a fully-grown cow?"

He raised a brow.

"Assuming it is the only way to rescue, say, a woman you fancied."

"Mayhap if the coo is attached to a winch."

Campbell was the least talkative of Broderick's brothers, but in the three days since they'd arrived in Edinburgh, she'd enjoyed his company best. He was quiet. Patient. Despite his gargantuan size, she found him less intimidating than Alexander and less exhausting than Rannoch. That mattered a great deal when her husband dictated that she be constantly guarded while he scoured the city in search of a "putrid pile of shite" named Kenneth Lockhart.

Kate's restlessness was nigh unbearable.

They'd arrived at this pleasant townhouse under the cover of darkness several nights earlier. Broderick's family had rented the place during his recuperation and decided to keep it as a secure base in the city. The house was four stories, fully staffed, and while modestly furnished, quite comfortable.

Still, being confined here with little to do apart from struggling to write the final act of her novel-play had been frustrating. She'd seen little of her husband, nothing of the city, and far too much of the guards Broderick had posted to keep watch.

Sighing, she turned back to the watery window that looked onto the wide, cobbled lane. A new guard appeared, huddled against the rain and furtively scanning the neighboring houses. "Campbell, are you certain we cannot—"

"I'm certain, lass."

"But, there is a vast park not forty yards from here. Surely we could take a short ramble without—"

"'Tis called the Meadows. And no, we cannae."

Broderick had given strict instructions that she was not to leave the house. "If Lockhart discovers ye're here, he'll have only to find a way in," he'd warned her two mornings ago. "Ye must stay hidden, *mo chridhe*. Ye must do as I tell ye."

She'd done precisely that. And certainly, he'd provided for her every comfort. Whatever she asked, he or his brothers delivered it to her within hours—bolts of tartan wool, reams of paper, a full-length tub for bathing, a warmer pair of gloves for Janet. Anything except a blasted half-hour outside this house.

She stabbed her pen back into its holder and shoved away from the desk. "Perhaps I shall make you another scarf." She'd spent the previous day making one for each of the MacPherson men.

Campbell grunted.

Unsatisfied, she wandered to the chair nearest him and sat, examining his carving. The astonishing detail of a bird's wing taking shape beneath his blade made her blink. "Heavens, that is splendid. What sort of bird is it?"

He paused. "An owl."

"Oh! How lovely. Do you know, there is a tree on Broderick's land with a whorl that resembles an owl. I've tried to capture it, but I've little talent for sketching."

"Aye. I've seen it."

She met his gaze. Campbell's features weren't as handsome as Rannoch's or Alexander's. They were blunter. Rougher. But his eyes had stories in them.

Kate adored stories.

"Have you never wished to marry?"

He stilled. "Ye ask a great many questions, lass."

Perhaps it was the mind infection, but she couldn't fathom why such an exceptional man as Campbell MacPherson hadn't married long before now. "Well, I think a woman would be very fortunate to capture your heart." She patted his wrist. "Now, are you certain you couldn't lift a cow?"

A deep frown furrowed his brow. His heavy jaw flexed, but he didn't appear angry. "A coo weighs a thousand pounds."

"Yes, but you are extraordinarily strong."

"Is the beastie alive or dead?"

"Oh, very much alive."

"Then, no." He resumed whittling.

She let several minutes of silence pass between them. "What about a bull?"

He blew out a breath. "A bull is twice the weight."

"What if it was very young? And your dearest love stood directly in the animal's path? And the only way to save her was—"

"I'd lift the lass, nae the bull."

She blinked. Memories from the night Broderick had saved her from death-by-falling-tree-limb flew past her mind's eye. Her heroic husband had knocked her from her horse then taken the brunt of their fall upon himself while wrapping her in the safety of his arms.

"Good heavens. Of course!" She leapt to her feet and rushed back to the desk, frantically digging through her manuscript for the tenth chapter. Immediately she set to work, crossing out lines and writing new ones. Time passed swiftly, and before she knew it, she'd written two chapters, the rain had stopped, and the guard on the street now leaned casually against a lamppost.

She blinked a few times and squinted to bring the young man into focus. Was that a pistol in his waistband? He adjusted his cap and peered toward her window. Just then, he stiffened, glanced behind him, and dashed off as though chased by a Highland bull.

How odd. Perhaps he'd had urgent need of the privy.

Distantly, she heard the front door open and close. Alexander entered the morning room, unwinding the blue-tartan scarf she'd finished for him yesterday. He shrugged out of his damp greatcoat and gave her a nod. "The songbook ye asked for will be delivered later today, lass."

She smiled. "You're very kind, Alexander. Thank you."

His grin was wicked. "I'm nae even a wee bit kind, but ye're most welcome." He held up his scarf. "I'm obliged to ye for this. Standin' in the pissin' rain for three hours isnae as pleasant as it sounds."

Early that morning, Broderick had asked Alexander to watch Lockhart's residence and report back on the movements of both Lockhart and his sister.

Campbell stood. "Did ye see anythin'?"

Alexander's expression took on a sardonic glint. "Aye. She played the pianoforte. Drank three cups of tea. Sent a maid to the shops. I dinnae think she's eaten aught but a dry biscuit in three days, but by God, she'll have her kid gloves and satin bonnets, eh?"

"Any sign of Lockhart?" Campbell asked.

Alexander shook his head. "If he's inside, she's keepin' him well hidden." Unexpectedly, he chuckled, but the sound was dark. "I did see somebody I wasnae expectin', though."

Kate stood. "Who?"

"Sergeant Neil Munro of the Inverness constabulary."

Dear heaven. Munro was here? Was it because he was working for Lockhart?

Campbell's granite jaw flexed, his huge frame tensing. "Bluidy hell. Why?"

"Dinnae ken. He came to the door; she answered. They spoke for a wee minute, then he left." Frowning, Alexander glanced around the room. "Katie-lass, have ye aught that's warm to drink? Parts of me shouldnae be as numb as they are."

She crossed her arms over her bosom. "Munro is my concern, too, you know."

"I ken."

"I'll not be kept in the dark. I know him better than any of you."

He ran a hand through his hair. "Might we discuss this when I'm nae freezin' my ballocks off?"

Noticing that his lips were, indeed, much paler than normal, she clicked her tongue and moved to pour him a cup of tea from the tray on the desk. "Now, did you see her give the sergeant anything? A purse or a package? Did they appear friendly? Did she smile at him?"

Drinking from his steaming cup, Alexander raised a brow at her. "Ye ask a lot of questions."

"Do you intend to answer any of them?"

"Mayhap when I can feel my face again."

She scoffed. "Rubbish. You haven't been out in the cold any longer than the new guard outside, and he hasn't complained once."

Both MacPhersons suddenly went still. Dangerously still.

"What new guard, Kate?" Campbell's voice was a low rumble, his tone deadly.

She blinked. "The man across the lane. Gray coat, black cap. He's been watching the house off and on ..." A trill of alarm washed over her skin. She swallowed. "For hours."

Campbell's expression turned thunderous. "Stay with her," he barked to his brother.

"Be careful," she warned. "He has a pistol."

He nodded. Long strides carried him swiftly from the room. The front door slammed moments later.

Alexander set his cup on the tray and took her elbow. "Come away from the window." He tucked her beneath his arm, positioning his body between her and the window. Then, he guided her out of the morning room and took her to a small sitting room near the master bedchamber.

When she sank down onto a settee, she watched Alexander demonstrate why he was the brother-in-law she found most intimidating.

He moved like a ghost. Minimal motion. No expression. Perfect concentration. She'd seen Broderick behave similarly from time to time, but he was never as coldly precise as Alexander.

It gave her shivers.

He pulled up a wooden chair and straddled it to face her. "Now, Kate. Tell me about the man ye saw outside. Did he see ye?"

She nodded. "I think so."

"How long was he there?"

"Since early this morning. He arrived shortly after Campbell and I settled into the morning room."

Alexander's eyes were dark, like Broderick's and Campbell's. But right now, they were as flat and cold as a frozen blade. "Did ye see him leave?"

"Yes. Just before you came in. I thought he had to use the privy." She was relieved to see a tug of amusement at the corner of his mouth.

"Likely saw me comin'."

"Alexander," she said, struggling to keep her voice steady. "Does this mean Lockhart knows where I am?"

"Aye, Katie-lass. That's what it means."

A sick wave of fear washed over her. "Where is Broderick?" She wanted her husband. Needed him desperately.

"He'll be back soon. He and Rannoch have been trackin' Lockhart's business partner. If we can cut off the bastard's finances, he'll have nothin' to fund his favorite sport."

And no way to plague them after his death.

Kate had never wished death on anyone. She'd never hated anyone this much. But Lockhart's twisted schemes had maimed the man she loved. They'd made Annie's life and the lives of the MacPherson men a landscape of dread. In too many ways, Kate believed what Annie had told her: *The devil won.*

She would do anything to ensure he didn't win again.

"I want to help," she said.

"Best ye keep safe."

"Yes, of course. But—"

"Broderick wouldnae survive losin' ye."

That startled her. "I think you're overestimating his attachment."

Alexander simply stared at her with the intensity she found so intimidating.

"He survived losing Magdalene Cuthbert," she pointed out, deliberately ignoring the hot pang of jealousy. The woman was dead. She must stop resenting her place in Broderick's heart.

"She wasnae his wife. Besides, he only learned of her death months later, after he recovered his strength."

That couldn't be right. She'd assumed Broderick had witnessed the attack. "How did he find out?"

"He asked Rannoch and me to find her, make certain she was well."

Why had he waited months to discover what happened to the woman he loved? He didn't love Kate, and yet, she couldn't imagine him patiently waiting to discover if she were alive or dead. The man had promised to chop down every tree along a mile of road to ensure her safety, and he merely *lusted* after her.

"Ye look confused, lass."

"Yes, I … How did you learn Magdalene had been killed?"

"We found one of her attackers. He told us they abducted a woman down the hill from the prison."

"A woman." She puzzled at the vagueness. "Did he describe her?"

Alexander shook his head. "'Twas dark and they were sotted when they took her."

A suspicion tickled the back of her mind. "So, you believed a man who was too drunk to recall what she looked like?"

His smile sent chills down her spine. "He was beggin' to preserve his manhood at the time, so aye. We believed he'd done what he claimed."

"No, I meant, how do you know it was Magdalene?"

"We dinnae ken for certain."

The walls shifted around Kate. Her heart stopped then restarted. Hope and anguish warred inside her chest.

Magdalene might be alive. This very minute, the woman whose death had imprisoned Broderick's soul in a bleak, dark cell might yet be found alive.

"Lass, I see what ye're thinkin', but ye're wrong. We tracked her to a kirk near where they left her for dead. The minister said she wore the same color gown as Magdalene wore, though it was in tatters."

"What color?"

He frowned. "Gray."

She waved a dismissal. "Too common. It means nothing."

"There was nae sign of Magdalene Cuthbert after that day. We looked."

Kate's stomach churned. She should leave it be. Resurrecting Broderick's lost love would tear her heart into pieces. Kate might lose him. Worse, she might be forced to watch while her husband suffered the mind infection for another woman. Either way, unendurable pain awaited her.

And, yet, how could she leave Broderick to suffer in the dark?

"Magdalene would not use her real name to find employment." Kate barely squeezed the words through her tight, aching throat. "She was imprisoned for theft. No employer would have her."

Alexander eyed her sharply. "Aye. We assumed so." He explained how they'd scoured the areas of the city where she might have found employment, and no one had recalled a woman of Magdalene's description. "Nothin' is certain, but we spent a fortnight searchin' for signs of her. Naught was found."

"We must search again."

"We? Nah. Ye'll be stayin' here."

Kate raised her chin, ignoring the voice that screamed for her to let Magdalene Cuthbert remain dead. "Lockhart already knows I'm in Edinburgh. If he seeks to target me, he will do so regardless of my location."

Alexander's dark eyes flashed. "He'll bluidy well die if he tries."

"Alexander, we must find Magdalene." Her belly twisted painfully. She laid a hand over her midsection to stifle it. "For Broderick's sake. Please."

It took a half-hour of coaxing to win his agreement, but he would only agree to conduct the search himself. After an additional half-hour of persuasion, he agreed to take her along on the condition that she must wear a disguise, and at least two MacPhersons must accompany her at all times.

Kate had won many arguments in her life. But never had victory tasted so bitter.

Two days after learning Lockhart had sent a man to spy on his wife, Broderick wanted blood. Instead, he donned a cravat, tailcoat, breeches, and waistcoat to escort Kate to the theatre.

He was bloody well choking. And not because of the cravat. His rage simmered too close to the surface.

Kate was afraid. He saw it every time she looked at him, the way she worried the edges of her shawl and twirled the curls near her temple. Her fear maddened him. He'd told her over and over that he would keep her safe. He'd whispered it in her ear as he'd made love to her. He'd murmured it at breakfast and at dinner and later, while he held her on his lap by the fire.

She would smile. Nod. Reassure him that she believed him. Then, she'd swallow or glance away or sigh, and his frustration grew.

Even now, as they sat together in an ornate box watching her beloved "Scottish play" onstage below, she wound a curl around her gloved finger and nibbled her lower lip. None of her fretfulness made her less beautiful, of course. His wife was so bonnie, he struggled to catch his breath sometimes.

Tonight, she wore ice-blue satin. It gave her skin a soft, creamy sheen that matched her silk gloves. Those dense lashes lay against her cheeks, and a faint smile curved her tempting lips.

God, how he wanted her. But just when he thought her heart was his, he'd catch her sending him uncertain glances or pretending to sleep when he knew she was awake. Then, there had been her nonsensical tantrum before they'd arrived in Edinburgh. Baffling woman.

Plainly, she wasn't yet his. Not completely. And it was driving him mad.

His campaign to make her fall in love with him had shown signs of success—she often touched him with tenderness, and since that morning at the inn, she'd declared her affection several times. But it felt like dry toast when he longed for a feast.

During their marriage, with a few exceptions, he'd restrained his appetites, limiting the tupping to two or three times a night. She was a passionate, responsive woman and often sought to please him. But the intensity of their lovemaking alarmed her. She still fought her own desires, withholding crucial parts of herself, and he didn't know why. He'd done everything he could think of to win her—gifts and pampering, conversation and compliments, pleasure and restraint. He'd even asked Rannoch for advice.

Rannoch had laughed. Then he'd suggested Broderick try "letting the lass out of the house, man." Every so often, his youngest brother said something sensible.

He'd purchased a box for that evening's performance at the Theatre Royal in Shakespeare Square on Princes Street. He'd presented the playbill to her at breakfast, expecting her to light up and leap into his arms. Instead, she'd given him a false smile and a halfhearted, "How lovely. Thank you, Broderick."

Now, partway through the scene in which Macbeth learned of his wife's death, Kate's eyes shimmered with tears, and Broderick wondered if this had been a shite idea. What the devil did he know about winning a woman's heart? He'd only ever done it accidentally.

She sighed. Pressed her lips together. A tear tracked down her cheek.

"'Tis nearly over, lass."

With a startled glance, she blinked up at him and gave his hand a pat. "Never mind me," she whispered. "This part always makes me weep like a ninny."

He handed her a handkerchief.

She dabbed her cheeks, wiped her nose, and turned back to the stage. When the play finished, she pressed her hand to her bosom. "No matter how many times I see it, I am still moved."

Behind them, Rannoch snored.

She giggled and shot Broderick a blushing grin. "Perhaps we should take a stroll before the opera begins, hmm? I find it helps improve stamina."

He had no need of stamina. If anything, a cold drenching was in order. Nevertheless, he wanted to please his wife, so he stood and offered his hand. She hesitated the briefest second then slid her fingers into his grasp.

After he nudged his daft brother awake with his boot, Rannoch dutifully fell in behind them as they headed toward the saloon on the lower level. The room was too crowded for his liking, but Kate remained close, and he remained vigilant.

Suddenly, she stopped. Gasped. Murmured in a high pitch, "Can it be? *Francis?*"

Frowning, he scanned the crowd. He followed her wide-eyed gaze, searching for the friend Kate had described as "very amusing," the one who'd given her a bottle of her favorite scent for her birthday. Oddly, he only saw a pair of gentlemen conversing with a fruit seller. Nobody in that area was female.

"Where, lass?"

She pointed to the pair of gentlemen. "Come, Broderick." She tugged eagerly, more animated than she'd been all evening. "We *must* say hello."

Confused, he searched for the woman she considered one of her dearest friends. As she dragged him toward the men, his suspicions mounted. Then, closing the last few feet, she pulled free and rushed toward the taller of the two. That man turned at the last second, a surprised grin lighting his face.

His unearthly *handsome* face.

Kate squealed and launched herself into the man's arms. "Francis, I cannot believe you're here!" she cooed as the distinctly male Francis embraced her.

Everything inside Broderick went dark. And red. Mostly red.

Rannoch clapped his shoulder. "Steady."

It took all his strength, but he managed to control himself.

The blond dandy was well-dressed, he noted. Finely tailored blue coat. Gold silk waistcoat. Polished boots that likely never touched a pasture's muck.

"Francis Prescott, Lord Teversham, may I present my husband, Broderick MacPherson, and his brother Rannoch."

The interloping bastard's blue eyes flared as they took in Broderick's size and patch and scars. And, yes, probably his expression. He felt ready to kill.

Then the dandy flashed a white-toothed grin. "Such splendid serendipity! I am heartily gratified to meet the"—he glanced at Kate—"how did you phrase it? Ah, yes. 'The consummate confluence of all superior Highland attributes.'"

Kate blushed berry-bright. "A tad exuberant, perhaps."

"Nonsense. Your letters epitomize eloquence, my lady." The dandy affected an elaborate bow.

Kate tapped the man's arm with her folded fan. "No silliness, if you please. You must tell me what brought you to Scotland."

"Did you not receive my last letter?" When she shook her head, Francis waved forward the man behind him, whom he introduced as his valet, George Parker. The brown-haired, pleasant-featured Parker was shorter and less handsome than his employer, but equally lean. "George's grandfather, unfortunately, passed away, necessitating a visit. And, as I cannot be without my valet for longer than an afternoon, I have taken the occasion to visit the city of his birth."

Kate murmured her condolences to George and asked after his family. Broderick might have thought it odd that she would show such friendliness to a servant, but he'd seen her with Janet and Mrs. Grant. Kate's warmth with everyone, regardless of rank, was one of her many admirable qualities.

Francis touched Kate's elbow, twisting Broderick's gut into a burning knot. "Dearest Kate." The dandy smiled at her with too much affection. "After Edinburgh, we had planned to venture into the Highlands to see you and your new home."

"Oh, yes. Francis, you must come for a visit."

Broderick's ears began to roar. His fists clenched. Rannoch's grip on his shoulder tightened. "Easy, brother," Rannoch whispered.

"Clarissa, too?" the dandy asked. "Her last letter said she and her grandmother feel the need to escape Ellery Hall for a sojourn in Scotland. I hope you don't mind that I invited her to make the glen her destination. She's keen to join us for Christmastide."

Kate bounced on her toes. "How lovely! Of course, Broderick and I would adore it."

The dandy sent Broderick a cautious glance before turning back to Kate. "Now, about the play. Did you laugh when the cauldron overturned? George thought it was intentional, but I assured him witches prefer their cauldrons open-side-up."

The two chatted about actors and stage props and severed heads for several minutes before Broderick had had enough. Shrugging off Rannoch's staying grip, he slid an arm around his wife's waist, yanked her against him, and caught the dandy's sky-blue gaze. That gaze turned wary in a flash.

Good.

"Sounds as if the music is startin', Teversham," he said softly. "Ye wouldnae wish to miss the show, eh?"

Broderick's intimidation appeared to be working, as he watched "dear Francis" grow increasingly alarmed. Much like a stag who'd heard the cocking of a hunter's rifle.

"Francis, I insist you and George join us in our box." That was Kate. Friendly. Oblivious. Broderick squeezed her waist tighter. Her only response was to pat his arm and continue, "We have ample room. You simply must. German opera is your favorite."

The dandy raised a brow, but he didn't answer. Didn't take his eyes from Broderick's face.

"Rannoch, take Kate back to the box," Broderick said. "I'll be along soon."

Kate sputtered a protest, but Rannoch murmured, "Best ye do as he says, Katie-lass. Limit the damage."

"Damage? Don't be silly. Oh, is that woman selling oranges? I am a bit peckish." Their voices faded as Rannoch guided her away.

Finally, Broderick stood alone with the dandy. "How long have ye been 'dear friends' with my wife, Teversham?"

"Three years," he answered, sizing up Broderick's frame. He glanced to his valet and back to Broderick with a sheepish expression. "Look, MacPherson. Whatever affection you perceive between Lady Kate and me is purely platonic, I assure you."

"Right."

"George, tell him." The plea sounded a bit desperate. "Have you ever seen a single impropriety—"

Broderick interrupted, "What would a valet ken about it? He folds yer drawers and shaves yer whiskers."

"Before he was my valet, he was my footman, and often about when Kate and Clarissa visited." Francis gestured to the other man, who nodded.

"It's true, Mr. MacPherson," George confirmed, his voice shy yet firm. "Lord Teversham would never countenance a slight against Lady Katherine's reputation. They are fond of one another, but that is all."

Footman. George the footman. A bell of familiarity rang in Broderick's head. Everything crystallized. Looking between the unearthly handsome Lord Teversham and the former footman, he finally noticed what he'd missed in his red haze. Francis's hand repeatedly brushed George's. The angle of their positions was close, with Francis's being the more protective.

Bloody hell. *Francis* had declined Kate's proposal. *Francis* had been caught kissing his footman behind a hedge. Because he didn't want her—nor any woman.

Like an unraveled rope, Broderick's tension abruptly slackened. His gut relaxed. His chest untightened. His vision cleared.

Relief flooded in. Francis was no rival. In fact, he'd done Broderick a great service by refusing to marry Kate.

"Plainly, I've misjudged ye," Broderick admitted at once, offering his hand.

Francis darted a glance at his companion then accepted the handshake with a confident grip and a steady gaze. He smiled wryly. "No harm done. A man in love is part halfwit, part lunatic. Happens I know something about that."

Feeling a wee bit ashamed of his daft, uncontrolled jealousy, Broderick nodded to both men. "Kate's right. Ye must join us."

An hour later, Kate sat at the front of the box between Rannoch and George. All three raptly focused on the incomprehensible caterwauling onstage. Meanwhile, seated well behind them, Broderick conversed with Francis. The dandy was, in actuality, quite a decent fellow. Good-humored, sensible, intelligent. And a fount of knowledge about Kate.

Broderick found the last quality particularly useful.

"So, havin' a pianoforte would be important to her, then?"

"I can scarcely imagine Kate without one," Francis murmured. "Whenever she is distressed, she must either play music or ramble. Stifle her too much, and she sinks into melancholy."

"She said the two of ye often sang together."

Francis chuckled fondly. "Indeed. Her voice falls into a rather unfortunate middling range, neither alto nor soprano nor a pleasing blend of both. She's lamented this fact many times, but her dearth of talent cannot persuade her to abstain from that which brings her joy. I would have it no other way." He leaned closer and nodded toward where Kate clapped in delight. "A joyful Kate is the loveliest sight imaginable; don't you agree?"

Broderick had to catch his breath as she beamed a happy grin at him over her shoulder. "Aye. The bonniest creature in heaven and earth."

Francis fell silent. When Broderick managed to tear his gaze away from his wife, he found the blond man assessing him with a wry smile.

Broderick frowned. "What?"

"She's worked her magic with you, too, hasn't she?"

Oddly, he felt his face heating. "Nah."

"Oh, yes. She does it with everyone. Nothing to be embarrassed about."

"I'm nae embarrassed." It was warm in the theatre. That was all.

"Take our mutual friend, Clarissa Meadows, for example." Francis casually gestured. "Kate, as previously noted, is lovely. Everyone agrees. But in her first season, a family scandal relegated her to a seat amongst the wallflowers."

"Aye. She told me."

"Clarissa had been a wallflower for seven years." Francis pointedly caught Broderick's gaze. "Seven. Years. That is an eternity for a young woman to sit on the fringes of the ballroom and watch her matrimonial prospects wither."

"What was wrong with the lass?"

Francis waved away his question. "A bit overplump in her youth. Perhaps a bit too frightened of leaving her grandmother's side. In any event, Kate befriended her in a trice, as Kate does. Within a year, she transformed Clarissa Meadows from a plump gosling into an elegant swan." Francis chuckled. "The thing of it is, Clarissa didn't realize what was happening. Kate simply listened to her. She discovered her love of dancing. Then, Kate dragged me to her house every day so we could practice together. Soon, Clarissa's confidence brightened, her form trimmed, and her fashions became eminently more suitable. I may have had a hand in the last bit, but the rest was entirely Kate. She senses what people need, what they desire most, and she finds a way to deliver it to them, all without anyone the wiser. I don't even know if *she's* aware she's doing it. It just seems to … happen."

Nothing of Francis's story surprised Broderick. This was what he'd seen. Facilitating a romance between her lady's maid and Stuart MacDonnell. Recommending Mrs. Grant's sister as a new cook for Annie. Teaching Rannoch to improve his table manners beyond those of a donkey. Kate's generous heart changed everything for the better.

He cast a curious glance at Francis. "What did she do for ye?"

The other man's eyes began to glow with profound emotion. He nodded to where Kate chatted with George, patting the valet's hand and avidly explaining the German caterwauling.

"That," said Francis. "She accepted me. An innocent girl who had just been rejected by the man she wanted to marry. She did not understand, but she accepted. Then, she warned me that real, honest love is a treasure, and only an 'addlepated ninny' would fail to claim it, whether society thought it acceptable or not." His gaze dropped. "She could have ruined me, you know. Instead, she gave me magic and asked nothing in return."

That was Kate. Pure magic. It was why he must win her. He must keep her safe. He must defeat Lockhart and then spoil his wife until she never suffered a single doubt about where she belonged.

"Guard her well, MacPherson."

Surprised at the man's grim tone, Broderick shot him a glance.

Francis's gaze turned steely. "She shared a bit about your current troubles in her letters. If you have need of my assistance, consider me an ally."

"I'm grateful for the offer." He huffed out a chuckle. "I dinnae suppose ye ken a man named Kenneth Lockhart."

"No, I'm afraid not."

"Ah, well. 'Twould be an odd day for my luck to turn."

"Lockhart is the man we must protect Kate from, yes?"

"Aye."

"She indicated you'd already done him some injury."

"Aye, but it willnae stop him. Rannoch and I have been trackin' his business partner, a man by the name of Rob McKenzie. McKenzie runs a club for men of particular appetites. Lockhart is a silent partner, livin' off his share. But he also uses his knowledge of the club's members to coax them into doin' his bidding. If we can get inside and locate McKenzie's member list, we can use it to shut down the club and render Lockhart's blackmail schemes worthless."

Francis's brow furrowed. "What is the name of the club?"

"Second Circle. Somethin' to do with the levels of hell, I take it." He grunted. "Apt way to describe a house on the fouler end of Cowgate. Nevertheless, they've secured the place well. Nobody comes in or out without membership, a code, and bein' on that night's list. I've none of those."

Francis leaned forward to catch Broderick's eye. "I've heard of the Second Circle. Or, rather, George has. His former employer was a member there."

"Can he help us gain entry?"

Francis smiled. "For Kate? Consider it done."

CHAPTER SEVENTEEN

Kate took a moment to adjust her mask before she descended the staircase to join her husband. He might not agree to this, but she must try. Did Lady Macbeth sit idly by while her husband charged into the fray? No.

Drat, perhaps that was not the best analogy. Regardless, she intended to bring Lockhart down, and helping Broderick infiltrate a scandalous club was one small way to do so.

She smoothed red silk over her hips and tugged her cape into place before making her way down to the parlor, where Francis, George, Broderick, and Alexander had gathered. All four men wore frowns. Those frowns deepened when she entered. "Gentlemen, I am coming with you."

A chorus of denials erupted.

She sniffed and adjusted her gloves. "The decision is made. You need a female, and I am female."

"Kate," Broderick growled. "We discussed this. The first time ye have to lie, ye'll give us away."

"I shan't speak. We'll pretend I'm the timid sort cowed by her domineering husband."

Said husband snorted and rolled his eye. "Might as well say ye're a bottle of whisky."

Francis tried next. "Kate," he said reasonably. "The Second Circle is a den of iniquity. You will see things there you'll heartily wish you hadn't."

"What things?"

He cleared his throat and cast nervous glances at the other men. "Even to explain them would shock your sensibilities."

"Rubbish. This is important, Francis. To enter the premises, we must be a group of four men and one woman. That is what you said, is it not?"

He sighed. "Yes."

She tilted her chin, eyeing the men. "So, which of you would care to wear a gown?"

Alexander grinned. "Mayhap Rannoch could do it."

Broderick cursed.

"Now, do stop behaving like missish old women and be sensible." Kate waved at the four of them. "Surrounded by all of you, I shall be in no danger whatever."

Broderick stalked toward her, stopping only when they were inches apart. "Listen well, lass. There is nae way on God's earth I shall take ye into that place. And that's my final word on the matter."

An hour later, sandwiched between Broderick and Francis in the coach, Kate leaned forward in an attempt to catch her first glimpse of a notorious "den of iniquity." From the outside, it appeared rather more modest than she'd anticipated.

"Are you certain this is the right house, Broderick?" she inquired. "It looks ... plain."

He didn't answer. He'd been sulking ever since she'd forced his hand by calmly threatening to hire a coach and follow them after they left. When he'd threatened to lock her in their bedchamber, she'd raised the stakes with a promise to lock *him* out of their bedchamber—after she bribed one of the kitchen lads to release her.

Now, the coach halted, and all the men except her husband exited onto the street. Jaw flickering, Broderick gritted, "Ye'll stay by my side, do ye ken? I want ye close as my bluidy skin. At all times, some part of ye must be touchin' some part of me."

"Stay close. Yes, I understand."

"Nae close," he growled, his eye flashing in the faint light from a nearby streetlamp. "Touchin'."

"Yes. Touching."

"Dinnae get curious. Dinnae speak. Dinnae remove yer mask for any reason. If somebody touches ye apart from me, they'll lose whatever part did the trespassin'."

She caressed his flexing jaw with her gloved palm. "Everything will be fine."

He yanked away and tied on his mask—a gold full-face mask with a blank expression. Then, he exited the coach and reached for her, lifting her down with breathtaking ease. He looped her arm through his, clasping her hand firmly against his body.

They approached the quiet, modest house not from the front, but along the side, where a dark, narrow close led to a service entrance. Francis removed his glove and knocked in an odd rhythm. The door opened. Francis murmured something nonsensical about ships and mutton to the bald man inside. The man opened a small book and peered down through reading spectacles. He asked for Francis's name, and Francis replied, "Robin Goodfellow."

It was one of the names for the mischievous Puck in *A Midsummer Night's Dream*—Kate's suggestion. She'd liked the whimsy.

The bald man eyed their group with squinting skepticism. He appeared puzzled by the unusual height of two of their party. "Ye were noted as havin' a lass among ye."

Reluctantly, Broderick drew her forward into the light.

The bald man nodded and waved them inside. "This way, sirs. Madam."

They passed through a small, gold-hued antechamber occupied by two masked men who rivaled the MacPhersons in size. The bald man unlocked a black door with a pair of overlapping circles painted in gold. They entered a long, taper-lit corridor that ended in a staircase winding down. Broderick's arm squeezed her waist until her ribs nearly merged with his hand. She tapped him and wheezed. Beneath the edge of his mask, she saw his jaw flex, but he loosened his grip.

They descended two flights and entered a long room that smelled of lilies and musk. The open chamber was lit by red lanterns and white chandeliers, casting the space in an odd, pink glow. Rose-red velvet daybeds, black divans, and the occasional gilded chair formed conversation areas and lined the walls.

But the furnishings were far from the most riveting sight in the room. No, indeed. That distinction belonged to the dozens of people in varying states of undress from naked to somewhat naked, frolicking on said furnishings.

Kate wanted to ask why a man would beg a woman to use her riding crop on his backside and then ride him like a pony, but her curiosity would have to wait. Broderick was hauling her through the crowd as if it were a leper colony. To be fair, among the shockingly lewd acts carrying on before her eyes, some were revolting. Others, however, were intriguing.

She'd never considered using her mouth to pleasure Broderick in a way similar to the woman kneeling on a pillow nearby. The recipient of her attentions appeared most appreciative, moaning his ecstasy while fondling her bosom. Later, Kate must ask Broderick if he would enjoy such an act. She felt certain she would.

Leading their path through the crowd, Francis stopped at a door hidden behind a giant urn. He used a key from his pocket to open a passage, waving them through. "We've a quarter-hour to search before they discover our ruse." He withdrew his watch. "Return to the coach by half-past. Good luck, lads."

As Alexander started down the long corridor glancing this way and that, Francis and George veered to the right, following a different passage. Broderick bent down and whispered, "Dinnae look at anythin', ye ken? Keep yer eyes on me."

She tried to do as he'd instructed, but the sounds emanating from the chambers along the corridor were disturbing. She heard groans of ecstasy similar to those in the pink room, certainly. But also, screams of pain. Whimpers for mercy. Cracks that sounded distinctly like whips or straps striking flesh. She managed to keep her eyes on the carpets as Broderick hurried them along.

But, since each chamber had a window, she glimpsed movement in her peripheral vision. Automatically, she glanced up.

And instantly regretted it.

She tugged at Broderick's arm. Dug her fingernails into his muscle. "That—that's—dear God, how—"

"Haud yer wheesht," he hissed, dragging her past the room she never wanted to see again.

"Dear God." She felt her gorge rise. Burying her face against Broderick's shoulder, she clung to his arm and tried to keep pace.

He turned them left into another passage. Soon, he muttered, "Stairs, lass."

She opened her eyes but kept them directly on the floor in front of her. The stairs in front of her. The landing and the next flight and the new carpets in front of her. She thought they must be on the ground level, now. She could still hear moans and rhythmic thuds emanating from chambers along this new corridor. There were no screams, though. No whimpering. Soon, all sounds quieted.

"The chambers on this end appear empty," Broderick whispered, pausing to listen. "We may be close."

They were searching for McKenzie's quarters, reputed to be in the less frequented area of the house. Kate's heart pounded as Broderick rushed them forward then abruptly halted when, twenty feet ahead, a couple emerged from one of the chambers. The man was short and muscular, the woman tall, slender, veiled, and white-blonde. The man's face was unmasked, his gingery hair only covered by a top hat. In his hand was a valise. The pair murmured to one another as the man turned to lock the door.

Suddenly, Kate found herself lifted against Broderick's body, turned so her back was braced against the nearest wall, and her bosom crushed by his chest, her thighs straddling his leg. Broderick lifted his mask only enough to clear his mouth before slamming it down upon hers.

Her head spun. He hadn't kissed her since that morning, and the impact was potent. Firm, skillful lips caressed hers while a sleek tongue slipped inside her mouth, pulsing and pleasuring. A large hand moved from her waist to her breast, kneading with insistent pressure. Distantly, she realized his purpose must be subterfuge, but that didn't change how it felt.

Like an erotic fantasy, the way he touched her—with such silent, masterful command—set her body afire. Before long, she was panting and whimpering against him, running her hands beneath his cloak and around his waist to draw him closer. She felt his hardness rise against her thigh, felt his hands clasping with greater urgency, his tongue plunging in a mimicry of lovemaking. His breathing turned harsh, his grip tighter.

He withdrew enough to whisper against her mouth, "God, woman. What ye do to me." More harsh panting. "Look to yer right. Are they still there?" He kissed her again, lighter this time.

She struggled to clear her head of its lustful fog and follow his instruction. The corridor was empty. "They're gone," she whispered.

He nodded but didn't immediately release her. "Bluidy hell. Too close."

"They wouldn't have recognized us, would they?"

He didn't reply. Rather, he drew back, flicking her cape closed and his mask back into place. Then, he took her hand and pulled her to one of the nearest doors. After listening for a moment, he placed a finger to the mouth of his mask to signal silence, then opened the door a scant inch. He peeked inside, found it empty, then pulled her behind him into the chamber. The room was scarcely even a bedchamber. It had a bed, true, but it was a tiny space with only a small washstand and a single chair. A lantern glowed from a shelf.

Broderick closed the door behind them. "I need ye to wait here for me, lass."

Kate blinked. "Why? I thought you wanted me close. I thought we were looking for McKenzie's quarters."

"Aye, that's why. The man we saw was McKenzie, and I suspect the door he locked leads to his chambers. He's gone now, but for how long? I cannae delay, cannae search for Alexander to guard ye." He cupped her face in his hands.

It was strange to gaze up at him and see only a gold mask. She wanted to see his face. Wanted him to kiss her again.

"I need ye to stay in here until ye hear me knock thrice. Lock the door behind me. Dinnae open it for anybody else. Ye ken?"

She nodded, swallowing the anxious lump in her throat.

"That's my brave lass. If aught happens, and an hour passes without me or Alexander comin' for ye, then do yer best to find yer way out of this place. Anybody asks what ye're about, say yer husband left ye behind. Hire a hack to take ye back to the house. Tell Campbell what happened."

"No," she rasped, clinging to him. "We shan't need any such plans because you'll be fine. Everything will be fine. It must be." She forced herself to smile up at him, though her eyes were welling like a perfect ninny. "You are *legendary*, Broderick MacPherson. More than Sir Wallace. More than any man I've ever known. You will find a way into McKenzie's chambers. You will locate the list. You will defeat Lockhart."

He huffed out a chuckle. "Dinnae ken about legendary, *mo chridhe*. But if there's breath in my body, I'll always find ye. No matter where ye are or how dark it seems." He raised his mask to kiss her once more, then lowered it to slip out into the corridor.

With shaking fingers, she turned the lock. With shaking legs, she lowered herself onto the bed. And waited.

A quarter-hour came and went. Then another.

Her stomach began to cramp. She cradled it and rocked back and forth.

Another quarter-hour passed, and she began to pace the tiny chamber, listening at the door, wondering if she should try to find Broderick or wait until an hour had passed. She looked again at the small watch she'd pinned inside her corset. Ten minutes remained. What must Francis, George, and Alexander be thinking? Were they searching for her and Broderick? Had they left already?

Just then, a knock sounded at the door, startling her. Had that been three raps or four? It didn't matter. It must be Broderick. She rushed to unlock the door. "What took you so ... long?"

Oh, heavens. It wasn't Broderick. It was a woman. The veiled woman from earlier.

All blood in Kate's veins went cold. Her heart pounded. Her breath stopped.

"I recommend letting me inside," the Scotswoman said calmly. "McKenzie doesnae tolerate intruders. I dinnae think ye wish to be seen."

Kate staggered backward, and the blonde woman followed, closing the door. "Who are you?" Kate demanded.

"My name doesnae matter."

It was hard to see the woman's eyes through the dense, black veil, but Kate felt them examining her closely. "What do you want?"

The small hat perched on the woman's white-blond hair resembled a riding hat, but it was covered in black satin and a fountain of black lace. The woman's gown was green, her posture elegant. Kate suspected if she lifted the veil, she'd reveal beauty.

"Ye're his wife, then?"

Kate paused. "Of whom are we speaking?"

The woman's soft voice turned waspish. "Broderick MacPherson. Dinnae pretend. I saw the two of ye earlier."

A suspicion of the woman's identity tugged at the back of her mind. "What do you know of him?"

"Oh, I ken him. I ken every inch of him."

A wash of acid flooded Kate's body. It stung like hatred. Tasted like hot poison. "You're Lockhart's mistress," she whispered.

The woman lifted her veil with an abrupt motion. And, yes, she was beautiful. Ethereally, unbearably beautiful. "Ye'll never please a man like Broderick. Weak, cold English tea; that's all ye are. He'll get bairns upon ye, aye. He'll let ye have his name. But ye'll never have his heart. No woman will."

The charge was a bullet that pierced Kate's chest. One woman had, although that woman was not in this room. She should answer, but she couldn't breathe. Hatred and jealousy warred with pain. Finally, she marshaled every Huxley resource in her body. Wound up to fire a bullet of her own.

"At least he married me. You couldn't even manage that much."

Sea-blue eyes flashed fire. "I *managed* to persuade him into my bed in an afternoon. Can ye say the same?"

No, she couldn't. She'd had to beg him to kiss her, demand he touch her. His own wife. Sickness roiled in her stomach. Her hands curled into claws.

A triumphant smile curved the woman's exquisite lips. "When ye kiss him, remember I kissed him first. When he touches ye like ye're made of spun glass, remember he touched me first. When he whispers his sweet, bonnie words in yer ear whilst he tups ye, and turns yer head with his Gaelic poetry, remember others have heard it all before and likely will again."

Kate's jealousy receded just enough for confusion to intrude. Spun glass? Sweet, bonnie words? Gaelic poetry? Were they still discussing Broderick? Perhaps this white-blonde tart was thinking of another man she'd "persuaded" into her bed "in an afternoon."

In Kate's experience, Broderick touched her with passionate command. He scarcely uttered more than ten words when they made love, and those were far from "bonnie" or "sweet." Erotic, yes. Guttural. Raw. And the only Gaelic he used with her was *mo chridhe*. He said that fairly often, but as far as she knew, it was a common endearment, much like darling or dearest. Certainly, he'd never bothered to cite poetry.

Perhaps he knew it was unnecessary. He knew she would beg for his attentions. Why expend the effort to treat her like spun glass?

Her sickness deepened, her vision shifting. The white-blonde tart's expression disappeared behind a lowered veil.

"He'll be here soon," the other woman said. "If you care to keep him safe, best the two of ye leave quickly. McKenzie returns at three. Tell Broderick I willnae help him again."

Kate narrowed her eyes as the woman turned to open the door. "Why didn't you help him before?"

The woman froze.

"You must have known what Lockhart might do." Kate's chest felt crushed. "Did you know before it happened?"

The woman lowered her head.

"Yes, of course you knew. Yet, you did nothing. Not even a warning." Kate moved closer. "Do not speak to me about my husband's nature. *Lockhart's* nature would have been obvious to you, and yet, you risked Broderick's life. You stood by whilst an envious demon tormented a man you claim to love. I don't know why you're helping us now. But it is far too little and months too late."

"Ye ken nothin' of my reasons."

"True. But I know this: I would sooner die than watch him suffer. And I would not stop fighting until he was free of that place, no matter the consequences. Because love means you value him above yourself." She paused before repeating the woman's earlier words back to her. "Can you say the same?"

The woman didn't answer. Instead, she left the chamber, quietly closing the door.

Alone again, Kate stumbled to the bed and collapsed. She held her middle and rocked. She waited to hear him.

Then, came three raps. She surged to her feet, dizzy and sick. She managed to open the door a split second before he gathered her up into his arms, crushing her to him.

"Thank God," he murmured. He held her tightly while she breathed him in, burying her face in his neck and clinging with all her might. "Time to go, lass."

She nodded. Loosened her arms reluctantly. He set her down carefully. Then, with a curse, he lifted his mask, clasped her neck, and brought her mouth to his. The kiss swiftly turned desperate before he tugged away with a low growl. "By God, ye madden me."

Finally, he locked her arm inside his and tucked her close against his side. After checking the corridor, he led her out, keeping his pace swift and steady.

Her thoughts whirled, but she kept up and kept her gaze pointed down. A short while later, they exited through a different entrance—this one at the rear of the house. A blast of cold rain struck her face.

Then, she heard Francis's voice, and tears began to choke her.

Dear, dear Francis. He'd waited for them. She stood on her toes to kiss his cheek.

Suddenly, Broderick scooped her up and carried her into the coach, settling her on his lap and ripping his mask off. Dimly, she heard him explaining that he'd had to force his way into McKenzie's chambers and search six rooms for the documents he sought. That had been the delay—they'd been hidden inside a book on a shelf behind a sculpture of a kelpie.

"But ye have them," Alexander asked.

"Aye."

Broderick's hands didn't stop stroking her all through his conversation. Her arms and her back, her nape and her cheeks. As the coach turned onto a new street, he removed her mask, cradled her head, and encouraged her to rest against his shoulder.

Shaky and exhausted, she let him hold her, needing the comfort.

An hour later, she sat in their bedchamber while Janet brushed her hair and debated whether bairns fathered by Stuart MacDonnell would inherit his "bonnie red hair." Kate took comfort in her maid's conversation. She'd also bathed earlier, enjoying the sense of normalcy and routine. It felt important to wash away the remnants of that dreadful place.

Downstairs, Broderick and his brothers continued poring over the documents he'd stolen and made their plans to choke off Lockhart's finances. While they'd been infiltrating the club, Campbell and Rannoch had been tracking Munro. They'd spotted the constable meeting with Sabella Lockhart at an inn near Lawnmarket. Once again, the conversation had been brief, and Sabella had left Munro looking frustrated. It remained unclear whether Munro was hunting Lockhart or working for him.

What did seem clear was that Lockhart's mistress— Cecilia Hamilton, according to Broderick—had been ferrying funds between McKenzie and Lockhart. Having recognized Cecilia in the corridor, Broderick had quickly concluded that she was still controlled by Lockhart. Kate had started to tell him that she'd spoken with Cecilia, that the woman had known he was there and might have protected them. But the words had choked her.

Meanwhile, the men had continued discussing their plans, and she'd retreated upstairs to gather her thoughts.

Kate wanted this to work. She prayed it did. But she still felt sick. The cold, slithery feeling refused to go away, despite the bath and her cheerful maid's chatter.

Janet finished tidying up then laid a hand upon Kate's shoulder. "All will be well, mistress. The MacPhersons are no wee, puny men. Only look at yer husband. All he's survived." She gave Kate a reassuring pat. "That blackguard fired every weapon he had at Broderick MacPherson, and all he did was make him stronger."

Kate didn't know why, but a tear tracked down her cheek. She squeezed her eyes closed and nodded.

"Summon me if ye have need of anythin', ye ken? Even if I'm sleepin', I'm never far away."

She nodded again. A moment later, she heard the soft click of the door. Despair crept in like smoke beneath a door. It filled her with a dreadful ache. Tears kept coming, and she kept swiping them away. With a sniff, she gathered Broderick's plaid around her shoulders and drifted to lie on the bed.

God, how she hated wallowing. But all she could see when she closed her eyes was Cecilia Hamilton's exquisite face. All she could hear was Cecilia's taunting description of Broderick's lovemaking. The knowledge that he'd gone to her bed so readily, treated her so differently.

What did it mean? Perhaps nothing.

He wanted Kate. She need only kiss him, and his body told her that much. He'd worked hard to please her and keep her safe—to a maddening degree, one might say. He was a good man. Noble.

Yet, her despair would not abate. She loved him. But by all evidence, he did not love her. Perhaps he'd loved Magdalene. Perhaps he'd treated her the same way he'd treated Cecilia—with gentle kindness and Gaelic poetry.

Perhaps with Kate, he'd resigned himself to being her husband and, needing wifely comfort, he'd simply taken what was offered. Seduction? Unnecessary. Wooing? Why bother? She was already his—her body, her heart.

Now, she buried her face in a pillow and chided her own stupidity. What had she expected? She'd all but forced the man to marry her, to consummate their marriage and pretend it was real.

The door opened and closed. Boots fell in a quiet, hitching rhythm. Clothing rustled. Water splashed. A sigh. The cooling scent of his liniment wafted toward her. The mattress depressed behind where she lay curled up. A gentle hand stroked her hair. "Are ye awake, *mo chridhe?*"

She nodded.

"I'm sorry I took ye to that place. I should have locked ye in here and taken the key with me."

"Don't be silly," she rasped. "I forced your hand. I do that a lot, don't I?"

He fell quiet but kept stroking her hair. "Do ye care to tell me what has ye in such a state?"

Her breathing shuddered. She considered not saying anything, but she must tell him about Cecilia. He needed to know. She rolled over and sat up, hugging her knees to her chest. "I spoke with Cecilia."

A frown. "When?"

"Whilst you were searching McKenzie's quarters. She knocked, and I thought it was you."

"What the devil did she say?"

"She recognized you in the corridor." Kate swallowed. "I think she made certain we wouldn't be discovered. I expect she still has feelings for you."

He scoffed. "Aye, well. Fat lot of good that did me last time round."

She blinked at his cavalier tone. "Y-you knew that she ...?"

"Cecilia came to see me at the warehouse in Leith an hour before the exciseman was shot. So, aye. I've nae doubt she kenned what would happen. Mayhap if I hadnae rejected her, she'd have warned me of his plans."

Her chest tightened. "How can you not hate her for what she allowed him to do to you?"

"Cecilia is damaged, lass. She was damaged long before she met Lockhart or me."

"I don't care. I hate her."

A small smile tugged at his mouth. He stroked her hair and her cheek. "I can see that."

"Keep her away from me. If I see her again, I shall rid her of that appallingly colorless hair and demonstrate my facility with a *sgian-dubh*. She'll need a veil then, by God."

He chuckled. "My ferocious Kate. I like this side of ye, lass."

She laid her cheek atop her knees, loving his smile. A piece of her despair wisped away.

"Now, then," he said. "I've a notion ye were upset by somethin' else she said."

"It doesn't matter."

"Kate—"

"No, really." Her mouth quirked. "She was jealous. She wanted to hurt me. That's all."

His eye narrowed and flashed. "Hmm. Ye willnae mind lettin' me tup ye before we sleep, then." He stripped off his shirt.

Blinking, she sat up straight and scooted away, shaking her head. "Wh-what has one thing to do with the other?"

"Dinnae lie to me," he snapped. "Ye havenae been up here weepin' because she said somethin' that *doesnae matter*. And I willnae let ye sleep until we settle on what's distressin' ye so badly."

"I'm just tired, Broderick. Please, can we change the subject?"

"No. We cannae."

"Everything she said was predictable. I could have written it myself."

He crossed his arms. "Aye? Recite it to me."

"I don't want to."

"Why?"

"Just ... stop, Broderick." She rolled forward onto her knees, intending to leave the bed.

He grasped her waist and dragged her close. "Did she claim I loved her? Because I didnae."

"No." She shoved at his chest, wriggling to free herself. She shoved and struggled, succeeding only in making herself hot and breathless. In the end, the plaid fell away, and her breasts flattened against his chest while his arm banded her backside. She writhed and shoved again, arousing her nipples and lowering the neckline of her shift several inches. "Let go of me!"

He held her fast. "Tell me what she said, and I will."

Her hands clawed into his chest. "God, you are infuriating!"

"Say it."

Incoherent rage surged. "I. Don't. Want to!"

"Why not?"

"Because if I say it, I'll know it's true! And I can't bear to know for certain, you arrogant, impossible Scot!"

"Nothin' that's true should distress ye, lass."

She screamed through gritted teeth and pummeled his shoulders with impotent fists.

He squeezed her tighter and braced her nape, his eye flashing like lightning amidst thunderous black. "I'll nae tolerate yer pain, *mo chridhe*. Ye must glow for me. My heart. My light. 'Tis all I have to keep me sane."

She collapsed in his arms. Buried her face in his muscular neck and slid her tired arms around him. An inarticulate whimper escaped her throat. "You read her poetry, Broderick. You touched her like spun glass."

He stroked her back, her neck, her hair. "What else? Tell me."

"She won you to her bed in an afternoon." A sob. She was choking. "I—I had to beg you to kiss me. I had to dose your whisky with Mrs. MacBean's stoat tonic."

Firm lips kissed their way from her temple to her cheek. They caressed and coaxed as strong hands kneaded her shoulders, back, and nape. "Good thing that wasnae what ye gave me, wife," he whispered while pressing tiny kisses beside her ear. "Ye wouldnae have walked properly for a bluidy fortnight."

She clung tighter, his hands and lips and heat draining some of the ache in her chest. "I only wish you considered me worthy of Gaelic poetry."

His hand slid down to lift her shift and caress her bare backside. "Nah. Ye dinnae."

She caught her breath as long fingers pressed, slid, dipped between her thighs, and sank inside her sheath. First one. Then two. "Broderick," she moaned, her fingers digging into his nape at the shocking pleasure of his invasion.

"Shall I tell ye why?"

"Oh, God."

"Before I met ye, I had ways of seducin' a lass. Most of 'em were pure rubbish." He ran his tongue along her throat, then captured her lips for a long, deep kiss before continuing. "A few bonnie words in Gaelic worked well enough. But my head had to be clear to recall the lines, ye ken? Likewise, I took care to handle a lass gently lest my strength frighten her away." He kissed her again, his fingers pulsing inside her, winding her tighter. "No chance of clear thinkin' with you. I cannae recall my own sodding name until ye scream it for me."

Her head fell back as pleasure climbed and climbed. She groaned.

"Aye, ye feel it, too. Comes on like a storm." His mouth dragged across her throat, suckling and nibbling. Suddenly, his fingers withdrew. He lifted her, stood, and lowered her onto the bed. Then, he shoved her shift above her waist and stared down at her with molten intensity. "I cannae hear. I cannae think. I cannae touch ye like glass, my bonnie Kate, because I'm so bluidy mad for ye, 'tis like havin' my ballocks in a vise. Thank God ye dinnae mind too much."

He dropped to his knees beside the bed. Then, he dragged her toward him and draped her legs upon his shoulders. "I feel yer skin," he rasped, smoothing his palms over her knees and thighs. Her hips and belly. "I hear ye breathin' and watch ye blush, bright as berries." He angled his head down and kissed her inner thigh. Licked her skin. Inhaled on a deep draw. "I smell yer scent. Sweet. So sweet, *mo chridhe*. Makes me hungry."

She arched her back and used her legs to pull him closer. "Broderick. I need you so much."

"Aye. But I'm nae done explainin'." He shot her a wicked grin as his fingers began to play. "Ye had to beg me to kiss ye because I kenned this was how it would be. Once I had ye, I'd never stop. Never be satisfied." He teased her swollen nub with the tip of his finger, pressing in tiny pulses. "I'd want to drive ye to the same depths of madness I feel. Just so I wouldnae be alone, here in the dark." He spread her folds and placed his open mouth directly upon her center.

Pleasure exploded in a riptide as he suckled and laved her, ravishing her senses and making her scream his name. *Broderick.* Over and over and over. She tore at her shift. The blankets. His hair. When he growled and refused to let up, she arched and begged.

Finally, he raised up, his lips shining, his skin flushed, and his eye filled with the fires of Hades. "Mayhap, one day, I can be easy." He kissed her inner thighs. First one, then the other. The kisses were soft, almost reverential. "I've tried to restrain myself. Nae more than thrice a day, I said, like meals or whisky. Because I ken how it frightens ye, what's between us. But if I gave ye a moment's doubt about what ye are to me, *mo chridhe*, let me set ye straight." Very gently, he eased her legs down. Then, he dispensed with his trousers and stripped away her shift. Finally, he settled on top of her, heavy and hard, holding some of his weight on his elbows but otherwise, not giving her an inch.

She moaned as heat pulsed everywhere his skin touched hers. The roughness of his chest hair against her breasts. The weight of his belly pressuring hers. The width of his hips spreading her legs. The silken stalk seeking to fill her. Every part of him was pure, arousing pleasure. As usual, the sensations overwhelmed her every lucid thought.

"Aye, my bonnie Kate." He kissed her brows and played with her curls. "Ye feel it. Then, ye fight it. But ye shouldnae be afraid. Because I'll always need ye more than ye need me."

She shook her head. "No. Don't you understand?" Her hips writhed to force him closer, bring him inside. "I love you. I love you so much, I would die for you. And the pleasure is too strong. It makes me think you could love me, too. But I know that's not true. I know you don't."

"But I do."

"No. You didn't want to marry me."

He chuckled. "Aye, lass. I did."

"Don't lie."

"How else could I have brought ye to my bed, ugly monster that I am?" He kissed her. Raised her knees up on either side of his hips. "How else could I plant my bairns in yer womb? One or two, remember? I wanted more. Ye looked at me with a spark that said, 'Ye might be big, but I'll handle ye just fine, Highlander.'" He grinned. "God, it felt like I'd been struck by lightnin'. I wanted ye enough to set fire to stone."

He slid his hard length along the seam of her folds, drawing forth long, aching, exquisite sensations that drove her mad.

"More than that, I wanted ye safe from everythin' that comes with bein' my wife," he whispered in her ear. A kiss. A caress of her nipple. Another stroke between her thighs. "So, I fought it, the way ye're fightin' it now. But ye might as well fight the tides. 'Tis too strong, *mo chridhe.*"

"But I'll always love you more," she despaired, cradling his beloved face and tracing the scars along his brow and mouth. "You own my heart, Broderick. I'll never have yours."

"My heart? Christ, woman, dinnae ye realize yet?"

"Realize what?"

With a single thrust, he forged inside, driving a pleasured gasp from her throat. "'Tis *you*, Kate Huxley MacPherson. I didnae have a heart before ye wandered into the dark and decided ye belonged here." He began thrusting rhythmically, forcefully. "Do I love ye? Aye." More thrusts. His hand tangled in her hair. He lowered his head and breathed deep. "I love ye. But that's a weak fucking word for what I feel, Kate."

She heard him, but more than that, she felt him. The hard desperation of his thrusts. The need grinding in his muscles. The gravel-and-caverns rumble of his voice. She felt the truth in him trying desperately to plant itself in her.

Suddenly her chest expanded like a sunrise, hot and bright and splendid.

He loved her. And not just a little. He loved her more than he could express. The same way she loved him.

Her pleasure magnified tenfold. She grasped his nape in both hands and brought his mouth to hers. Slid her tongue inside and demanded his in return.

He grunted his surprise, his hips quickening. Hammering. Harder and harder.

"Yes, my darling," Kate purred against his mouth. "That's it. Give me everything."

"Bluidy hell, lass."

She laughed, her joy spilling over and joining the glorious pleasure of her husband's deep, pounding thrusts. "I love you, Broderick MacPherson."

"Aye," he panted, his muscles straining. "I can feel it. Ye've stopped fighting. Ye must come soon. I cannae last. Yer laugh sets me afire, *mo chridhe*."

"Do you want to feel me come around you?"

"Aye," he growled.

The sound sizzled through her veins, spiraling along with the pleasure in their joining. "Then, make me, husband."

His eye flared with a kind of madness. He rolled them both until he lay on his back and she sat astride him. His hands slid up to her breasts and thumbed her nipples. "Ye favor ridin', aye? Take yer pleasure and give me mine."

Uncertain at first, she learned that if she braced her hands on his chest, she could sink down upon him slowly and deeply. The rich pressure inside, along with the angle of his penetration, had her gasping. Trembling. Poised on the edge of an abyss. Her body shocked her by welling up into an incandescent explosion. It took mere seconds in this new position for the pleasure to peak. But it didn't stop quickly. Oh, no. It went on and on and on in a glittering cascade.

"Ye light my sky, *mo chridhe.*"

She beamed down at him, seeing now what she'd missed by thinking she was alone. His wonder. His love. His heart, shining back at her. She collapsed into his kiss. Moved her body to pleasure his. Caressed him. Kissed him. Showered him with every drop of affection she'd been holding back out of fear.

As his peak drew near, she whispered what she wanted to try next.

It made him roar her name. Gravel and caverns. A man claimed. And a reassurance that whatever else he might be, whoever else had come before, he belonged to Kate, now. Her forever man had found his way home.

CHAPTER EIGHTEEN

Broderick watched as a brand-new Kate spun in the center of the morning room. He'd thought her enchanting before. Now, she glittered like a sea of diamonds.

"What do you think, my darling?" she inquired innocently, smoothing her hands over the blue velvet of her gown as she grinned over her shoulder. "Too elegant for a day of shopping with one's husband?"

The gown nipped in at her waist, flowing across her hips and backside in a way that made him want to tear it from her body so he could devour her whole. "Bonnie," he rasped, swallowing against a dry throat. "Ye dazzle me."

She laughed—crack, hitch, and tumble—then rushed to him and threw her arms around his neck. After a deep, long kiss, she sighed. "I could spend the next month making love to you, and it would still be insufficient. You are positively delicious."

His head spun. His chest heated. Expanded. The old Kate had intoxicated him. Freed from doubts, confident in his love, this new Kate held him in thrall. He hadn't understood the difference it might make until he saw it for himself.

She was happy. Beaming, shining, sensual. In the three days since he'd taken her to the club, she'd showered him with constant touching, frequent singing, and adventurous lovemaking that left him speechless.

Two nights ago, she'd insisted on taking him in her mouth. The walls still resounded with his roars. Last night, she'd explored his body so thoroughly, he'd begged for mercy. She'd grinned up at him from between his thighs, her eyes glowing with sensual fire, and crooned, "Not until you give me everything, Broderick MacPherson."

His knees were still weak.

He'd won her heart, but the need to please her in all ways remained fierce. Taking her shopping had been her idea, but it was a good one. Christmas was less than a fortnight away, and she'd mentioned wanting to find gifts for her family. After some maddening wifely persuasion, he'd agreed, provided they take precautions for her safety.

Now, she kissed his chin, sighed, and pulled away to fetch her bonnet. The deep brim shadowed her face even before she lowered the blue lace veil.

He hated covering her bonnie face, but it was better than her being spotted by Lockhart's men.

"Ready?"

She nodded and slipped on her gloves, then took his hand in hers. For a moment, she paused, her eyes scarcely visible through the lace. She drew him down and traced a gentle finger between his brows. "Everything will be fine. Don't worry so."

He cupped the small of her back and breathed in her lush, flowery scent. It reminded him of something he'd been meaning to give her. "Wait here a moment. I have a surprise for ye."

"Oh?" Her eyes lit up. She tossed back her veil and bounced on her toes. "I adore surprises."

"Aye. So I've been told."

He retrieved the small bottle from one of his trunks and quickly returned to the morning room. "Here. Now, ye'll have nae need to wear a scent purchased by another man."

She shot him a dubious look from beneath her lashes. "Broderick. Francis gave me that perfume. He is not *another man*. Precisely. I mean, he is a man, but you know very well he hasn't those sorts of feelings toward me."

He crossed his arms and nodded to the bottle Mrs. MacBean had prepared for his "bride" before she'd even arrived in Scotland. "Open it."

"Really, darling." She loosened the cap. "We had Francis and George to dinner only last … night." Her nose flared as she caught a whiff of the scent inside. Her eyes closed and she breathed deeper. "Oh. Oh, my. It is … heavenly. Tuberose and jasmine, bergamot, clary sage and …" Another breath. "You." Her eyes flared open and fastened upon him with a powerful lust. "It is us. Together."

"Aye. Are ye surprised?"

"Oh, yes."

"She did say ye'd love surprises." He grinned and shook his head. "The auld crone willnae let me hear the end of this one."

"We're going to be late for our shopping excursion, husband."

"How late, lass?"

She drew him down for a kiss and whispered against his lips, "Very."

Two hours later, he entered their first stop on the shopping excursion, a music shop on Princes Street, and found his wife chatting animatedly with the proprietor. As planned, he'd sent her inside separately with four of his men posing as footmen. If she were seen with him on the street, Lockhart would have no trouble identifying her. Targeting her. That must not happen.

Blast, he needed to find the blackguard. He and his brothers had already enacted their plan to choke off his funds. McKenzie had shuttered the Second Circle Club and fled Edinburgh. John Huxley's contacts here in the city—along with a few well-placed allies of Broderick's—had acted swiftly, seizing the club's assets and sending its members into a panic. A dozen or so had been cooperative, providing evidence of Lockhart's blackmail. Lockhart would be left with only the funds he had on hand, which would run out eventually.

In the meantime, Lockhart was still missing. Still dangerous.

Broderick took a deep breath and let Kate's delighted laughter soothe his dark tension. This was her day to enjoy a wee bit of normalcy, and he meant to give it to her.

He approached her slowly, admiring her slim curves beneath blue velvet. They were as graceful as those of the grand pianoforte she caressed with reverent fingers.

"Reinforced with iron, you say? How extraordinary."

"Aye, indeed," answered the proprietor. "A recent innovation from Broadwood. See, when ye stabilize the frame in this way, 'tis less prone to goin' out of tune. Sturdier in transport, too."

Her hand caressed the dark, polished wood the way she'd caressed Broderick's chest earlier that morning.

He shuddered in a breath.

"The rosewood veneer is lovely. May I play?"

"Of course, my lady." The proprietor positioned the bench and gestured with a bow. "Any song in particular?"

"No. I prefer to be extemporaneous." Gracefully, she sat and removed her gloves. For a moment, she fussed with her wedding ring. A secret smile curved her lips. Then, she positioned her fingers and began to play.

Rich, full chords sang out from the depths of the instrument. Her touch was light, sensual. Her pauses were perfectly timed to lift tension, her use of the pedals perfectly measured to layer resonance beneath stirring beauty.

Broderick watched her face—her closed eyes, the tiny motions of her brows and lips as she wrought emotion from an inert object. He saw his wife play, and he imagined their future.

He would place the pianoforte in the drawing room, facing the stag he would hunt for her.

He would listen to her sing nonsense songs in her in-between warble.

He would light her up with pleasure and swim naked with her in the moonlight and lay his hands upon her belly, swollen with his bairn.

He would take her to Edinburgh for the theatre and to Nottinghamshire to visit her family and to any other place she wanted to see for the sheer adventure of it.

He would work like a sodding draft horse to make the distillery a success so that his wee, bonnie wife could boast about him to her sisters.

In all the months since the Bridewell, Broderick hadn't allowed himself to think past killing Lockhart. He hadn't imagined a future because he hadn't believed he had one.

But now, here, he saw it as clearly as Kate's blue velvet gown. He must not fail her. He must eliminate the threat and come home to the woman he loved.

He moved to her side, ignoring the proprietor's horrified gasp as the man caught sight of him. Caressing her shoulder, he murmured, "Ye play beautifully, *mo chridhe.*"

Her tongue darted over smiling lips and her lashes fluttered upward. She finished her tune with loving strokes then clasped his fingers. "Do you think so?"

"Aye." He glanced at the proprietor. "How much?"

"Broderick," Kate hissed, tugging his hand. "You mustn't."

The proprietor named a staggering sum.

Indeed, Broderick would be working like a sodding draft horse. He might also be delaying the new stables he'd planned. But it would be worth it. "Can ye ship it to Inverness?"

"Aye, sir."

"Broderick," Kate gritted. "May I speak with you privately?" She stood and dragged him to the opposite corner of the showroom, where a row of violins gleamed in the light from the window. "You cannot purchase that pianoforte."

"Why not?"

"It is far too extravagant."

"Well, now, if ye kenned the plans I have for it, mayhap ye'd feel differently."

"What plans?" She waved her hands. "Never mind. It doesn't matter. You cannot spend a year's wages on—"

"Who claimed that's a year's wages?"

She blinked. "I—I assumed—"

"Nah. Half a month's worth, mayhap."

Her lips worked into an O. "The distillery is ... that successful?"

"Aye. And the farms. The rents." He grinned at her bewildered reaction. "Should I be offended that ye thought me poor, lass?"

"No, I didn't ... that is, I ... good heavens, Broderick." She blushed and played with her ring. "I meant no offense. Still, I cannot accept a gift of such magnitude. There are square pianofortes just there."

"Nah. Too wee. I cannae tup ye properly on one of those."

Her blush intensified. She inched closer, chiding, "Do not say such things. What if someone should overhear?"

"Then, they'd ken how much I want ye. If they've eyes in their head, they'll see why."

She weaved into him. "Good heavens."

"Ye said that already."

"You are ... this is ... you're seducing me. Right here in a music shop in broad daylight."

"Ye sound surprised."

She nibbled her lower lip and shot him a melting look from beneath her lashes. "Perhaps we should discuss this in the coach."

"Can ye wait that long?"

Her breath caught. "Provided you make our conversation ardently persuasive."

He grinned. "Ye're in luck, lass. Ardent persuasion is just what I had in mind."

Sabella exited the perfumery with her maid by her side. Today, Princes Street was bustling. Whenever the rain lifted, the shops teemed.

"Is he still there?" she murmured to her maid.

"Aye."

Sabella swallowed and lifted her chin. The "footman" Kenneth had assigned to watch her made her skin crawl. The way Cromartie leered, as though eager to set his hands upon her and cause her pain, was a threat of its own. Kenneth may have ordered the gin-swilling cretin not to harm her unless she ran, but if she did? What then?

She'd been too afraid to attempt it more than twice. Her luck had never been that good.

Her maid shifted the packages beneath her arms. "Shall I take these to the carriage?"

Sabella nodded. "Join me in the bookshop when ye're finished."

The maid curtsied and rushed to comply, heading for the carriage three shops away. The bookshop lay in the opposite direction. Sabella had no desire to purchase books, but the farther she could get from Cromartie, the better.

As she started forward, the door to the neighboring shop opened, and a shockingly tall man strode out. The man walked with a long, hitching gait. He wore a leather patch over one eye. He had dark hair, a lean-yet-massive frame, and scars through his brows, mouth, cheeks, and jaw.

Dear God. Her heart stuttered. It was Broderick MacPherson. He glanced to his left and started in that direction.

She must speak with him. She must warn him. Where was his wife?

Fear coiled around her insides, cold and slithery. Someone jostled her elbow as they passed. She dared a glance behind her toward her carriage. Her maid was distracting Cromartie with the loading of packages.

Heart pounding, she knew she must try. There might not be another chance.

Her feet carried her forward. Muscles stiff with fear, she was too slow at first. Then, seeing how swiftly his long strides increased the distance between them, she quickened her pace. Soon, she was nearly running.

A woman backed into her, slowing her pace and knocking her reticule from her hand. The woman apologized, but Sabella kept going. No. MacPherson was disappearing around the corner. She mustn't lose him. She must tell him what Kenneth had planned.

She opened her mouth to call out to him.

Something hard crushed her belly. Something painful drove the air from her lungs. A fist, she thought. The agony was explosive. Flashes floated in her vision.

A cretin who smelled of gin dragged her backward, ticking a chiding sound in her ear. "Now, now, Miss Lockhart," he whispered. "Feelin' poorly, eh? Time to take ye home. His lordship wouldnae care to have his sister speakin' to strangers."

Kate smoothed her hands over her gray wool bodice and cringed. "Are all your gowns this stiff, or have you decided I should be dreadfully uncomfortable for my foray into domestic service?"

Janet laughed and pinned a white cap over Kate's hair. "The wool isnae so fine as what ye're accustomed to, but ye'll fit right in, mistress. Just dinnae say aught other than 'aye, sir' or 'no, madam,' and ye'll be fine."

Kate rehearsed her lines for a few more minutes while Janet tied her apron in place. Next came the white kerchief tucked into her neckline and a black hooded cloak for warmth. She blew out a breath and retrieved her reticule. "Remember, not a word to my husband. If I'm wrong, I do not wish him to ever know what I've been doing. Promise me."

Janet smiled and retied the cloak, forming a perfect bow. "What ye're doin' for him is … 'tis a splendid gift, Mrs. MacPherson."

Warmth suffused her. Impulsively, she hugged her maid. "Thank you for helping, Janet. I love him. I would do anything for his happiness."

Embracing her with a pat, Janet chuckled. "Aye, and he's mad for ye; that much is plain." She pulled back and retrieved a length of coppery tartan wool from the chair nearest her dressing table. "Now, dinnae forget yer scarf." Janet fussed with the folds before giving her reticule a dubious glance. "'Tis a wee bit fine for a maid."

"Oh." Kate held it aloft. "Do you think so?" It was embroidered with an elaborate thistle design in gold and black thread on black silk velvet. She'd purchased it on her shopping excursion with Broderick several days earlier.

"Here." Janet retrieved Kate's brooch to pin the reticule to the lining of her cloak. "Now it willnae show." She found a pair of plain deerskin gloves and handed them to Kate.

Kate realized she'd been twisting her wedding ring around her finger again. Lately, she'd been preoccupied with the knot design, which matched her brooch. For some reason, the metal sometimes felt overwarm, as it did now.

"It belonged to his mam, ye ken," Janet said.

Startled, Kate paused before donning her left glove. "Th-the ring?"

"Aye." She smiled and tapped the central knot, which swirled in an infinite pattern. "Her father—Mr. MacPherson's grandfather—was a metalsmith. He made it for her. Had a wee touch of the sight, some say. All I ken is my mam said she wore it 'til the day she died."

Emotion choked her. She'd thought Broderick had purchased the least expensive ring he could find. Instead, he'd given her one he considered precious.

A knock sounded. "We dinnae have all day, Katie-lass," grumbled Alexander. All the brothers had started calling her by Annie's endearment. It made her feel part of the family. "Campbell will only keep Broderick occupied 'til four."

It was not yet eight in the morning, but still, he was right. They had a great deal to do and not much daylight to get it done. "Wish me luck," she murmured to Janet, who sent her off with a reassuring grin.

Kate and Alexander met Rannoch in the entrance hall and, together, they climbed into the coach. As she settled into place, Alexander rattled off his instructions. "Let's be clear on one thing, lass. Ye're nae to do anythin' risky. Ye go in, pose as Rannoch's maid, ask yer questions, and leave. That's it. Dinnae linger. Dinnae stray too far from Rannoch. In and out, that quick. Ye ken?"

Nervousness fizzed in her stomach. Nodding, she sat back and watched the streets pass as they made their way toward the orphan hospital.

For the past week, Rannoch and Alexander had done as she'd asked, retracing their steps to verify whether Magdalene Cuthbert was dead, as they'd thought, or alive, as she suspected.

Two days ago, the brothers had found Kate in the morning room shortly after Broderick departed for a meeting in Leith. Rannoch's eyes had flashed with excitement. "We have somethin', Katie-lass. Could be nothin'. But it might be somethin'."

Exasperated, she'd prompted, "Well, tell me."

"The woman found near the kirk was a prostitute."

Alexander had nodded, looking dreadfully weary. "We questioned the minister again, and somethin' didnae seem right. He admitted he recognized a birthmark she had in a …" He'd rubbed the back of his neck. "Delicate location."

Setting aside precisely *how* a minister acquired such intimate knowledge of a prostitute's body, this meant there was no reason to believe Magdalene was dead. Which meant they must find her.

Kate had called in Janet to help, quizzing the maid about how a woman recently imprisoned for theft might find domestic employment without references, funds, friends, or the use of her real name.

"Och, that's a riddle," Janet had mused. "Is this for yer story?"

After Kate explained about Magdalene, Janet had suggested eliminating finer households from their search. "She'll find better luck with the middlin' ones. The sculleries always need lasses." Finally, she'd asked whether Magdalene had "kin," which had reminded Kate that Magdalene had been raised in an orphanage here in Edinburgh. If anyone at the orphanage remembered Magdalene, they might know where she would go to find shelter, support, and employment.

Janet had cautioned them against revealing too much in their search for Magdalene. "Even scullery positions arenae easy to land. If anybody discovers she's a thief, that'll be the end of her. Best ye avoid drawin' too much attention, fine lady that ye are."

"Perhaps I could pose as a maid asking after a friend," Kate had suggested. Predictably, Rannoch and Alexander had argued it wasn't safe for Kate to accompany them, but she'd pointed out they were both too big and intimidating to do anything other than frighten their best sources of information. Upon hearing several *excellent* Shakespeare quotes about underestimating women, they'd conceded, and the current plan had been set.

Now, as they came to a halt in front of the rambling stone building that housed the orphan hospital, Kate recalled why she'd never trod the boards at Drury Lane. Her face was already hot.

Rannoch disembarked first, tugging at his fine blue coat and extending a hand like a proper gentleman. With a trembling smile, she accepted his assistance and stepped down onto the muddy lane.

"Ye dinnae have to say anythin'," he murmured. "As far as they ken, ye're my maid, helpin' me search for more maids."

She took a deep breath and nodded.

A line of small boys marched past carrying buckets. Their little faces were drawn and serious. Kate's heart squeezed when she saw one dark-haired boy, in particular, frowning fiercely as he struggled to raise his bucket to his chin. Would Broderick's sons look similar? She longed to find out.

Rannoch led her inside, where a young woman with spectacles took his name and left to fetch the matron of the orphanage. Inside, the place felt cavernous with a resounding echo, high ceilings, and polished wood floors. It smelled of vinegar, beeswax, and oats.

The matron—a short, round-cheeked woman with red hands and pinched lips—arrived moments later. Her name was Mrs. Hogg, and she seemed remarkably averse to "subjecting my lassies to interrogation."

Rannoch glanced around with a wry expression. "Isnae yer purpose to place these lasses with an employer?"

"Aye," Mrs. Hogg retorted with a sniff. "But I dinnae favor placin' them in the home of an unmarried man such as yerself."

"That's why I brought my current maid." He tugged Kate forward. "Miss Rosalind. She'll be helpin' me interview the lasses."

The woman's eyes narrowed upon Kate. "How long have ye worked for Mr. MacPherson?"

Kate swallowed. "Three years?"

"Are ye askin' or sayin'?"

"Saying?" Blast. Her cheeks were afire and her voice an octave higher than normal.

Rannoch flashed one of his wicked grins at the matron. Good God, the man could flirt with anyone. "Aye, she does grand work, too. My cravats have never been starchier." He angled his head in a cajoling way. "Alas, there is but one Miss Rosaline."

"Rosalind," Kate murmured beneath her breath. She'd selected the name of the heroine from *As You Like It*, who disguised herself as a young man. The boldness of the choice had seemed brilliant at the time.

"I plan to elevate her to housekeeper."

"Oh, that's clever," she muttered beneath her breath.

"But I cannae do so until her duties are delegated to a proper staff."

"Excellent improvisation," she breathed.

The matron glared at both of them, evidently immune to Rannoch's charm. "I've four lasses of age to take positions. Two are fourteen, two thirteen." She glared hard at Kate. "Ye may speak to them. Come." The last word was a bark issued with authority.

Kate and Rannoch started to follow the woman, but Mrs. Hogg spun and pointed at him. "Ye'll stay there."

He frowned. "As their potential employer, I must insist—"

"Ye may stay there, or ye may leave."

Kate flashed wide, pleading eyes at Rannoch. She could see his reluctance to let her go alone, but this might be her only chance to garner confidences from the orphanage's employees. He nodded, and she mouthed a "thank you" before dashing to catch up with Mrs. Hogg.

"So, Mrs. Hogg. How long have you worked here?"

"Two years. Are ye lookin' to hire me, with all these questions?"

Kate blinked. She'd only asked one.

"I ken what's what." The matron sniffed. "He's a braw man. Many lasses would do the same."

Frowning, Kate scrambled to keep up both figuratively and literally. Mrs. Hogg walked at a grueling pace. "I'm afraid I don't—"

"He wants to make ye his mistress but doesnae want to pay for separate quarters. Take my advice, Miss Ross."

"It—it's Rosalind."

"Men that bonnie dinnae marry their housekeepers. Ye'd do well to find a new position before he leaves ye with a bastard in yer belly. We've too many of those here already."

"Oh, I think you've misunderstood our—"

"Here we are." Mrs. Hogg abruptly turned right and opened a door into a room filled with steam. Large vats of scalding water occupied the center of the space, along with lines strung with dripping sheets and at least twenty females ranging from five to fifty. All had red faces. Some stirred the laundry vats with large paddles while others tended the fires, hauled water, pinned bedding and assorted garments to the lines, and scrubbed other garments in washtubs. One little girl dropped an armful of wet stockings when she tripped over a wayward paddle.

Without thinking, Kate crossed to her and helped the poor mite to her feet. The little girl's lower lip quivered. "Not to worry, little one," Kate soothed, giving the girl a smile and a pat before retrieving the overturned basket. "We'll have this tidied up in a trice."

Another woman, this one pinning a large sheet a few feet away, cast a nervous glance in Mrs. Hogg's direction before crouching to help stuff the stockings back into the basket. The woman nodded her thanks to Kate and ushered the little girl toward the door leading out into a small garden.

"This way, Miss Ross," snapped Mrs. Hogg, indicating the four girls lined up along one of the walls. "Ye have ten minutes."

Kate blew out a breath. This visit was not what she'd hoped it would be. Mrs. Hogg was far from forthcoming and likely had never met Magdalene Cuthbert, given she'd only worked there two years and Magdalene had left at least eight years before that. All the other women in the place appeared harried and oddly silent. How was she to ask her questions? The girls along the wall were too young to know anything.

Nevertheless, she "interviewed" the girls about subjects she presumed maids must be required to know: their preferences in solvents, their opinions about starch, their tolerance for onion chopping. When one of the girls asked what sort of work would be required, she kept her explanations vague. "My employer, Mr. MacPherson, prefers a clean house. You mustn't be squeamish or easily alarmed. Oh, and he likes onion gravy."

At the end of ten minutes, Mrs. Hogg cleared her throat loudly.

Kate sighed. Really, the woman was insufferable. "Mr. MacPherson will be most impressed with such well-trained young ladies," Kate said, giving them an approving smile. For Mrs. Hogg's benefit, she added, "He's a very successful, entirely legal and licensed distiller of fine whisky, you know. An *important* man."

The wide-eyed girls curtsied, and the matron led her out of the steam-soaked room and back into the cool corridor.

A failure. That's what she was.

Her gown itched. Her chest hurt. And like most things, investigative inquiry was not her strong suit.

Rannoch was pacing when they reached the entrance hall. "Anythin'?"

Kate gave a shake of her head.

He sighed and thanked Mrs. Hogg before escorting Kate outside. Rain was drizzling, and wind gusted it into her face. She tugged her scarf higher around her cheeks. The lane had emptied while they'd been inside.

"It's nae yer fault," Rannoch murmured, guiding her around a puddle toward the coach. "The odds were always low."

Her throat and eyes burned. "I wanted this too much. I am dreadful at deception. And singing." She began to choke. "And writing. Blast. I am dreadful at everything."

"Nah." He halted in front of a garden wall and clasped her shoulders. "Listen, now. If ye hadnae pressed us to go back and retrace our steps, we wouldnae have discovered Magdalene might be alive. That's somethin', aye?" When her tears started flowing, he drew her into his arms and patted her back. "Nae more tears, Katie-lass. We havenae failed yet."

Her answering smile trembled, but she swiped her cheeks and raised her chin. "Quite right." She sniffed and looked toward the coach. "Where did Alexander go?"

"Och, likely takin' a piss. Or stayin' out the rain."

Neither one sounded like something Alexander would do. The man was preternaturally vigilant.

From behind them came the whining of gate hinges, then a shy voice. "A-are you … Mr. MacPherson?"

They turned. Kate recognized the woman as one of the laundry maids—the one who'd stopped to help the little girl with the stockings. The young woman had a long, prominent nose and a narrow face, full lips that covered what looked to be large teeth, and wide gray eyes that rounded as they lit upon Rannoch's face. Faint color flagged near-translucent skin. Kate might think it the result of cold rain or hard labor, but she'd seen this before. Most females blushed around Rannoch.

"Aye," he replied to the woman's question. His gaze ran up and down, taking in her dishevelment. The woman tugged to straighten her slumped cap then retied her hastily knotted shawl—twice. Rannoch's brow lifted in amusement. "Can I help ye?"

Mouth working, the woman took a step closer then stopped. Her voice cracked into a squeak. She covered her lips, mottled red flooding her cheeks.

In his usual fashion, Rannoch sought to set her at ease by teasing, "Is that a wee mouse caught in yer throat, lass?"

The woman shook her head, her eyes flaring with an odd emotion—half hope, half fear. "I—Is he … is he well?"

Rannoch frowned. "Who?"

"Broderick," she whispered. "Ye're his brother, aye?"

Kate's head reeled.

"Ye look very much like him."

CHAPTER NINETEEN

Wandering closer, Kate blinked at a miracle. "Magdalene?" She swallowed as the woman's gentle eyes focused on her. "Magdalene Cuthbert?"

Glancing warily at the garden gate, the woman murmured, "Aye, though I beg of ye not to tell anybody here. Mrs. Hogg would not look kindly upon—"

Kate rushed forward and clasped Magdalene's red, bony hands, much to the other woman's astonishment. But she couldn't help it. She laughed. "My dearest Miss Cuthbert. We have been searching and searching. Thank heaven you're alive."

As Magdalene backed away, Rannoch clasped Kate's shoulders. "Easy, Katie-lass. We dinnae wish to frighten our wee mouse." With a charming grin, Rannoch drew Magdalene's attention back to him. "'Tis true I am Broderick MacPherson's brother. And this is his wife, Kate."

Magdalene's breathing quickened to a pant. "Then, he is all right? I heard dreadful things. I've been so worried, but …" Another quick glance behind her. "This position is all I have."

Heedless of the young woman's reticence, Kate clasped her hands again. "Broderick is very well. Scarred from his time in the Bridewell, but strong. So strong."

Magdalene's expression softened. "He always was."

Kate beamed. Her eyes welled. "Yes. He looked for you. He thought you'd been … well, he thought you hadn't survived." She glanced at Rannoch and back to Magdalene. "He will be overjoyed to see you. Come with us. Oh, you simply must."

"'Twould be splendid to see him, but I cannot leave. Mrs. Hogg has tolerated me until now, but—"

"Nonsense. You will come with us to see Broderick. Then, you will return to Glenscannadoo and stay with us. Our house has ample room and the most charming little loch." Kate tilted her head. "Or, would you prefer a cottage of your own?"

"Kate?" Rannoch said. "Ye're gettin' a wee bit overexcited."

Indeed, Magdalene appeared alarmed by her enthusiasm. "I couldn't possibly."

"Oh, but you must!" Kate shook her hands up and down. "Broderick will insist. And you will adore the glen. Really, who wouldn't? It is magical."

Magdalene opened her mouth to speak, but once again, only a squeak emerged.

Unexpectedly, Rannoch chuckled. "There's that wee mouse again." He angled closer. "Look, lass. I ken this came out of nowhere. But Kate isnae mad. Broderick sent me and our brother to find ye because he cares for ye. He'll wish to see ye, be it here or at our house in

Buccleuch. Either way, he'll nae tolerate ye workin' yer hands raw as a washerwoman." Rannoch's eyes hardened as they dropped to her red, chapped hands. "Neither will I."

Looking back and forth between Rannoch and Kate, Magdalene frowned. "I—I must retrieve a few belongings."

Triumph surged inside Kate's chest. "Yes. Yes, yes, yes." She squeezed the young woman's hands. "Shall I come with you? I should love to see the look upon Mrs. Hogg's face when you tell her you're leaving."

"Kate," Rannoch warned. "Ye'll wait in the coach."

"Oh, but—"

"I'll nae have ye wanderin' about. I'll take ye back to Alexander where ye'll be safe."

"Blast. Very well, then. Must keep Kate *safe*." She rolled her eyes.

He grinned. "Aye. That's the notion."

She huffed. Clicked her tongue. Gave Magdalene's fingers one last squeeze. Suddenly, she recalled the small tin Mrs. MacBean had given her. She reached inside her cloak to dig through her reticule then offered the salve. "Here. It's excellent for chafing."

Mrs. Hogg chose that moment to appear at the garden gate. Immediately, she castigated "Miss Smith" for laziness and implied her week's wages would be reduced. When Magdalene merely gave a dejected nod, Kate bristled.

So did Rannoch. "She's leavin' yer employ, Mrs. Hogg. I've decided to hire her."

Glaring at Magdalene, Mrs. Hogg harrumphed. "After all I did for ye." She shifted to Rannoch. "Fine. Ye can carry that ingrate's heavy trunk out of here. I never want to see it again. Nor her."

Rannoch shot Magdalene a puzzled glance.

"It's a long story," she sighed.

In the end, Rannoch agreed to accompany Magdalene after he deposited Kate safely inside the coach. Kate argued the coach was only twenty feet away and she could find her own way inside, but he insisted.

She greeted the coachman, who tipped his hat.

"Jack," Rannoch barked as they approached. "Where is Alexander?"

"Inside, sir."

"Doin' what?" He nodded to the closed curtains. "Havin' a nap, for God's sake?"

"Aye, sir. I believe so."

He reached for the door handle.

Kate patted Rannoch's arm. "Don't wake him. Go on and help Magdalene. I shall wait inside with our somnolent guard dog."

Rannoch frowned.

"Somnolent means sleepy," she clarified.

He rolled his eyes and started toward Magdalene. "Get inside, Kate," he called over his shoulder. "Dinnae linger."

"Yes, Papa."

He shook his head as he strode away.

Jack started to climb down from his bench, but Kate waved him off. She opened the door and immediately saw Alexander's long legs sprawled awkwardly between the seats. There was something strange about the position.

Something odd about the smell inside. Like … gin.

"Join us, Lady Katherine," a chilling voice said from the darkest corner. A click sounded. A gloved hand held a pistol to Alexander's chest. "I insist."

Her veins froze, stalling her heart. She wanted to scream. Frantically, she gasped, trying to draw air, mouthing Rannoch's name. She managed to turn, but Rannoch had already disappeared inside the orphanage.

"Now, now," the voice said. Beneath the aristocratic diction, it was faintly Scottish, yet slurred and distorted, as if he was chewing his words. "Come along."

Another man's hand grasped her upper arm and dragged her inside. This man, swarthy and mean, was the source of the gin stench. He forced her onto the seat beside him and latched the door.

Kate couldn't stop staring at the pistol. Head spinning, she tried to see whether Alexander breathed. When she noticed the faint movement of his chest, her own lungs filled. A whimper was the result.

She didn't want to look at the man who held the gun, but she must.

Ah, God. He was ... hideous. His left brow slumped into his eye socket. His jaw was sickeningly large. His teeth were largely absent, his lips bisected, his nose angled in at least three directions.

Broderick's fists had been thorough.

She could scream. Jack would hear her. Why hadn't their driver noticed these men entering the coach? Why hadn't he seen them attack Alexander? Why—

Sickness hit her in a wave.

Jack would do nothing. Because Jack worked for Lockhart.

Dear God. Broderick had surrounded her with guards and the MacPhersons. He'd hidden her away, taken every possible measure to ensure her safety, but none of it mattered a jot.

Lockhart had always known where she was. He could have killed her at any time. Killed Broderick. Killed Alexander or Rannoch or Campbell. Or Annie.

Jack had been John and Annie's coachman first, after all.

The black and silver interior warped around her. Lockhart's grotesque face twitched as he pounded the ceiling. The coach lurched into motion.

Rain fell in buckets.

Cold froze her through.

And Kate wondered if anything she did could have changed this, or if her fate had been sealed the moment she'd set foot in Scotland.

"We've a bit of a drive, Lady Katherine. Make yourself comfortable."

Her stomach twisted. "I prefer Mrs. MacPherson."

Green eyes burned with unnatural fire. "What a coincidence. So do I."

Breathing without pain had never before seemed a luxury to Sabella. But as she spied the coach below her bedchamber window, her starving lungs and pounding heart reminded her that anything could be a luxury, given sufficient deprivation.

Air. Safety. Love.

Below, in the garden, her brother's blond hair glinted gold in the watery light. Hair like her own. She remembered how he'd plaited her hair for her when they were wee. In their basement room beneath a weaver's shop, he would brush her hair gently with his fingers then tell her delightful stories about their mother's silk gowns. It had drowned out the hunger for a time.

She squeezed her eyes closed and opened them again to see he'd donned his hat. The coachman and Cromartie struggled to remove something from inside the coach. Cromartie was the one who'd broken her ribs. The physician had said she was fortunate they hadn't punctured her lungs.

Fortunate. Some might assume so, she supposed.

Her maid poured her another cup of tea. "I waited at the shop like ye asked, mistress. He werenae there." She transferred a slip of paper, folded in eighths, into Sabella's hand beneath the saucer.

Sabella closed her eyes again, taking care not to gasp or breathe too deeply. Another failed attempt to warn the intrepid constable from Inverness. The man was going to die if he weren't more careful. Worse, MacPherson's wife was going to die. And she couldn't help her. She couldn't even help herself.

Below, the two men carried what looked to be a third between them. The third man was dreadfully long and, given the strain on the coachman's face, dreadfully heavy. One of the MacPherson brothers, no doubt.

Banging resounded from downstairs—Kenneth's new favorite way of summoning her. She stiffened and handed her tea back to her maid. "Fetch the blue wool pelisse. I've a feeling today will be quite cold."

Minutes later, she entered the parlor overlooking the rear garden. Seated at a small desk near the fireplace, Kenneth scraped a spoon across the bottom of his soup bowl and handed it to a footman before dabbing his chin with a napkin. Nearby, sprawled on a large sofa, was an unconscious MacPherson male.

She laced her fingers at her waist, tightening them against the odd desire to wipe away the blood streaking from dense, dark hair down a square jaw and along a thick, muscular neck. He appeared enormously strong, so she had hope he would survive. For the moment, however, she could not rush to his rescue. She must focus on keeping her brother's temper calm.

"Who have you brought into our home, Kenneth?"

"Alexander MacPherson." He gave her a bone-chilling smile. "Ye remember, do ye not? I believe you enjoyed watching him toss stones over a bar and remove his shirt for a swim during the Highland Games last summer."

Her heart quickened. She struggled to control her breathing. "Did I? I'm afraid I don't recall."

"No? It was the same day your *friend* Annie Tulloch engineered my humiliation. He was present for that, too."

Silence fell between them filled only by the sigh of rain outside. "Why did you bring him here?" she asked.

"Because you enjoyed watching him so very much." Kenneth's ravaged lips twisted into a sneer. "Don't you wish to see him once more before he dies?"

She swallowed, her mind scrambling, her heart pounding, pounding, pounding. "He is nothing to me. Why would you assume otherwise?"

"Well, that much is true. He is nothing. Which makes yer interest in this rustic monstrosity a fair mystery, sister."

Every breath she took hurt like stabbing knives, but the pain of watching the brother she'd loved, who must have once loved her, deteriorate into madness was unbearable. "Kenneth. Please. I don't know him. We've never spoken."

His eyes softened. He sat back, glanced out the window, and gave her a broken grin. "Do ye remember the year I taught ye to ride?"

Grief welled up from a chasm. "Aye. I remember."

He'd been so patient. Eighteen and handsome, already amassing his fortune. She'd been eleven, cosseted as a crystal vase, and fearful of getting too close to such large animals. *Nothing to fear, Sabella,* he'd assured her, sunlight beaming down on his golden head. *All ladies must learn to ride. I shall catch ye if ye slip. Have I ever failed ye before?*

"You couldn't fathom why I would force ye to mount an animal large enough to crush you," he said. "But my reasons were the same then as they are now." His smile faded until his eyes turned sharp. "You are the daughter of Lady Lockhart. Your blood demands you behave as ladies are required to do." He gestured to the unconscious giant on their sofa. "He is beneath you, Sabella. All the MacPhersons are, including the red-haired bitch you betrayed me for."

"I didn't betray you."

"Anne Huxley is still alive. Somebody warned her about the man I sent."

"N-not I. Ye're my brother. I love you," she whispered, watching blood seep down the column of

MacPherson's neck. Wait. Had his breathing quickened?

"Love is not required. Loyalty, however, must be given in full measure." Kenneth withdrew a pistol from inside his coat. He aimed it at MacPherson's chest.

Sheer horror drained the blood from her head. A deep gasp sent knives slicing through her abdomen. "No!" She flew into the gap between the two men just as MacPherson reared up and, roaring like a beast, withdrew a blade from inside his boot.

She couldn't stop her momentum. She collided with MacPherson's arm just as he readied to throw his blade at Kenneth. Another roar sounded as the knife flew wide, grazing Kenneth's arm.

Darkness swarmed her vision as she struggled to breathe. A massive arm banded across her throat, drawing her back against a warm, heaving stone wall. His hand cradled half her head.

"Where is Kate?" MacPherson demanded. "I swear to Christ, Lockhart, if ye dinnae tell me where she is, I'll snap this one's neck."

Sabella could have told him Kenneth valued his goals far more than her life, but she couldn't breathe properly. MacPherson's grip was surprisingly gentle, but the collision and the pain in her ribs had flattened her lungs. Dimly, she heard the man shouting, "Tell me where she is!"

"Nowhere ye'll ever find her," Kenneth snarled, cradling his wounded arm. "*Nobody* will find her. But I shall so enjoy watching the hunt."

MacPherson's arm flexed as he maneuvered her sideways. The motion twisted her ribs, making her cry out. Stars floated in her vision.

His hands loosened as she sagged into him. "What the devil is wrong with ye, woman?"

Blackness rushed in when his arms caught her waist.

Pain exploded. She screamed, a puny wail without the force of breath behind it. Hard hands grasped her arms instead, turning her into the sofa and lowering her down.

The next thing she heard was a crack. Deafening. Resounding.

Watery light swirled as her gorge rose.

Red bloomed on MacPherson's broad back. One of the strongest men she'd ever seen staggered forward. Bent at the knees. And crashed to the floor.

Kenneth stood above him with a chilling smile and a smoking pistol in his hand.

Broderick returned to the house in Buccleuch to find Sergeant Neil Munro waiting for him.

"Bluidy hell, man. Dinnae ye have aught that's useful to do?"

The constable glowered at Broderick, but when Campbell dismounted, he backed up a step. "I need yer help, MacPherson."

"Ask somebody ye didnae try to send back to prison." He handed his mount to the stable lad with an order to send Connor to him at once.

Munro trailed them inside. "Lockhart has somethin' big planned."

Campbell grunted. "Keen work, Sergeant. A wee bairn could have told us that much."

"He means to flee Scotland, mayhap by ship."

In the entrance hall, Broderick paused, listening for Kate's voice. Nothing. Where was she?

"Saw trunks bein' loaded from his house into a cart yesterday," Munro continued, following them into the kitchen. "Day before that, a physician visited. I suspect 'twas for Miss Lockhart."

While a kitchen maid poured them cups of cider, Broderick snagged one of the lads carrying kindling from the garden. "Fetch Mrs. MacPherson."

"She's gone, sir. Left this mornin'."

Frowning, Broderick snapped, "Gone where?"

The boy tugged his collar. "Dinnae ken, sir. They took the coach."

Connor entered through the scullery. "Ye wished to see me?"

"Where did my wife go? And why arenae ye with her?"

"She went with Rannoch and Alexander. They didnae ask me to come." Connor lifted his cap and scratched his head. The young man looked bone-weary. He'd been manning the night watch of late.

"Were they takin' her shopping?" He'd thought she'd done all she wished on their Princes Street excursion. "Or mayhap for a visit with Lord Teversham?"

"All I ken is Alexander rousted me from my bed to help Jack Murray prepare the coach. He didnae say where they were headed."

Broderick questioned him further but learned nothing useful. He sent Connor back to the stable and the lad to fetch Kate's maid then turned back to Munro. "Tell me what ye suspect."

THE TAMING OF A HIGHLANDER

There was a chance Munro was working for Lockhart and that he'd come here to lure Broderick into a trap. But the more he and his brothers had watched the constable, the less likely it seemed. Munro had spent most of his time in Edinburgh doing the same thing they'd been doing—watching Lockhart and his sister from a distance, waiting for the adder to slither from his nest. Besides which, Munro had met with Sabella at least twice. Broderick happened to know Sabella's true alliances.

Now, Munro straightened his shoulders. "I came here to find Lockhart, to return him to the jail."

Campbell finished off his cider and clapped the cup onto the table. "Ye mean so he might wait a few more days in his bluidy royal chamber before he's released by the judge on his payroll."

The constable's whiskers bristled. "I didnae ken anythin' about that. My job is to find the prisoner and return him—"

"Yer *job*," Broderick snapped, "is to keep rabid animals in their cages so they dinnae terrorize the countryside. So far, *Sergeant,* yer performance is shite."

"Perhaps if ye bluidy MacPhersons didnae crack open the cages—"

"Just tell me what ye ken."

He appeared to bite down on his hatred. "Three days ago, I saw Lockhart's man—one of Gordon's auld contacts from his days in Glasgow—carryin' Miss Lockhart into the house in Charlotte Square. She looked … in a bad way." The constable rolled his shoulders and raised his chin. "Limp. White. Thought at first she might be dead, as he carried her over his shoulder, but I heard her moanin'."

This seemed to disturb the constable greatly. The man's fists kept clenching by his sides until he finally clasped them at his back. "Nae lady should be treated thus. Particularly Miss Lockhart." Munro cleared his throat. "I saw the same man deliver a physician to the house the next day, and the day after, he was loadin' crates and trunks into a cart."

"Did you follow him?"

"He didnae take the cart anywhere, but aye. I followed him to a house in Queen Street. He gave a package to the woman there."

Broderick met Campbell's gaze as understanding passed between them. "Cecilia Hamilton."

"I've a suspicion Lockhart's been stayin' in that house, though I havenae seen him directly."

Broderick had suspected the same, particularly after he'd seen Cecilia at the Second Circle Club. "Likely it's one of several places he's been stayin'. We've also spotted his man visiting a storehouse in Leith."

Munro nodded. "That's why I suspect he means to bolt. Reportedly, he has resources in Amsterdam."

Bloody hell. Broderick hadn't known about Amsterdam. Cutting off Lockhart's club funds and blackmail schemes would do little good if he had access to a new reserve on the Continent.

"Three ships depart for Amsterdam in the next seven days," Munro continued. "I cannae search them all myself, nor watch his house round the clock. Ye have men. Ye want Lockhart found as badly as I do. I'm askin' for yer help."

"Mighty desperate, eh? Not so long ago, ye were bent on provin' I'd murdered the bugger. Now ye want my help to find him."

Munro's fist landed on the table, rattling their cider cups. "Damn ye, man! Miss Lockhart hasnae sent word in days! She might be injured. Or worse. This is nae time for grudges."

Broderick arched a brow at Campbell, who looked equally surprised. Sabella Lockhart had been even more subversive than they'd thought.

Just then, Janet entered. "Ye rang, sir?" Her eyes narrowed on the constable. "What is Sergeant Whiskers doin' here?"

"Never mind him. Where is Kate?"

She blinked. "She—she hasnae returned?" Glancing out the kitchen window at the swiftly falling darkness, the maid swallowed. "I expected her before ye arrived home, sir. I was stitchin' another of her shifts, which do have the strangest habit of gettin' torn, by the by, and I lost track of time."

The darkness outside was nothing compared with the looming, thunderous unease inside him. "Answer my question. Where did she go?"

The maid hesitated, eyeing first Campbell then Broderick.

"Janet!"

"They meant to start at the orphan hospital. 'Tis where she suspected Miss Cuthbert might seek help after leavin' the Bridewell."

The maid might as well have brained him with the iron pan hanging beside the hearth. His bewilderment must have shown, because Janet rushed to explain, "She wished to return yer friend to ye, Mr. MacPherson. She loves ye that much."

His throat closed, his chest squeezing. Magdalene was dead. She'd been murdered by Gordon's men.

Hadn't she? He looked to Campbell, whose expression was oddly sheepish.

"We didnae want to tell ye, brother. In case it werenae true." Campbell grimaced. "No sense losin' her twice."

Briefly, Campbell explained why they'd been misled about the woman attacked by Gordon's men and how Kate had been the reason they'd bothered to retread old ground in the first place.

By God, he wanted his wife. Needed to hold her. Thank her.

Even if Magdalene could not be found, the fact that Kate had gone to such lengths to search for her was … well, it was just what Kate would do, wasn't it? Restore a man's soul and ask nothing in return.

"Rannoch and Alexander are with her," Campbell said, frowning at the clock on the sideboard. "But they should have returned by now. I told them we'd be gone 'til four. 'Tis half-past."

A queasy sensation struck him, passing from his middle out, turning his skin clammy. He hadn't felt this way since the Bridewell.

A clatter arose from the direction of the entrance hall. He heard Rannoch's voice, but it sounded urgent. Winded.

At once, they all rushed toward the sounds.

Ah, God. No.

"Janet!" Rannoch snapped as he and Connor hauled a blood-soaked Alexander between them. "Boil water. We need bandages. Thread and needle. Go. Now!"

While Connor left to fetch a surgeon, Broderick and Campbell helped carry Alexander upstairs. Only after they'd settled him in his bed and cut away his bloody clothes did Broderick notice the two women who had also entered the room behind them.

One was a bonnie blonde with leaf-green eyes. Sabella looked like death, her lips bloodless, her arms wrapped around her torso, her eyes fixed upon Alexander. She swayed in place, her gown obscenely soaked in blood.

Beside her was a much plainer woman. A beloved friend. Someone he'd thought dead.

"Miss Cuthbert?" he breathed.

She smiled. Warm gray eyes filled with tears. "Mr. MacPherson," she choked.

He knew she didn't like to be touched—such a chaste, tidy woman—but he gathered her up in his arms anyway. "Ah, lass. I've never been so glad to see someone breathin'."

She patted his arms and shoulders then swiped a knuckle beneath each eye. "We must do this later. Yer brother needs me now." With brisk efficiency, Magdalene Cuthbert took charge. She ordered everyone about in her soft, calming voice, commanding a maid to boil a pair of tongs, Rannoch to bring her the strongest spirits he could find, Janet to tear more sheets into bandages, and Campbell to lift Alexander's slack body so she could remove the rest of his clothing.

Broderick hadn't felt the rage rise until he saw his brother's wound, stanched by wads of blood-soaked cloth, exposed. The hole, located high in Alexander's chest, overflowed with more blood. He heard a gasp from the doorway.

Sabella had slumped against the casing. Munro braced her elbows, a fatherly frown on his whiskered face.

Broderick stalked to where they stood, though Sabella kept her gaze fastened to the bed. "Miss Lockhart." Nothing. "Sabella." He took her blood-smeared hand in his.

She jolted. Looked at him with lost eyes. "I—I never meant … Kenneth … the pistol."

Dark rage surged higher. Broderick forced it down. "Aye. Where is yer brother, lass? Where did he go?"

"I don't know. He left after …" Her eyes strayed to the bed.

"Where is my wife, Sabella?" He shook her, causing a moan.

Munro bristled, shoving him back. "Mind yerself, MacPherson."

Rannoch approached. "I'm so bluidy sorry, brother." He ran a hand through his hair. "I lost her."

Broderick's stomach lurched until he wanted to vomit. There was only one "her" who was missing.

Rannoch explained how the coach had disappeared from the orphan hospital. How he'd scrambled to find a hack in that part of the city. How he and Magdalene had searched for Kate and Alexander in vain until he'd decided to seek out the adder in its nest. They'd gone to Charlotte Square and found Sabella frantically pressing a linen tablecloth into Alexander's wound.

"The lass was out of her head," Rannoch murmured. "I couldnae get answers from her."

Broderick would. He moved to Sabella. "Where is Kate?"

She shook her head listlessly. "That's just what he asked. Alexander." She stared at the bed, eyes stark. "Kenneth said ye'll never find her." Her brow crumpled. "Oh, God." Bloodstained fingers hovered over her mouth. "I couldn't stop it. I tried. Nothing can stop him."

Broderick gripped her arms hard and forced her hands down. "What did he have planned for her? What did he say?"

"He—he said he waited for ye to love her. To consider her yours." Her throat reflexively swallowed. Her lips flattened. "He wants ye to feel what it's like to lose your greatest prize to a thief. To know she's near and that ye cannot have her."

Anguished rage turned the world black. Not Kate. Not his wee, bonnie wife.

The roaring in his head swallowed all reason. Black slowly became red.

Campbell joined them, speaking in his quiet rumble. He and Rannoch questioned Sabella and traded information with Munro. Distantly, Broderick listened. Munro had a theory—something about two ships leaving for Amsterdam the following day.

But he knew only one thought. He must find her. He must find Lockhart so he could find Kate. Without his light, there was only the black. The silence. The roar. And pain that was both everything and nothing at all.

CHAPTER TWENTY

Kate couldn't decide whether she was awake. Blackness surrounded her. The air smelled of liquor, ash, and wood. She was damp. Cold. Her head ached abominably. Her knees were folded up against her chest, restricting her breathing and turning her feet numb.

At first, she struggled. Scraped her elbows on the wood. Rapped her knuckles and forehead on the rounded walls and flat ceiling. It was tiny, her prison. She could scarcely breathe.

"Hellooo?" She gathered more air. "Is anyone there?"

Soon, she thrashed and pounded the wood. Solid. No give. She braced her knees on one side and her shoulders against the other and shoved with all her might. She strained and gritted and, very soon, sweated. No crack. No give.

"Blast." She gathered another lungful. "Somebody!" She banged her fist on the wood above her. Harder. Both fists now. "Somebody *help me!*"

Silence. Blackness. Where was she?

Panic took hold, quickening her pulse. Frantically, she pounded away until her hands hurt too badly to continue.

Muddled from the fumes and the tightness, she fell back. "Please," she whimpered, resting her forehead against her knees. Beyond the wood, she heard nothing. Not even wind.

How much air was in her tiny prison? Blast, she couldn't see anything. The smell of alcohol and a faint hint of char made her sick. This must be … a cask?

She pressed the round interior again, wedged her hands against the top and pushed. Not even a squeak.

Huffing, she carefully scooted around, inching her fingers along the lower third of the cask. Somewhere, there should be … ah, yes. She found the bung. It was coated in something. Wax, perhaps. She tore off a glove and began digging. Soon, her fingers were sore, and she'd encountered something harder than wax. Cork, she thought.

Exhausted, dizzy, and sick, she rested for a moment.

Broderick would find her. He would, he would, he would. But if she ran out of air, she'd be dead by the time he arrived. She mustn't die. She had a husband to love. Children to create. A novel to finish—or perhaps a play.

Fighting the queer sensation of spinning inside a black void, she redoubled her efforts to claw at the stoppered hole that might be her one good source of air. Long minutes later, a sob gathered in her chest. It was no use. Her fingernails were broken past the quicks. Her legs were cramping. She suspected she'd lost consciousness at least once, for she'd somehow drooled upon herself.

But she could not give up. Because Broderick would never give up on her. She knew that as well as she knew William Shakespeare was the greatest playwright ever to put pen to paper.

With her knuckles, she shoved at the cork. Again. Again. Desperate for any sign of give, she strained and seethed, repositioning her shoulder for a better, though much more painful, angle.

No give. In fact, it seemed the harder she pushed, the harder it became. With a shrieking cry that sounded pathetically puny, she covered her eyes and wept.

After a while, she drifted. She didn't know how long. But she felt half-asleep when she heard the whisper. *Pull instead of push, lass.*

Her eyes popped open. Her heart skipped a beat. That might have been from the oxygen deprivation, but nevertheless, she felt a glimmer of hope. What if the bung had been corked from the inside? Pushing would only wedge it harder into the hole.

"Bloody hell," she muttered, uncaring of the obscenity. No one was around to hear it. And she needed the release because she'd just realized that the part of the cork she might have used to "pull instead of push" was the very part she'd spent the past hour or two clawing into tiny bits.

"Bloody hell!" She slammed her fist into the wood. Again and again. She screamed foul nonsense, using every curse she'd ever heard spoken in England or Scotland.

Then she remembered the reticule. And the spiral-shaped charm Mrs. MacBean had made her promise to carry with her.

"'Tis yer bride charm, lass," the old woman had whispered in her ear. "Promise ye'll always keep it with ye. Wear it round yer neck, if ye must. Promise me."

She'd promised. Now, with painful, bloody fingers, she fumbled for her reticule. Felt inside. And found the bride charm shaped very much like a corkscrew.

Then, she laughed, loud and long. "Oh, Broderick, my love." Another laugh. "Mrs. MacBean will never let either of us hear the end of this one."

Of all people, Broderick would not have predicted that a weak-chinned, ginger-haired MacDonnell would be the key to finding Lockhart. But Stuart MacDonnell had spent a great deal of time in the treacherous Jack Murray's company. And, as Stuart rarely spoke more than a few sentences each day, the coachman had made free with the whisky and blethered on more than he should in Stuart's presence.

When Janet had informed Stuart about Murray's true employer, Stuart had straightened his shoulders and quietly announced, "I may ken somethin' useful."

Apparently, Murray had taken to "explorin' the city a wee bit" when he'd been off duty. One of the places he often went was to a warehouse in Leith, near the waterfront.

"I asked why, and he said that's where he found the real riches." Stuart had thought it an odd thing to say, so when the man sobered the following day, he'd asked what Murray had meant by it. "He brushed it aside, sir. Said he was sotted and referrin' to whores. But mayhap that's where he was meetin' with Lockhart."

Broderick braced the young man's earnest, solemn face between his hands and gave him a grateful shake. "By God, ye're the best of the MacDonnells, lad."

Janet wore a smug smile. "Didnae I tell ye?"

It took less than five minutes for Broderick, Campbell, and Rannoch to mount up. Munro insisted on coming, too. The weather was foul, dark had fallen an hour past, and the constable talked of Dutch shipping schedules for the entire ride north.

Broderick cared for none of it. When pain was everything, it was nothing at all. And this pain—the very thought of losing her—was pure anguish like he'd never known. It had a sound. A vibration. It echoed in his skin.

By the time they neared the waterfront, the vibration had reached a numbing pitch. He would do whatever was necessary. Torture Lockhart. Let Lockhart torture him. It didn't matter.

Nothing mattered but her.

A row of warehouses loomed ahead. Which one could it be? There were at least five near the water. Four of them were unsecured by more than locks on the doors. The fifth was routinely used by a fellow whisky runner—one without a license but a great belief in securing his goods. Lockhart wouldn't find sanctuary there.

Which left four possibilities. "We must each take one," he said. Rannoch and Campbell grunted their agreement.

Munro protested. "Are ye mad, MacPherson? He'll nae doubt be armed, as will his men be." The constable sat straighter and wiped his damp whiskers with an agitated hand. "We're better off bein' patient, searchin' for signs of occupancy first. Mayhap—"

"We dinnae have time," Broderick said softly. "*She* doesnae have time."

"If one of us finds Lockhart and dies, then what?"

"Then, we're down a man. And the rest will ken where to go."

"Use yer head! Bluidy hell, I ken she's yer wife, but we willnae find her if we cannae *reason*. If we dinnae *plan.*"

Oddly enough, Broderick's numbness had sunk in deep and generated a strange calm. He listened to Munro. Munro made sense. "What do ye have in mind?"

"We'll split up, as ye say. But each of us will take a different building and circle round the outside to look for signs of occupation. Bottles and rubbish piled near doors. Signs of horses and lanterns, laundry or beds."

Broderick breathed out. His breath was white, he noted. It was damned near freezing, the ground turning slick beneath his mount's feet. He didn't feel cold but, rather, warm, as if a blanket covered him. "Done. Each of us will scout the grounds of the four likely warehouses. Then, we'll meet at the corner of Constitution and Bernard. Nae more than a quarter-hour, ye ken?"

They all nodded. Munro looked impressed.

Twenty minutes later, they all convened as planned. "Anythin'?" Broderick queried.

All three men shook their heads.

He uttered a foul curse. There'd been no signs of anything apart from darkness and frost. "Could it have been a different spot? One closer to the docks?"

Munro answered first. "The ships leavin' for Amsterdam dock on opposite ends of the port. 'Twould take us all night to search both places."

"We could start with the nearest one," Rannoch suggested.

"Is he more likely to choose one over the other?" asked Campbell.

"I dinnae ken," answered Munro. "He's leavin' for Amsterdam. 'Tis the only place he has resources to draw upon. That's what Sabella said. Er, Miss Lockhart, that is."

Rannoch and Campbell slanted the older man a wry look. Broderick didn't give two shites if Munro fancied the young woman. What he cared about was finding Kate.

Something tickled the back of his mind. Amsterdam was in … Holland. "Munro, are both ships bound *directly* for Amsterdam?"

The sergeant scowled. "One is. The other docks in Newcastle first."

That spoon's straight from Holland with no stops in between.

"We'll start there, then."

They found Lockhart in a warehouse on the west side of the port, roughly a mile from where they'd started. The splash of waves could be heard in the distance. The air smelled of fish and refuse.

And the sign above the small brick warehouse's door read, "McKenzie Imports & Fine Silver Goods."

"Ah," breathed Broderick. "The spoons."

Campbell gripped Broderick's nape as their da often did. "Rannoch and I will take the back. Munro should take the south entrance. Ye should take the north. I've a notion he's anticipated yer arrival."

"Why?"

Campbell nodded toward a lit lantern placed beside a familiar coach.

"Doesnae matter. He'll tell me where she is. If he kills me, ye must promise ye'll find her."

"God, brother—"

"I'll have yer word. You as well, Rannoch."

Both men vowed they would find Kate should Broderick fall. Then, they each took their positions and slipped inside the building as silently as a shadow. Broderick's vision worsened in the dark, but the warehouse was half the size of others he'd used— perhaps fifty feet long by thirty deep. Windows lined the top story, which allowed faint moonlight to slant down upon stacks of crates and long shelves.

Broderick picked his way past a worktable littered with packing straw and barrel staves. When he saw a shadow move in his peripheral vision, he swung around to find Rannoch creeping between two tall shelves. Broderick gave him a questioning look, and Rannoch shook his head.

They continued to search the building until it became clear Lockhart was nowhere on the ground floor. That left only a series of offices on a mezzanine level above. Broderick took the lead.

Lockhart was behind the second door he tried.

"My, my," the blackguard sneered. "Punctuality is not your strongest suit, is it? Or perhaps it's cleverness that's lacking." He sat on a stool behind a desk. When he lit a lantern, Broderick saw he wasn't alone.

"Cecilia. Ye dinnae have to go with him, lass."

She looked as bonnie as ever. As sad and broken as ever. "I made my choice," she replied. "I chose him."

Nodding, Broderick held up his hands. "What will it take, Lockhart? What must I do?"

A gruesome grin appeared. "Suffer. Beg. Oh!" Green eyes flared as he leaned forward. "Weep. I should love to see it. Does an eye still shed tears after it's gone? I must admit to a certain curiosity."

"Ye have Cecilia by yer side. She's loyal to you."

"Aye. She's mine. But we've had an arduous task in restoring our affections. Haven't we, dear?"

Cecilia's lashes fluttered oddly. "Aye," she breathed.

Distantly, Broderick noted the sounds of fighting—MacPherson grunts and fists, pained cries from the poor, wee victims of said fists.

"Just tell me what I must do," he said, stepping further into the room. "Give me the price, and I'll gladly pay it."

"You know, in some places, thieves are punished by removing their hand."

Broderick raised his arm. "Take it. If ye tell me where she is, ye can take it now."

"Oh, but you haven't merely stolen a loaf of bread." Leaf-green eyes went colder. Colder. Ice. "You were inside her. The violation was absolute."

The calm that had been keeping Broderick sane cracked. Pain intruded through the fissure, spiking above the numbness. Lockhart had no intention of telling him anything. The man would spend his last breath taunting Broderick. Punishing Broderick.

"I see you've realized your conundrum," the bastard said. "Kill me, and she dies. Don't kill me, and there's the slightest chance I'll tell ye where to find her. But will it be in time? Now, there's the thorny bit. Perhaps she's dead already, in which case, this conversation is naught but a delightful diversion on a wintry eve."

Behind him, he felt his brothers arrive, flanking him like a wall. A faint, coppery smell came through the door. MacPhersons were not to be trifled with.

"What do ye need, brother?" Campbell asked.

"Nothin' yet. He has a pistol trained on me."

Lockhart grinned and raised his hand above the desk. "I wondered if you'd noticed."

"Ye've only one shot."

"One is all I require. Ask Alexander about that."

More sounds from the open door. Shuffling and a pained groan. "Och, cease wailin' like a wee bairn, ye worthless traitor." Munro dragged a bloodied Jack Murray by his collar and shoved him forward. "Tell MacPherson what ye told me. Go on!"

The coachman wiped his bloody nose with his wrist. "She isnae here."

"Where, then?"

"Another warehouse. I dinnae ken which one. I only helped with the cask."

Cold whistled through him, bringing pain as vast as a frozen sea. "What cask?"

"The one w-we sealed her up in."

Broderick faced Lockhart and saw the truth in his eyes. His gloating, triumphant eyes.

"We spared no expense for your bride, MacPherson. Previously, that cask housed some of the finest whisky in Scotland." He leaned an elbow on the desk as though holding the gun was wearying. "It's a wee bit larger than the ones you use, so, provided she doesn't thrash about too much, I'd say she has about four hours before running out of air." He made a show of looking at the watch that sat near his left wrist. "Oh. Oh, dear. Well, this is regrettable. It seems *eight* hours have passed since we sealed her up." He clicked his tongue. "Punctuality. A virtue without equal."

A fissure ruptured. A monster roared. The devil raised a hand to fire. That hand shook and bled. A woman with flaxen hair and rosebud innocence screamed the monster's name and clawed the devil's face. The devil cast her off. Pointed his weapon. But never fired.

Instead, he wore the monster's blade, which the monster had thrown with beastly force into the devil's eye.

The devil fell.

Too late. Too late. Too bloody late.

The monster roared again but heard nothing. Saw nothing. Felt nothing but the blackness.

Still, he must find her. He would always find her, even in the darkest place.

With savage blows, he turned on the betrayer, demanding to know where they'd hidden his light. The coachman wept pathetically, vomited blood, sobbed that he didn't know.

Then came a soft voice. "He doesnae ken, Broderick. Ye can stop now."

The monster turned. Focused.

"He doesnae ken," she said, the blood of her lover smeared across her pristine cheek. "But I do."

CHAPTER TWENTY-ONE

In a sea of darkness, Kate floated between worlds. One was cold. The other warm. One was quiet. The other a symphony. One promised pain and smelled of burnt wood and heady liquor. The other promised rest and felt soft as down.

But Kate had never been one to laze about in bed when there was something better to do. And what was better than fighting?

She was fighting for Broderick, after all. Broderick and all the "wee bairns" they would make together. Would a dozen be too many? She must ask him.

Stay awake, Katherine Ann Huxley MacPherson. You may sleep when you have his arms around you, and not before.

Because pain was better than softness. And silence was better than music. And cold would do fine, thank you, for she was far from done.

No more wallowing.

With numb fingers that no longer shivered but barely followed her commands, she fumbled with the brooch for the hundredth time, working the torn strip of tartan back through the metal knot and cinching it tight with her teeth. It wasn't much, but she suspected her tiny prison was sitting in a sea of other casks, and if she wanted Broderick to find her, she must offer him some sort of banner. The tartan was red, so that would help. Of course, she still didn't see any daylight coming either through the bung or the seams between staves.

She threaded the tail end of the tartan through the hole before shoving the wadded length as far as it would go. Then, she tried to loosen it from the brooch so she could fasten it to the wood.

Her fingers refused to comply. She couldn't see them or feel them, but she thought perhaps they were wet. The brooch slipped. Clanked through the hole. Pinged, metal against metal.

What did that mean? Confusion turned her head into porridge. What had she been doing?

The cold was turning warm again. Her eyes were open and closed again. The music was drifting closer again.

And far in the distance, beyond the dark and the wood, the numbness and the pain, a gull heralded a new day. If only she could stay awake to see it.

As Broderick entered the warehouse where the exciseman had been killed, he expected to feel dread or grief or fury. Something. But once again, he felt nothing apart from urgency.

As though she could be saved. Impossible.

Nevertheless, he couldn't shake the feeling. He barked orders at Munro and his brothers, telling them to look for signs of oddities. The massive building housed several thousand barrels. His wife was inside one of them, and he would find her.

They spread out, taking a fast initial sweep of the lengthy, towering rows. None of them noticed anything odd. Outside, gulls had started their loud greetings.

Broderick closed his eye, bracing a hand on the nearest cask, and prayed he might find her alive. An impossibility. But how could he go on if she were ...

No. His eye flew open. He would not give in. She was here. He must find her.

Their second and third sweeps likewise yielded no clear anomalies. Lockhart had said the cask he used was slightly bigger than those used by the MacPherson Distillery, so that narrowed down the search to roughly fifteen hundred.

A fourth sweep had them opening three casks with odd markings. Nothing but whisky.

Frustration ate at his guts. He couldn't see well enough in the dark. Finally, in desperation, he went outside to the coach they'd brought with them and took down one of the lanterns.

Kate liked the light, he recalled. She liked to look at him and kiss his scars.

For a moment, he reeled beneath an onslaught of pain. Staggering sideways, he caught himself on the loading platform. *Must force it down*, he thought. *Must find Kate.*

Returning inside with the lantern, he performed a fifth sweep and a sixth.

388   ELISA BRADEN

On the seventh, something glimmered. He wouldn't have noticed if it weren't for the lantern. But a wink of metal lying between two casks caught the light just so. When he looked closer, he saw a pattern resembling his wife's wedding ring. The one that had belonged to his mother.

The following minutes blurred into a stew of pounding heart, frantic shouting, and desperate calls to his wee, bonnie Kate. He found her cask behind two others. When he saw the strips of MacPherson plaid streaming from the bung—a bung which had been somehow unsealed from the inside, his shouts grew louder. Joyful. She might be alive.

He and Campbell lifted her down from atop a platform while Rannoch raced to retrieve tools to open the cask. A hammer was all he found.

A hammer would do.

Broderick tore into the wood. The metal hoops. Tore the cask apart with hammer and hands until he saw her bonnie brown curls. When he saw her skin was blue, he roared her name. Reached for her. Carefully unfolded her body from its cramped position. Lifted her in his arms and raced for the coach.

All the while, he kissed her, hoping to feel her breath. She was like ice, but he would make her warm. She was still and silent, but he would hold her until she awakened. He whispered his love and begged her to stay.

He needed his light to awaken and dance for him.

But as the coach lurched into motion, his brothers wore grieving expressions.

Broderick held her tighter. Prayed harder. And waited for her return.

The dark place shifted around Kate. She'd been warm. Then cold. Then shivering. Then still.

Now, her body shied away from the pain, but something wanted her to stay. It bound her with knotted ropes. It wouldn't let her go.

After a time, it started singing. Or, rather, he did. A wondrous male voice, deep and rich and faintly rough. Gravel and caverns.

He sang words she didn't understand. The song was a lovely air. She wanted to sing it with him, for it was both joyful and mournful at once. Like a plea made out of love.

Aching pain moved closer. Other sensations returned—a warm, strong hand holding hers, the weight of blankets, the brush of fingers at her temple.

"Le cùmhnanta teann 's le banntaibh daingeann. 'S le snaidhm a dh'fhanas 's nach trèig."

She didn't understand the words, but the tune was lovely. Who was singing? He had the voice of an angel.

Gentle lips caressed hers. "Ye must awaken, *mo chridhe*. I'll nae stay here without ye."

Her eyes wanted to open. She wanted to kiss the man who sang so sweetly. The one who called her his heart. She tried to wake.

The singing resumed.

Her eyes fluttered. Light shone through her lashes, white and gray.

"Lass?"

Eyelids should not be this heavy. She pushed them open with a grunt. The world looked like a mirror spread with grease. She blinked again. Focused on the man who, evidently, had been bold enough to take up half her bed. He lay stretched along her side, one hand holding hers and the other tickling her cheek.

"Aye, there ye are."

Everything hurt now that she was awake. But something in this man's face made her glad. Pain was small. Inconsequential. What mattered was that she stayed. For, he needed her. She saw it in his eye.

"I kenned ye'd come back to me. How do ye feel?"

She drew a breath and sighed. Drew another and tried to remember. "Thirsty," she rasped.

He gestured to someone else. Gentle, reddened hands came to help her drink. First water. Then tea.

But Kate could not take her eyes from the man. He was badly scarred. Yet, she'd never seen anyone handsomer. She wanted his arms. She wanted his mouth. She wanted him to sing again.

Love shone from him like a lighthouse in a storm. She reached for him. Her hands were bandaged, but it didn't matter. He folded her close, aligning their bodies perfectly.

Suddenly, her chest ached with the need to weep. Relief and tenderness overwhelmed her senses. She buried her face against his throat and released a small cry.

"Shh, *mo chridhe*. Ye're safe. Ye're home." He stroked her, offering comfort with his hands. But the greatest comfort was his scent. Cooling. Wondrous.

"B-Broderick?"

"Aye."

"You found me?"

"Aye, lass. I'll always find ye, no matter how dark it seems."

For a long while, she simply absorbed the blissful safety of his arms, the warm strength of his body. "Did you see the corkscrew?"

He chuckled, the sound deep and reassuring. "Aye. Rannoch brought it with us. He was very impressed."

She snuggled closer, wanting his skin and her skin to be touching. "Well, it was impressive. We must thank Mrs. MacBean when next we see her."

He hummed his agreement.

She stroked his cheek with her bandaged hand, wishing she could feel him. Perhaps after she'd healed. "You sing beautifully," she whispered, kissing his throat and the underside of his jaw. "What did the words mean?"

"'Tis a love song. A man's praise for his bride. The first verse speaks of a knot that remains unfailing. Their marriage, ye ken?"

"Hmm. Why have you never sung to me before?"

For a moment, she wasn't certain he would answer. And then, he did.

"The music left me. But for ye, I'll sing." He held her tighter and warmed her through. "For ye, *mo chridhe*, I'd sing forever."

"Mmm. Forever is a very long time."

A kiss. A smile. A man who loved her well. "Not long enough."

&PILOGUE

Kate squealed as Clarissa Meadows stepped down from her grandmother's coach. She ran to the curvaceous blonde and threw her arms around her. "Oh, how I have missed you! Happy Christmas, dearest."

With a radiant smile, Clarissa immediately launched into breathless chatter. "Scotland is everything you said, Kate. The mountains. The water. And the haggis! Simply dreadful. Grandmama still hasn't recovered."

Lady Darnham descended from the coach with the aid of Stuart MacDonnell, who had recently transferred his position from Glendasheen Castle to Kate and Broderick's household, which Kate had decided would now be called Rowan House. Broderick objected to the name on the grounds that "all those bluidy nuisance trees will have to be cut down sooner or later," but Kate believed she could convince him. She was very persuasive where her husband was concerned.

Emerging from inside the house, Mama and Papa— who had surprised Kate by being at the castle when they'd arrived home from Edinburgh several days earlier—crowed greetings to Clarissa and Lady Darnham. Soon, Francis and George came outside, as well. The conversation continued in lively fashion until Broderick stalked outside.

He made straight for Kate and, without a word, scooped her into his arms.

She yelped. "Broderick!"

"I willnae have ye standin' about havin' a blether when it's this cold, lass." He carried her inside, refusing to set her down until they'd entered the drawing room. He lowered her to a spot near the fireplace.

"Our guests are going to think me terribly rude."

"Nah. Me, mayhap. You? They'll just think ye're married to a great beast with nae manners."

She laughed and cupped his face to draw him down for a kiss. "They wouldn't be far wrong. But oh, how I adore my beast."

Surprisingly, Broderick's scars, size, and manners hadn't put off Mama and Papa, who had already invited him to call them either Meredith and Stanton or Mama and Papa. "Mama and Papa are preferable," Mama had advised only yesterday. "It saves on confusion, dearest boy."

Kate thought Broderick might already be growing accustomed to Mama's long hugs and Papa's questions about the whisky business, though he had assigned Rannoch to take Papa for his third tour of the distillery.

Alexander had survived his wound and continued his recovery at Rowan House, thanks to Magdalene's surprising capabilities. The young woman had bashfully confessed her interest in medicine. She'd spent much of her time after leaving the Bridewell acquiring books on the subject from the orphan hospital's surgeon. She'd brought a trunkful of the tomes with her when she'd returned with them to the glen.

Unfortunately, they hadn't been able to persuade Sabella to return with them. She'd been determined to stay in Edinburgh and clean up after her brother. Munro had volunteered to stay and help her; he'd promised to write if they required MacPherson assistance.

Cecilia had disappeared the day after Kate's rescue. They all speculated that she'd kept her passage on the ship to Amsterdam, but none of them wished to pursue the matter, least of all Broderick.

"'Tis time to write the end of this bluidy chapter," he'd said. "We've much happier endings to look forward to."

Today was Christmas, so Annie, John, Mrs. MacBean, and the MacPhersons all arrived within an hour of Clarissa, making for a lovely sort of chaos. As scents of Mr. McInnes's planned feast wafted through the house, Kate, Broderick, and their guests gathered in the drawing room to exchange small gifts and tell amusing stories. Papa had just finished an anecdote about Kate's first attempt at ice skating when Janet entered carrying Kate's gift for Broderick.

She thanked her maid and cleared her throat to draw everyone's attention. "I have one last gift to offer." She stroked the tartan fabric covering the package then caught her husband's eye. "This one is conditional."

He raised a brow. "Aye?"

"You must promise to sing for me at least once per day. And when my new pianoforte is delivered, you must agree to a duet."

A frown tugged. He glanced at the package she held out to him. Then, he took it carefully in hand, unwrapped it, and sat still, staring down at the case. "When did ye …?"

"On our shopping excursion." She swallowed, waiting for him to open the case. Would he be pleased?

It took far too long for him to reveal what lay inside, but Kate was rewarded for her patience when he lifted out the gleaming violin.

In the room, gasps and *ah's* of delighted approval sounded from Huxleys and MacPhersons alike. Francis exclaimed, "By Jove, man, that is a fine instrument. I didn't realize you played."

Angus replied, "My son plays like a bluidy angel. Inherited his mam's talent for music."

Rannoch added wryly, "Aye, and his da's temper. He smashed his last fiddle into kindling. Best nae do likewise with this one, brother."

Broderick stroked the gleaming wood with reverent fingers. He looked at Kate, and her heart squeezed hard enough to stop her breath. "For ye, I'll sing, *mo chridhe*."

Tears filled her eyes until the light through the windows wavered and his beautiful face swirled. "And for you, my darling, you must play."

He plucked out the bow, tucked the violin beneath his chin, and began to play. The tune was the same one he'd sung to her before. A love song that spoke of knots never to be undone.

Later, as everyone sat around the dining table— rough Highlanders and elegant Englishmen, bold charmers and brash lasses, wild-haired old crones, soft-spoken laundresses, and fascinated ladies—Kate marveled at the family she'd managed to create.

"Dinnae fash, laddie," Mrs. MacBean said from Broderick's opposite side. "I'll make ye a fertility charm.

I gave one to yer wee sister, and now look at her. Carryin' twins!"

Down the table, Annie gasped and John choked. Annie was the first to reply. "Ye told me yesterday 'twill be a son, auld woman."

Mrs. MacBean frowned, her good eye wandering away from her blind one. "I did?" She shook her head. "Must have been the mushrooms."

Annie snorted. "Twins. Pure rubbish."

"Mayhap I was thinkin' of somebody else." The old woman's milky eye wandered toward Kate. Soon, her good eye joined in, and she stared pointedly at Kate's middle. "Aye."

Alarmed, Kate placed a hand upon her belly. Mrs. MacBean might be half-mad, but Kate had learned well not to underestimate her. "Are you—are you certain?"

The old woman shook her head as though awakening from a sleep. For a moment, confusion entered her eyes. "Certain of what, lass?"

"That I shall have twins."

"Who said that?"

"You did."

"I did?"

Kate blew out an exasperated breath and looked to Broderick, who was fighting amusement. "Dinnae bother," he advised. "Ye'll drive yerself as mad as she is tryin' to make sense of it."

"Must have been the mushrooms," Mrs. MacBean repeated. "Take my advice, lass. Never eat the orange ones."

"I suppose we must simply wait to discover what lies in our future, hmm?" Kate gave the old woman a gentle smile.

"Och, aye. Still, I'll plant another two rowans outside, shall I?"

"No, really, that's not necessary," she answered in vain.

Mrs. MacBean had already turned toward Rannoch to explain why dallying with French women brought nothing but disease and misery.

Kate turned a grin toward her husband and found him staring at her. Blushing, she reached for his hand. "Do you suppose we shall have more than one or two, my darling?"

"Aye, lass."

"How many, do you think?"

"How many do Sir Wallace and his fair Fiona have, now? Ten, by my last count."

She grinned. "There's always room for one or two more. And we Huxleys are prolific, after all."

"Ah, but ye're a MacPherson now. And we MacPhersons tend to go bigger rather than smaller."

"Hmm. Yes. I find I do prefer bigger. And being a MacPherson."

He raised her hand to his lips and kissed her fingers tenderly. His thumb brushed over her ring. "How ye dazzle me, Mrs. MacPherson. I'm fair blinded every time I look at ye."

She swallowed, her heart aching with love for her forever man. "How perfectly ironic, my love." She kissed the hand that held hers and smiled. "Every time you look at me, I feel found."

Watch for the next book in the
Midnight in Scotland series

COMING SOON!

MIDNIGHT IN SCOTLAND: BOOK THREE

THE TEMPTATION OF A HIGHLANDER

BY

ELISA BRADEN

MORE FROM ELISA BRADEN

*Be first to hear about new releases, price specials,
and more—sign up for Elisa's free email newsletter at
www.elisabraden.com so you don't miss a thing!*

Midnight in Scotland Series
*In the enchanting new Midnight in Scotland series,
the unlikeliest matches generate the greatest heat.
All it takes is a spark of Highland magic.*

THE MAKING OF A HIGHLANDER (BOOK ONE)
Handsome adventurer John Huxley is locked in a land
dispute in the Scottish Highlands with one way out: Win the
Highland Games. When the local hoyden Mad Annie Tulloch
offers to train him in exchange for "Lady Lessons," he agrees.
But teaching the fiery, foul-mouthed, breeches-wearing lass
how to land a lord seems impossible—especially when he
starts dreaming of winning her for himself.

THE TAMING OF A HIGHLANDER (BOOK TWO)
Wrongfully imprisoned and tortured, Broderick MacPherson
lives for one purpose—punishing the man responsible. When
a wayward lass witnesses his revenge, he risks returning to
the prison that nearly killed him. Kate Huxley has no wish to
testify against a man who's already suffered too much. But
the only remedy is to become his wife. And she can't possibly
marry such a surly, damaged man…can she?

Rescued from Ruin Series
*Discover the scandalous predicaments, emotional
redemptions, and gripping love stories (with a dash of Lady
Wallingham) in the scorching series that started it all!*

Ever Yours, Annabelle (Prequel)

As a girl, Annabelle Huxley chased Robert Conrad with reckless abandon, and he always rescued her when she pushed too far—until the accident that cost him everything. Seven years later, Robert discovers the girl with the habit of chasing trouble is now a siren he can't resist. But when a scandalous secret threatens her life, how far will he go to rescue her one last time?

The Madness of Viscount Atherbourne (Book One)

Victoria Lacey's life is perfect—perfectly boring. Agree to marry a lord who has yet to inspire a single, solitary tingle? It's all in a day's work for the oh-so-proper sister of the Duke of Blackmore. Surely no one suspects her secret longing for head-spinning passion. Except a dark stranger, on a terrace, at a ball where she should not be kissing a man she has just met. Especially one bent on revenge.

The Truth About Cads and Dukes (Book Two)

Painfully shy Jane Huxley is in a most precarious position, thanks to dissolute charmer Colin Lacey's deceitful wager. Now, his brother, the icy Duke of Blackmore, must make it right, even if it means marrying her himself. Will their union end in frostbite? Perhaps. But after lingering glances and devastating kisses, Jane begins to suspect the truth: Her duke may not be as cold as he appears.

Desperately Seeking a Scoundrel (Book Three)

Where Lord Colin Lacey goes, trouble follows. Tortured and hunted by a brutal criminal, he is rescued from death's door by the stubborn, fetching Sarah Battersby. In return, she asks one small favor: Pretend to be her fiancé. Temporarily, of course. With danger nipping his heels, he knows it is wrong to want her, wrong to agree to her terms. But when has Colin Lacey ever done the sensible thing?

THE DEVIL IS A MARQUESS (BOOK FOUR)

A walking scandal surviving on wits, whisky, and wicked skills in the bedchamber, Benedict Chatham must marry a fortune or risk ruin. Tall, redheaded disaster Charlotte Lancaster possesses such a fortune. The price? One year of fidelity and sobriety. Forced to end his libertine ways, Chatham proves he is more than the scandalous charmer she married, but will it be enough to keep his unwanted wife?

WHEN A GIRL LOVES AN EARL (BOOK FIVE)

Miss Viola Darling always gets what she wants, and what she wants most is to marry Lord Tannenbrook. James knows how determined the tiny beauty can be—she mangled his cravat at a perfectly respectable dinner before he escaped. But he has no desire to marry, less desire to be pursued, and will certainly not kiss her kissable lips until they are both breathless, no matter how tempted he may be.

TWELVE NIGHTS AS HIS MISTRESS (NOVELLA – BOOK SIX)

Charles Bainbridge, Lord Wallingham, spent two years wooing Julia Willoughby, yet she insists they are a dreadful match destined for misery. Now, rather than lose her, he makes a final offer: Spend twelve nights in his bed, and if she can deny they are perfect for each other, he will let her go. But not before tempting tidy, sensible Julia to trade predictability for the sweet chaos of true love.

CONFESSIONS OF A DANGEROUS LORD (BOOK SEVEN)

Known for flashy waistcoats and rapier wit, Henry Thorpe, the Earl of Dunston, is deadlier than he appears. For years, his sole focus has been hunting a ruthless killer through London's dark underworld. Then Maureen Huxley came along. To keep her safe, he must keep her at arm's length. But as she contemplates marrying another man, Henry's caught in the crossfire between his mission and his heart.

ANYTHING BUT A GENTLEMAN (BOOK EIGHT)

Augusta Widmore must force her sister's ne'er-do-well betrothed to the altar, or her sister will bear the consequences. She needs leverage only one man can provide—Sebastian Reaver. When she invades his office demanding a fortune in markers, he exacts a price a spinster will never pay—become the notorious club owner's mistress. And when she calls his bluff, a fiery battle for surrender begins.

A MARRIAGE MADE IN SCANDAL (BOOK NINE)

As the most feared lord in London, the Earl of Holstoke is having a devil of a time landing a wife. When a series of vicious murders brings suspicion to his door, only one woman is bold enough to defend him—Eugenia Huxley. Her offer to be his alibi risks scandal, and marriage is the remedy. But as a poisonous enemy coils closer, Holstoke finds his love for her might be the greatest danger of all.

A KISS FROM A ROGUE (BOOK TEN)

A cruel past left Hannah Gray with one simple longing—a normal life with a safe, normal husband. Finding one would be easy if she weren't distracted by wolf-in-rogue's-clothing Jonas Hawthorn. He's tried to forget the haughty Miss Gray. But once he tastes the heat and longing hidden beneath her icy mask, the only mystery this Bow Street man burns to solve is how a rogue might make Hannah his own.

ABOUT THE AUTHOR

Reading romance novels came easily to Elisa Braden. Writing them? That took a little longer. After graduating with degrees in creative writing and history, Elisa spent entirely too many years in "real" jobs writing T-shirt copy ... and other people's resumes ... and articles about giftware displays. But that was before she woke up and started dreaming about the very *unreal* job of being a romance novelist. Better late than never. Elisa lives in the gorgeous Pacific Northwest, where you're constitutionally required to like the colors green and gray. Good thing she does. Other items on the "like" list include cute dogs, strong coffee, and epic movies. Of course, her favorite thing of all is hearing from readers who love her characters as much as she does. If you're one of those, get in touch on Facebook and Twitter or visit **www.elisabraden.com**.

Made in the USA
Monee, IL
17 March 2023

30093479R00236